praise for james earl hardy's
love the one you're with

Black Issues Book Review
Best of 2002 Recommended Fiction

"The light storyline is generously studded with slangy vernacular and a host of barbed, campy one-liners, especially during the warm and wicked gay-friends-as-surrogate-family gatherings. A well-documented 'soundtrack' (Hardy knows his music) and scenes with Pooquie's young son lend a soft glow to the story."   —*Publishers Weekly*

"Hardy's greatest strength has always been chronicling the lives of what he calls 'same-gender-loving men,' and he adds subtle shading to the portrait here, revealing how a group of friends functions as a family."   —*Kirkus Reviews*

"Hardy's crisp and authentic dialogue, biting humor, heartbreaking drama, and unabashed celebration of culture makes this book a genuinely good treat from start to finish."   —*Venus*

ABOUT THE AUTHOR

An honors graduate of the Columbia University School of Journalism, JAMES EARL HARDY is the author of the bestselling novels *B-Boy Blues, 2nd Time Around, If Only for One Nite,* and *The Day Eazy-E Died.* He lives in New York City.

james
earl
hardy

LOVE
THE
ONE
YOU'RE
WITH   a novel

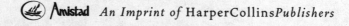 Amistad *An Imprint of* HarperCollins*Publishers*

A hardcover edition of this book was published in 2002 by Amistad, an imprint of HarperCollins Publishers.

FIRST AMISTAD PAPERBACK EDITION 2003

DESIGNED BY SHUBHANI SARKAR

Printed on acid-free paper

The Library of Congress has catalogued the hardcover edition as follows:
Hardy, James Earl.
Love the one you're with : a novel.—1st ed.
p. cm
ISBN 0-06-621248-0
1. African American Gays—Fiction. 2. New York (N.Y.)—Fiction.
3. Gay men—Fiction. I. Title.
PS3558.A62375 L68 2002
813'.54—dc21 2002066630

ISBN 0-06-051239-3 (PBK.)

03 04 05 06 WBC/QW 10 9 8 7 6 5 4 3 2 1

Pooquie, Little Bit, Li'l Brotha Man & I would like 2 thank . . .

God

Bam Bam, for continuing to remind (God)Daddy what life is really all about

Lonnell "LW" Williams & Prince Albert, my "Jood Judys" for being so lovely and so looney!

John McGregor, for the brotherly representation

Kelli Martin, for the sisterly, editorial eye

Manie Barron, for bringing us to Amistad and respecting my vision

the *ph-ph-ph-phyne* Bruthaz of *Rundu* and *Champion Men*, for the *inspiration*

Aretha, Luther, Dionne & Friends, Mary Jane Girls, Meshell, James, Oleta, the O'Jays (two times!), Minnie, Grover & Bill (and Will), Lady T, Donny, Stevie, Uncanny Alliance, Maria, Karyn, Jennifer, and Jermaine, for helping us "name" each chapter

and to all readers around the world who have adopted us. Thanks for letting our family become a part of yours. . . .

"THIS IS . . . for THE *cheater* IN YOU . . ."

LOVE
THE
ONE
YOU're
WITH

1

I picked up the receiver before the phone could ring once . . .

"Hi, Pooquie."

"Hay, Baby. How you know it was me?"

"Who else would be calling me at this hour? Besides, I could tell it was you by your ring."

"My ring?"

"Yes. The phone rings in a special way when you call me. It sounds like you when I'm bangin' that booty."

He giggled. "You *cray*-zee, Little Bit."

"About you? Most definitely."

"I ain't wake you up, did I?"

"No. I've just been laying here, waiting for your call. So, I see you got there okay."

"Yeah."

"And how was your first flight?"

"It was da bomb!"

"Oh really?"

"Yeah."

"You didn't pass out?"

"Nah."

"You didn't throw up?"

"Nah."

"No? There wasn't any turbulence?"

"Nah, Baby. It was a smooth flight."

"You didn't even get queasy sitting by the window?"

"Nah. Shit, that was one of tha best parts."

"Okay. What were some of the other highlights of the trip?"

"Yo, they know how ta treat cha in first class. I had a brotha servin' me."

"Mmm. I bet he was all too happy to see you."

"He sho' 'nuff was: we was tha only Black folks up in that section."

"Doesn't surprise me . . ."

"And he made sure I had as many blankets and pillows as I wanted, that my glass was never half-full, and I always had some eats on my table. Ha, if I had asked him, he prob'ly woulda served his ass on a plate. He was all in it."

"Hmm, I can't blame him."

"He wanted ta give me his digits. Told me if I wanted a tour guide ta give him a call. But I told him my Baby wouldn't like me acceptin' a stranger's phone number up in tha air."

"And what did he say?"

" 'What if I give it to you when we land?' "

We laughed.

"Then he asked if *you* was my Baby."

"He did?"

"Yeah. He said he saw us checkin' in."

"And what did you tell him?"

"I told him yeah."

I beamed. "Did you sleep on the plane?"

"How could I wit' him checkin' up on me ev'ry five minutes? And tha brotha can *talk*. By tha end of tha flight, I had him and that other flight attendant in first class sayin' *jood*."

"Ha, you're gonna have the whole world sayin' that word soon."

"Yeah. After tha movie went off, he came ta collect my headphones, saw tha look on my face, and said: 'I take it the movie wasn't jood, huh?' "

I giggled. "What movie was it?"

"*Forrest Gump.* They shoulda called it Forrest Junk. Only white folks would go fuh some American-pie bullshit like that. And tha movie is too damn long!"

"Well, the movie aside, it was an all-around jood experience, huh?"

"Yeah. It was real excitin' and a lota fun. Tha only minus was my ears poppin' when we took off. Couldn't hear a thang fuh like a minute. That Big Red was no match fuh it."

"I'm glad your first flight was such a success. I just wish I could've taken it with you."

"Me, too, Baby. Me, too."

We sighed together.

"Did they have a car waiting for you?"

"Yeah, a black stretch limo, Baby. And a *sista* was drivin!"

"Really?"

"Yeah. And she was su'prised I was a brotha. Said she always be gettin' them stodgy, white studio VPs. She was able ta finally turn on some hip-hop and turn up that volume. We had madd fun just cuttin' up. She from Boogie Down."

"You should request to have her take you back when you leave."

"I will."

"Was someone from the studio at the hotel when you arrived?"

"Yeah. This white girl named Clemmy."

"Clemmy?"

"Her name is Clementine. She say ev'rybody calls her Clemmy."

"Clementine? As in 'Oh, my darling'?"

"Yup."

"Ha. I bet she is whiter than white bread, too."

"You know it, Baby. And she got this orange hair."

"Orange?"

"You heard. It matched that hoochie halter she was wearin'. Her hair is really spiky but short. And speakin' of short—she like a Munchkin and shit. And she was wearin' these seven-inch black platforms."

"Mmm . . . I bet you two were a sight to see at that front desk. What does she do on the project?"

"She a producer's assistant."

"Uh-huh. A gofer."

"Ya know it."

"And since she was wearing, as you put it, a hoochie halter, I take it the temp is high . . . ?"

"Yeah. It's like seventy-five."

"Nice. It's in the teens here."

"What? Yo, I'm glad I'm outa that deep freeze. As soon as they said we was about ta land, I took that sweater and them slacks off."

"Hmmph, no wonder you had folks trying to give you their digits up in the air. But don't get too used to that summer weather. Remember that you'll be coming back to this deep freeze in a couple of weeks."

"Ha, don't remind me."

"Oh? So you've been there all of a few hours and want me to send you the rest of your things?"

"Nah, Baby. This just tha first time in my life I ever been able ta wear shorts in February."

"Mmm-hmm. How is the hotel?"

"It's like Trump Tower and shit. Chandeliers, crystal, and stainless-steel glass ev'rywhere. And tha elevators are outside."

"They're outside?"

"Yeah, you know, you get a view of tha whole hotel as it goes up."

"Oh. That must be nice."

"And I got a phat room. It's got two double beds, queen size, plus a separate livin'-room area wit' a kitchenette. I'm gonna be nukin' that chicken you cooked fuh me in a minute."

"Well, they just givin' you the Tom Cruise treatment, ain't they?"

"Baby, if I was gettin' *that* kinda treatment, I'd be stayin' in the Presidential Palace not the Governor's Suite."

"Ha, indeed. But it sounds like you on your way there."

"I guess."

"It's almost ten o'clock out there. You've got a big day ahead of you. If you're not too tired, you can call me back after you eat and get settled."

"You gonna be up?"

"Mmm-hmm. Waiting for your call."

I could feel that smile. "A'ight. I love you, Little Bit."

"I love you, too, Pooquie."

2

"Well, well, well . . . if it ain't Miss Jean Brodie!"

There was Gene, right where he said he'd be: sitting at the bar in Pizzeria Uno, a rather trendy restaurant just blocks from Christopher Street in the West Village (aka Homo Ville). Besides dishing up some very jood pizza, it's also one of the prime locales in the city where the homiesexuals go to meet one of the Children. While their unsuspecting girlfriends or wives wait for them to take a leak, they're usually exchanging digits with one of us in the bathroom or by the bar. Gene loves to have a ringside seat for the festivities. He's been coming every Friday night for the past three years (given how much green he spends in the place, he should own some stock in the company). On a slow night, he sees a half-dozen love connections—and he's usually making at least one of them himself (although in his case it would be lust).

We hadn't seen each other in over two months—mainly because I stopped speaking to him. We had a major blowup just after Thanksgiving. Gene and I had never really had a fight before; we argued, even had a couple of shouting matches (in each case over the two things folks should *never* discuss—religion and politics), but our disagreements didn't end up with one of us so angry at the other that we decided to cut off all ties. But that almost happened this time. And it was Gene's "big-azz mutha-fuckin' mouth" (as Pooquie calls it) that started it.

The incident that almost broke up our friendship happened at my place. We—meaning Pooquie, Gene, B.D., Babyface, and I—had all settled into the living room after a very jood Sunday dinner. I made the turkey and dressing; B.D., the ham; Babyface, the peas and rice; Gene, the string beans and potato salad; Pooquie, the biscuits, with my help (he can't cook . . . not in the kitchen, anyway); and the cheesecake was courtesy of Junior's. Pooquie and B.D. were anxious to trounce Babyface and me in *Jeopardy!* for the fourth straight time. One would think Babyface, a Manhattan district attorney, and I, the award-winning journalist-turned junior-high-school writing teacher, would be the doubles tournament champs: Pooquie is a high-school dropout, while B.D.—a dancer with his own company, Nia—is a little ditzy (his initials stand for Barry Daniels—or *Brain Dense*, depending on who you talk to). But since Gene was with us this eve, we decided to play Truth or Shade. Instead of the verbal challenges players face in Truth or Dare, each person writes down a question or two on slips of paper and they are put into a bowl. If anyone believes that the person hasn't answered the question they've chosen truthfully, they will be thrown *shade* and the group will vote on whether to believe the challenged or the challenger.

To my surprise, Pooquie not only wanted to play but, after everyone wrote down their questions, volunteered to go first. But after reading over his question silently, it looked as if he wished he hadn't.

"What do you like better: fuckin' someone or bein' fucked?"

No doubt Gene came up with that one and the person he wanted to pick it did. He had inquired about our sexual proclivities on more than one occasion and I would've shared them but knew that he was the *last* person Pooquie would appreciate knowing.

"Uh . . . I don't think I could choose one over tha other." Pooquie looked at me. "Variety is definitely tha spice of life wit' my Baby."

I think Gene was thrown by his response; he assumed that Pooquie got done ("The *B* in B-boy *really* stands for *booty*, and that's something those boyz know how to give up") but probably didn't expect him to admit it. And the goofy grins on both of our faces were all the proof everyone needed to know he was telling the truth.

B.D. was next. "Have you ever slept with a woman before? If so, when and why did you do it? If not, why not?"

I knew who contributed that question—Pooquie. And I'm pretty sure he wanted me to pick it. He had asked me in the past if I had and I don't think he believed me when I told him no (he thinks that *every* man—gay or not—has or at least thought about doing it). He probably figured that presenting it in this forum would force me to disclose that I had in fact done it, especially if I admitted it to any of the others.

But B.D. got the query, and since everyone assumed he would answer no and respond to the *Why not?* with a *Why would I?*, we were all ready to move on. In fact, Babyface (yeah, he's got the cutest little . . .) had already shifted on the sofa where he and B.D. were entangled (legs and arms looped) so that he could draw his question next, when B.D. matter-of-factly declared . . .

"Yes."

As I've often heard Gene say during shocking moments like that one: It was so quiet you could hear a rat piss on cotton.

Pooquie ended the silence. *"You* been wit' a female?" Even though Pooquie didn't know B.D. that well, what little he did know (B.D. is the epitome of a muscle queen) made this revelation unbelievable even to him.

Gene was floored. "I cannot believe you've actually used what's between your legs for something other than relieving yourself—and sometimes I can't believe you do *that.*"

"Surprise, surprise. Contrary to *un*popular belief, it hasn't just been hanging there all my life like mistletoe."

"You never told me about that, Baby," piped in Babyface, who knows better than anyone that B.D. has "decorative dick"—meaning he never *touches* it during sex. (But at least he will let Babyface touch it; Gene and I have swapped stories about boyz who became completely undone when we attempted to blow, crank or, God forbid, ride their stick—and in every case, we're talking about a *stick,* dick down to the knee. Yeah, a waste.) "When did this happen?"

"When I was seventeen. I've blocked it out of mind."

"Uh-huh. The kind of thing you try to forget, right?" Gene smirked.

"Well, not really. I mean, it wasn't a bad experience."

"So, you enjoyed it?" Pooquie asked.

"Mmm . . . not exactly. I don't regret doing it. The girl . . . her name was Autumn."

"Don't tell me she has a sister named *Summer!*" Gene chuckled.

"No. But she does have a brother named August."

"August? What were their parents named: Mother Nature and Father Time?" joked Gene.

"August was the one I was after. He was my age; Autumn was a year younger than us. She had a big crush on me; she would've done anything I wanted."

"Apparently," I interjected.

He shook his head. "Nope. Doing it was her idea."

"Really?" groaned Gene. "Ain't that somethin': Autumn wanted to take a Fall!" Even Pooquie giggled at that one.

"I felt it was important that I finally come clean with her."

"You mean, you told her you were after her brother?" I asked.

"Yes. I had to. She had followed me around like a lost puppy for three years, wishin', hopin', prayin' that I'd ask her to marry me. But I wanted to marry her brother!"

"So, what she say when you told her?" Pooquie queried.

"First she thought I was joking. Then she thought I was just being mean, that I was using that as an excuse not to admit I wasn't interested."

Gene frowned. "You kept the girl at bay for three years—*that* should've been her hint that you weren't interested."

B.D. nodded. "Then she realized I was telling the truth but came up with a solution: 'You just *think* you're gay. Sleep with me and you'll see you're not.' "

Gene, Babyface, and I nodded at B.D. and each other. We had all been there before: Every gay man has (or will have) at least one hetero woman say to him that all it will take is one night (or, in some cases, one hour) with her and he'll see *and* feel the light. How ironic that Babyface, the "masculine" one in their relationship, has never slept with a woman, but B.D., the "feminine" one, has.

B.D. continued. "She got it hard. She put the condom on. She guided it in. And she did the bumpin' and humpin'."

"Why am I not surprised *she* did all the work," Gene giggled.

Pooquie's eyes narrowed. "You enjoy it?"

"I *enjoyed* the way she would slap my ass as she bumped and humped. All I could picture was her brother doing that to me. And it didn't help that she looked just like her brother, so when I looked in her eyes . . ."

"So you didn't cum?" asked Pooquie.

"Yes, I did. But not because of how being inside her made me feel."

I could tell by the look on Pooquie's face that he didn't buy that. He's from the school where, if you can get it up and off with a woman, that means you can't be gay. But a man can get hard if the wind blows the right way against his dick—and it doesn't matter what way he swings. And, given all the gay men who function as straight and their wives or girlfriends don't know it—and, when they do find out, can't believe it, since he performed in a way that never gave them cause to pause—such a masquerade isn't hard to pull off.

"Did she think her experiment was successful?" Gene questioned, even though he already knew the answer.

"She did. But she also saw her spell didn't last long. She came home a week later and found her brother and me fuckin'."

"No!" I squealed. "How did *that* happen?"

"Well, she made the mistake of telling her brother about us. And he confronted me about it."

I was on the edge of my seat for this one. "And what did he say?"

B.D. smiled. " 'If you wanted it, all you had to do was ask!' "

We all cracked up.

"Now, *that* must have truly been traumatic for her," I managed to get out between chuckles.

B.D. shrugged. "I guess seeing it with her own eyes was. But in the end, she accepted her brother being gay and us being a couple. The way she saw it, it was better she lose a man to her brother than another woman!"

"Ah. The dick that got away couldn't be hers to begin with," I added.

"You go it," B.D. agreed.

"My, my, my: The power of the pussy fails again!" announced Gene.

As we cackled and Pooquie groaned "Uh-huh," Babyface correctly surmised it was time to move on. He stuck his hand in Pooquie's X cap, and chose: "Have you ever dreamed about having sex with someone in this room other than your significant other?"

We would later find out that B.D. jotted this one down—and that Babyface was his intended target.

"Well . . ." Babyface began, looking at the floor, "I've had this dream . . . a few times . . ."

Given that we had gotten busy on the very couch he was lounging across, I knew he was going to say me (as part of their "one more fling before we exchange rings" deal, B.D. and Babyface each slept with someone else—and I was Babyface's pick). But when he looked up, his eyes trailed past me . . .

. . . and fell on Pooquie, who was just as surprised as Gene and I. "Man, you fuh real?"

"Yup."

Being the not-so-modest person he is, Pooquie naturally wanted to know . . . "What you dream about?"

Babyface wore a slight grin. "Well . . . we're going over your contract, and after we're done, you say: 'Well, it's time for me to pay up.' Then you stand up, rip off your shirt, unzip and drop your pants, knock the contract on the floor, climb atop the table on all fours, and say: 'A'ight, Counselor: It's time to chow down and throw down!' "

Everyone fell out, except Gene. "Well, it's clear how you wish to be paid for *your* legal services." He rose and went into the kitchen.

B.D. waved at me. "Can ya believe it? Our husbands having an affair!"

I pointed to Pooquie and Babyface. "I think we may have to keep an eye on you two." They blushed.

Hmm . . . knowing firsthand how well Babyface works that tongue and dick, I glanced in the kitchen and could clearly see Pooquie planted on the countertop with his chocolate pound cakes spread and Babyface chowing down before throwing down. It didn't rub me the wrong way, it rubbed me the *right* way—my dick got hard.

I was next.

"Tell someone something about them that bothers you the most."

That was easy. I turned to Pooquie. "I wish you were at a place where you could tell your family about yourself—and us." He and I had talked about this a lot. The nod he gave me affirmed he's slowly starting to realize that, after integrating me into his life the way he has, there's no way that his mother or his son's mother doesn't suspect we could be more than just friends.

I handed the hat to Gene, who had just returned with a cup of coffee—but he wouldn't take it. He was throwing me shade.

And, yes, I was gagging. "What?"

"Now, you know that ain't what you told me a few weeks ago."

I wasn't looking in his direction, but I could *feel* Pooquie tense up.

"Uh-oh, a challenge!" exclaimed B.D.

"What are you talking about?" I asked.

"You told me that the thing that bothers you the most about Pooquie is his being a drama queen."

I could see Pooquie out of the corner of my right eye freeze: he clutched the armrests of the easy chair and his head was titled down on a ninety-degree angle, avoiding everyone's gaze.

"I didn't say that," I laughed, trying to inject some humor into the haze of doubt filling the room.

Gene sucked his teeth. "Oh, no? Then what *did* you say?"

I struggled. "Well . . . if I remember correctly, I said that . . . that Pooquie sometimes has the bad habit of . . . of being a little too dramatic about some things, that he sometimes acts *like* a drama queen."

"That's not what *I* remember," declared Gene, crossing his arms and his legs. "Now, you did say that he has the bad habit of being a little too dramatic, that he sometimes overreacts to things—throwing a tantrum, storming off, running away. But you also said it bothers you a lot, and the last words out of your mouth were: 'I wish he wasn't such a drama queen.' "

I was playing it over in my mind and, yes, that was what I said. But I certainly didn't want to own up to it now. "Gene, you misunderstood me."

"I didn't misunderstand a thang. I know what I heard."

"Well, even if I did say that—"

"*Which* you did," he insisted.

"—I certainly didn't mean that he *is* a drama queen, as you originally stated."

"Ah, a stickler for details. The journalist in you is coming out. How convenient."

I was more than testy now. "Well, if you're going to quote me, quote me verbatim. As we see, one or two words can make the difference."

He huffed. "He *is* a drama queen, he acts *like* a drama queen . . . a distinction without a difference if you ask me. No matter how you try to break it down or rework it, it basically means the same thing."

Pooquie agreed. He, along with Gene, voted that I wasn't telling the truth. (B.D. sided with Babyface, who believed that the context was important, and since it was unclear based on our different accounts, they couldn't vote either way.) Pooquie simmered, but he did a jood job of keeping his top. But after they left (which wasn't long after the argument; it threw a wrench into and ended the game, and put a damper on the rest of the day), he blew up. He was more hurt and embarrassed than angry, and I could understand why: I would've felt the same way if I discovered in front of others (even if they were extended family like B.D., Babyface, and Gene) that my mate viewed me in such a way. But, in classic Pooquie fashion, he carried on about it (yeah, like a drama queen), accusing me of "insulting" his manhood and wondering out loud how he could fall in love with someone who thought of him that way. And, as is often the case when he is put out or off by me, he chose to sleep on the couch for the next six days (absolutely the longest he can go without being touched by or lying next to me).

The day after all of this drama unfolded (a Monday), Gene called and left a message on my answering machine at home. I didn't return it. He did the same thing Tuesday; again, I didn't respond. Wednesday night he called me at home; I wouldn't pick up. When those three days turned into a week, B.D. and Babyface stepped in to re-unite us, but nothing they said or tried worked. Gene showed up at my job just before Christmas and followed me home (I live just three blocks away from the junior high school I teach at); as he pleaded with me to talk to him, I wouldn't even acknowledge him, closing my front door in his face. And I brought in the New Year for the first time in six years without him (he called five seconds after 1995 began, wishing me the best).

"You think you makin' him suffer when you makin' yo'self suffer," Pooquie argued—and he was right. (That was advice he himself had to take to heart: He tried to punish me by holding back on the lovin,' but that "I ain't givin' you none" eventually turned into *"Yeah, mutha-fucka, bone it like you own it!"*) Pooquie saw how the separation from Gene was affecting me, and while a part of him may have been pleased that Gene was out of the picture (they've always butted heads because they have the same domineering personality and believe they should be number one in my life), he knew that I—and *he*—would continue to be miserable so long as Gene and I weren't speaking. So he "tricked" me into talking to him again: he called up Gene, placed him on speakerphone, and after Pooquie got me to admit how much I missed him, Gene entered the discussion with: "I miss you, too." Gene and I made up that night. I was still a little angry at him, but the bottom line was that I blamed Gene when I was really angry with myself for not thinking such a thing could come back to haunt me (not to mention coming up with that question in the first place; I didn't want any particular person to choose it, but I certainly didn't expect to have to answer it myself). Yes, Gene can be a wise-ass, but I hadn't told him this in confidence; I didn't swear him to secrecy. So it was fair game in the game we played. And it wasn't worth losing my best friend, the big brother I never had who served as my mentor "in the life" (i.e., the Black gay world), over.

Although Gene and I patched things up a few weeks ago (placing Truth or Shade on that list of things we will never partake of again), our schedules didn't allow us to hook up. But I planned to spend the entire weekend (which included the observance of Dead White Male Presidents' Day) with him—shopping, clubbing, and doing a whole lot of catching up and kee-keeing.

It was jood to see him again and he obviously felt the same way: He stood as I approached him and didn't give me the chance to put my bag down, almost snatching me up in his arms. I had to admit, the bear hug felt very jood; I hadn't realized just how much I missed him until then. How ironic that Phyllis Hyman's "Old Friend" happened to be playing at that moment.

He finally released me. "So . . . now that the dog's away, the pussy can come out and play, huh?"

I frowned. "Not funny."

"Believe me, that *wasn't* a joke."

"So, where's B.D.?" I asked, peeling off my leather jacket and placing it around the back of the stool.

"In the ladies' room." He sat back down.

I joined him. "To do more than just wash his hands before dinner, I'm sure."

"Indeed."

"Oh, how *fagulous!*" B.D. cried as he sashayed toward us. "It's so wonderful to have our three-for-T circle together again." He hugged us both by the neck.

Gene pushed him off. "Yeah, yeah, save it for Sally Messy Raphael, okay? I need another drink." He signaled for the bartender. "You want something, Mitch?"

"No. I'll wait till we eat. I'm starving."

Just then, a brother who was the embodiment of "tall, dark, and handsome"—probably six-six and three-hundred-plus pumped-up pounds, sporting a diamond stud in his right ear and a black fedora on his bald head, and wearing a bloodred turtleneck and scandalously tight black leather pants—scooted by us, winking at B.D.

B.D. licked his lips. "So am I."

I, too, was drooling. "Is *he* who you were busy with in the bathroom?"

"Uh-huh." He sighed.

About to sip his gin and tonic, Gene stopped. "And just how busy were y'all?"

"Ha, not *that* busy. But we were *very* busy years ago." He had a flashback. His whole body trembled. "Lawdamercy. If I weren't a married woman . . ." He turned to me. "And speaking of being a married woman: What kind of mischief do *you* plan on getting into now that the hubby will be out of town for a spell?"

"I'm not getting into any mischief."

"You're not?"

"No."

"Why not?"

"Why would I?"

"Why *wouldn't* you? I mean, a little bit of flirtin' and flashin' never hurt anybody."

Gene lifted his glass in a toast. "I'll drink to that!"

"But why would I do that? Pooquie and I, we're committed to each other."

"No, you two should *be* committed," Gene corrected.

"I'm committed to Babyface but, as you see, haven't retired from enjoying and engaging in the sights," testified B.D.

"Well, that might work for you, even Babyface. But that's not how it is for Pooquie and me."

B.D. folded his arms against his chest. "Oh? How do you know?"

"Because I know him. And he knows me. And we have that understanding."

B.D. gave me a quizzical look. "Uh, is this something you two have discussed?"

"Uh . . . well . . . no."

They grinned at each other. "Uh-huh."

I went on the defensive. "But it doesn't *have* to be discussed. It just is."

B.D. balked. "You are assuming that he feels the same way and wouldn't participate in any extracurricular activities, is that it?"

I was at a loss. "Well . . . well . . ."

"Chile, you can't assume, you gotta *know*." B.D. leaned on the bar. "You don't think Pooquie might, uh, stray while he is away?"

"No, I don't."

He looked at Gene. "And I thought *I* was the dense one in this family." He turned back to me. "Mitch, hon, you know I like Pooquie very much. But we're talking about a man who is three thousand miles away making his first film in a town where almost every person he meets or sees will be just as P-H-Y-N-E as him. You don't think he might be just a *little bit* tempted to taste a *little bit* of someone else?"

"No, 'cause *this* Little Bit gives him every *little bit* of what he needs," I confidently stated.

"I'm sure you do, dahling. But there's just one problem: You are *here* and he is *there*. And you know what they say: 'If you can't be with the one you *love* . . . ' "

Gene, the reigning president of the "Love Don't Live Here Anymore" Club, spit out his drink. B.D. giggled.

"What we have is strong enough to keep us for two weeks," I argued.

B.D. pointed to Gene. "Well, I hate to sound like the jaded queen that we all know and *sometimes* love who is seated at this very bar—"

"Shut up, bitch," snarled Gene, who was wiping his mouth with a tissue.

"—but, when you can lust the one you're with, what's *L* got to do with it?"

I accepted the challenge. "Well, *I* hate to sound like the helpless romantic that we all know and love who is seated at this very bar—"

Gene nudged B.D. "Hmmph, more like a *hopeless* romantic!"

"—but *L*'s got *everything* to do with it!"

B.D. shrugged. "Maybe so. But temptation knows everybody's name, hon. You don't stop being human 'cause you in *love*." He giggled as Gene visibly cringed. "Besides, you two are due."

"We're due?"

"Yes. There comes a time in every relationship where you get that . . . *itch*."

"You mean . . ." Marilyn Monroe came to mind . . .

. . . and being sort of a dumb blonde himself, he must've sensed it. "Yup, the seven year itch. But, in fag years, it's seventeen months."

"Seventeen months?" I repeated.

"Yes. If a couple makes it there, they are what you could call serious candidates. The not-so-serious last no more than seventeen weeks." He looked at Gene. "And the *un*serious?"

Gene gladly took that one. "Seventeen *days*."

B.D. nodded. "See. Too many of us fall in the latter category, so you know it's a surprise when ya reach the second plateau."

"Ha, and a *miracle* when you reach the third," Gene snickered.

"After all, how many gay couples do *you* know who have been together seventeen months or longer?" B.D. asked.

Hmm . . . I could only think of one.

B.D. grinned. He cut his eyes at Gene. "And *some* said we wouldn't last seventeen *hours*."

"Ha, it ain't over till the fat-*ass* lady sings," shot back Gene.

B.D. drew his claws. "But it *is* over for some of us, isn't it?"

I couldn't believe he went there. Gene broke up with Carl, the guy he had been seeing for over a year, last October. Gene still won't tell us why; B.D. and I figure Gene said or did something to fuck it up. But whatever happened, it wrecked Gene, even though he tried hard not to show it.

Gene glared at B.D. "*Any*way . . ."

"Uh-huh. An-ty-way . . . if my calculations are correct, you two have officially been together as a couple for seventeen months. And while y'all have been through a hell of a lot together, the real test—

infidelity—hasn't reared its head"—he suspiciously eyed me—"as far as we know. So, if neither one of you has creeped yet, it could happen very soon."

"I don't think so," I said in a very dismissive tone.

B.D. grasped and shook my arm. "Chile, you better snap out of that dreamworld, thinking it can't happen to you. *Every* man is capable of it."

"Every man?"

"Yes, every man."

"Even Babyface?"

"Well, he's a man. And, as quiet as it's kept, *I* happen to be one, too." Gene was about to jump in when B.D. cut him off: "Don't *even* go there."

"Uh . . . you've cheated on Babyface?" I asked.

"No, I haven't. But that doesn't mean I haven't thought about it, haven't been tempted—or haven't come close to it."

Gene and I moved in closer to him. "Really?" we both sang in unison.

"Yes, really."

"With who?" we echoed.

"If you two must know, Gerrold Garrett."

Gene wasn't impressed. "You mean the one with no neck?"

"Yes. And what he does not have between his head and shoulders he more than makes up for in other areas."

I grinned, picturing "Jiggly Gerrold" (as he's been affectionately dubbed), a member of Gene's dance troupe, in nothing but his tights and a thong. "Ha, he sho' nuff do!"

"I don't know if Babyface has," B.D. confessed, "but I'd be more than naive to think he hasn't thought about it, hasn't been tempted, or hasn't come close to it, also. Hell, he's *dreamed* of doing it with another man, as I am sure you're aware."

I nodded.

"And, if he *did* do it—and chances are that he has—I wouldn't want to know about it."

"You wouldn't?"

"No, I wouldn't."

"Why not?"

17

LOVE
THE
ONE
YOU're
WITH

"So long as he is treating me right, treating *us* right, why should it matter if he was, is, or will be with someone else? What we have isn't a moment in time, but what he would have with them *would* be.

"And, besides," he began, glancing at Gene, who declared right along with him, "He's a man."

"Just like *Pooquie*," enunciated Gene.

"Uh-huh. Just like you," added B.D.

YEAH . . . JUST LIKE ME.

We all like to think that what we have with our significant other has never existed before, that it's special, different—and I would have to say that my relationship with Pooquie *is* all of those things. It's not conventional. It's not typical. It's not average. It's not ordinary. Some (like Gene) would say that it's a *miracle;* after all, we're diametrically opposed opposites—he, the homie from Harlem; me, the buppie from Brooklyn. Yet that may be why we're so jood together: despite (or in spite of) the differences, we've grown to appreciate the other for who he is and not what we wish he would be (as the card he sent that I found in my mailbox just before I went to meet Gene and B.D. sang: "I Love You Just the Way You Are").

But, as the discussion with B.D. (and the ad-libs from Gene) illustrated, what we have is, like any relationship, vulnerable. And the truth is that I have always recognized this—it's just something I haven't had to focus on. After all, the world we've created together is so . . . cozy. It's far from perfect and we each have our own baggage to carry (and sort through), but we've found a groove that gives us the room to be ourselves, and with the addition of Junior, Pooquie's six-year-old son, it's made us a family. After roughly a year and a half, we've settled down. And it just doesn't feel jood to be with him; it feels . . . *safe.*

But given Pooquie's new public profile, that safety is slowly being . . . I guess the word is *threatened.* He doesn't "belong" to me anymore; his world has gotten and continues to get much bigger with every new modeling and acting job he gets. With that new world calling on him more and more, I'm seeing less and less of him—and others are trying to step in. He's gotten "love letters" from fans, not to mention a few pro-sports figures and hip-hop artists. While he has shared all of this with me (not to mention the edible underwear one rapper sent him) and finds it comical, I am fully aware that the more he is drawn into the spotlight, the more attractive this world may become—and the more likely it is that someone he meets in this new world could sweep him off his feet.

Funny thing, though, is that I never seriously considered that someone could sweep me off *my* feet. I've never met anyone like Pooquie, never *loved* anyone like him; no one has ever made me feel the way he makes me feel, and in the time we've been a couple, I've never considered being with someone else, never considered that there could *be* someone else. But *that* was all about to change. As B.D. warned, "Temptation knows everybody's name"—and I was about to find that out in a very big way . . .

3

Gene lives many, many, *many* miles from the Bronx Zoo, but his apartment could still be its souvenir shop.

The sign pasted below the bell on his door announces: IT'S *MY* HOUSE . . . AND *I* LIVE HERE. But the moment you step inside, there is evidence everywhere that he doesn't occupy the three-bedroom co-op alone. A bearskin rug welcomes you. Walk a few feet up the hallway and there's a shark fin dangling from the ceiling. Venture a few more feet, and at the end of the hall, you'll be greeted by Eloise, his wild boar head that is mounted on a closet door. Turn left, walk two yards, make a sharp right, go down three steps and you'll be in the sunken living room, where a panther lies in the center of the floor, its mouth wide open. Dancer and Prancer are on opposite walls, facing each other. Over the fireplace are four peacock tails encased in a gold frame, and four elephant tusks have been grafted onto the red brick, forming a horseshoe. On the coffee table is a six-foot-long coiled cobra and on either side of that lie two turtle shells that can be used as ashtrays. And, in his bedroom, directly over his king-size bed, is a lion's head, which is flanked by baboon masks.

The only things missing? Bugs, Daffy, Porky, Sylvester, and Tweety.

"Are you gonna be okay out here?" he asked.

"What do you mean?"

"What I just said . . . it's been some time since you've seen the children. You might wake up in the middle of the night and think you're having a nightmare."

"No, I'll be fine."

"Okay. Chile, I am going to bed. I am exhausted. I'll see ya in the mornin'."

"Okay. Jood night."

"*Jood* night?" He shook his head. "Lawd." He disappeared into his bedroom.

There were two pillows and a blanket on the mahogany leather sofa. I pulled off my boots, socks, jeans, and sweater, then headed to the bathroom to splash my face with some water before crashing.

I opened the pantry to get a washcloth, forgetting this would be the last place I'd find one. Like Imelda, Gene loves shoes—*really* loves them. His pantry doesn't have a single hand or bath towel in it, just eight rows of every designer name you can think of. There's over a hundred pairs in every color of the rainbow except orange, yellow, and pink ("The entire world can tell by looking at me I'm a fag; I don't need to broadcast it on my feet"). Sometimes, when searching for a particular pair, he discovers he has two of the same. He may not have worn them in a while and, seeing them again in a store, forgets he already has them. I've been shopping on three occasions with him when this has happened.

I closed up his shoe factory and found a washcloth where I should've looked: on the top shelf in one of his hall closets. I quickly scrubbed up.

Tossing and turning for an hour, I couldn't sleep. So I crept to the kitchen and dialed up Pooquie. I'd memorized the hotel's toll-free number.

"Good evening, the Beverly Hilton, how may I help you?"

"Yes, Room 1215, please."

"Hold on, please."

She connected me. Pooquie picked up on the first ring.

"Hello?"

"Hi, Pooquie."

"*Hay, Baby.* I'm *so* glad it's you. You musta known I wanted ta hear yo' voice."

"Oh? Then why didn't you call?"

" 'Cuz, I wasn't gonna have Gene cussin' me out, callin' his spot at three A.M."

I chuckled. "He wouldn't mind. After all, you're the reason why Gene and I are speaking again."

"Yeah well . . ."

"You sound exhausted. You had a long day?"

"A long, *hard* day, Baby. I just got back in like fifteen minutes ago."

"Wow. They're not kidding when they say eighteen-hour days, huh?"

"Nope. And we didn't even shoot today. At least I didn't. They just went over my lines wit' me, and had me practice some of my moves on tha court."

"Like *you* need practice when it comes to that?"

"I know, right? But, as that director said: 'We know you got the right moves; we just want to make sure the moves you got are right for us.' "

"And were they?"

"You know it, Baby. He's havin' their writers add two scenes so I can show 'em some mo' of what I got."

"Ah. Impressin' him already and he hasn't even filmed you yet. I'm so proud of you."

That's right, Pooquie . . . *blush*.

"But does that mean you won't be home in two weeks and two days?"

"Nah. They said it'll probably be like a extra minute of screen time, so hopefully it won't take longer than that ta film."

"Ah. Jood."

"So what y'all do tonite?"

"We had dinner with B.D."

"And how was that?"

"Jood. And we stopped off in Harry's. Gene met one of his old running buddies there who was in town for the weekend."

"You . . . have a jood time?" By the sound of his voice, he was hoping I didn't.

"Not really. It was just the same old faces wearing the same old drag and standing in their same old places. Even the same music was playing."

"Not Sylvester!"

"Yes, Sylvester. It was like I was just there last night, not two years ago. Ha, I was in *my* same old spot."

"By tha jukebox?"

"Yup."

"Anybody try ta talk ta you?"

"Mmm-hmm, that same old, *tired* Thompson Williams."

"Thom Thom?"

"I guess that's his nickname. You were chatting with him the night we met."

He was quiet for a few seconds; I guess he was going back in time. "You remember that?"

"I remember *everything* about the night we met."

I could feel that smile.

"I guess that's why I didn't enjoy myself. It wasn't the same without you. But it was nice being there and kind of reliving that first time."

"What Thom Thom hafta say?"

"The same old tired lines: When are we going to get together, I need to give him a chance, I know I want him—"

"And you gonna say yeah one day and he'll be waiting when ya do, right?"

We cracked up.

"That mutha-fucka is just so late. He ran that same shit down on me ev'ry time *I* fell up in there."

"Just imagine how he would feel if he knew we were together!"

"Yeah."

Silence.

"Little Bit?"

"Yes?"

"I miss you."

"I miss you, too, Pooquie. I can't believe you're three thousand miles away. You sound so close."

"I'm always close ta you, Baby. No matter how far I am."

"I know."

"Well, it's goin' on one here and I gotta be up and out by six."

"Oh. Then you better get some z's. Have a jood night."

"You, too, Baby."

"Dream about me."

"You all I dream about."

"I *better* be."

"What you say?"

"You heard."

"Uh-huh, talk that ying-yang all you wanna now. You ain't gonna be trippin' wit' that lip when I get back."

"We'll see."

"No, you'll *feel*, when I spank dat azz."

"If talkin' ying-yang will get me a spankin', you gonna have to keep a scorecard!"

We giggled.

"I love you, Little Bit."

"I love you, too, Pooquie. Talk with you tomorrow?"

"You know it. Bye." *Smack.*

Smack. "Bye."

My throat was kind of dry, so I went for the handle on the refrigerator, but I knew better than to look inside. I don't understand why Gene has one—it's always bare, as are the cupboards. He always eats out or orders up; the tool drawer is filled with menus and flyers from dozens of neighborhood eateries and diners (his cookware consists of a single cast-iron skillet, which he once used as a weapon when a piece got beside himself). And the one food item he always has in stock— whipped cream—isn't kept in the kitchen. Like Blanche Devereaux, it can be found in his bedroom.

But, to my complete shock, there were liters of Coke and Canada Dry ginger ale, a quart of Tropicana orange juice, two sixteen-ounce bottles of Snapple raspberry iced tea, and a dozen Entenmann's mixed doughnuts (plain, white powdered, and chocolate) in a cardboard box on the top shelf. Attached to the box was a big red bow and a note:

> *I knew you'd look in here, so I thought I'd make it worth your while . . . for once. Welcome back.*

I grinned.

I WAS SHAKEN OUT OF SLEEP BY A FAMILIAR SOUND: Patti Labelle, crowing in a very accusatory tone, "If you want somebody to be your slave . . ."

Gene starts off every day with his anthem: "Get You Somebody New." While it's a killer track (when Patti, Nona, and Sarah screamed *"I can't stand it!"* for close to three minutes without so much as a breath between them, you just know that studio's foundation *shook*), it is a bit intense for the A.M. hour. But a man with such quirky (some would consider weird) hygiene rituals *would* have such an off-the-wall morning theme: He opts for baking soda instead of toothpaste ("It don't matter if it comes flavored or in a gel, the shit is still nasty"); applies Neat to his face instead of shaving cream and a razor ("I don't plan on having acne under my chin when I'm older"); blow-dries his pubic hair ("I *hate* being damp in that area"); and uses milk of magnesia as an astringent ("If it's good enough to clean your insides . . ."), then waxes and buffs that face as if it were a hardwood floor (he borrowed this regimen from the opening of *Mommie Dearest*).

By the time he's done, the song will have played six times—and I, like LaBelle, am ready to shout, *"I can't stand it!"*

"Mornin', mister," he sang, flouncing out of the bathroom.

"Mornin'. Have we finished beautifying ourselves?"

"Yes. As Kathleen Battle chirped during her concert with La Norman: 'I Feel Prit-*tee!*' "

"Well, let's not deprive the world the pleasure of seeing it for themselves—I'll be ready in a bit."

"Good, 'cause we got a little shopping to do today. The sooner we're out of here, the better . . ."

For gay men, there is no such thing as a *little* shopping, for even when Gene says "a little" he still means a lot. I know I have to wear my walking shoes—we'll be out at least four hours. (If he said, "We goin' shoppin'," I would snap on my hiking boots, for we'd be in the streets a *minimum* of six.) But when he informed me just how little shopping he would do, I gasped.

"You're not buying a thing?" We were chomping down on doughnuts in his living room.

"Nope." He took a swig of his morning power drink: a mimosa.

"No cologne?"

"Nope."

"No jewelry?"

"Nope."

"Not even a handkerchief?"

"Nope."

Those were his hallmarks—if he didn't get anything, he purchased one of if not all three. "Why?"

"Because, darling, all the things I would buy are going to be given to me next week at the birthday party. Each person has been told what to buy, where to buy it, how much it costs, and whether or not the store will take a pint of their blood instead of currency, credit, or a check as payment."

"You didn't tell me what you wanted me to give you . . ."

"Chile, *you* are the gift I want from you for my birthday."

We nodded.

"So, what are we going shopping for, then?"

"We'll be doing something I've never done before—window-shop. I want to show you all the things I'll be getting next week."

And so he did. After we got manicures and pedicures at his favorite Korean-owned salon, Finger Tips & Toe Dips, he took me on the sightseeing tour: Willi Wear leather pants, a Ralph Lauren cashmere sweater, two Geoffrey Beene dress shirts, a Donna Karan athletic suit, dark brown Bruno Magli loafers, a bottle of Calvin Klein's Obsession, a twenty-four-karat-gold money clip, a Gucci clutch, and special multiple CD collections by the Maestro of Love, Barry White, and the Queen of Rap 'n Raunch, Millie Jackson. And he "presented" the merchandise as if he were one of those models on *The Price Is Right*.

Given that we didn't have to push or bum-rush our way through the maddening crowds to catch a sale or test our patience waiting in line to pay for anything (I didn't make any purchases either), the little shopping we did was a whole lot peaceful.

It was during our two dining experiences of the day, though, that the true melodrama unfolded.

For lunch we had Kentucky Fried Chicken, and it never fails—every time I go into a KFC, they get my order wrong. I specifically ask for a two-piece meal, original recipe, thigh and wing, and I always get a wing/breast or a thigh/leg combo.

This time they really screwed it up—I received a leg and a breast, the two pieces I never eat. And the way the cashier was acting out, you'd think *I* was the one who fucked up, not her.

"That's what you ordered, that's what you got," she snapped, after I approached her about the order being wrong. Her French curl had blond and cherry highlights, and she sported those grotesque, gargoyle-like claws these B-girls have the nerve to call nails (which made it hard for her to handle money).

As Gene would say: She wasn't ghettofied but ghetto*fried*. And he was about to turn up the heat under the frying pan.

Before I had a chance to respond to her—we had been in this same position several times before, but not with someone as belligerent as her—he jumped in. "Look, *Ugly*meesha, or whatever constipated name your mama gave you," he began, ignoring the name tag that said TRAYMEESHA and causing her to twirl her head back and suck her teeth while those around us giggled, "the customer—who is *always* right—asked for a thigh and a wing."

"No, he didn't," she barked.

"Oh, no?" Gene presented a microcassette recorder. He pressed the play button.

"Can I take your order?" her annoying voice repeated on the tape.

"Yes, I'll have a two piece meal, original, a thigh and a wing, with mash and potato salad as the sides, and a medium orange drink please."

He clicked off the recorder. "You were saying, Miss Thing-a-ma-jig?"

All eyes on her, she was paralyzed. The employee who fixed the order—a long, lanky, light-skinned Latino gent—stepped in. "Uh, I'll get that for you right away, sir."

"Thank you," I replied.

"Do have a good day," he advised, handing me my tray.

"I will. You do also."

"Oh, and remember," Gene directed toward her, "you're supposed to say, '*Good* afternoon, welcome to KFC, *may* I take your order, please?'—okay?"

As we sat down, he shook the recorder triumphantly. "I *knew* this might come in handy. I'll carry it with me again if we take any future trips into a Krazy Fried Chicken." He dropped it in his pouch and pulled out what I thought he was reaching for at the counter: his hot sauce. Like Patti, he never leaves home without it. I laughed as he twisted off its cap.

"What the hell is so funny?" he grumbled.

"Uh, nothing. It's . . . it's just great to see you again."

"Ya know, you are always picking the worst time to get mushy on me. Let's eat our fried flour so we can get out of here."

Gene's not good at handling tender moments. But this time he softened: He picked up his drink, motioning for me to do the same. We clinked.

Dinner at Anita's, a steak house and pub near Lincoln Center, was a mess for a whole nother reason. The meal itself was great (we both had shrimp platters). And the waiter, Ethan, was not only gracious but attentive; we never had to request that our drinks be refreshed, and he was at our table every five minutes to ensure that everything was satisfactory. I hate eating out and having to do the work of the person waiting on you; I shouldn't have to call on the host to locate the waiter/waitress to take our order, or ask the server for something simple like ketchup (the little things do mean a lot).

But then the check came.

Since Gene took care of lunch, this was my treat. Things just didn't add up: It appeared that an appetizer had been included that we didn't order.

I was trying to get Ethan's attention when Gene reviewed the check. "Ah . . . I see what the problem is."

"What is it?"

"Mr. Thing added his tip."

"Say what?"

"That eight dollars and eighty-five cents is what he *believes* he should receive as a gratuity."

I took the check from him. I studied it. "Well, what he *thinks* he should get and what he *will* get will be two totally different things."

The check was $38.75, minus the tip. I got out my calculator, multiplied that figure by 0.15 and came up with $4.48. I rounded it off to $4.50 just to be nice.

Naturally, when Ethan saw that the funds on the table were lower than the actual total he submitted, he confronted us. "I'm sorry, but there seems to be a mistake."

"Uh-huh, and you made it," Gene snickered under his breath.

I tried not to laugh. "What's the problem?"

"You didn't pay the full amount."

"Oh, we did. I do believe my dining partner and I were more than satisfied with the service"—I glanced at Gene, who nodded—"but you added a gratuity to the check when you had no right to."

He got rather indignant. "I do so have that right. I'm given that discretion by management."

Uh-huh . . . the discretion to discriminate. The stereotype in the service industry is that you can't count on Black folks to tip correctly (if at all), so some businesses take it upon themselves to make sure we do—even if it means breaking their own rules regarding tipping and the law.

Well, I wasn't having it. "It doesn't matter what discretion you are given by the management. If it's not in writing, it doesn't apply. Your menu clearly states that you can take such action with parties of five or more and/or after ten P.M.—and, as you can plainly see, we are not such a party, nor is it after ten P.M."

"Excuse me?" The voice came from a table a few feet away from us. The man it belonged to stood up and walked over with a check in his left hand. "I couldn't help but overhear . . . was a tip placed on your check by this waiter, also?"

I was so mesmerized by him—he was a live ringer for Mario Van Peebles, except he was a shade lighter, bald, and had a much bulkier frame—that Gene had to respond for me. "Yes, it was."

"Well . . ." He surveyed the dining hall and turned to the waiter. "I certainly hope this didn't happen because we're the only Black people in here."

Ethan turned beet red.

Another white man—fiftyish, frumpy, and freckled—jumped into the fray. "I'm Howard, the assistant manager, and I certainly hope you're not suggesting you've been treated differently because of skin color, sir."

The mystery man frowned. "I am not *suggesting,* I'm *inquiring,* Howard."

"This establishment does *not* discriminate," Howard emphatically declared.

"Well, if that is the case, I surely hope that every single party in this restaurant receives a similar computation on their check—otherwise you will be answering to Public Advocate Mark Green, the Better Business Bureau, the New York State Council on Civil Rights, and the NAACP."

Flustered, Howard fell into passive-aggressive white-boy mode. "Sir, you're getting a little too excited and there's no need to make threats. I would hate to call the authorities if you and this other gentleman refuse to pay."

Ain't that just like white folks: They want to call the cops because you have the nerve to expect to be treated like a human being.

Well, this white man was in for a *big* surprise.

"You won't have to," the mystery man advised as he held up his badge.

Now Howard's face, like Ethan's, had turned a beet red. He focused on the badge. "Officer Rippington?"

"*Detective* Rippington," he corrected.

As Gene chuckled, Howard stumbled. "Uh, I, we, um . . . let me, uh . . . please, excuse us for just a moment." He grabbed the waiter by the arm and they huddled, speaking in hushed tones. They probably depended on Black customers not putting up a fight and just paying the bill; surely, the police wouldn't buy their claims of racism and they would be viewed as criminals for attempting to skip out without paying. And, of course, the restaurant can continue the practice, knowing that the law will inadvertently protect and preserve their right to mistreat us.

Not this time, motherfucker.

Howard now had that phony-ass smile white folks wear when they know they've been caught in their shit. "I, uh, am so sorry for this . . . mix-up."

"Adding a tip to a check when you have no right to is *not* a mix-up," I argued.

"Uh . . . well, then, let's say, a misunderstanding."

"And that ain't true, because we understand exactly what happened and why it happened," Gene huffed.

"Uh . . ." The lightbulb went on; Howard clasped his hands together. "I'll tell you what: Why don't I just take those checks and refigure the amounts, and if you wish to, you can leave the waiter a tip . . ." He reached for them.

"I'll tell *you* what," Detective Rippington began, "why don't you be a smart man and pay for our meals. Better to pay for your fuck-up now than to pay for it later."

Howard didn't like that suggestion, but given what could happen, he reluctantly agreed to it.

Detective Rippington—first name, Mykle—got Howard's full name, as well as Ethan's, and warned them both that if he received any reports that they were still treating Black customers in this manner, he'd make good on his threat. But, as he admitted to us outside the restaurant while his dining partner—his younger brother, Jarome, who was equally handsome—went to get their car, he intended to make good on them anyway.

"I would love to get your information . . . so that the officials who handle this sort of thing can contact you." While there may have been some truth in the last part of his statement, even he didn't totally buy it; that smirk gave it away.

"Sure." I gave him my name and number.

"Thanks. Here's my card."

I took it.

"I'm sorry we had to meet under circumstances like this."

"Me, too. Thank you for stepping in when you did."

Jarome pulled up, honking his horn.

"I've got to go. Great meeting you."

"You, too."

We shook hands. He did the same with Gene. We watched as they sped off, he waving good-bye.

Now, *he's* New York's *phynest*.

And Gene noticed that I noticed. "Uh-huh," he cooed in his best Jackée "Sandra Clark" Harry voice.

"And what does that mean?"

"That means your man ain't been out of town forty-eight hours and you're already actin' like a ho."

"I am not."

"Like you don't know what effect batting those very long eyelashes have. Chile, *please*. He was swept all up in it. And you, barely able to talk when you first saw him."

"He just . . . caught me by surprise."

"Mph. Is this the same man who said just last night that no other man could catch his eye?"

"I didn't say that."

"You may as well have."

"I can admire from afar, can't I?"

"Darling, you were doing more than admirin' that man. And you certainly weren't taking him in from a distance; y'all were so far up in each other's face I thought you were gonna start tonguin' each other down right here on the sidewalk."

I shrugged. "All right, I can admit being . . . turned on by him."

"Ha, if Detective Rippington called you, you would no doubt return that call—and then *you'd* be turned out by *him*." He took the card. "I'll hold on to this."

"Why?"

"Well, since you're a married woman, why would you need it?"

"We might file a complaint against the restaurant, and—"

"Yeah, right, save it for *The People's Court*, okay?" He placed the card in his wallet. "There's no sense in inviting temptation in, is there?"

No . . . I guess there isn't.

AFTER I VIEWED AND WATCHED HIM REENACT ALMOST every scene from *All About Eve* for the thousandth time on the giant-screen TV in his entertainment room, we retired to Gene's bedroom with the other half of the chocolate marble cheesecake he purchased at Veniero's. We finished it as we watched his *Roseanne* tape. That he likes the show surprises me—a sitcom about the travails of a white working-class family in a bum-fuck hick town in the Midwest doesn't quite complement the other shows he adores (*I'll Fly Away, Cagney & Lacey, Maude, Dynasty*, and—of course—*The Golden Girls*). And given that he grew up around a lot of poor white trash in Fairfax, Virginia, that he had no tolerance for, his warming up to the Conners was truly Twilight Zone–ish. But what he really loves about the show is Roseanne—or rather, her mouth. He relishes the verbal barbs she spews. Well, in actuality, he's watching himself: If Gene was, were, or came back as a white hetero woman, he'd be Roseanne (the quips that fire out of her mouth are so similar to things he has or would say). As he put it: "This is probably the closest I'll ever come to seeing myself on TV."

I enjoy the way the show debunks the myth of the harmonious, homogeneous nuclear family (which is why many industry folk and family-values nuts can't stand it), and many of the shows he's recorded are some of my favorites: Roseanne's grandmother disclosing at Thanksgiving dinner that her mother had Roseanne out of wedlock; Roseanne's father dying and how she finally makes peace with him; Roseanne denying the Halloween spirit and being visited by the past, present, and future ghosts of the unholy holiday, à la *A Christmas Carol;* Roseanne getting breast-reduction surgery; Becky and Darlene being overly nice to Roseanne on Mother's Day in the hopes she'll allow them to attend a concert in another state; Roseanne's mother deciding she wants to move to Lanford—to the dismay of Roseanne and Jackie; Roseanne teaching Darlene's home-economics class the art of feeding a family of five on a nonexistent budget; Roseanne clashing with her new, snooty, stuck-up neighbor; Roseanne imploding when she discovers that Dan's had lunch with an old flame; the two-parter when Dan's bike shop goes belly-up and Becky elopes; and, Gene's all-time number one: when Joan Collins guests as Roseanne's rich cousin Ronnie (*"I'm* a bitch? I *bow* to the queen of *all* bitches!"*).

We were watching the episode where Roseanne learns Jackie has been physically abused by Fisher, her much-younger beau, when Gene asked without so much as looking at me through the corner of his eye: "He hasn't hit you again, has he?"

We hadn't broached the subject of Pooquie's punching me since it happened. Gene was against our getting back together and warned that if he did it once, he'd do it again. So I was happy to report that . . .

"No, he hasn't," I stated confidently.

He nodded.

Just then, the phone rang. He picked it up. "Speak . . ." His eyes widened. "*Ah* . . . your ears must have been burnin', 'cause we were *just* talkin' about you . . . oh, nothin' major. How are things going out there in Earthquake Country?" He winked at me. "Uh, don't get testy with me, mister. The executive producer of *Hard Copy* happens to be a *jood* friend of mine, and all I gotta do is dial them digits and we'll be seeing a two-part exposé on you next week . . . all right, that's better . . . yes, he's right here. Break a leg, or two. Hold on."

I covered the receiver's mouthpiece. "Gene, do you mind . . . ?"

He huffed. "*Damn. I'm* getting thrown out of *my* bedroom so *you* can exchange *sour* nothings with *your* man. Something is wrong with this picture." He hopped out of bed, turned, and bowed. "I'll be in the kitchen if you need anything, Your Majesty." He closed the door behind him.

"Hi, Pooquie."

"Hay, Baby. How u be?"

"I be jood. And you?"

"I be *very* jood."

"Oh really? Why?"

"You know why."

"I do?"

"Yup. I found it."

"You found what?" It clicked. "*Oh.* Well, it took you long enough!"

"Yeah. I was lookin' fuh my shavin' cream and there it was in my kit."

"I thought you were going to shave when you got in Thursday. That's why I put it there."

"I was, but I fell asleep. And then I was gonna do it last night, but then a producer said that shadow on my face gave me a rougher look and that I should keep it. But I guess one of them other actors thought I was stealin' *their* look and complained ta tha director."

"Ah. Show business."

"Uh-huh. I been list'nin' ta it tha past two hours, over 'n' over."

"So, you're enjoying it, I gather?"

"You gather right."

"I'm glad. Any song you like in particular?"

"All of 'em are smokin'. But that first one on side A is *workin'* me. I ain't never heard it befo'. What is it called, 'Wait Right Here'?"

" 'Til I See You Again.' "

"Ah. It's Gladys and the Pips, right?"

"Yeah. It was on their last album for Columbia Records. Most folk haven't heard of it. It's the best song on that album, and I'd rate it as one of the best they've ever done."

"I agree. It's up there wit' 'Neither One of Us . . .' and 'If I Were Your Woman.' I love it. I can hear you singin' it ta me."

"When you get back, I will."

"Nah, I wanna hear you sing it *now.*"

"*Now?*"

"Yeah. You don't sing that kinda song up close 'n personal."

Jood point. But . . . "Right now?"

"Yeah. Please, Baby, please, Baby, *pleeze?*"

One thing about Pooquie: He *ain't* too proud to beg. And I'm a sucker for it every time. I gave in.

When I was done, he moaned a sigh. "*Mmm* . . . that just makes me feel so jood. Thanks, Little Bit."

"You're welcome. Uh . . . you're tingling, aren't you?"

He giggled.

"Yeah, you're tingling," I replied, answering my own question.

"You know singin' ta me turns me on. I get hot like fire."

"Uh-huh, and that's exactly why I didn't want to do it: I ain't there to put the fire out. Guess you're gonna have to take a cold shower."

"*Hell*-fuckin'-no. I'm gonna do tha beef jerky!"

I laughed. "Pooquie, you're a mess."

"Ha, I plan ta be when I'm finished, b*elieve* me, Baby."

"I believe you, I believe you."

"Uh, I guess I better get some sleep. I gotta be on tha set at three."

"In the morning?"

"Yup."

"Damn."

"We shootin' some late-nite b-ball and hangin'-out-in-da-'hood scenes."

"Okay. It's almost nine there. You better go."

"Yeah. Thanks fuh thinkin' of me, Baby. And thinkin' of me that way."

"There's no other way to think of you, Pooquie. And think of me while you're, you know, jerkin' da beef."

"You know I will be."

"I love you."

"I love you too."

We exchanged a lot of smacks and a couple of pops.

"Jood night, Pooquie."

"Jood nite, Baby."

Right on cue, Gene reentered the room. He had two jelly glasses.

"Lawd, I thought you two would *never* stop," he cried, handing one to me.

"Were you listening?"

"Of course I was. I couldn't help *but* listen, *Gladys*."

"I made him an 'I'll Be Missing U' tape. That was one of the songs on it. He wanted me to sing it for him."

"I know. I heard. And so did the rest of the neighborhood."

"I wasn't loud."

"You were loud enough. And all that saliva swapping . . . I bet the surgeon general would declare *that* unsafe."

I sipped; it was some of his famous rum punch. "Thanks for the drink."

"You're welcome. You're gonna need it."

"Huh?"

"I have something I want you to see . . ." He walked over to his dresser drawer. He pulled out a piece of paper. He sat near me, on the edge of the bed. He handed it to me.

In bold type, it said:

LAST WILL & TESTAMENT

I glanced at him.

"Yes, it's my will," he confirmed.

I certainly didn't want to finish reading it. It's one thing to know you're going to die one day—it's another to actually plan for it. I put the drink down on the nightstand and went on . . .

> I, Eugene "Gene" Roberts, being of very sound mind and exquisite body.

My eyes darted from the paper to him.

He knew why. "Well, it *is* exquisite!"

I shook my head and continued:

> hereby bequeath all of my earthly possessions—my apartment
> and all of its contents, any and all funds in my bank accounts,
> and even the pocket change found in between the sofa cush-
> ions—to Mitchell Sylvester Crawford.

I looked up.

"Yes, I am leaving *everything* to you. That sorry-ass sperm dona-
tor identified as father on my birth certificate ain't gettin' *shit*.
You'll no doubt want to keep the record collection, maybe even the
fuck films. The animals you can officially turn over to the Bronx
Zoo. And you can donate all the clothes and shoes to homeless
shelters. Goodwill and the Salvation Army ain't makin' no green
off of me."

I was speechless. "Gene . . . I . . . I don't know what to say."

"How about 'Thank you'? I ain't dead yet, but I wouldn't be
insulted if you showed a *little* joy over hitting the lottery."

"But . . . why are you showing me this now?"

"Well, why not? May as well know you're in the will. Ha, you *are*
the will. But just don't get any ideas: I ain't Doris Duke, and I do plan
on dying a natural death, okay?" He cackled. When he saw I hadn't
joined him, he stopped. "What is it?"

I hesitated. "Are . . . you all right?"

"What do you mean?"

"Are you . . . all right?" I repeated, more solemn than the first time.
He knew what I meant.

He sighed. "I . . . I had a lump . . . on my back. Just below my
neck. I . . . had a biopsy. Last December."

As my eyes grew large, I inhaled with dread.

"No, I don't have cancer," he assured me.

I exhaled my relief.

"But just the idea . . . it scared the shit out of me. Still does."

"So . . . you . . . had to go through it alone."

"B.D. and Babyface, they were around. And Carl . . . tried to be."

Ah . . . I'd finally get the lowdown on why they broke up. "He tried
to be?"

"You know how I am. I can't be the vulnerable one, the needful one. Even after I got beat up . . ." His voice drops and trails off whenever he brings up the night he was gay-bashed, two summers ago in the Vill. They caught the three punks who did it; they pleaded guilty to a variety of charges, including several counts of aggravated assault and assault with a deadly weapon (they took turns punching and kicking him while one knocked him out with a bottle of Coke he had just purchased at a store), and are each serving a minimum of five years. Because he suffered a concussion, a cracked jaw, a broken nose and right arm, fractured ribs, and a damaged left testicle, he had to take a two-month leave of absence from his position as a publicist at Simply Dope Records to recover. But I know the physical healing happened faster than the emotional.

He heaved. "I . . . I let him in, but not all the way. But with something like that I had to and . . . I just couldn't put my pride aside."

"You mean your ego," I corrected.

He frowned. "Thank you for the clarification." He sighed. "I pushed him away. So, yeah, I kinda went through it alone."

I took his hands in mine. "Oh, I'm so sorry, Gene."

"Chile, why are *you* sorry? *I'm* the one who's sorry. I let this motor run and almost lost you because of it. You were the one I needed, and when I needed you the most . . . I had no one but myself to blame you weren't around, that you didn't want to be around me. I realized just how much you mean to me. Not having you in my life . . . I don't know what I would do."

We hugged. Tighter and tighter and tighter. Our shirts were soaked with the other's tears.

Then it hit me: This is why I haven't seen a cigarette in his hand the last two days. He would've gone through three packs by now. Last night at dinner with B.D. and tonight at Anita's, we sat in the smoking section but he didn't light up.

"Did you quit?"

He pulled away. "Ha, sometimes you can be just as slow as that Brain Dense child."

I smiled. "How long has it been?"

"Exactly two months."

"Did you join a support group? Are you a patient at a clinic that helps people kick the habit?"

"Hell no. I just stopped."

"Cold turkey?"

"Yup."

"Gene, you've been smoking since you were fifteen."

"I know. I was there."

"You just can't stop like that."

"I *can* just stop like that. *I* can do anything, have you forgotten?"

"Yeah. I guess I have. But given how much you love it and how long you've done it . . . not having one for more than two hours is one thing, but two months? You should've exploded or something by now."

He giggled. "Yeah, spontaneous combustion. Hell, I ain't cured. And I still get the craving. But anytime I get really weak, I just remember the pain of them sticking that needle in me." He gently stroked the upper left part of his back. "No doctor or nurse is *ever* going to do that to me again."

"It wasn't malignant, but . . . are you out of the danger zone?"

"Given my history, the doctor says it's no wonder my lungs don't look like the sky on a foggy Frisco day. They're going to monitor me over the next few months."

"Well, if you want me to go with you—"

"I do."

Silence.

"Why didn't Babyface and B.D. tell me?"

"Because it wasn't their place to tell you. This was something I had to handle. But if it turned out I did have it, I would've told Pooquie."

"You would?"

"Yes. When I got that phone call from him last month . . . he proved that he is worthy of my respect."

"He'll be happy to hear that."

"No, he won't, 'cause you ain't gonna tell him. He's still on probation."

"Probation?"

"That's right."

"And when will that be over?"

"When you two have celebrated your *fiftieth* anniversary."

We laughed.

"How do you think Babyface and B.D. will feel about your leaving everything to me?"

"Babyface doesn't care. He helped me draft it." He pointed to Babyface's signature on the document; I didn't recognize it since I've never addressed him by his given name (Courtney Lyons) in the five years I've known him. "But I'm sure B.D. will be flabbergasted. He's always had his eye on my fake mink stole. You can give it to him."

"Why don't you just put it in the will?"

"Because if I left *him* something, then everyone else would trip."

"Ah. So have everybody angry with me, right?"

He elbowed me in the side. "You got it." He leaned against me, his head resting against my neck. "I don't *ever* want to be missing you like that again."

I lowered my head onto his. "You won't."

4

"It's the only thing—besides you—that could get me to venture into Crooklyn."

So says Gene about Body & Soul, a dance held every Sunday night in Brooklyn. I hadn't attended it in some time. In fact, I haven't been to a club since Pooquie and I closed a spot called UnderCover up in the Bronx the summer we started seeing each other. (UnderCover is exactly that: a place where all those boyz who are very *under cover*—including those homiesexuals in hip-hop—can go to jam.) Body & Soul lives up to its name: You don't come to dance; you come to Dance. You will sweat the stress, wash the worries, abandon the angst. You won't just work that body—you'll set your soul free. And, while the slammin' sounds of the disco/dance era take you on that trip to Redemption, you won't find the aloofness, antagonism, and attimatude that pollutes much of the Black gay club scene. No muscle heads or cutie pies whose noses rise three inches in the air if you talk to them—or whose eyes hold you in contempt if you don't. No crafty cretins whose main purpose is to break up other people's happy homes because theirs is so *un*happy. No Geritol Granddads preying on the Embryos (or vice versa). No homiesexuals holding up the walls, standing guard like pit bulls and wearing menacing stares that would make Medusa turn to stone. No Queens *without* a Country holding court on a stool they rent nightly, being way too catty and way too loud. And, what do you know, not a single "cool" or "hip" Caucasian, or a Snow Cone hangin' on his arm who feels out of place because there's way too much Negritude in the room (but, like his man, watches us in awe as if they are on safari in Africa).

Just the brothers coming together to do the Chic cheer: *Dance, Dance, Dance*.

For Gene, it just isn't about the Dance. The party reminds him of the very festive and fierce Paradise Garage, the dance-club landmark that preceded Body & Soul, the H(e)aven away from home for Black and Latino gay men in the seventies and early eighties. Gene met many of his friends there and, after the club closed its doors, saw many of those friends die—of AIDS. He'll well up when certain songs are played—most notably, Patti LaBelle's "Music Is My Way of Life." He's recognized that while they may be gone, the music didn't die inside *himself*. It's left up to him to celebrate the lives they lived and the life he has. As Patti testifies, "When the music plays, I gotta keep dancin' . . ." And so he does.

Before we headed to Brooklyn, though, we made a pit stop that was truly the pits. Gene had comps for Dizzy's, which claims to be "the only club in America where disco isn't dead." I wasn't too thrilled about going; given who was on the flyer (a chiseled white man in white Calvin briefs . . . how *unoriginal*), I knew we were not going to see the type of folk or hear the type of "disco" we would hear at Body & Soul.

And, when we pulled up in front of Dizzy's, the song that greeted us confirmed my suspicions: the Bee Gees' "Night Fever," which the deejay introduced just before the first verse with: "And here are the true innovators of disco." *Huh?* If there is any "white" act that could be called a disco innovator, it'd have to be K.C. & the Sunshine Band (and they were a mixed-race group). White folks finally decided disco was worthy of being respected when *Saturday Night Fever* hit, but the Bee Gees' work was truly cheesy and lacked the grit and soul of *real* disco (listen to the other *Fever* soundtrack contributors—Kool & the Gang, Tavares, and the Trammps—to hear the proof). I've always argued that if disco died, *they* were to blame: because of their hokey misappropriation it's no wonder that, twenty-five-million-plus albums later, the world overdosed on them and wished the genre itself would go away.

So, I wanted us to, as Soul II Soul once chanted, "Keep on Movin'."

"Let's just go to Brooklyn, Gene," I insisted, tugging on his arm as he paid the taxi driver.

"Chile, we won't stay long." He opened the cab door and stepped out. "Besides, it's always good to see how the other half is *not* having fun."

After checking our coats and passing through a makeshift museum that housed a gold record of the Bee Gees', the Golden Globe Paul Jabara won for "Last Dance" (the theme from the not-as-celebrated disco flick *Thank God It's Friday*), and the velvet ropes used outside Studio 54, we entered the main room—and were assaulted by the lights. Strobe beams flickered green, red, and yellow in every direction. A giant, silver-studded, spinning disco ball hovered above the center of the dance floor, which itself blinked on and off. All the flashing annoyed the hell out of us but didn't seem to bother the rest of the clientele.

"This would be a sniffer's paradise for those who love cocaine," Gene observed.

"You got that right." In fact, you could count the Negroes on two hands—and you know I counted them (yes, I included Gene and me). Most of the two-hundred-plus white men seemed out of place in that bland and boring white-short-sleeved-T-and-faded-blue-jean ensemble. There were a few preppies (khakis, varsity sweatshirts, and loafers) and a lone punk sporting purple spiked hair, slashed denims, and black Doc Martens. But some *did* keep in tune with the spirit of the place: several had on platforms and bell-bottoms, there was a Village People incarnation (the Cop, the Construction Worker, the Sailor, and the Indian, who was a *very* pale face), a Donna Summer drag*on* queen (he was a beast), and, of course, a half-dozen John Travolta wannabes, dressed in silk shirts and white polyester suits. Unfortunately, everyone (including the few colored folk) were doing that white-boy shuffle: moving and clapping off beat, some so erratically you'd think they were on drugs (they probably were; the only way some folks can listen to disco is if they *are* fucked up).

We got our complimentary drinks and stood directly below the deejay booth. We were hoping our distaste for the selections would be felt by her and the music would get better. It didn't. The Bee Gees were followed by Leo Sayer ("You Make Me Feel Like Dancin' "), Leif Garrett ("I Was Made for Dancin' "), Rod Stewart ("Do Ya Think I'm Sexy?"), and, the ultimate horror of horrors, Rick Dees ("Disco

Duck"). If *this* is the music that people define disco by, it's no wonder there were well-publicized and well-attended events where stacks of disco records were demolished and/or torched (hell, I would've volunteered to drive the bulldozer or start the fire). It was odd that we hadn't heard any Black female artists; Diana's "Love Hangover," Thelma's "Don't Leave Me This Way," Gloria's "I Will Survive," and almost anything by Donna are staples at white gay clubs. Whether these ladies were already played or coming up next, we didn't plan on sticking around to find out: as Cher began pleading "Take Me Home," we made our exit.

The best things in life aren't always free.

Three dollars is all the folks who put on Body & Soul charge and it's a criminally low sum to pay for the very jood time you know you'll have. Frankie Knuckles, undoubtedly *the* greatest deejay and mix master ever, was on the turntables this eve, so we knew he'd be crankin' out those classics nonstop (jood thing I wore my dancin' shoes: a pair of black Rockports that are also great for walking). We arrived just as the horn-howling intro to *the* "let's get this party started *right*" tune blared: Cheryl Lynn's "Got to Be Real." Frankie continued on a Disco Diva run: Evelyn "Champagne" King ("Shame"), Aimee Stewart ("Knock on Wood"), Anita Ward ("Ring My Bell"), Miss Ross ("The Boss"), Karen Young ("Hot Shot"), Candi Staton ("When You Wake Up Tomorrow"), and Taana Gardner ("Heartbeat"). And, as it always does, Patti's "Music . . ." caused Gene to go into a trance, his body jerking as if he were having a seizure. By the end of the song I was rocking him like a baby, as he sobbed. But he did a three-sixty on Loleatta Holloway's "Hit & Run" (unlike Loleatta, Gene believes in stickin' but not stayin').

Then Frankie proved the beat *did* go on when the eighties rolled in, serving us treats like Atlantic Starr's "Circles," Two Tons O' Fun's "Just Us," Womack & Womack's "Baby I'm Scared of You," Denroy Morgan's "I'll Do Anything for You," Teena Marie's "Square Biz," Fonda Rae's "Over Like a Fat Rat," Gwen Guthrie's "Ain't Nothin' Goin' On but the Rent," Imagination's "Just an Illusion," Young & Company's "I Like What You're Doing to Me," Indeep's "Last Night a DJ Saved My Life," Patrice Rushen's "Forget Me Nots," D-Train's remake of "Walk On By," and back-to-back jams from Alicia Myers:

"You Get the Best from Me (Say, Say, Say)" and "I Want to Thank You," which *everyone* sang—including Gene, who is an atheist (that dance floor *can* take you places you wouldn't normally go, but the conviction with which he recites those lyrics makes me wonder if he's a closet Christian). When Alicia repeated the song's verse a second time, Frankie cut the music as we swayed to our own voices and drummed the beat with our feet. And the Amen Corner—the Children who come straight from afternoon church service in their Sunday best—provided us with the hand clappin' and tambourine slappin' on this and every other song.

It was on "Funky Sensation," when Gwen McCrae breaks it down ("move your left leg . . . throw your right hand in the air . . . lean left, lean right, lean front, lean back, c'mon . . ."), that *he* appeared. Gene would later tell me that he saw him checkin' me out from afar, dancing just close enough to peep me. He joined Gene and me as we and dozens of others heeded Gwen's instructions.

As Gwen gave way to Carl Carlton's "She's a Bad Mama Jama (She's Built, She's Stacked)," he stepped in my purview but off to my left side. *Mmm* . . . Shiny, rich, dark caramel skin. A U-shaped head, topped by a neatly styled short afro. Very thin eyebrows that sat above his very big brown eyes. A large, broad nose, the nostrils flared. Lips that weren't full and plump but fat and pouty, not to mention glossy. Cheeks that seemed to be invisible, they hid so well in the plumpness of his face. His facial hair consisted of a thick mustache, stubble on his chin, and sideburns that stopped at his earlobe. And the ears: almost Mr. Spock–ish. He was a little taller (a couple of inches) and a little stockier (not bulky or muscle-bound, just slightly toned and smooth) than me.

An *extraordinarily* ordinary-looking man.

He wore a uniform that made him stick out in the crowd: military fatigues. (Was he in the armed forces? On leave for the weekend?) But it was the azz—that's right, *the azz*—that really made him stick *out* in the crowd. Now, I thought I had a big booty for a guy my size, but his was nearly twice the size of mine. It sat so far from *and* off his waist it had to have its own zip code. It seemed so firm you could probably bounce a *roll* of quarters on it. And those fatigues were having a hard time containing it—the trousers sat a jood two inches *below* his waist, exposing the ribbed top of his boxers. Talk about a low-slung booty!

Uh-huh, he was a Bad *Papa* Jama—built *and* stacked. Just as *PHYNE* as he could be.

Our eyes met; I smiled. He turned away, but I could make out the outline of a grin.

We repeated this scene twice more; was he going to do something? Say something? Since I'm attached, it would be wrong for me to. I wouldn't want to lead him on.

The sign he was waiting on came when Gene spotted his ex, Carl, and proceeded to do da butt *on* his butt.

If Military Man thought Gene and I were together, he didn't anymore. He wasted not another second.

He didn't say a word—he let his hips do the talkin'.

When making that contact, some will dance up *to* you; some will dance up *on* you; and some will dance *around* you, hoping you'll grab them and stop them from going in circles.

Military Man did none of these things. He took two steps to the right, groovin' directly in front of me. Then he danced himself—or rather, that azz—up *into* me.

What a military maneuver *that* was!

He didn't put a booty rush on me; he did it gradually. Baby-steppin' his way back, pokin' it to the left, pokin' it to the right, pokin' it out a little, and a little more, and a little more, and a little more until he was doin' a little rub-a-dub-dub on my nub.

I did what any red-blooded American man in this position would do: I let my nub follow his rub.

And Frankie knew just what to play at this moment: Rufus & Chaka's "Do You Love What You Feel?"

I sho' 'nuff did.

But that wasn't even an appetizer considering what lay ahead: He showed me "He's the Greatest Dancer" as we got "Lost in Music." We bumped to Grace Jones's "Pull Up to the Bumper." We shook it up on Cheryl Lynn's "Shake It Up Tonight" and shook our bodies *all* the way down to the ground on the Jacksons' "Shake Your Body Down (to the Ground)." We got funky on Peter Brown's "Do You Wanna Get Funky with Me?" and funked up with Sylvester's "Do You Wanna Funk?" We *rocked!* and *freaked!* off of GQ's "Disco Nights." We took our time on the S.O.S. Band's "Take Your Time" and *fixed it* with Ashford & Simpson's "Found a Cure," on which he seemed to catch the Holy Ghost: head extended up to the heavens, eyes closed, right hand bent in the air at a forty-five-degree angle, body bobbing on his toes, and mumbling some very unintelligible yet sexy words. We *really* got our Praise on with Tramaine Hawkins's "Fall Down," Vanessa Bell Armstrong's "Pressing On," and the Clark Sisters' "You Brought the Sunshine." We boogied on Heatwave's "Boogie Nights" and boogie-oogied on A Taste of Honey's "Boogie Oogie Oogie." We had a better-than-good time on Chic's "Good Times."

And the Gap Band summed up the entire experience: "Outstanding."

Believe it or not, with all this bumpin', shakin', funkin', rockin', freakin', and boogie-in' goin' on, I kept my distance—emotionally speaking. I let him initiate everything that happened—and he had no problem performing that role.

I didn't place my arms around his waist—*he* placed them there.

I didn't pull off his shirt—*he* had me do it (he didn't wait for an invitation, though, to unbutton and remove my black Polo).

I didn't plant my hands on and massage his chest, teasing those pointy nipples as I bumped him from behind—*he* planted them there (he returned the favor, nipplin' and nubbin' me).

And *I* didn't grab ahold of his ass . . . okay, I *did* do that on my own, but *only* because he had ahold of mine (and I could tell by that gleam in his eyes that that's what he wanted).

The only sounds that came out of his mouth were gruff *Ahs, Ohs,* and *Mphs* (I released some myself). But that changed as McFadden & Whitehead's "Ain't No Stoppin' Us Now" faded out and MFSB's "Love Is the Message" began. We were in what had become our favorite position—his arms stretched out on my shoulders, his meaty thighs squeezing mine, my left hand palming the small of his back, and my right hand glued to his left butt cheek—when he leaned in and brought his lips close to my ear. He inhaled. He was about to say his first words—but they weren't what I expected.

"Can you Tango Hustle?" he cautiously asked in a creamy baritone voice.

We had done every dance you could think of—the Snake, the Wop, the Electric Slide, the Bus Stop, the Tootsie Roll, the Running Man, the Wave, the Drop, the Smurf, the Cabbage Patch, the Funky Chicken, even *very* old-school moves like the Shake, the Mashed Potato, the Jerk, and the Twist. And we did them without discussion or negotiation—we naturally fell into each groove, reading the other's mind and knowing which foot (and what other body parts) to put forward (or backward). That he'd query me about this one signaled he'd probably come across few (if any) who knew how.

I wasn't one of those people. "I sure can."

He was happy to hear that.

Once again I let him take the lead. We glided throughout the crowd, never missing a turn, spin, or dip (we each got dropped).

After a dozen other "love" tracks—Stephanie Mills's "What Cha Gonna Do with My Lovin'?," Phyllis Hyman's "You Know How to Love Me," the Jones Girls' "You Gonna Make Me Love Somebody Else," René & Ángela's "I Love You More," Inner Life's "I'm Caught Up (in a One Night Love Affair)," Third World's "Now That We Found Love" (on which we salsa'd it up), Evelyn minus-the-"Champagne" King's "Love Come Down," Slave's "Just a Touch of Love," and double takes from Change ("The Glow of Love" and "A Lover's Holiday") and First Choice ("Love Thang" and "Dr. Love")—he gently clutched my arm as First Choice, on their third go-round, exclaimed *"It's-not-oh-ver!"* for the fiftieth time on "Let No Man Put Asunder," and asked . . .

"Would you like to get a drink?"

I was beyond parched, and like him, the sweat was pouring off of me. "Sure."

We headed for the bar, walking arm to arm. He took the liberty of getting us both bottled water. I presented him with the two dollars mine cost, but he refused it. "I won't take your money, but I *will* take your hand." He held out his. "My name's Montgomery. Montee for short."

His hand was sweaty and strong, and the shake *seismic*—my whole body quaked. "Hi. I'm Mitchell. It's a pleasure to meet you."

"Mmm-hmm, I'm gonna make sure it is." He winked. I smiled. He paused before letting go of my hand. He tapped my water bottle with his.

I took a couple of gulps; he literally poured the H_2O down his throat.

"I was thirsty," he explained.

"So I see . . ."

He ordered two more, dunking one of them (with his head back, he held the bottle over his mouth, the water falling out as if he were drinking from a faucet).

"Ah . . ." he breathed. "I would ask you to shower me with the other one, but it wouldn't be right to get their floor all wet."

I grinned.

He put the other bottle down on the counter. "You're a *great* dancer."

"Thanks. So are you."

"Thanks. Where did you learn how to Tango Hustle?"

"I'm ashamed to admit this, but . . ."

"*Saturday Night Fever,* right?"

We laughed.

"You, too?" I asked.

"Yeah. It wasn't that bad a movie. I couldn't help thinkin' throughout it that if a brother was cast, they wouldn't have had to teach him how to dance. It might be a stereotype, but we just got it in our blood. Everything he did, I could do ten times better—including Tango Hustle. Up until then, I didn't know there was such a dance."

"Me neither."

"Brothers look at you like you crazy when you ask 'em if they can do it. This must be my lucky night." He eyed me. "I haven't seen you here before. Is this your first time?"

"No. I just haven't been in a while."

"Ah. I come one Sunday every month, usually a holiday weekend. Just dance the night away and prepare for the battles I know lie ahead of me . . ."

"Is that why you're dressed like that?"

He chuckled. "Yeah. When I'm on the dance floor I take no prisoners."

"I know."

We smiled.

He gently clutched my right arm. "Pardon me. I have to use the rest room. I'll be right back."

"Okay."

As he walked off, the T-shirt draped over his left shoulder, I noticed he was bowlegged. That wobbly stride made his ass jiggle like Jell-O. *Lawdy*.

A few minutes had passed when Gene reappeared. "Chile, you ready?"

"Uh . . . no."

"No?"

"That guy I was dancing with, Montee. He said he'd be coming right back."

"For what?"

"I . . . I don't know."

"Uh-huh. Does *Montee* know that you're somebody else's guy?" Jocelyn Brown just happened to be gettin' off her high horse at that moment . . .

"I didn't have the chance to tell him."

"You didn't have the chance to tell him . . . you've been dancing with him all night!"

"Exactly. We were too busy dancing."

"So, is that what you're going to tell him when he returns? Given how he's dressed, I wouldn't be surprised if he declared war on your ass. Y'all just weren't shakin' booty, y'all were *bakin'* it."

"We were just having a good time."

"I know. I saw the whole sordid, seedy, *sin*ful mess."

"I just don't want to leave. That would be rude."

"What would you rather be: dissed in absentia or dissed to your face? At least with the former he can *save* face; the latter he can't. And if he's that heartbroken that you left—and I doubt he will be—he's in the right place to have it mended. There are many Children here who'll be glad to show the sergeant a good time."

"Well . . ."

"Believe me, it's better this way. Besides, Carl is giving us a lift back to Chelsea."

That was jood news; we wouldn't have to wait on a train or hail a cab. "And will you be giving *him* a lift when we get to your place?"

"No, dearest, I won't be. We are just friends now."

"Ha, y'all weren't actin' like it out on that floor."

"We were just having a good time," he mocked.

"Uh-huh."

"Anyway, he'll also be dropping off Ivan, the boy he met here to-night."

"He is?"

"Yes."

"Uh, won't that be kind of . . . awkward?"

"What's so awkward about it?"

"I mean . . . him having the new and the—"

"*Old?* Who you callin' *old?*"

"*You* know what I mean."

"They aren't dating or fucking—yet. But they are sweet on each other. I think Carl wants to know what I think of him, wants me to check him out."

"You mean interrogate him."

"Exactly."

"Well . . . I'll just wait here until you get our coats. In case he comes back."

"Of course. But don't say I didn't warn you."

Five more minutes went by and still no Montee. I thought of venturing toward the bathrooms, but didn't. It made no sense to search for him when I wasn't searching for someone. Now, if I had been single, I probably would've hunted him down, ditched Gene (although *ditched* is the wrong word; he would've insisted I rope him and, just to be safe, take one of his "safer than sorry" condom/lube packs), and danced that last hour with him. Afterward, we could've gotten some dessert at the twenty-four-hour diner across the street from the Y and, who knows . . .

Montee's not coming right back made me feel less guilty about leaving. After all, how long was I supposed to wait? I'm sure the line for the bathroom wasn't *that* long. Did he run into someone he knew—or someone else he *wanted* to know? I finished my water and took the one he left on the counter.

The Whispers' "And the Beat Goes On" began to play as we all climbed into Carl's midnight-blue Lexus. I wondered: Would Montee hook up with someone else and forget about me? But as Carl shot across the Manhattan Bridge and Gene gave Ivan the fourth degree, I had to shake myself (not to mention quit stroking that bottle of Deer Park): I was doing a *lot* of daydreaming about Montgomery aka Montee aka Military Man aka this stranger. You'd think we had swapped digits and he made a promise to call on a certain day at a certain time so we could set a date. *I* may as well forget about *him*. I had a jood time—in fact, a *better* than jood time—but that's all it was and that's all it could be. Maybe we'll bump into each other on another dance floor someday, but chances are that I'll never see him again.

Or so I thought.

5

He was late—again.

I was sitting at a table in Rory's, an upscale yet crassly decorated espresso shop on the Upper East Side (the fake Victorian chairs and sofas clash with the walls, which are a nauseating pea green, reminding you of the soup Linda Blair threw up in *The Exorcist*). It's been a hangout for the post-yuppie crowd since the eighties ended, a spot for them to lick their wounds after the financial boom went bust and regroup while making those connections to rebuild their empires. If one wanted to be in the know (or be the one *to* know), this would be the place to show your face. And given the social-climbing, status-hungry personality of my ex, Peter Armstrong, I'm not the least bit surprised he wanted to meet here. He'd chosen the same spot for our first meeting, nearly four years ago . . .

IT WAS THE FALL OF 1991 AND I, LIKE SO many other Americans, was glued to my television, watching the Clarence Thomas confirmation hearings—or, as Babyface dubbed it, "Uncle Thom's Cabin(et) Show." And what a show: it was eerie seeing white folks who normally don't give a damn about Negroes (Republicans/conservatives) go to war over one of us against those who profess to be our allies but do little as possible to help advance our cause because then we wouldn't be dependent on them (Democrats/liberals). (As I've often said: We know we're gonna get screwed by both Democ*rooks* and Republi*klans*, but at least the Dems will wear a condom.)

And then there was the parade of Black Republicans testifying before the committee and giving their own thoughts on Thomas, Anita Hill, and the state of Black politics on the various news-analysis programs. Given the alarmist reactions of many white folks, you'd think aliens had landed, à la *The War of The Worlds*. Up until then, it was rare to see any self-appointed or white media-annointed Black leader deviating from the usual post-civil-rights song-and-dance Negroes were expected, even encouraged, to perform. White America was shocked when they finally realized we all don't think alike (although, considering the views many of these Kneegrows hold, I'd rather they believe we were a monolithic group). Problem was, what these Black Republicans had to say wasn't practical—too often, they were (and still are) parroting a party platform that dismisses or ignores Black folks. And that platform is a classic study in hypocrisy: Republicans claim to be "pro-life," yet are gung-ho about the death penalty (shouldn't one be pro-life for *all* life, no matter how wretched or despicable it may be?); they're against affirmative action, yet don't have a problem when it benefits one of their own ilk—*especially* if he/she is highly unqualified (i.e., Uncle Clarence); and they're the champions of "less government" but don't see a contradiction in restricting what folks can and cannot do in the privacy of their own bedrooms (hence those sodomy laws, which are rarely, if ever, enforced against heterosexuals). They talk a good game plan, but it's like a block of Swiss cheese: full of holes. Many have fallen for the piffy, feel-good platitudes, but I'm interested in sound policy, *not* sound bites.

Because much of what I heard and read leading up to and after Uncle Clarence's confirmation did little to illuminate who Black Republicans were or why they thought the way they did, I decided to profile one but from an angle I'd yet to see anyone tackle, let alone mention: what it was like being a Black *gay* (or lesbian) Republican. Publicly acknowledging that *that* particular brand also walked amongst us, I knew, would really send folks over the ledge and get me a byline that would stand out from the rest on the subject.

But I had to find one first. There were several Republican groups that catered to Blacks and a few for queers, but none for both. And the response I received from both entities (as well as those that were white and heterosexually identified) about the particular stripe I was searching for was the same: "You want to talk to someone who is *what*?"

Luckily, Gene had a friend at work who knew such a man. I had him pass my info along so he could contact me and we could hook something up. We played phone tag for a week until I told him to pick a day, time, and place for us to meet. Rory's was that place. The day was a Monday.

He said six o'clock; I got there at 5:55. At 6:30, I started packing up my notebook and recorder when . . .

"Are you Mitchell Crawford?"

"Yes, I am."

"Hi. I'm Peter Armstrong."

I was *flabbergasted*. He didn't "look" like a Black Republican. I'd never seen one who wasn't on the not-so-shy side of ugly. Not just nerdy but *turdy*, possessing a face that, yes, *only* a mother could love.

But I guess there *is* a first time for everything, huh?

The man in front of me was *phyne*. Almond Joy skin, curly short-cropped black hair, dimples in both pinched cheeks, pretty purplish lips, a lean, *mean* swimmer's build, and a soccer-ball booty.

As Carol Burnett purred about Albert Finney in *Annie:* "For a Republican, you're sinfully handsome."

"*You're* Peter Armstrong?" I couldn't believe it.

"Yes. Why?"

"I . . . I didn't expect . . ."

"Well, I know you didn't expect me to be *white*," he joked.

"No, no. I didn't expect you"—*Think fast*—"to show up now. It's going on seven and you did say you had another appointment at seven-thirty."

"That's why I'm late. I was able to handle that project before I left the office, but it took me a little longer that I expected. Do forgive me."

"Sure."

After he purchased us both a hot chocolate (his with whipped cream, mine without) and the bio was revealed (born in Seattle, oldest of three boys, Harvard grad, architect with Goodman Designs), we got down to his political philosophy—and if I was blindfolded, I'd swear I was listening to a *very white* white man. He rattled on about limited government, less taxes, and individual responsibility. How could someone who was so appealing a view spout such *un*appealing views?

He was reading straight from the Republican talking-head script—and I planned to rip it up. "Have or do you feel any conflict as a Black gay man being a member of the Republican Party?"

"Conflict?"

"Yes. The party isn't exactly welcoming or accepting of those who are not white, not male, not heterosexual, and not, at the very least, middle-class."

"It may not appear that way, but it is."

"Oh? How?"

"The party doesn't believe in individuals thinking or behaving like they are a part of a group."

"Doesn't that mean you have to not just assimilate but erase who you are in order to join the club?"

"No. They just don't want any part of this identity politics, where-oppression is used as a calling card."

"Could you explain that?"

"That's how the Democrats deal with minorities: Trade in on your victim status as a disenfranchised group and we'll be your friend. Ha, a lot of good that has gotten minorities over the past several decades with them, especially African-Americans."

"If Democrats, as you have indicated, have taken minorities for granted, it appears Republicans have ignored them altogether."

"I wouldn't say that. It's just that the party sees me as an individual and not a member of any minority group. And I like that."

"But, Mr. Armstrong—"

"Please, call me Pete."

"Pete?"

"Yes. Everyone does."

"Okay. Pete." *Pete* . . . it sounds *so* white. "You *are* a member of a minority group—*three* to be exact—and some would argue that your unwillingness to demand the party see you for all that you are makes it convenient for them not to take the concerns of so-called minority groups seriously. Treating you like a victim is one thing; ignoring that certain groups do not have the access or opportunity others do is another."

"I think the party does take our concerns seriously. Minorities want the same things whites and heterosexuals want: crime-free neighborhoods, good schools, jobs, homes, a family. The American Dream."

"I'm sure. But some of those things are harder to attain because of who one is *not*—and the party doesn't make it any easier when they continually block efforts that would enable those who don't have the advantages the so-called majority groups have always had."

"Well, people cannot expect the government to make things easier. That's just the nature of a free marketplace. It's not the government's job to give a handout or a hand up."

Now, how did I know he would go there? I was ready . . . "It's not about offering a handout or a hand up, but a hand*le*."

That one slapped him across the face—his head actually swung left as if I backhanded him.

I went on. "The playing field isn't level, yet the party acts as if it is. And it isn't going to change so long as the status quo is protected. What are you, as a Black gay man, doing on the inside to change that?"

His face was blank. "Uh, could you excuse me for a moment? I have to use the rest room."

"Sure." I shut off the tape.

He returned five minutes later. His face was glistening. I guess he'd doused it with cold water.

"May we continue?" I asked.

"Yes, we can."

I turned it back on. "When we left off—"

"I think it's important to play by the rules if you want to make inroads in any industry or institution, and that's what I'm doing in the party. My being Black and gay are incidental. They don't have to be brought to the table."

"Are you saying that your being Black and gay just aren't important—at least to the party—and because of that you won't bring it to the table?"

"I'm saying neither one has to be nor should they be made an issue."

"If that's the case, then can one say that you aren't making any inroads as a Black gay member?"

"I wouldn't say that. I see myself—and I believe they do also—as a member who *happens* to be Black and gay."

"But you just don't *happen* to be who you are. You do, however, *happen* to be a Republican at this moment. You may not be tomorrow. Or next week. Or next year."

He considered this point, tapping his cup. "On the outside they may see a Black gay man, but they soon realize I can be just as dedicated to the cause as they are. That speaks volumes."

Uh-huh: You're a sellout.

"So, then, your being Black and gay *do* matter."

"What do you mean?"

"You want them to see a Black gay man who is just like them— whoever *them* is."

"I guess you could say that."

"So I go back to my original question: Have or do you feel any conflict as a Black gay man being a member of the Republican Party?"

He hesitated. "No."

"So then it doesn't bother you that quite a few members of the party are white men who have direct or indirect ties to white supremacist groups?"

"Uh . . . one shouldn't judge a man solely by those he knows but by what he does."

"Given how the party has demonized Black people, isn't it possible that at least some of its more vocal members feel the same way about Black people as their racist friends or acquaintances in hate groups do?"

"I don't think the party can be held accountable for what some members say or do."

"It can if it does not disassociate itself from such imagery, and it hasn't. In fact, it has thrived on racist messages, from Ronald Reagan's welfare queens to George Bush's Willie Horton to Jesse Helms's dishonest attacks on affirmative action."

"Those are just three examples. I don't believe they represent what the party is all about."

"Then what does the party say to you about Black people?"

"To me?"

"Yes, to you."

He pondered. "That I have just as much right to the American Dream as anyone else and that my color doesn't have to be a hindrance."

This man was truly in denial.

I decided to switch the topic. "Does it bother you that the party has been vigorously fighting, along with the Religious Right, gay civil rights laws across the country?"

"Well, those laws are really unnecessary. All Americans are currently protected under the law from discrimination."

"What about those gay and lesbian Americans who are fired from a job, denied a place to live, and harassed at work or school because of who they are? They are not included under the Civil Rights Act of 1965."

"I doubt very seriously if that's happening to many gays and lesbians."

Is he for real? "Even if it is happening to just *one* person, isn't that reason enough to ensure that the majority does not trample on their rights?"

He shrugged. "Majority rules. It can't be about what special-interest groups want, for then government becomes a fractured mess trying to cater to the whims of every subgroup out there."

I was waiting for that phrase to come up . . . "Isn't everyone, in his or her own way, a special-interest group?"

"Huh?"

"Well, each person has specific interests that they want met. No one person is a single thing, as you can testify to, nor do they only occupy one station in life."

Looks like I pimp-slapped him again. "Uh . . . uh . . . I would say . . . you might be right."

"Well, then, how can the party go on and on about the Dems being the home of special interests when they have particular groups, like the Religious Right, in their front pockets, as well as millions of other Americans, like Jerry Falwell and Pat Robertson, each one with a special-interest agenda of their own? And, mind you, the majority of those folks make up one of the biggest and most powerful special-interest groups in the country—white men."

He was on the ropes now. "I, uh . . . I think that there is a . . . I don't believe that the two groups . . . special interests are organized blocks that work for the good of themselves and not the country as a whole."

"A while ago you said that the party doesn't believe in individuals thinking or behaving like they are a part of a group. Yet judging from who has benefited the most from its agenda, one could argue that the party is a special-interest group working for the good of itself—its good white-male self."

He was on the mat; the countdown began . . . "Uh . . . uh . . . uh . . ."

Click.

The first side of the tape was finished—and so was he.

As I started to turn it over, he pushed back from his seat. "You know, I'm sorry. I really have to go. I just remembered that there's another project I promised to work on weeks ago and haven't begun yet. I . . . maybe we can pick this up sometime tomorrow." He threw on his coat.

"Okay. Call me, for I would really love to finish." Ha, I'd really love to finish *annihilating* your ass.

"Uh, uh, I will." He stuck out his hand. "Nice to meet you."

I shook it. "Same here."

And he literally ran out of the shop.

I didn't think I'd hear from him again, but I did. That next day he left a message on my machine:

"Hello, Mr. Crawford. This is Pete, Pete Armstrong, from yesterday. Uh . . . I was hoping you'd . . . well, I don't want to be featured in the article. Because of my position and the chance that this article could be in a major paper . . . I don't think it would be wise for me to . . . be so public. I hope you understand. If you have any questions, just call me. Thank you."

Yeah, I understood: He didn't want to look like a fool in print.

Normally, I would've ignored such a request (I'd received it a couple of other times from folks who regretted saying certain things, but since they had given consent to the interview—*on tape*—what could they do?), but decided to let him off the hook. I could make the salient points I needed to without humiliating him. Besides, the next day I interviewed a Black lesbian Republican who made more sense than he did. She understood what kind of group she was a member of ("I have no doubt some of those folks would love to see me swinging from a tree") but argued that it was important for African-Americans to be represented in both parties so that there was someone in the room who could point out the obvious ("You motherfuckers are racist and you need to check that shit") when no one else would. She also set a timetable on how long she would stick around ("I've been in it for three years and will give it another three; if I don't see any concrete steps being taken, I'll be joining the Reform Party."). Now, *that* I could respect; while I still didn't agree with her choice, at least she was clear about who she was and realistic about what kind of group she was dealing with and what her role in it could be.

Peter, however, was more concerned with impressing his white/hetero cohorts (can you say *house nigger?*). And he was just as evasive and transparent as many of those Caucasian Republicans I'd had the displeasure of discussing these issues with over the years. But one thing made that forty-five minutes we spent not such a total waste—he was cute. Confused, but cute.

A few weeks later, after the *Village Voice* agreed to run the article, I was at home watching *L.A. Law* when the phone rang.

"Hello?"

"Uh, hi. Mitchell?"

"Yes. Who is this?"

"This is Pete, Pete Armstrong. Remember, the guy you interviewed."

How could I forget? "Yes?"

"I . . . uh . . . this may seem a little . . . I don't know, out of place. Even weird. But . . . I was wondering if . . . if you'd like to maybe, uh . . . get together sometime for a drink . . . or dinner . . . or something."

I was *stunned*. "Are you asking me out on a date?"

"Uh, well . . . I guess I am."

Silence.

"When?" I inquired.

"Uh . . . I don't know. Whenever you'd like to. I'm flexible."

"How about this Saturday night?" Did I just say that?

"Oh, okay. What time?"

"Eight o'clock?"

"That'll be fine."

"Where will you be taking me?" That's right, where will *he* be taking *me*. After all, *he* asked *me* out . . .

"Um . . . where would you like to go?"

"A movie and dinner would be fine."

"Okay. It's a date."

Dinner actually came first, at this quaint but not so little Italian restaurant named Luigi's. Then we saw *Jungle Fever*. Then we ventured back to his place. And after we guzzled down a bottle of white zinfandel, I turned him the fuck out.

To my knowledge, he was the first Black gay Republican I ever got busy with. But he upped me in the "first" department—I was the first Black *man* he ever slept with.

I knew it before he officially confessed. The dead giveaways? His comments about the film ("I don't know why Spike had to come down so hard on black men who date interracially; it's not always about the stereotypes and the myths"). The men he'd found attractive over the years (Montgomery Clift, Sylvester Stallone, and Tom Cruise). And, what he grunted while I was going down on him ("Oh, yeah, suck that big, black cock!") and he was going up in me ("Yeah, ya like that big black cock up in ya, huh?").

I nicely told him that any more declarations like those would *kill*, not spoil, the mood, so he'd have to come up with something new—and he did. He replaced the racist rhetoric with lots of *golly gees, God dangs, oh shoots,* and *mother-fredericks*.

But he wasn't so polite when I feasted on his two big Bon Bons ("Oooh, yeah, lick that ass like a lollipop!") and banged him in three different positions—doggy, f.d.a.u. (face down, azz up), and propped over the kitchen sink, as his head occasionally banged against the wall (his line during each: "Oooh, yeah, motherfucker, do that nasty all up in me!"). When he said he was flexible, he wasn't lying—I bent, folded, and stretched that limber, wiry body as if it were a rubber band.

"I've never experienced *anything* like that before," he puttered, still trying to catch his breath as his head lay on my chest after his first plugging.

"Oh really?"

"Yes. I . . . I always thought that sleeping with another Black man would be like . . ."

Oh, boy . . . here it comes.

". . . like sleeping with my brother, even my father."

I've heard *that* bullshit before from way too many other snow queens. As far as I'm concerned, it's a convenient excuse self-hating Black men use to justify rejecting other Black men. After all, when was the *first* time you ever heard a white man say he couldn't be with other white men because it'd be like fucking a family member?

"It's not that I never wanted to *be* with a Black man; it's just that . . . it never happened."

Uh-huh . . . 'cause you never *wanted* it to happen.

"I really am color-blind; I don't see color."

Uh-huh . . . you're so color-blind that you only "see" those who don't have any.

As repulsed as I was by the admissions, I wasn't repulsed by the sex—it was some of the best I ever had. And, subconsciously, I believed I was helping him face and hopefully conquer his inhibitions/fears/demons about being with Black men, and that made me feel . . . well, superior. I got so arrogant that when I wore that ass out the second and third times that night, I'd boast: "Uh-huh, I bet none of them white boys could work it like this, huh?" But he didn't mind; it just got him going even more.

I was still spooked, though, over our getting together. Our verbal exchange made me . . . well . . . *wet.* I don't know if I was turned on by him or turned on by the debate we had or turned on by the fact I was grinding him into a fine powder *and he knew I was,* or maybe it was a combination of all three, but I was turned on. And he admitted that that was why he contacted me—being in the hot seat not only made *him* hot, it made him hot for *me.*

And, so, we became fast fuckers, fast friends, and fierce foes, in the figurative sense of the word. It was after we had one of our most heated debates (it almost always had something to do with the two R's: Reagan, who he feels is the greatest president of the twentieth century; and racism, which he believes is no longer an obstacle for Black folks because those on the receiving end of it today are allegedly *white*) that we'd heat up the bedroom (or the kitchen, or the bathroom, or the living room, or his car). I'd eat that ass with a vengeance, making his ears wiggle like a hummingbird's wings, and fuck him until he was screeching like a pig caught in a fence. He no longer had a problem telling the difference between me and his former (white) pieces, and his groove got so good that I'd egg him on with "Be *real*

Black for me, Daddy, *yeah*" (and he had the nine-inch-long, five-and-a-half-inch-thick dick to be real *with*).

Gene gasped when he heard we had hit it—and *gawked* when he learned the blaze had lasted longer than a night. But he warned: "Chile, no matter how good you're givin' it to him and no matter how good he's givin' it to you, he will eventually leave you to go back to the *white* House."

Well, he did leave me—for Wiley House, a major high-tech design and production firm in Beverly Hills that constructs movie sets for the studios. His high-five-figure salary would be doubled, and he'd have the title of a VP after his name (something he'd always wished for). When he asked me to move with him, I didn't know what to say. Despite his being culturally unconscious, I liked him; he had a gentle, funny side that I cherished (he did a laugh-out-very-loud impersonation of Tim Conway as Mr. Tudball from *The Carol Burnett Show*). I loved being with him—and I loved being *with* him. But did I love *him*? And was I in love with *him*? My feelings for him, my feelings for us, didn't run deeper than my feelings for what we *did*. We were the ultimate fuck buddies: two people with little to nothing in common but who could hang out—and let it *all* hang out.

We weren't "dating"—unless one considers a relationship that's ninety percent sex and ten percent other activities "dating" (as much boot knockin' as Pooquie and I did during our first month and a half together, it paled in comparison with the number of carnal conquests Peter and I engaged in in our first few weeks). So as much as I liked the idea of being invited to join him (it's not every day you receive what is basically a "marriage" proposal), I declined the offer. He seemed somewhat heartbroken that I did. Initially, the distance didn't put out the flame, it just intensified it. For close to a year, we visited each other, probably trying to find *something* that would finally convince us that what we had was more than a physical thing. But that something never revealed itself and the fire fizzled out. After two years without any contact, I thought I'd never hear from him again . . .

. . . UNTIL HE CALLED ME UP LAST WEEK. HE SAID HE'D be in town and would like to see me. Pooquie didn't mind if I went out with him for coffee—"so long as he know you ain't available." Pooquie knew he could trust me—we had gone through this when I went to my high-school reunion and faced my first love, former gymnastics coach and current Rikers Island resident Warren Reid (he's awaiting trial for raping one of his male students). But would Pooquie's being out of town during this reunion make a difference?

I figured that after several years, Peter would have changed in some way. But I knew one thing would remain the same: his tardiness. So, I had enough sense not to show up at the time he specified. He said 6:30; I got there at 6:50. And I wasn't there a minute when he glided through the door.

"Mitchell," he crooned, embracing me. "It's so good to see you."

"You, too."

After we separated, his eyes darted up and down. "You look fantastic. Have you been working out or something?"

"A little." I'm not a gym queen like B.D. (who works out five days a week) and I'm not even a member of a gym, but after watching Pooquie crunch it up every morning, I decided to join him. Those push-ups, sit-ups, and leg lifts have paid off: My body is now as firm as it was when I was a gymnast in high school.

And he could tell. "It shows."

"You're looking good yourself." And he was. He shook off his gray tweed coat to reveal an emerald-green, long-sleeved Polo shirt and black Eddie Bauer trousers, tightly wrapped around his frame.

"I'm so sorry I'm late," he apologized. "I had a client who wouldn't stop talking. I hope you weren't waiting long . . ."

I wasn't but he didn't have to know it. "As a matter of fact, I was. Some things never change." I smiled.

He did, too. "Hopefully, I can make it up to you."

"We'll see."

He ordered a hot chocolate (with whipped cream, of course). I switched gears and had strawberry mint tea.

"So, with you looking so good, I'm sure life is treating you the same way."

"Yes, it is."

"Well, we haven't really talked in almost two years. Tell me what's been going on . . ."

I did. The new job and how I'm suing the old one. My new side gig as a session singer. And, of course, Pooquie and Junior. I proudly presented my wallet-size pic of them.

"Hmm . . . they're a strikingly handsome pair."

"I agree."

He approvingly shook his head. "This . . . this looks like the real thing."

"It is." I took it back. "They're something special to me."

"Was *I* something special to you?"

Hmm . . . now where was he coming from with that?

I decided to go with Archibald Bunker for my reply. "*You*, Peter, were something *else*."

I don't think he quite got it; he was blushing.

I moved the convo before it sank in that it wasn't a compliment. "So, how is L.A.?"

"L.A. is okay. I kind of miss the cold, though."

"You do?"

"Yeah. It just gets boring after a while. And if the temperature drops below sixty and clouds produce the faintest drizzle, people start shrieking and running for cover."

I chuckled. "I've heard about that."

"I wouldn't have believed it myself if I hadn't seen it. I thought an earthquake was going on but, because I wasn't familiar with them, didn't feel the tremors like they did."

"I'm sure if there was an earthquake, you most certainly would have felt it."

"Ha, I already have: the quake last year."

"You weren't hurt, were you?"

"No. But there was some minor damage done to my apartment. It was nothing compared to the rumblings going on in the city right now over that O. J. trial."

"Oh? What kind of rumblings?"

"Oh, you know: If he's found not guilty, we are going to pay for it."

"I'm sorry? We?"

"Yes, we. You know, Black Americans."

"We?"

"Yes, we."

"As in *you*, me, and the rest of us Negroes."

He laughed. "Yes."

"Well . . ."

"What?"

"That's the first time I ever heard you refer to Black folks and include yourself in the equation."

"See, I have changed."

"I suppose. But what would the party think, your viewing yourself as the member of a group and not an individual?"

He frowned. Guess that was one change he didn't want his party peers to know about.

"And, what exactly is it that *we* are going to pay for?"

"Come on, Mitch, *you* know. African-American jury, African-American high-profile defendant, white victims. If he walks, white people will not be pleased and we will feel it at the polls, in government, at work, at school, everywhere."

"Contrary to what the media keeps repeating, it is *not* an African-American jury; there are white folks on it, as well as a Hispanic. And, since when have white folks needed a reason, let alone an excuse, to *mis*treat colored folk?"

He giggled. "You know, that's one thing that I miss: that militant stance of yours."

"Not militant. Just conscious."

"Uh-huh. I do get a little bit of it from Brad. He's almost as radical as you. Would you like to see a picture of him?"

I took the photo knowing I would see a person of the Caucasian persuasion and that he would be a beast, but hoped just this *one* time I'd be wrong—and, unfortunately, I wasn't. Just under six feet (Peter is in the pic with him and they're the same height), Brad has peach-tanned skin, dull dishwater-blond hair, a rectangular shaped face that is dotted with acne, green eyes, a rail-thin frame, and a pierced belly button. Not the *least* bit cute.

With all those wannabe *International Male* models and *Baywatch* extras out there, he hooks up with *this*?

"And what makes him so radical?" I asked.

"Oh, he's always been a crusader for African-Americans . . ."

Uh-huh . . . he's a *cruise*-ader for us, I'm sure.

"He's a member of the NAACP. He had us join the National Association of Black and White Men Together. And that picture was taken at At The Beach, the Black gay-pride celebration in L.A. last summer. We go to all the major Black gay functions in the city. Brad thinks it's important we do."

Yeah, *Brad* thinks it's important, not you. Maybe Brad goes to show his "support" (when a white man decides he's in our corner, nothing will stop him from doing just that—even if his "support" isn't needed or wanted), but I'm sure Peter's sole goal is to show up the other Black men ("Look at the prize I got! Don'tcha wish you had one, too?").

"And, of course, he loves Black men."

Of course. He *thinks* he loves Black *men* when he really loves black *meat*.

"You two make a handsome couple," I managed with a straight face, handing the photo back to him.

"Thanks. He's a bartender."

Which means he's more than likely an actor; L.A. is overpopulated with them. And Peter didn't mention his education *first*—which is what he does with everyone—so he more than likely didn't go to college. His other white lovers—Chad, Josh, Howie, and Bart—were also blue-collar men without degrees. Hmm . . . is it *just* a coincidence that when he decided to be with a Black man, he had a master's degree and a corporate job?

"How long have you two been a couple?"

"Just over a year. He's my apple tart and I'm his cupcake."

How fitting: He's a glazed fruit and you're a Hostess—chocolate on the outside with cream filling on the inside.

"He knows we're meeting tonight."

The way he said *we're meeting tonight* . . . "And what does he think about our meeting tonight?"

"He's all for it."

"He's all for *it*?"

"Yup."

"What is *it*?"

"You know, for us. *Meeting*." He placed his left hand on top of my right.

He's *got* to be kidding. I removed my hand. "We are not *meeting*."

He frowned. "We're not?"

"No, we're not. And I don't understand why you would think, *how* you could think we would be."

"Don't you wanna rock me for old time's sake?" He smiled. "*Roll* that tongue up in me for old time's sake?"

"I have someone else to rock-and-roll, thank you."

"But . . . he doesn't have to know. It would be our secret. I would have no reason to tell him."

"*I* would."

"And Brad would understand. He knows there are needs he can't meet and is okay with me having them met elsewhere."

"Brad is okay with you sleeping with other men?"

"Not other *men*. Just you."

"Me?"

"Yes, you."

"He is all right with you sleeping with your ex-lover?"

"Yes. I've told him all about you."

"Oh, have you?"

"Yes. He's not good like you are."

"Was that a compliment?"

"Yes, it was."

"Didn't sound like one to me."

"Well, it was. I have to practically do everything with him. He's so passive that he doesn't even initiate sex. And I'm sure I don't have to tell you that he's not . . . well . . . packin' and stackin' like you. Ha, his behind is so flat you could use it as an ironing board! And the *cock*?! As he's said about his kind: 'When God got to us in that department, he didn't break the mold; he forgot it!' "

I don't know what disturbed me more—his use of the word *cock* (I guess a zebra can't change his stripes) or the racist humor.

"He knows the chances of you two meeting are slim. I think the fact that you're not in the same city or state makes it easier for him to accept this arrangement."

This arrangement. Other Black gay men (most notably, public figures like activists, artists, even porn stars) have such "arrangements." They are hitched to a Caucasian so they can sip (they could never taste) the power, privilege, and prestige white men have as a birthright, but get their kicks with us—with their white massa, uh, man's permission. They get to have their trophy *and* their trick—in some cases at the same time.

The message: We're good enough to bed but not to wed.

"I'll be in New York once a month starting in April. I'll be helping them set up the office here, and I'll need to—"

"Excuse me, *Pete*," I interrupted, "but has it ever occurred to you that maybe what you *need* to do is drop Brad and find someone you can really show off with *and* throw down with, like, say, I don't know . . . a *Black* man?"

Judging by the stupefied expression on his face, it hadn't.

"You know what? This time, *I'm* going to be the one to leave in a rush." I sprang up. I rummaged through my pocket and tossed a five-dollar bill on the table. I flung my coat over my right arm. "We had fun. We had laughs. But to paraphrase Lalah Hathaway: 'What we had is better as a memory.' "

He was *geeking;* his mouth opened but nothing came out except a sound similar to a baby's squeaky toy.

I flounced out without looking behind me.

"*THAT MUTHA-FUCKA,*" POOQUIE SNARLED.

I giggled. I had him on speakerphone. I was sitting up in bed.

"I can't believe he thought you would just go fuh some shit like that," he went on. "He better hope I don't run inta his Oreo ass when he come back out this way."

"Now, Pooquie."

"Now, Pooquie *nuthin'*."

"You sound more upset about it than me."

"I *knew* he wanted ta hit it. Why else would he wanna see you after all this time?"

"Well, he can only dream of hitting it now. And, he could never dream of hitting it—or loving me—the way you do."

"Ha, you know it, Baby."

"In a way, I am glad I saw him tonight," I admitted.

"Why?"

"Because it reminded me just how lucky I am to have you. It's jood to be with someone who isn't afraid of the person looking back at him in the mirror."

"Yeah. That mutha-fucka prob'ly scared of his own fuckin' shadow."

"I'm sure."

"So, did you 'n' Gene go out last nite?"

He knows we did; he left three messages on Gene's answering machine. We didn't get in until after four. He and I played phone tag the rest of the day. "We did. To Body & Soul."

He drew back a breath. "Uh . . . you dance?"

"Yes. Makes no sense to go to a party like that and not dance."

Silence.

I knew what was going through his mind . . . "Yes, Pooquie, I danced with someone: me."

I could *feel* that sigh of relief. Pooquie can be a little possessive, so the last thing he would want to hear is that I shook my shimmy with someone else. He also didn't *need* to hear something like that right now—being so far away, in a strange city, and given all the stress and pressure he's under, there's no sense in making him antsy or uptight. And I wasn't lying—I *did* dance with myself (before Montee showed up).

"And even if I *did* dance with someone other than myself," I reasoned, "you know that's all it would be."

"Yeah. I do."

I'm glad he did 'cause, for the first time, I wasn't too sure about it myself . . .

I recalled the convo with B.D. and Gene at the restaurant. "I know you worry about another man getting close to me. But if anyone should be worried, it's me."

"You?"

"Yes. *You're* the big-time model and soon-to-be movie star. And you *are* in the place where all the beautiful people play."

"Ah, c'mon, Little Bit. You know I ain't even inta any of that."

"Yes, I know. Which is why it doesn't even have to be brought up."

I could see him nodding.

"Oh, Pooquie, let me go. I have to call your brother-in-law before it's too late. We have to talk about our trip on Sunday."

"What trip?"

"Remember, we're going to see our father."

"Ah, yeah. Tell Adam I said hay."

"I will. My mom says to tell you hi. And *jood* luck."

He laughed. "Tell her I said thanks."

"Will do. Call me again the same time tomorrow night, okay?"

"What, you ain't comin' home straight from school?"

Ha, *he's* sounding like my father. "I'll just be dropping off my bag. I'm having an early dinner with Gene, then heading over to the Brotherhood meeting."

"Is he goin' wit' you?"

"No." Gene doesn't believe in being a card-carrying member of anything except American Express. As he put it, "*Being* a homo is enough of a political act—why join a group?" Pooquie would probably agree, but for a different reason: He (like all the homiesexuals I've ever known) doesn't identify as gay/bisexual/queer/——— (fill in the blank) and rejects the cultural history and political baggage surrounding them as identities. But neither has tried to convince me to quit; they've supported me (Babyface and B.D. have also—by joining—but their very busy careers have prevented them from being active in the group). I've been a member of the Brotherhood for a year and a half, and it's made me feel I'm part of a larger community of Black Same Gender Loving men. Sometimes we need to be a part of something that gives us a better sense of self—or a *new* sense of self—and the Brotherhood has done both for me. After quitting my job as an editor at *Your World* and suing the magazine for racial discrimination, I craved a space where I could fellowship with others who looked like *and* loved like me, where all that I am would be recognized and appreciated. Lawd knows I've never been a comatose Negro like Peter, or one of those deep-in-the-vault, tryin'-to-play-and-lay-"straight" boyz, but one doesn't have to fall in either category to seek affirmation from those who really know what it is like being you.

"A'ight. But just wait fuh me ta call, Baby, please? I just wanna hear yo' voice. *Pleeze?*"

There he goes, beggin' again. Yeah, I fell for it. "Okay, okay. I'll be walking in at three-oh-five, so make sure you call me by three-ten."

"I will."

"All right. I love you, Pooquie."

"I love you, too, Little Bit."

Smack. Smack. Smack.

"Jood nite, Baby."

"Jood night."

6

The Brotherhood has its weekly meeting on a Tuesday, which still seems odd to me. Most gay social groups in the city meet on the weekend. But when Ras Akhbar, the current executive director, came on board, this was one of the things he sought to change. He reasoned that most are in a party mood on Friday (the original meeting date), and the group would increase its membership if it met during the week. After surviving a manic Monday and a trying Tuesday, Ras knew the brothers would need to be emotionally and spiritually reenergized to get through the rest of the week—and his observation appears to have been correct. Before the switch, membership peaked at three hundred. It has since tripled. On average, one hundred men come out each week, and depending on the guest speaker(s) and/or subject being discussed, it can swell to two hundred.

Like tonight. I was a bit shocked at this particular standing-room-only crowd: the program wasn't exactly sensational (the "Whose Got the Power: Tops or Bottoms?" session exposed a very nasty divide between those who get done and those who don't), controversial (the two brothers who dared to extol the virtues of interracial dating were literally run out of that meeting), or explosive (there were so many tears shed during "Our Love/Hate Relationship with the Black Church" that someone had to go out and buy a couple of boxes of Kleenex). I surmised, though, that many in attendance wanted to hear for themselves the man that Ras had showered with so much praise. No, make that *doused*. You can't have a discussion with Ras without his reciting the line "And, according to the *honorable* Ahmad Khan . . ." The man isn't Elijah Muhammad (hell, he's not even a Muslim), but he certainly is in Ras's eyes. A former Black Panther who spent fifteen years in jail for the rape and attempted murder of a white woman (a crime he did not commit), Ahmad received a bachelor's degree in history behind bars and, since his release in 1991, has written three books: *The Soul of a Man,* his autobiography; *The Spooks Who Still Sit by the Door,* a critique of the failure of Black political leadership in America; and *Let My People Go,* sort of an instructional manual for Black folks on how to detect, treat, and eradicate the white supremacy that surrounds and lives within us. Unlike other self-proclaimed uplift-the-race philosophers like Dr. Frances Cress Welsing, Jawanza Kunjufu, and Neely Fuller, Ahmad does not view us—meaning homosexuals—as a group attempting to shirk our responsibility to Black women by "acting" like them, or a threat to the evolution and survival of the Black family. You know, *the enemy.* Ahmad believes the Black community can't really be a community (and grow into a nation) if it continues to sacrifice any of its members because of prejudices (most notably, sexism, classism, homophobia/heterosexism) that have their roots in the very evil (white supremacy) *all* Black people have to overcome.

Ras has sworn by Ahmad's prescription for our healing as a people, but his passion for the man's politics (and his incessant pronouncements about his love for "his tribe") have alienated many. He can be a little too abrasive and annoying in his quest to, as he puts it, "wake the masses up from their comas." Remember Spike Lee's *School Daze?* Ras reminds me of that film's super-pro-Black activist, Dap—*on speed.* No one can tell Ras he is wrong about *anything,* and if he feels that he is losing ground or can't convert you to his way of thinking, he'll resort to name-calling ("Don't be a fool"), and/or try to shame/humiliate you ("I'm so sorry that you've chosen to be culturally unconscious" and his favorite "I am offering you freedom and you'd rather be a slave"). Such rhetoric always stifles any debate and casts him, no matter how inappropriate his comments about a person's character or level of awareness, as the Great Emancipator trying to lead us, the ignorant and misguided souls, to the Promised Land. His antics have moved some to leave the group while others complain in silence. I've witnessed him perform several times and have called him on it—but not in front of the group.

Despite his well-intentioned but warped sense of advocacy, the brother's heart is in the right place and he does make a lot of sense. (And it doesn't hurt that he is a brawny man with light caramel skin, curly brown hair, green eyes, and dimples in both of his chipmunk cheeks; as one member remarked, "Yeah, he can be an asshole, but he is so fine it's hard to stay mad at him.") So, many of us have overlooked the high-handed, high-minded presentation and embraced his agenda, as well as Ahmad's teachings. His membership support, though, wasn't enough to convince the Brotherhood's board of directors it would be worth flying Ahmad in from Oakland and paying him $5,000 to do a lecture ("Claiming Your Throne as an African King"). But Ras was determined and resourceful: he offered his own place as lodging, would pay for Ahmad's meals, got a friend who works at Continental Airlines to arrange a very cheap round-trip fare, and convinced Ahmad to cut his fee in half. For Ras, Ahmad's appearance would be his crowning achievement at the Brotherhood. Over the past year, he's been molding and reshaping it to be something other than another pickup spot for the brothers. At a time when the group was embroiled in several scandals (the issue of whether white men could attend meetings reached a fever pitch, the treasurer embezzled $25,000, and the former executive director was arrested for "lewd behavior" in a public park), Ras won the ED job by appealing to the board and members with a practical yet profound plea: "It's time for the Brotherhood to live up to its name." With too many of us dying because of physical (from AIDS to cancer to heart disease) and mental (loneliness, depression, self-hatred, and malnourished spirits) ailments, the Brotherhood had to be a vocal voice to help fight our invisibility and possible extinction. And his pitch worked: even though he had no experience being in such a leadership position (he has a bachelor's degree in anthropology from the University of Massachusetts at Amherst), he got the job with a unanimous vote.

Since then he's worked to raise the morale of the rank and file, not to mention the group's profile (and, in the process, his own). Because just about all of us were born in, raised in, and still reside in a Black community, Ras felt the only way to ensure that our communities can know us, respect us, and love us as ourselves is if they *see* us. And the best way to show we are not only a part of the community but that we *are* the community was to represent at citywide functions and events, such as the African-American Day Parade, held each September in Harlem. As you can imagine, there was a *lot* of resistance to this. Unlike others apprehensive about joining the contingent, my biggest fear wasn't being verbally or physically assaulted by other marchers or the public (although that *was* a concern given that no openly gay group had marched in the parade before)—it was Pooquie. Since he and his family live in Harlem, he was convinced someone would see me and his cover would be blown. Naturally, he didn't want me to march and gave me the silent treatment—verbally and physically—when I refused to drop out of it (it lasted six days).

But Pooquie had nothing to worry about (if I was spotted by anyone, they haven't spilled the beans), and neither did the eighteen other members who decided to march. Although we did receive a few quizzical stares, our participation was welcomed (one woman, who had set up a little barbecue hut in front of her brownstone, gave all of us free dinners for our courage; turned out she had recently lost her son to AIDS). We also signed on nine new members. It was a jood lesson for all of us: Don't underestimate your own people.

Ras also moved the meetings from the gay and lesbian community center in the Vill to the Marcus Garvey House in Harlem; had a bylaw passed banning white men from meetings and running for office (a couple of Caucasians have threatened to sue for "reverse discrimination," but since the group is a private organization, they wouldn't prevail in a court of law); and got rid of the Brotherhood symbol—a rainbow flag in the shape of Africa—and changed it to a black-and-white profile of two brothers in silhouette, locked in an embrace. This new Afrikan-centered shift has strained our relations with other groups. The Brotherhood and the multiracial, multiethnic Color Blind Queers (CBQ) used to be "sister" organizations (an alliance that, to some observers, made the Brotherhood more of an extension of CBQ than a group with its own identity, particularly given that some white CBQers felt they had the "right" to participate), but that all changed when they asked us to join a "boycott" of a bar called Wing Dixie because of their racist "carding" of Black clientele (while whites are granted automatic entry, we're expected to produce anywhere from one to four pieces of identification, depending on the mood of the doorman that night). Ras laughed in their faces ("We have more important things to fight for than the right to have access to the playpens of white gay men to be their toys"), arguing that the real problem is not getting into white establishments but how we are treated inside (and outside) of them. As he stated in an article about the bar's unspoken but well-known policy that ran in *The Rainbow Times*, a weekly lesbigay newspaper in the city: "Why is it that a white gay man who sits at a bar alone is a paying customer but a Black Same Gender Loving man is a customer who wants to be paid—as in *hustler*? It is insane for any Black man to *beg* Caucasian queers to take our money so they can either exoticize or criminalize us." After rebuffing their call for support and dismissing their efforts in print, CBQ (which Ras often refers to as the ABSQ—the Amalgamated Brotherhood of Snow Queens) has been more than cool toward us (which suits him just fine).

And now, with Ahmad's visit, the Brotherhood would receive the type of validation Ras had been chanting for (he's a Buddhist). The group had never hosted such a "mainstream" (i.e., Black heterosexual) figure in its eight-year history, and it was somewhat historic— reporters from the New York *Amsterdam News* and the *Village Voice* were in the house. Ras hopes the exposure will encourage other Black leaders to open up and nurture a dialogue with Same Gender Loving people (and he's already laid the groundwork for that by inviting the Reverend Al Sharpton to be on a panel to discuss that very topic in April).

Above all else, Ras would finally get to present to an audience of his peers (well, I'm sure we're viewed more like his pupils) the man whose political leanings and cultural ideals helped fashion his own. And to prove just how special this evening was, he didn't show up in one of his usual revolutionary war T-shirts (i.e., FREE MUMIA, FREE GERONIMO PRATT, I DEMAND MY 40 ACRES & A MULE) and blue jeans but a maroon turtleneck, black pleated corduroy pants, and black leather monkstraps. And the silver hoop he often wears in his left ear was gone (this fashion decision no doubt influenced by Ahmad, who frowns down on men and women adorning themselves with jewelry). After preliminary announcements, Ras took the floor—and was he in his glory. We knew what was coming first: "We are very luck' to have with us tonight the *honorable* Brother Ahmad Khan . . ." And then, he went on for almost five minutes, recounting how he came across Ahmad's work and how it has changed his life (as if ninety-five percent of the people in the room didn't already know). Gushing and grinning as if Ahmad were a movie star, he stepped aside and took a seat not three feet away from him, his eyes glued to him during the entire presentation.

For a forty-eight-year-old, Ahmad is very well preserved. He favors Keith David, the actor: tall, thick, bald-headed, and incredibly sexy. His advice on how we can claim our own throne really came down to common sense: have faith in a Higher Power; respect yourself and your brethren (and sistren); keep those around you who feed your mind and spirit; know and celebrate your people's history so you can truly create and live your own. He used his own life as an example, tracking his journey to self-discovery. He didn't recount the harassment and violence he encountered as a Black Panther from the government, nor his being railroaded by the system (he was framed by white policemen, had a district attorney try him who was more concerned with being reelected than with seeking justice, was represented by an ineffective white defense lawyer, convicted by a white jury, and sentenced by a white judge), with any bitterness. He couldn't denounce all white folks: he has a few to thank for his being released (a team of lawyers raised the funds to get a DNA test done and it cleared him).

However, he did warn us about falling for the white man's game—and the white man himself, calling an attraction to Caucasians "unhealthy and unnatural." While I would be the *last* person to support Black men and white men being together, I don't think desire is something you can will or wish into being; it just is. While it can be impacted by different factors (and there is a difference between being attracted to a person and having a fetish for the group they belong to), it is more internal than external. For Ahmad, though, it's not the attraction itself that is dangerous but the "delusion of inclusion" we as Black folks too readily accept, thinking the white people we have relationships with couldn't possibly harbor white-supremacist tendencies.

As he put it, "So long as people who call themself white have white-skin privilege, they cannot be allowed the privilege of sampling us."

Yeah, this went over well with the audience, especially Ras, who threw his hands up as if to say *Amen*. He's convinced that if you find *any* white person attractive, you have accepted, as Meshell NdegoOcello would put it, "the white racist standard of beauty." I think his obsessive preoccupation with not seeing Black men with white men (he's gone so far as to answer personal ads placed by brothers looking for white men, "pass" as white, and, when he met them in person, blast them for being so self-hating) might have something to do with his nonrelationship with his own father. When asked about him, he gave an answer that closed the door on the subject forever: "He's white. He lives in Chicago. And I haven't spoken to him in eight years." I've wondered why he disowned him—or whether that shoe is on the other foot (he's the youngest of five and Daddy might not like his only son being a homo). Ras didn't appreciate my being so inquisitive (it's the reporter in me) about the basis of his theory but decided not to attack me to my face. I'm sure he's the one who started the rumor that I have or am presently dating a white man (it ain't none of these folks' business who I was or am seeing and I tell them so—but in a polite way). You ask a question and you're suddenly sleeping with the enemy . . .

When Ahmad touched on our lives as Same Gender Loving men, thank God he didn't attempt to appease us with a story about how he came across many of our kind behind bars (although I bet he had many of those stories to tell). He admitted his ignorance around issues pertaining to SGL people but a willingness to learn. And, since he wasn't very specific about it in any of his books, I looked forward to hearing his thoughts on homophobia—and I have to admit that it did surprise me when he testified it is very much alive and well in Black America. (Mind you, I didn't say *Black homophobia;* I don't believe in couching Black people in the negative, and that's what monikers such as this that purport to describe our behavior do.) Ras doesn't believe it exists *at all*. As he argued: "When was the last time you ever heard of one of us being killed by a brother or sister because of who we love?" Granted, there may not be many documented cases of it, but such crimes *have* happened. And denying that homophobia does exist in Black America and can manifest itself in a way that could lead to violence is just as dangerous as claiming, as some have, that Black people are *more* homophobic (than *whom*, no one ever says). As Ahmad expressed, the trick is getting Black heterosexuals to see how their language and behavior help sustain a culture that is heterosexist at its core and that, if left unchecked, can fuel homophobia. While Ras's body shifted a little during this part, his eyes never left Ahmad.

Overall, Ahmad was an impressive public speaker. He talks exactly the way he writes—clearly, succinctly, and without any air of pomposity or arrogance. Ras could take some cues in this area: he is very long-winded, goes off on tangents, and loves to hear the sound of his own voice.

But then, just before the discussion was opened up to us . . .

"This is why I encourage all of you brothers to not forget that, even if you are that way . . ."

Huh? Did he say what I thought he did?

". . . the community needs you. While there are many in the community who would and probably have rejected you because you are that way . . ."

Yeah, he said it. *Twice.*

For much of the night, he used *homosexual, nonheterosexual,* even *Same Gender Loving* a few times (he must've been coached by Ras on the latter). *Gay* never crossed his lips, and Ras was probably behind that, too: since it's a white-constructed label, he strongly discourages us from using it. But *that way*? This really threw me for a loop. One could argue that it really wasn't a big deal; I mean, they're only words, right? You can't expect even the most open-minded or progressive heterosexual to know or get *everything*. But it still bothered me that he would choose such a phrase to describe us. And while I wasn't going to let something like it ruin what had been up to that moment a very positive experience, I had to know why.

Ras asked the first few questions. Given that he was on Ahmad's jock, I knew he wouldn't ask about it. I saw how others reacted to Ahmad's saying the phrase and thought one of them would address it. They didn't.

You know who had to.

I raised my hand. I guess Ras knew I was going to go there: he tried to pretend he didn't see it.

"Well, if there are no more questions . . ." he began, looking everywhere except in my direction.

Of course, his ignoring me puzzled just about everyone, including Ahmad, since I was seated in the center of the very first row and my hand was the *only* one raised.

"I think Brother Crawford has a question," said Rasaad Badu, aka Preston Werner, who was seated directly behind me—in two chairs. He's just over four feet tall—and nearly four feet wide. His DSLs (that's Dick Sucking Lips) are his most attractive attributes, and I heard through the grapevyne (Rasaad is the operator on the group's main line) that Ras has been putting those lips to jood use. There are two things on this earth Ras loves—to be worshiped and high-yellow boys (when B.D. attended only his second meeting with me a few months ago, Ras walked around with the most visible hard-on for most of the night—until Babyface showed up and B.D. introduced him as his husband). So he hit the Lotto jackpot with Rasaad. But Rasaad's cultish worship of Ras is frightening. After moving to New York from Cleveland last spring, he saw Ras in action and came back the following week having adopted a variation of Ras's name and volunteering to be his personal assistant (he also started letting his hair grow natural; he wants a headful of short locks like Ras).

But he doesn't just make sure Ras's mail is opened, his schedule is organized, and his pencils are sharpened: he also finds it necessary to come to Ras's aid when others dare to challenge him. Ras can be downright rude, yet Rasaad will overlook his behavior and chastise others for throwing back at him what he dishes out (his favorite line being "That was an *un*principled attack"). He's yet to do it to me; he must know that wouldn't be wise.

Even after his cheerleader acknowledged my hand, Ras was still reluctant to call on me. He halfheartedly nodded in my direction.

I rose from my seat. I turned my attention to Ahmad. "I'd like to thank you for coming to our meeting. You've been very affirming of us as Black *men*. We usually aren't afforded that from heterosexual brothers. To be reminded that we are indeed a part of the community and that we have a rightful place in it . . ."

Ras's expression went from a frown to a half smile. Guess he was no longer disappointed that he called on me.

"But—"

His body jerked with dread.

"—I was wondering why you used the term *that way* when referring to us."

I could feel many exhale; the subject was finally broached. But Ras visibly cringed, and what little color he had all but drained from his face.

Ahmad was caught off guard. "Oh. Is there a problem with it?" He turned to Ras, a little concerned (or was that a cry for help?).

"Well, it could be viewed as problematic," I offered.

"Ah." He was intrigued. "Would you say the phrase is a slur?"

"I wouldn't call it a slur. But it isn't a term of endearment. I'm sure many of us have heard it before, and it wasn't expressed with love." Several brothers nodded in agreement. I could vividly see Olivia Cole saying the phrase with a distorted face and a voice dripping with contempt when describing the relationship between Paula Kelly and Lonette McKee in the miniseries *The Women of Brewster Place*. "I guess you could say it's pejorative."

"I see." He pondered the notion, stroking his goatee, which was speckled with gray.

"It's also sort of a code word," I continued. "I've heard heterosexual people use it because they are uncomfortable actually *saying* the word *homosexual*. Not that you fall into that category . . ."

The room was silent as he considered what I said. His eyes grew wide. "Now that you say that . . . I distinctly remember hearing my elders using it when I was young. And it wasn't used in an affirming way." He smiled. "In my haste to use those identifiers I believed were appropriate, you could say that . . . well, it just slipped out."

"Sure. That's understandable." And it was.

"As I've already explained, I'm not the kind of man who believes in using euphemisms. So I will check that." He scanned the membership. "And I certainly didn't mean to insult anyone."

"I'm sure you didn't mean to," I assured him. "And speaking for myself, I wasn't insulted. Just a little thrown by it. Thank you for the explanation." I sat back down.

He smiled. "And thank *you*, brother. In order for us to truly conquer the isms and phobias that affect and infect us, we have to make sure the language we use is correct and just. Actions do speak louder than words, but words very much impact our actions. So I'm glad you pointed that out."

And *I* was glad he took my query seriously and didn't respond with that "*If* I insulted you . . ." bull that people who make offensive comments often say, implying that your reaction, not what they said, is the real problem. He was very sincere and honest about it, and understood that while it may have been a small thing, it was worth addressing and analyzing. The members appreciated this, also; there was a collective sigh in the room that that cloud had been lifted.

Ras, of course, was not pleased. I dared not only to question but to *school* his idol in front of the entire group. While Ahmad didn't at all seem embarrassed or bothered by it, Ras was. After Ahmad gave his closing remarks, folks got the chance to talk with him individually—and with each other (despite Ras's attempt to turn the Brotherhood into a gay Black Panther Party, you can never get a roomful of fags together and not expect digits to be exchanged). As I was welcoming a couple of brothers who were there for the first time, inquiring about whether they enjoyed the meeting and would come again (I guess you could call me the hospitality committee), Ras approached us.

"I gotta talk to you," he almost snarled.

"Okay. In a minute."

He grasped my left arm. "Now."

Not wanting to cause a scene and give these brothers a reason not to come back (not to mention something to gossip to their friends about), I graciously smiled at them. "Would you two excuse me for a moment?" I guess they were so stunned by Ras's abrupt behavior they couldn't respond. I handed them membership applications. "Why don't you both just look this over and if you have any questions, I can answer them when I return." I lightly jerked my arm from Ras and started walking away from him.

He walked along with me, whispering directly into my ear. "What you did was uncalled for."

"What are you talking about?" I said out of the left side of my mouth, all the while smiling at folks as we passed them.

"You know damn well what I'm talking about."

I stopped. I glared at him. My voice was low but forceful. "You would want to change your tone and refrain from using such language with me." I continued walking and headed out of the meeting room and toward the office, for I knew the volume would be turned up on this exchange. He followed me.

He closed the door behind us. He sat against his desk. "You just couldn't leave well enough alone."

"I just asked for clarity, which, I might add, he was happy to give."

"That wasn't about clarity, it was about clownin'."

"Excuse me?"

"You heard, clownin'. The man comes all this way to help us in our efforts to make this group stronger, to make each one of us as individuals stronger, and you get all bent out of shape over a couple of words he says."

"First of all, I didn't get all bent out of shape. Secondly, I wasn't the only person in that room who was taken aback by what he said. And third, if you weren't taken aback by it, you *should've* been."

He now wore that smug grin that I hate so much. "Well, unlike you, I'm secure enough not to let a couple of words break my spirit."

I started to laugh uncontrollably.

He was baffled by my reaction, not to mention disgusted. "And the very fact that you think this is funny tells me just how much of a fool you are."

Yeah, I stopped laughing. "You know, you are just so predictable it's pathetic. Or is it the other way around?"

"What?"

"*And* you are such a *hypocrite*."

"A hypocrite?"

"Yes."

"What do you mean?"

"Uh, what part of those statements do you *not* understand? You are always so hell-bent on setting folks straight, particularly since you *think* you know everything. But because I questioned someone you admire, there's a problem. And, we know that if you admire someone, they can't, like you, be questioned, right?"

"Listen, Mitchell—"

"*And,* if there is a fool in this room, I'm looking at him. Did you think I would just put down my hand because *you* decided there would be no more questions? We already have one dictator in this town and he's at City Hall; we don't need another. Don't get mad with or try to insult me because you made a fool of *yourself*. Now, if you don't mind, I have members to recruit."

I was out the door before he could finish saying my name.

He caught up with and hurried by me, approaching the two young men I was speaking with. "So, do you brothers wish to join our group?" he asked.

They were both, again, startled. The shorter one spoke. "Uh, yeah. But I thought, uh, Mitchell was—" He pointed to me.

"Oh, Mr. Crawford no longer handles membership here."

They looked at him. They looked at me.

"What?" I almost yelled, causing folks around us to turn and look.

"You have been relieved of your duties. I will handle this from now on."

I caught my breath. I smiled. "Oh. I see. Because I refuse to be one of these little groupies who fawn over you, who believe every word you say, and who do as they are told, you have no use for me, right?"

Just like clockwork, his number-one groupie—Rasaad—interjected. "Oh, is there a problem?"

I rolled my eyes at him. "No, there isn't. Ras can handle himself. He doesn't need *you* to come to his aid, okay?"

Ras put on that condescending, consoling cape. "Mitchell, I believe you're being a little too emotional—"

"And *don't* you tell me what I am or am not being, either." By this time all eyes were on us.

And this was what he was counting on. Now he went into p.a.m. (passive aggressive mode). "You are taking what I said the wrong way. What I told you was said—"

"For my own good, right? Stop putting on a front for these folks, okay? They know a self-absorbed, manipulative, narcissistic tyrant when they see one." Some gasped.

He still pressed on with that tired performance. "Brother Mitchell, I am so sorry that—"

"I feel this way, right? You're sorry, all right—you're one *sorry* motherfucker." Some giggled; others nodded their heads, realizing they had seen this scene played out many times before—except the person he said this shit to just took it.

Well, you know that I ain't the one.

"And *don't* call me brother, 'cause you *don't* mean it," I barked. "I am so *fucking* tired of your Malcolm X–wannabe, Blacker-than-thou ass." One person laughed out loud; a few others followed suit.

I noticed Ahmad, who appeared dumbfounded by this spectacle. I walked over to him. "I'm sorry, Mr. Khan. I know that we shouldn't address each other as men of African descent in such a way, but *believe* me, there was no other way to respond to his subterfuge." I held out my hand. He shook it. "I enjoyed your presentation very much. If only your protégé *really* knew what it meant to be a Black man with principles. It was a pleasure to meet you."

His mouth opened; nothing. Then . . . "Uh, you, too, my brother."

With all eyes still on me, I walked over to the chair I had sat in, picked up my knapsack, and made my way to the exit. I stopped in front of Rasaad. "Oh, and for the record: Contrary to what *some* have been saying *behind my back*"—I gave him a once-over—"I've never been with a white man." I turned to Ras. I smiled. "But I understand this is something *you* cannot say."

Everyone's jaw—including Ahmad's—dropped. I learned this bit of information from Gene, who says that Ras used to go fishing for rich white men with one of his former best friends, Malik. Gene ran into them one night in the Vill and Ras was all hugged up on some six-tyish shribbled-up shrimp.

I nodded at the two brothers thinking about becoming members. "Good luck." I returned my gaze to Ras, who had that *busted* look on his face. "You're gonna need it."

When the phone rang—no, make that *screamed*—it almost knocked me out of bed. And I almost knocked over the nightstand reaching for it.

"H'llo?" I gruffly breathed into the receiver, regretting not turning the ringer off. I usually do that at night. But now that Pooquie is on the road, I leave it on in case of an emergency. So it shouldn't have surprised me when the voice on the other end asked . . .

"Little Bit?"

"Pooquie?" I perked up. "What's wrong?"

"Nuthin'."

I squinted at the clock: 4:05. Something *better* be wrong. "Nothing? Then why are you calling so late?" I was trying not to sound irritated but knew I wasn't doing a jood job. We had spoken for an hour before I went to bed around eleven. I told him about walking out of the Brotherhood meeting ("I bet they gonna be *beggin'* you ta come back, Baby; that mutha-fucka is gonna drive ev'rybody away, except that weeble-wobble he fuckin' ").

"I . . . I'm sorry, Baby," he apologized.

Silence.

"Little Bit?"

I was drifting back off. "Yeah, Pooquie?"

"I . . . I'm horny."

My eyes popped back open. "Excuse me?"

"I'm horny, Baby."

Well, he made it just under the gun—six days. But he certainly didn't have to call and tell me that the deadline had arrived. I snickered a sigh. "Well, what else is new, Pooquie? When *aren't* you horny?"

"Baby, I need some."

"Well, Pooquie, what do you expect me to do? You're not in Harlem, you're in Hollywood, remember?"

"Uh, talk dirty to me."

"Huh?"

"Talk dirty to me, Baby. Please?"

Hmm . . . now this is something I never got into. I'm a hands-on kinda guy: if a man is breathing heavy, he's got to be in the same room with me if he expects to turn me on. The only person I've engaged in phone sex with is my ex, Peter—and it was at his request. When we were trying to make a go of the long distance thing after he moved to L.A., he'd call me every Friday at five o'clock his time to get a fix (for some reason, doing it at work heightened the high; he always volunteered to lock up the office on this day and, five minutes after the last coworker left, would proceed to lock himself up in a soundproof conference room so he could let loose). While he enjoyed it immensely (the last few times I visited him he'd have me call him from his home office while he choked the chicken in his second-floor bedroom), I never even considered taking my own dick out and stroking along with him (although he believes I did; Meg Ryan's "orgasm" in *When Harry Met Sally* was really fake compared with how I performed). All the oohing and aahing, groaning and moaning through AT&T was truly an exercise, my effort to keep the home fire he had for me burning. It did absolutely nothing for me.

But the thought of getting verbosely vulgar with Pooquie made me get a little excited.

I threw the comforter and sheet off of me, my dick swinging up and ready for action. "Uh, where are you?"

"In bed."

"You lying down?"

"Sittin' up."

Uh-huh. And, no doubt, *it* is sitting up, too. "You naked?"

"You know it."

"Totally butt-booty naked?"

"Yeah."

"Well, put on your boots and cap."

"Huh?"

"Put on your boots and cap."

"Why?"

"Don't worry about why. Just do it."

"Uh. A'ight."

I heard him swing off the bed, slip into his Timbs, and place the cap on his head.

"A'ight."

I got comfortable, lying flat on my back. "Now get on all fours."

He obeyed, maneuvering the phone so he wouldn't drop it. "I'm ready."

"Ha, you sure you ready?" My voice dropped from tenor to baritone. I couldn't sound like Barry White, but I could do a jood imitation of Billy Eckstine.

And he loved it. "Mmm, I'm always ready fuh some of what you got."

"You better be ready to take *all* of it, not just *some* of it."

"Uh-huh. I want all of it."

"You better, 'cause you gonna take it all whether you want to or not."

"Bring it on, Baby, bring it *on*," he demanded.

"Hmmph. You strokin' it?"

"Yeah."

"You givin' that piece a *long, deep* tug, right?"

"Uh-huh," he huffed.

"Jood. While you jerkin' it, I'm lickin' the tip of that big old pretty head, goin' 'round in circles . . ."

"Ah, yeah . . ."

"Ya like the way that feels, don'tcha?"

"Yeah, Baby, you *know* I do."

"Uh-huh, and while you keep on doin' the jerk, I'm gonna start poppin' that big ol' head with my mouth . . ."

"Uh-huh, Baby, ya know I love that shit."

"Ha, that's why I'm gonna do it." I pursed my lips in and pushed them out.

"Ah, *day-um*, Baby. I can *feel* that shit."

"Ya can, huh?"

"*Hell*-fuckin'-yeah."

Well, then: *pop, pop, pop, pop, pop.*

"Umph! That shit feels *so* fuckin' jood!"

"Ha, you ain't felt nothin' yet, homeboy. *Ssss* . . ." I was feelin' it myself.

"Ah, it's feelin' jood ta ya too, huh, Baby?" He giggled.

"You know it is. Now point that big ol' bootay to the heavens."

"Hhhhh," he breathed.

"*Uh-huh,*" I repeated, pickin' up the pace pumpin' on my own piece. "Ah, now we gotta let a little bit of my breeze blow on that bootay. You know what to do."

He did. He got into a fetal position, his head bowed and his knees locked together so that his cheeks spread apart. "*Ummm,*" he heaved.

"Yeah, Pooquie. How that feel?"

"*Hot,*" he grunted.

"That's right. Ya want me to cool it off for ya a little bit?"

"Uh-huh."

"A'ight . . ." I blew into the phone. It started low and grew louder.

"*Uh,*" he quivered.

"Ha, makin' ya shiver, huh?"

"Yeah."

"Ya like the way that cool breeze is just blowin' on it, don'tcha?"

"*Uh-huh.*"

"Ya want some more?"

"Ya know I do."

His wish was my command.

"*Oooh,* Little Bit, *day-um.*"

"Ah . . . yeah. Now I'm gonna spread them cheeks wider and blow *up* in it."

"Yeah, Little Bit, do it."

"Ya want me to do it?"

"*Yeah,*" he groaned.

I did.

"*Oh!*" he yelped.

"Yeah, Pooquie, open up . . ."

"Ah, yeah, Baby," he whispered.

I followed suit. "Come on . . . open up."

"Uh-huh."

"Open up and let me *all* the fuck up in, come on now . . ."

After a few sputtering sighs, I heard a sound that was very familiar. I knew *exactly* what he was doing. "*Get* your middle finger out of there!" I ordered.

I guess he was shocked I could tell he was tinkerin' with his tunnel. "Uh, but, but, Baby, it itches—"

"Well, I ain't tell you you can scratch it," I snapped. "So stop."

He reluctantly removed it. He sighed in frustration.

"Besides, *I* know whatcha need up there."

"Do ya?"

"Yeah." I tripped my tongue, letting it lap on the receiver. I could see that big basketball bootay jump.

"Ooh, yeah, Little Bit, tongue that azz."

"*Lalalalalala.*" I lapped with my tongue as it darted in and out of my mouth at rapid speed.

"*Ooh ooh ooh,*" he squealed.

"Uh-huh, throw it at me, Pooquie, *yeah.*"

"*Umph, umph, umph,*" he barked, thrustin' it as he jerked.

"Ya want me to eat it?"

"*Uh-huh.*"

"Say *please.*"

"*Pleeze,* Baby, *pleeze.*"

I love it when he begs.

I did, slurpin' and slobberin'.

"Ooh . . . *ooh . . . ooh ooh ooh,*" he yodeled, pushin' it all up in my imaginary face.

"Ha, careful now, Pooquie, give a brother the chance to breathe, a'ight? Don't smother me with it . . . yet."

He slowed down his pace. "Ha . . . *ha . . . ah . . . ssss . . . yeah,* mutha-fucka, eat me the fuck *out. Woof.*"

"Ha, I'm gonna do more than eat you the fuck out. I'm gonna bang them boots the fuck *off.* You ready?"

"Baby, I been ready."

"Sure you want it?"

"Yeah."

"Sure you can handle it?"

"*Hell*-fuckin'-yeah."

"A'ight, then. But, just one more—"

Slurp!

"—for the road."

"*Ah,*" he exhaled.

"Now I'm takin' aim. I'm gonna rim that bootay."

He was gettin' antsy. "Nah, nah, Baby, don't *tease* me, now . . ."

"Ha, I can hear that bootay callin' me."

Womp, womp, womp.

"*C'mon*, Little Bit, I *want* it."

"Ya want it, huh?"

"*Yeah.*"

"Ha, don't sound like ya do."

"*I want it, I want it!*"

He wanted it—and he got it.

"*Hooooooh,*" he grunted, as I've often heard him express when I've made my entrance.

"Ooh *yeah*, I'm slidin' all up *in* that ass, Pooquie. Ya feel it?"

"Yeah."

"I can't *hear* you . . ."

"*Yeah.*"

"Ya want it all?"

"Uh-*huh.*"

"You *sure* you want it all?"

"Yeah, Baby, give it ta me, give it ta me *now.*"

I gave it to him.

"*Aaaah,*" we both sang.

"You diggin' that, huh, Pooquie?"

"Uh-huh," he snapped.

"But wait, don't get too excited just yet. We gonna take a slow groove, slidin' back and forth, back and forth, *back . . .* "

"*Ooh.*"

". . . and *forth.*"

"*Aaah.*"

"*Back . . .*"

"*Mmm . . .*"

". . . and . . . *forth.*"

He moaned. "Doin' me on tha sneak tip, huh?"

"Sneaky *and* freaky."

He giggled.

"Mmm, I'm all *up* in dat bad boyee now. Gettin' a *real* jood feel of this. *Yeah.* I'm gonna bang them boots off yo' feet."

"Yeah, work that azz, mutha-fucka."

"Ha, ya want me to work that azz?"

"Yeah, Daddy, *work it!*"

"Well, ya gotta work with me, Pooquie, so, come on and back that azz up, back it up!"

I could *see* him twirlin' that ass into me and *feel* it as he clutched that dick.

"Woo, woo, woo," he huffed.

"Ah, yeah, work it. You twist and clench while I bang and bump."

"Uh-huh, mutha-fucka, bang that azz, yeah."

"Yeah, I'm gonna dig a trench in that ass, wage a war, know what I'm sayin'?"

"Uh-huh."

I smacked my own thigh—he knew what that was.

"Oh, *yeah,* mutha-fucka, spank it while you swing it!"

You got it. *Smack, smack, smacksmacksmack.*

"Yeah, mutha-fucka, slap and tap that azz like ya know!"

"Ha, don't you worry, I will."

"Aaaaaaay, sss," he heaved.

"Ha, that's right, you wiggle it while I jiggle *all* up in it!"

"Ay ya ay ya ay ya," he stuttered.

"Uh-huh, Pooquie, I'm *housin'* that new jack bootay, ain't I?"

"Cha cha cha cha," he chattered as if he were freezing.

"Ha, you know how to give that azz up. I'm mountin' them bootay mounds and you just lovin' it, huh?"

"Mmm, take it all."

"Hmmph, I'm takin' it all and some more."

"Ssss . . . oomph," he screeched.

Uh-oh. I knew what *that* meant. "Ah, you 'bout ready to cum, huh?"

"Aw yeah."

"Me, too, baby boyee, me, too. So cum with me, come on with me, cum on . . ."

"Aw yeah, I'm gonna cum."

"You gonna cum?"

"Uh-huh."

"Well, then cum on now. Spray it *all* over, Pooquie."

"Ooh, yeah, I'm cummin', I'm cummin'..."

"Yeah, Pooquie, bring that tide on *in.*"

"Oh, Baby, Oh, Baby, oh, Baby, oh oh oh oh..."

"Oh, yeeeeeaaaaah!" I howled as my volcano erupted.

But Pooquie just didn't blow his top—he toppled off of the bed and onto the floor. At least that's what it sounded like.

"Pooquie?" I could hear him going *"Oomph Oomph Oomph"* over and over. I must've called him a half-dozen times before the receiver was picked back up.

He was out of breath, as if he'd just run a marathon. "Yeah, Baby. I'm here."

"Are you okay?"

"Hell yeah."

"You sure?"

"Uh-huh."

"What happened?"

Not only did he take a tumble, he brought the phone and the Yellow Pages that were on the nightstand down with him.

"Well, I wanted to knock your boots off, not knock *you* off!" I laughed.

"That's a'ight. It was worth takin' that fall, Baby. *Oomph.*"

I chuckled. "You still on the floor or back on the bed?"

"Sittin' against tha bed on tha flo'."

"Ah. Didn't have enough energy to pull yourself back up, huh?"

"Ha, nope."

"You still squirtin', ain'tcha?"

"Ya know it. *Day-um.*"

"Hmmph. Me, too." And I was. It was real thick and gooey. "Don't leave remnants all over that room now."

"I won't. I was ready. Wiped up some of it already."

"Jood. And that was *day-um* jood."

"She-it, that was *better* than jood, Baybay."

"Indeed. Folks gonna think you have somebody in there with you."

"Tha way that shit felt? Ya couldn't tell me you wasn't here."

"Same here. And I'm sure the operator got much more than an earful."

"I bet she was enjoyin' it, too."

"Ha, or he."

"Ah, yeah."

I looked at the love jism all over my thighs and stomach. "Who would've ever thought that you could get lovin' this jood over the telephone. *Now* I know why some folks are so crazy about it."

"Ha, me, too. But there still ain't nuthin' like tha real thang, Baybay."

"Mmm-hmm. There ain't. And don't you worry: when you come back home, we're gonna have an instant replay."

He giggled. "Uh . . . I guess you gotta go back ta sleep now."

"How can I, after a workout like that!"

We laughed.

I rubbed my dick. "Besides, we got up together, we gotta come down together."

We sighed a moan together.

"Thanks, Little Bit."

"Ha, thank *you*, Pooquie. I'll be tired, maybe a little cranky today, but I'll be smiling on the inside."

8

"So . . . guess who's going to be a millionaire?"

I was in the office of my lawyer, Jozette Wilkes, an attorney with Brandt-Myers-Albrecht, one of the most successful firms in the nation that specializes in discrimination cases. Interestingly, she's the only African-American *and* the only female at B-M-A— and those are two of the reasons why I hired her. When I decided to sue *Your World* for racial discrimination, I had been advised by many to get white representation because it would play better in front of a jury. Sadly, some studies show that white *and* Black jurists place more stock in the words of a Caucasian attorney than a Black one when it comes to matters of race; I guess the assumption is that if a white person sees it, it *must* be true and the Negro(es) leveling the charge isn't/aren't just crying wolf (as many believe we often do). But I didn't feel the least bit comfortable placing this in the hands of someone white; I felt that the person I was paying jood money to had to know, on some level, what it was like, what I had gone through. And in corporate America, no one knows more about the isms than the sisters, who have to wage war every day on two fronts. Add her being a homegirl from the 'hood (Red Hook in Brooklyn) and a Columbia alum like me, and Jozette was the perfect choice.

She's a diminutive woman (no more than five feet) with Milky Way dark skin, big light brown eyes, a cleft in her chin ("It's *real*, honey"), and a headful of auburn spaghetti braids that fall just above her waist. But don't let her size fool you: like Julia Sugarbaker on TV's *Designing Women*, she's been dubbed "The Terminator." Many have underestimated her presence and power—and have lived to regret it. She may appear delicate and soft, but she can be tough, even vicious. She joined B-M-A three years ago and has never lost a case; she won three multimillion-dollar judgments and settled her last two cases out of court. (Her wrath has other lawyers running scared; it's rumored that *Your World*'s company attorney, Teddy Levine, bowed out of representing them because he lost to Jozette two years ago and wasn't about to suffer another humiliating defeat.)

Because of her reputation, Jozette believed we wouldn't have to go to trial. And after almost ten months of talk, it looked as if *Your World* was ready to strike a deal. I was praying they would be: I really didn't want to go to trial, for it would've proven too costly (both in terms of money and time). While I had a jood shot at winning and relished the thought of watching Jozette destroying every one of their witnesses on the stand, there was always the chance that my efforts would prove to be less than fruitful. The jury could find in my favor but award me only a fraction of what we asked for since I am young and the discrimination wasn't blatant. (As Jozette explained early on: "It wasn't as if you were finding dead rats in your locker, nooses hanging over light fixtures above your desk, and the word *nigger* spray-painted on your car.") Or the appeals process could take so long that any monies I eventually received wouldn't be enough to cover my lawyer's fees. Or worse, I could lose altogether and really be left emotionally, spiritually, and financially spent. On top of the unknown outcome, I also would've had to take a leave of absence from my teaching job and I couldn't afford that (a "fuck-you fund" can last but so long). And, since I knew that few racial discrimination suits are successful (be it an in-court judgment or out-of-court settlement), the cons certainly outweighed the pros. But, as Pooquie argued, this was something I had to do: if I just shrugged my shoulders and walked away, that would give them the license to continue doing it and I would be indirectly saying it's okay to mistreat us because of who we are.

So I was more than pleased when Jozette called me last Monday, excited she had come across the evidence that would, as I've heard many a lawyer on television declare, "break this case wide open." And it came from a source I certainly wouldn't have expected . . .

Phillip Cooper.

Phillip and I were barely speaking when I left *Your World* a year and a half ago, mainly because he decided to become the User-Friendly Negro—you know, the kind of colored person who won't rock the boat, who will go out of their way to make white folks comfortable, who will be as nonthreatening, nonconfrontational, non-*Black* as possible. His very accommodating manner was directed at one person in particular: my nemesis, Elias Whitley, aka the Great White Dope. No matter how nonsensical and stoopid Elias's position was (yeah, it was usually both), he could always count on Phillip to be his yes-man, going along with whatever he said. Phillip stroked much more than Elias's ego, though. I hadn't told Jozette about catching them fucking; if confronted, both would surely deny it, and it certainly had no bearing on my case. But I guess his arrogance got the best of him: being the only Negro on staff, doing the boss, and not believing what happened to me could happen to him went to *both* of his heads. According to *Your World,* his performance was unsatisfactory the first six months of 1994, and after he was placed on probation, it didn't improve during the rest of the year. He was fired three weeks ago.

Phillip tracked Jozette down to see if she'd also represent him. Problem was he didn't have a case for racial discrimination; Jozette had to control herself from laughing in his face when he related his tale, a story that sounded very similar to mine except that he didn't have the credentials or documentation to back it up. Judging from some of the comments made about him in his employee file ("frequently misses deadlines, research skills are elementary, doesn't pay attention to detail, writing is uneven and unfocused"), *Your World* actually ended up accommodating him: my lawsuit might've helped him keep his job longer than he should've had it (letting him go the same time they were served with papers would've been a real public-relations nightmare). But in his haste (or desperation?) to convince Jozette to take him on, he was all too happy to turn state's evidence on them. We already knew about my being paid less than Elias even though I had more experience (not to mention talent). But he did provide us with a piece of information that *Your World* had managed to keep secret.

Last September, Elias won an Eddy, sort of the Pulitzer of the education journalism world. I had been nominated three years straight and won my third time around. That Elias also managed to snag one—and on his *first* nomination—was shocking. And I gagged when I learned what he won for: a feature about a high-school program in Newark, New Jersey, where Black male teen fathers are schooled on parenthood. Given how much contempt Elias has for Black people (including the ones whose dicks he sucks), I found it hard to believe that such a well-written, thoroughly researched, incredibly incisive (if not pathologically themed) article could have been penned by him.

My hunch turned out to be correct: he didn't write the story. The article in question had been published some five years before. This was discovered by a student at Elias's alma mater, who was doing a profile on him for the school paper. When the student did a Lexis Nexis search on the program, he found himself seeing—and reading—double (it was originally published in *The Eye*, an alternative newsmagazine in Newark, and the Associated Press picked it up). It was the exact same story; Elias wasn't crafty enough to change the title, subtitle, or find out if any of those quoted still worked at/with the school (or, in the case of one of the teen fathers interviewed, was dead). When the student (who just happened to be Black!) notified the folks who hand out the Eddys, they stripped Elias of the award and demanded the $2,500 prize that came along with it be returned in forty-eight hours.

But that's just the tip of that iceberg. The student also discovered something else: Elias wasn't a college graduate. He dropped out of Yale during the latter half of his junior year. That copy of a diploma with honors (summa cum laude) hanging up on his office wall is a fake.

Now, after being exposed as a plagiarist and a fraud, you'd think *Your World* would have fired Elias. Well, they didn't. In fact, according to Phillip, one month after all these revelations, he was given a promotion *and* a raise. The entire editorial staff—which, in addition to Phillip, included Editor-in-Chief Steven Goldberg, Managing Editor Andrew Goodman, Assistant Editor Dennis Higgenbotham (he replaced Denise Garafola, a white woman who left a month after I did and would be a witness for our side), and Simon Churday, an Indian-American who filled my associate editor slot—met to discuss what action should be taken against him, and no one voted for his ouster.

He only received a reprimand (i.e., a stern lecture from Steven) and a two-week suspension *with* pay. (I'm sure that if I or Phillip had been involved in such an unethical scandal and it was discovered that we lied about our education or experience, we would've been suspended without pay, if not fired on the spot.) Phillip claims he wanted to suggest a harsher punishment be meted out but feared doing so would've put his job in jeopardy (uh-huh . . . we know the *real* reason why). Two weeks after Elias's return (his suspension was just an extended Christmas vacation), Phillip was given his pink slip—and, yeah, it was delivered to him by Elias (and knowing how smug Elias is, if they were still fucking, he probably expected that to continue). So Phillip was all too happy to supply us with this ammunition.

Your World was pretty confident that I wouldn't be able to prove a thing in court: they were betting the bank on Elias, their star witness, to portray me as the difficult, combative militant he saw me as. But now they could not call him to the stand: how could they argue to a jury that, when deciding who to promote to senior editor, a liar and a cheat was the best man for the job? *Your World* must have found out that we knew because, the very morning that Phillip provided Jozette with all the materials related to Elias's charade, their lawyer faxed Jozette an offer: $300,000. Yup, it was unacceptable. For Jozette, the most unacceptable thing was the dollar figure: given that they deliberately underpaid me and my efforts changed *Your World* from a dry textbookish magazine into an enlightening and entertaining publication for teenagers, she believed compensatory damages should include retroactive pay for doing a senior editor's job on an associate editor's salary, as well as the annual salary and bonuses I would've received had I remained with the company for an additional five years and been promoted the way I should've been. Adding punitive damages, the figure clocked in at a cool $3 million, with half paid upon signing an agreement and the other half coming a year later. Naturally, a third would be going to Jozette (or, rather, B-M-A).

I didn't care about the money; it might address the betrayal and disrespect, but it wouldn't redress it. I deserved and wanted an apology—and this was something they didn't plan on offering. In fact, their offer stated as one of its conditions that the settlement in no way meant that they were admitting any wrongdoing (the other was that I couldn't disclose the details of the agreement). I was doubly insulted: they fuck me over and then expect me to sign an agreement that absolved them of any responsibility for doing it and, by extension, forcing me to leave (while I did quit, I had no choice given the unfair treatment I received). And even with their backs against the wall, they were still more concerned with covering their own asses and keeping an incompetent Caucasian like Elias on board.

Jozette argued that they would messenger us over a check for the three mill before they admitted they intentionally wronged me. So we went around this by requesting two things that would indirectly tell the world that they did in fact discriminate against me and were taking proactive steps to make sure it wouldn't happen again:

- they had to hire a full-time affirmative-action officer
- they had to sponsor a college internship and writing fellowship program

Jozette had suggested that the other usual suspect—"sensitivity training"—be included on this list, but I nixed that. Such an exercise would truly be a waste of time and money. Can you really teach people to *be* sensitive? I don't think so. Having someone come in once a month to convince employees the way they've been conditioned to think and feel about a particular group is wrong won't help create a better working environment, it'll just foster resentment and fuel whatever indifference those who are white, male, and/or heterosexual have for those who aren't white, male, and/or heterosexual. Like my aunt Ruth says: "You can change the laws but ya can't change people's hearts."

As they do with "sensitivity training," companies also bring in an affirmative-action officer to fight or fend off accusations of racism, but it's usually nothing more than window dressing, a cosmetic addition that has no internal effect on the company's institutional policies. And given its track record, *Your World* would certainly follow that lead and practice another form of tokenism by filling this position with a person of color (more than likely Black) but not giving them the power to really do their job. But thanks to item number two, that wouldn't happen.

Our plan would require them to employ two high-school seniors of color as summer interns (one must be Black) and two college seniors of color as writing fellows, one during the school year and one during the summer (and again, one has to be Black). But they won't be able to just bring a couple of us in, stick us in a corner and give us next to nothing to do, then bid us good-bye at the end of our stint yet still count us as "staff" when those "minority" numbers are tallied (I've been there). Every two years, they must have hired and retained one of their summer interns as a contributing editor and a writing fellow as a staff writer or editor (or filled these positions with individuals from outside of the company with the help of the National Association of Black Journalists). The other departments, though, won't be off the hook: summer interns of color will also be familiar faces in graphic design, marketing, advertising, public relations, sales/subscriptions, and yes, even the mail room (which remains all white). And every time they award a fellowship and host an intern orientation, they will be reminded of who forced them to do it—and that would give me more satisfaction than a million-dollar settlement.

But, of course, it's those seven figures that most matter to Jozette. "This will make me a partner. Ha, it *better*, or *I'll* be suing for racial discrimination."

I laughed. "You really think they're going to fork over three million dollars?"

"No. But you always gotta ask for twice what you think they'd go for so all the bases are covered. That way, *you* get a great payday, *we* get a great payday, and they *still* get screwed." Her phone beeped. She picked it up. "Yes? . . . Good. Put him through." She hung up. "Well, this is the moment of truth."

I nodded.

Her line beeped again. She pressed a button. She smiled. "Stan, how are you feelin'?" Stan being Stanley Weitz of Kragen, Weitz & Brooke. His firm was representing *Your World*.

"Not as good as you'll be feeling in a few minutes." His voice was deep but nasal.

Jozette's eyebrows rose. "Oh, really? Well, talk to me. I always love feeling good."

He cleared his throat. "I've discussed your counteroffer with my client. They are willing to accept the terms . . . but would like to put another figure on the table."

"I'm listening."

"Seven-fifty."

Jozette shook her head. "Nope."

"That's as high as they'll go, Jozie."

She wasn't buying it. "A few days ago they were only willing to go as high as three hundred."

"Look, they plan to implement all the programs suggested, but it's going to take a lot of resources."

"Oh, come on, Stan. We're talking about one of the few magazines in the universe that actually made a profit over the last few years."

Wow . . . I didn't know that.

She glared at the phone. "And I'm sure I don't have to remind you *who* is partly responsible for that."

He sighed. I giggled to myself.

"And you know and I know that *Your World*'s reputation as a publication with *integrity* has to be worth more than that." Jozette said she hadn't disclosed that she had the joods on them, but that must've been the closest she'd come to spilling those beans.

Instead of a response, there was paper rustling and then some mumbling. I guess the publisher, Martin York, or someone from the board of directors was listening in and strategizing with Stan.

"How about one-two?" Stan asked with some caution in his voice.

Jozette nodded at me. She smiled. "Make it one-five and we have a deal."

There was more mumbling. "It's a deal."

Jozette grinned. "Terrific. I'll let my client know." She winked at me. "Why don't you draft up something with the conditions and items we've discussed, we'll take a look at it, and if there are any problems, we'll work on it."

"Fine."

"Oh, and Stan, I want to keep this process as smooth and uncomplicated as possible. Let's try and have all this worked out before, say"—she began flipping through her desk calendar—"March twenty-second, exactly one month from now. I'm pretty sure your client wants this matter settled as soon as possible, and mine does also."

"Indeed. I'll have something to you in writing next Wednesday. How does that sound?"

"Sounds great. We'll talk then."

"Fine. Have a good day."

"With news like this, you know I will. Till next week." She clicked him off, then pressed another button. "Kent?"

"Yes?" It was her male aide, a brother from Nairobi who is in his second year of law school at New York University.

"We should be receiving papers from Kragen, Weitz & Brooke next Wednesday regarding Mr. Crawford's case. If they don't arrive by eleven-forty-five A.M., make sure you place a call to Serena O'Day, Stanley Weitz's assistant."

"Will do."

"Thanks." She clicked him off. She smiled. "You gotta catch folks while they're still in a working mood and that's usually *before* lunchtime." She frowned. "For somebody who heard with his own ears that he's going to be a millionaire, you sure don't look happy. I've seen more joy on the faces of husbands who've been sued for and lost everything to their ex-wives."

I shrugged. "It's . . . good news."

"Ha, it's *better* than good," she corrected me.

I chuckled to myself, thinking about Pooquie. "Yes, it is."

She leaned forward. "Mitch, I know it might seem like a hollow victory, but given what you will come out of this with and what they have agreed to do, this has to be one of the best settlement deals I've ever seen, especially for one individual. Be glad there aren't twenty or thirty other people attached to this. Litigation would really go on for years and you'd end up with pennies in the long run—if you ended up with anything."

"Yeah, I know."

"It'd be great if we did have the agreement signed and the first check within the month, but now comes the tricky part: coming up with language that says what it's supposed to and that everyone can live with. Sometimes a deal can fall through because the parties disagree over the inclusion or exclusion of one word. *One* word. So you can't go on any wild spending sprees yet."

I laughed. "I won't."

"Oh . . ." She searched her desk. She handed me a yellow stickie. "It's Phillip's number."

I frowned.

"He wanted me to give him yours. You don't have to call him."

"You know I won't." And I wasn't. Yes, he gave us the "smoking gun," but, as usual, he did for his own self-serving reasons. Some things—or, rather, people—never change.

Jozette shrugged. "Well, at least I can say I passed it on to you."

I looked at her desk clock: 4:25. "Well, I have to go. Got essays to read." I rose.

"Okay." She walked over and hugged me. "But make sure you take some time to enjoy this moment, okay?"

"Okay."

"Promise?"

"I promise."

"Good."

I smiled. "Thanks so much."

"No problem." She grinned. "*I* know what'll cheer you up." She linked her arm in mine. We started walking toward her door. "We've got a new UPS man on this floor and he should be here any minute. Let's go by the watercooler and lie in wait." She batted her eyes, her very long lashes flickering.

I giggled. "Sounds like fun."

We waited for five minutes, but he was a no-show. Either he came early or was running late. I didn't want to be caught in rush-hour traffic, so I said good-bye and headed for the elevators.

One was waiting for me. I got on. I pressed for the lobby and was about to tap the close button when . . .

"Could you hold that door, please?" a baritone voice sincerely asked. It sounded familiar. The man's footsteps came closer and closer.

It was Montee, the brother from Body & Soul. He must've been the man we were waiting for. He was dressed in a different uniform today—UPS. And, like the army fatigues he had on Sunday night, he wore it hellafied well.

He grinned. "So, we meet again."

I smiled. "So we do."

105

LOVE
THE
ONE
YOU'RE
WITH

He got on, his electronic tracking tablet under his left arm. "And I see you *do* know how to honor requests."

"Excuse me?"

"Normally, when I ask someone to wait for me, I expect to find them when I get back. Like I said, I was only going to be a minute."

"You were gone longer than a minute; ten to be exact."

"You were counting the minutes I was gone?"

"Not . . . exactly."

"Uh-huh."

"I waited. But my friend and I had to leave."

"Uh, the brother you were dancing with who looks like Arsenio?"

I hadn't heard anyone describe Gene in that way in some time. "Yes."

"Ah. Well, I ran into a brother I hadn't seen in a long time, and before I knew it, the minutes flew. I'm sorry. Can you forgive me?"

"Yes."

"Good."

Silence.

He sighed. "I just knew I struck out."

"You didn't strike out. I wasn't even pitching."

He considered it. "Yeah, that is true. *I* was the one throwin' it, and *you* were the one catchin' it." He winked.

I blushed. "I had a good time. It was fun."

"It was."

"Uh, I would've told you, but you rushed off so quickly. I'm involved."

"With?"

"You know."

"No, I don't."

"With someone."

"Ah."

We looked up at the elevator display. Eighth floor.

"So, when can we get together and do the bump *off* the dance floor?" He smirked.

I eyed him in disbelief. "Didn't you hear what I said?"

"Yeah, I did. You said you're involved with someone. But you didn't say *how*. I mean, I'm involved with a few people—"

"Are you, really?"

"Yeah. But in different ways."

All right, then . . . I can play along. "Okay . . . I am involved with someone in a relationship." He was about to respond, no doubt with *What kind of relationship?*, when I added: "A *monogamous* relationship."

He nodded. "You catch on quick. Well . . . ya can't blame a brother for tryin'."

"No. I guess I can't," I said to him, but more to myself.

We looked up at the display as it reached L. The doors opened. He gestured for me to leave first.

"Thank you."

"You're more than welcome."

I opened and held the lobby door, allowing him to walk outside first. He nodded. "And thank you."

I peeped the azz—*damn*. "You're more than welcome."

He turned with his hand out. "It was good seeing you again."

We shook; *seismic*, just *seismic*. "You, too."

Neither one of us wanted to let go. I forced myself to. "You enjoy the rest of your day." I smiled, walking away.

"I will. You do the same."

I could feel his eyes on me as I ventured by what I assumed was his truck. *Something* was calling me to turn around and catch him before he sped off (in the other direction). After reacting rather nonchalantly to learning that I'd soon be rolling in dough, I wanted to ask him if he'd like to help me celebrate my very jood news.

But I knew if I looked back, there'd be no turning back.

107

LOVE
THE
ONE
YOU'RE
WITH

9

Have you ever found yourself waiting to purchase groceries, toiletries, or clothing, and wondered why the shortest line—the one *you* happen to be on—moves the slowest?

It's the strangest, most aggravating phenomenon. You just know you've beat the crowd. There's just two, three, or four people ahead of you, and they each have the same number of items as you—or fewer. You've got the money in one hand, your items in the other, and you're all revved up to hustle out of there and take care of whatever other bizness you have to tend to.

And then you realize you've been standing in the same place for a minute (or two or three) while the other lines you bypassed have not only moved along, they've got a whole new set of customers who came in around the time you first got on line.

I've been playing this waiting game all day. Thursday is when I usually run all of my errands so that I can chill on the weekend. Now that Pooquie is on the road and I am working full-time, I make sure we have the right kind of quality and quantity time together—and I refuse to let our lazy Saturday or Sunday afternoons and evenings be interrupted because we've run out of toothpaste, soap, toilet tissue, Wheaties, orange juice, or, worse, condoms (nothing spoils the mood more than that).

Every other week, the post office is the first stop on my journey—and I'm sure it is the *last* place most people would want to visit before punching a time clock (next to the Department of Motor Vehicles, it's got to be the most stressful environment for one to work in *and* be serviced at). But the tension between employee and customer hasn't blipped on the radar that early in the morning; in fact, I've found postal workers to be very considerate and friendly in the A.M., not the snotty, condescending lot they are often viewed as. Some do live up to that reputation, but I can empathize with their being a little testy; some customers can be downright nasty (I'll never forget one man telling a clerk: "How many times did you have to *fail* the inkblot test before they gave you this job?").

I usually just pop in to buy some stamps from a vending machine. But today I had a package to send out to an editor at *Premiere* magazine in the hopes of being a New York correspondent. I was praying the line would be short when I arrived, and it was (well, there wasn't one—I was next). But there was only one window open, even though there were *four* other employees behind the counter who seemed to be doing next to nothing (one was sipping on coffee reading his paper and the other three were having a gabfest amongst themselves). Given that the woman being waited on had several large envelopes to mail and didn't have the right zip for any of them, I might as well had been last on a line of ten. But then another clerk opened up and took care of me.

Next, it's the bank at lunchtime. I receive my check when I walk in to work—and getting it a day earlier has been a lifesaver. I avoid the crazy crowds on Friday and use the newly installed automatic teller machine to deposit it (given how robotic a *real* teller can be, there is not much difference between the two). I'm usually in and out in a couple of minutes, but today a dozen other folks wised up and decided to follow my lead—the line for the ATM was just as long as for the regular tellers. To make matters worse, two of the three machines had some glitch: one wouldn't dispense cash, the other receipts.

The final stop of the day is the supermarket, where I am now. And one would assume that this would've taken no time at all—after all, I'm on the *express* line.

But the folks ahead of me . . . what a bunch they were. One didn't see why his having ten items on a seven-items-or-less line was such a big deal. Another ended up paying in cash (after putting back two items) when her two credit cards were declined and her personal check was rejected (she didn't have a picture ID). One wanted to pay for a Kit Kat with a hundred-dollar bill—and got uptight when he was asked for something smaller. And the last couldn't understand why she should have to shell out an extra nineteen cents for a can of Chicken of the Sea tuna when it was on sale for two for three dollars. As the manager, whom she requested to speak to, explained to her, "The list price is a dollar sixty-nine. But if you buy two, you save." She didn't want to save.

Then, when it was finally my turn, the receipt tape in the register had to be changed.

In any other case, I would've eased onto one of the other lines. But if I did, I'd miss getting my weekly discount from my favorite cashier.

Skye is his name. He's a seventeen-year-old senior at Brooklyn Tech, a bright young man who wants to be (what do you know) a journalist. He actually went to Tech to study engineering but found his true calling when he joined the school paper.

"You've been moving kinda slow," I teased.

"Ha, I haven't. The *customers* have." A woman was about to place her items on the counter when he told her, "Sorry, ma'am, this line is closed." After she rolled her eyes in disgust, she stomped off. We looked at each other and laughed. "I told her nicely and she *still* gets an attitude. I tell ya . . ." He took a sign that said CLOSED and put it on the counter behind my items. "That will take care of that." He grinned at me. "So, how are you?"

"I can't complain. How have you been?"

"Much better, now that my favorite customer is here." He winked.

Hmm . . . he had never publicly acknowledged me in that way. I didn't know whether to smile or not, but I did.

He continued tinkering with the register. "I see we've been busy this eve."

"Yeah." I had the dry cleaning over my left arm (Pooquie's cop uniform and tux, which he's worn as an extra on shows like *Law & Order* and *All My Children*) and a Music Mania bag in my right hand (I purchased a "Best of" collection by Melba Moore; for some reason, I couldn't get "You Stepped into My Life" out of my head after hearing it at Body & Soul).

"Will you need help taking all of this home? I can help."

I nodded no. "Uh, that's okay."

"Wouldn't be a problem. I'll be taking my break right now, anyway."

"No. But thanks for offering."

Hmm . . . he had never offered to help me before and there have been many occasions when I've been lugging much more than what I was at the moment. And performing such a task also isn't a part of his job description (last month he had to explain to one woman who moved to the neighborhood from the Upper East Side of Manhattan that this ain't D'Agostino's, where they deliver your groceries to your door, but D'Amato's, where you'll be lucky to get them bagged), so it certainly raised my eyebrows.

He started to ring me up. "Ah . . . I see we've only got one pound of ground meat. You must not have a heavy date this weekend."

Hmm . . . now where did *that* come from? Our brief conversations usually revolved around his high-school misadventures, his interest in journalism, and my trials as a teacher.

So, yeah, I was caught off guard. "Uh, uh, no."

"Well, you could have one."

Oh, really? I wasn't even going to touch that one.

But he was just getting started. "Ya know, I've got an article coming out in tomorrow's school paper."

"You do? What is it about?"

"Puff Daddy. Interviewed him and everything."

"Wow. Great. I'd love to read it."

"Okay. How 'bout if I stop by after school tomorrow and show it to you?"

Stop by after school?

After repeating it in my head, I had to repeat it out loud. "Stop by after school . . . ?"

"All right, cool," he squealed. "I can be at your place around five."

I had to step on the brakes 'cause he sure wasn't going to. "Hold it, Skye. That wasn't an answer in the affirmative."

"Oh. Would Saturday be a better day?"

"Uh, no, it wouldn't. I . . . I'm just a little . . . puzzled by all of this."

"Why? Haven't you ever been asked out by a tall, light, and lovely brother like me before?"

Well . . . it was finally official. I grinned. "Why, Mr. Robinson . . . I do believe you are trying to seduce me." That happened to be his last name.

111

LOVE
THE
ONE
YOU'RE
WITH

And his response was a laugh very similar to Anne Bancroft's in *The Graduate*. "I guess you could say that."

I couldn't believe it. "Why?"

"What do you mean?"

"Why are you interested in me?"

"Why wouldn't I be? I mean, you're smart, funny, attractive, got a great smile, a *very* nice-lookin' kaboose—"

I literally gagged.

"—and you don't look like you been shortchanged in that front pouch, either," he observed, focusing on my crotch.

I patted my chest, my heart was zoomin' so fast. "Well . . . thank you. But I also happen to be a decade older than you—"

"Hey, I don't mind dating an older man."

"—and you *are* a minor."

"I won't be at twelve-oh-one A.M. tonight," he stated proudly.

Oh, yes; last week, he did mention his birthday was coming up. Little did I know that he had a plan on how to celebrate it.

"Hmm . . . why do I get the feeling that you don't want to date me but mate *with* me . . . ?"

"Yeah, that, too."

"Well . . . I'm . . . flattered." And I was. "You're a really sweet young man—"

He frowned. "*Young* being the operative word, right?"

"Well, yes. I mean, I own pieces of paper that are older than you—like my birth certificate!" I chuckled.

He didn't find that amusing. "But I'm mature for my age," he defended, leaning in closer and flashing those teeth, "in *all* the right places."

That I could not argue with. Black and Chinese ("Blasian," as he puts it) with skin the color of Sahara sand, diamond-shaped hazel eyes, pretty pursed lips, and a lean, toned two-hundred-pound physique, he's no slouch in the kaboose (looks like he's got *two* soccer balls attached to his lower back) or front pouch (uh-huh . . . swingin' *very* low, sweet chariot!) departments, either (I'm sure the elder Mr. Robinson had something to do with both). As Gene cracked when he first laid eyes on him: "Now *that's* what I call fresh produce."

I had to laugh. "Yes, you are. But—"

"And we have a lot in common." And we do.

"Yes, I know. But—"

"And—"

"Will you let me finish a sentence!"

"Oh . . . sorry."

I sighed. "I'm in a relationship."

Now he was really wounded. "You . . . you're in a relationship?"

"Yes. For almost two years now."

He turned toward the register. "Oh."

"But if I weren't and if I didn't have any qualms about dating someone your age . . . I would gladly accept your invitation."

"You're just sayin' that," he mumbled.

"No, I'm not."

He glanced at me.

I playfully jabbed him in his thick left arm with my right fist. "After ringing me up for seven months, you know I wouldn't just say that."

He considered it. He nodded. "Yeah. I do."

This was an awkward moment; neither one of us knew what to say next.

"Hey, Robinson, when you goin' on break?" shouted his supervisor, Andy, who was in his cubbyhole of a manager's station a few yards away.

"As soon as I finish up here," he called back.

"Well, hurry and finish up. I need you to help restock the bread."

"Okay." He turned to me. "Uh, that'll be eight-sixty-six."

I gave him a ten. He allowed his hand to brush mine as he took it and then placed the change in my palm.

I smiled. "Thanks."

"You're welcome." He started to pack the groceries.

"Can I ask you a question?"

"Sure."

"How did you know about me?"

"Well, you never mentioned a girlfriend . . ."

Hmm . . . come to think of it, neither had he.

". . . and I always had this feeling . . . from the first time I waited on you."

113

LOVE
THE
ONE
YOU'RE
WITH

I leaned in. "Gaydar, huh?"

He chuckled. "Yeah, I guess so."

"Uh . . . how long have you known?"

"Ha, forever."

"Well, if you ever want to talk about it . . . I know how it can be . . . just let me know."

"I will. Thanks."

That's when it hit me: *Now* I knew why he'd been giving me a discount for the past eight months.

"Does this mean I can't look forward to any more deals in the future?" I winked.

He blushed. "Of course you can."

"Good. You have a good night."

"You, too. I'll see you next week."

I picked up the bag and started walking away. I stopped. I turned. "Uh . . . on second thought . . ."

He was taking out his cash drawer. He turned. "Yeah?"

"I think I do need help carrying all this home."

There was that Kodak smile. "Let me log this and get my jacket."

10

If I had a son, I'd want him to be just like Junior.

Well, one could say that he *is* my son; after all, I am his godfather. I was both floored and flattered when, just days after we reunited, Pooquie announced that I would be filling this role, previously held by his deceased best friend, Derrick "D.C." Carter. He didn't ask me if I would do it; he expected me to. And, well . . . why wouldn't he? He knew how much I cared for Junior and how enamored Junior was of me. Although deep down I knew that this was another way for him to show that he was sorry for the terrible things he had said and his violent outburst, more than anything his gesture clearly illustrated that he was serious about us and that, as a guardian to his son, he wanted me to become an integral part of not just his life but his world.

If *that* ain't love, I don't know what is . . .

But Junior has made filling this role easy, not to mention exciting. At first, I wasn't sure how I should approach this new relationship. Godparents usually step into their godchild's life when tragedy strikes (i.e., the parents are missing in action or die). I haven't seen my godparents, Elijah and Elaine Cooke, in eight years; high-school sweethearts and childhood friends of my parents, they moved to Richmond, Virginia, when I was about to graduate from high school. The last time I talked with either of them on the phone was three years ago (and I can't recall whether it was one or both). And what few memories I do have of them aren't motherly or fatherly; my aunt Ruth and uncle Tweedle have acted more as guardians (whenever an emergency arose, they were called, not the Cookes). I've seen and heard of the same scenes played out in other families. More often than not, the title *godparent* is given to people because they've been a great friend or simply because they are a family member.

Looking back on the time Junior and I spent together, I was already a fatherlike figure to him, so the new designation just made it official. But in his own way, he revealed that this was something I shouldn't take lightly . . .

"Mitch-hull?"

"Yes?"

"You believe in God, right?"

"Yes, I do. Why?"

"Well, you my *God* daddy. You *have* to believe in God."

Whoa. Now, as often as that title is bestowed upon folks, I don't think most of us really give it that much thought. Of course, one doesn't have to believe in God to be a godparent—or does one? That Junior would make such a connection didn't surprise me. He is a very sharp little boy, a razor, as his daddy would say. But sometimes, when he puts two and two together, it's as if I'm learning that it equals four for the first time.

Which is why I always look forward to our spending one weekend together a month—I know there'll never be a dull moment. Of course, Pooquie usually rounds out the trio. But even though he'd be out of town, Junior still wanted to keep our date. And while we would only be able to hang out Friday and part of Saturday (I have to hot-tail it over to Gene's Saturday night to help him prepare for his birthday bash), that didn't matter to Junior—half a weekend at my place is jooder than no weekend at all.

When I arrived at his grammy Grace's (Pooquie's mom), his bag was packed and he was armed with his copy of *My First Webster's Dictionary*. It was one of my Christmas presents to him. He's been learning a new word a day, and I knew he couldn't wait to fill me in.

"*Hi, Mitch-hull!*" he screamed, nearly strangling me as I hunched over to hug him.

"Young man, didn't I tell you to wait until he gets into the apartment," Ms. Rivers scolded. His tackling me before I've had the chance to say hello has become a hallmark greeting.

He let me go. "I'm sorry, Grammy. I'm just happy to see him."

"I know. But let the man breathe first." She *smiled* at me. "Hello, Mitchell," she sang, allowing me to enter the apartment. After she closed the door, she gave me a hug. We had gotten a little close over the past few months—and the closer we get, the closer she gets to asking about *that* . . .

During Junior's birthday/graduation party at her home last summer: "So, Mitchell . . . how long have you and my son been *friends*?"

At her home for Thanksgiving dinner: "Mitchell, I just can't believe a handsome young man like you isn't married. You mean you've never even been engaged?"

And at Pooquie's celebration when his first TV commercial for All-American aired: "You came without a date? Now, there's got to be *someone* in this city you could've brought with ya!"

Not only does a mother know her child, she also knows *about* him. The last person Pooquie spent this much time with was Junior's mother, Crystal aka Sunshine—and she and Pooquie haven't been "together" since Junior turned one (they were high-school sweethearts). And then there's Junior, who has literally adopted me (which has probably made it easy for Ms. Rivers and Crystal to welcome me into the fold). When she looks at the three of us, she sees a family. Pooquie doesn't think she does, but that *smile* says it all.

I *smiled* back at her. "Hello, Ms. Rivers. It's jood to see you."

"It's jood to see you, too."

"I see we're all ready to go, huh?" I observed.

"Yes," he chirped.

"He's been ready to go since last weekend—that's when he started packing," she added.

"Oh, really?"

"Uh-huh," he grinned.

"And it's all he's been talking about. Before you know it, you could soon have a permanent houseguest."

I shrugged. "I wouldn't mind. He's the perfect kind of guest: a *jood* one." I pinched that nose. He giggled.

"Junior, go to your daddy's room for a moment. I want to talk to Mitchell about something."

He gazed at us. "Oh . . . it's grown-up talk?"

"Yes, it is."

117

LOVE
THE
ONE
YOU'RE
WITH

"Okay. Let me know when you ready, Mitch-hull." And off he ran.

"Please, take off your jacket. Would you like something to drink or eat?" she offered.

"No, thank you. I'm okay."

"All right. Please, have a seat." She pointed toward her dining-room set. I obeyed her, wrapping my brown leather jacket around the chair.

She sat across from me. "I . . . I wanted to ask you about something . . ."

Uh-oh . . .

"It . . . it's been heavy on my mind for some time . . ."

. . . ooh-ooh . . .

"I know I should be talking to Raheim about this . . ."

. . . look out . . .

". . . but I figured you might have some . . . insight on it. Might even be able to tell me how to approach it and . . . well . . . approach him about it . . ."

. . . here it comes . . .

"Uh . . . I'm not sure how I should say this . . . uh . . ."

Just say it already! The suspense is killing me!

"I know how close you two are . . ."

And?

". . . and that he values your opinion, as I do . . ."

AND???

". . . and, I just have to know the truth . . ."

I'm gonna faint, right here, right now. I shoulda had that beverage!

"Do you know if he is . . ."

INHALE . . .

". . . in a position to spend all that money?"

HUH???

My head was spinning from the false shock. "I'm, I'm sorry?"

"You know, on this co-op he wants to buy. Do you think he can really afford it?"

Yeesh. What was she trying to do, give me a heart attack?

"Uh, uh, yes, yes, uh, he can, Ms. Rivers," I stammered. "He's been very practical with his money." I chuckled. "And he knows how much you want to see him off that high-riser and out of that bedroom."

She nodded. "Well, I do want to see him out on his own, but I don't want him to feel that he has to rush into something because he thinks I want him out. It's just that his being in the business he is in . . . he needs his own space, where he can entertain and take care of his business. But I don't want him spending his whole life savings on a piece of property just to make that move. I'd let him set up a business line and convert that little sewing room at the end of the hall into his office first."

I caressed her left hand with my right. "Don't worry about him, Ms. Rivers. Not only is he financially ready to make this move, he's emotionally ready, too. And why wouldn't he be? Look who raised him."

She gushed. "Oh, Mitchell."

"It's true. And given who raised him, I'm sure he wouldn't want to leave the comfort of this home. But he knows it's time for him to make his own home, and he won't be in the doghouse when he does."

She breathed a big sigh of relief; the worry was gone from her face. "Well, thank you. I appreciate that. I guess . . . knowing he's actually going to do it . . . I'm happy for him but sad at the same time, you know?"

"I do."

"I'd appreciate it if you just kept this between me and you. He's a grown man—hard to believe, but he is—and I wouldn't want him to know that we were talking about something like this."

"I think he'd be flattered that you wanted to discuss it with me." The word I wanted to use was *flabbergasted*. If this doesn't prove that she knows, I don't know what further proof he would need. She's actually treating me like his significant other.

"I know how proud he can be—just like his father—and I also know that if something was or did go down, I'd be the very last person to hear about it."

"I won't say a thing."

"Thank you." She palmed my hand into hers. "My son is very lucky to have a relationship with a friend like you."

Well . . . *a relationship with a friend like you?*

Junior reappeared. "Excuse me, Grammy. Are you and Mitch-hull finished?" He was wearing his black leather coat and cap.

"Young man, you have some timing, you know that?" She winked at me. She rose.

119
LOVE
THE
ONE
YOU'RE
WITH

I did, too. "Yes, you do."

"You're so anxious you just couldn't wait for one of us to call you, huh?" she asked.

"Anxious?" he questioned.

"Yes. That's when you can't wait for something to happen," she explained.

"Oh, yes, that's what I feel!" he declared.

We laughed.

"Well, you have a jood half a weekend, okay?" She zipped him up and fixed his scarf.

"I will."

She hugged him. "And you be a jood boy."

"I will."

"I love you." She pinched his cheek.

He returned the gesture. "I love you, too, Grammy." They giggled.

I finished putting on my jacket and buttoning up. "You have a jood weekend, Ms. Rivers."

We hugged.

"You, too. And take care of my grandson."

"I most certainly will." I picked up his bag. "You ready?"

"Yes!"

"Okay. Let's go."

"Bye, Grammy." He waved as we walked out the door.

"Bye." She waved back, with *that* smile.

"SO, HOW WAS SCHOOL THIS WEEK?"

"It was jood. I learned to count to ten in Spanish!"

"Really?"

"Uh-huh. You wanna hear me?"

"I'd love to."

"Ooh-no, dohs, trey-s, qua-tro, seen-co, say-s, see-yet-tay, oh-cho, new-ay-vay, and *dee-ez*!"

"Wow, that's great. I bet you'll be able to count to twenty in Spanish by the end of next week."

"I'm gonna do it by Sunday!"

"Oh really?"

"Uh-huh. Anjelica, Uncle Angel's daughter, is gonna help me."

"Ah . . ."

"And we talked about Black History today. Every Friday this month is Black History Day."

Hmm . . . it's bad enough the celebration takes place during the shortest month in the year. But to delegate any acknowledgment or discussion of Negro achievements and contributions to just *one* day per week in February? "Oh, did you? And what did you all talk about?" Please, *not* Dr. King.

"Martin Luther King."

Of course. "And what did the teacher say about him?" Please, *not* that he had a dream . . .

"That he was a great civil-rights leader who had a dream . . ."

Of course. White folks have reduced his entire life into that one catchall phrase, a condensation that is palatable and digestible for *them*.

". . . that one day people would be judged by their character and not their color," he predictably finished.

"Mmm-hmm."

"But I raised my hand."

"You did?"

"Yes."

"And what did you say?"

"I said, 'He had more than a dream.' "

I grinned. "And what did your teacher say?"

"He said, 'What do you mean?' And I said, 'He didn't just dream about it. He worked to make it happen.' "

Uh-huh . . . just like a razor. "Yes, he did."

I'm sure that teacher was thrown by his insight. He may only be six, but Junior has no problem comprehending things that may be complex—and also knows that, when someone is trying to present something in too simplistic a way, they aren't telling him the whole story. He also interacts with adults like he is one of the elders and likes to discuss things that are very grown-up in nature. I know that one should encourage a child to be inquisitive, but whenever he questions me about an issue I think would best be handled by his parents—such as Susan Smith killing her kids ("How can a mommy drown her own children?")—I'll say, "Well, I think you should ask your mommy or daddy about that." But he always comes back with: "I already know how

121

LOVE
THE
ONE
YOU'RE
WITH

Mommy feels, I already know what Daddy thinks; I wanna know what *you* feel/think."

We were heading into Brooklyn on the A train going over those words in *Webster's* (he's on the *D*s: desk) when I sensed he wanted to have one of *those* talks again.

He studied me intensely. "Mitch-hull?"

"Yes?"

"Can I ask you something?"

"Sure." I braced myself.

"Um . . . do you have a grampy?"

Well . . . he finally brought it up. After walking out on him and his mother seventeen years ago, Pooquie's father reentered their lives last year. Although they've talked on the phone a couple of times, Junior hasn't met him—yet. Pooquie says that they will after he and his father sort some things out. Of course, Junior can't wait to meet him—he's always wanted a "grampy."

I sighed. "I had a grandfather. He's in heaven now."

"Oh, I'm sorry," he consoled, rubbing my hand.

"You don't have to be sorry . . ."

"When did he go to heaven?"

"When I was twenty-one."

"And you twenty-eight now?"

"Yes."

He tapped his temple and the tip of his left thumb went into his mouth. "He's been in heaven for seven years."

"Yes, he has."

"Did he get shot like Uncle D?" That's what he called D.C.

"No. He had cancer."

"Cancer? I know what that is."

"You do?"

"Uh-huh. Cancer is a disease that can start in one part of your body and go to another."

"That's right."

"Grammy says it causes a lot of pain. Was he in a lot of pain?"

"Yes, he was."

"He won't feel pain anymore, being in heaven," he assured me.

I nodded. "No, he won't."

"Did you have fun with him?"

"Yes, I did. A lot of fun."

"What did you do?"

"Oh, we went to the park. He would push me in a swing. We would play catch. And then we'd go for an ice-cream cone."

"Ooh, what kind?"

"Chocolate."

"Oh, my favorite!"

"Mine, too. And then he would place me on his shoulders and carry me home."

He sighed. "I'd like that."

I know he would.

"You know, you two had something in common."

"We did?"

"Yes."

"What?"

"He *loved* Michael Jackson."

Those little eyes grew wide. "He did?"

"Yes."

"Wow."

"When we get home, I'll show you a picture of him."

"Okay . . . um . . . do you miss him?"

I nodded. "Yes, I do."

"I miss Uncle D, too."

"I know. I do, too."

He held my hand the rest of the ride home.

After I located that photo ("Wow, Mitch-hull . . . you look just like him!") and he quickly inhaled two plates of spaghetti and turkey meatballs, we watched *The Jacksons: An American Dream*. I knew he wouldn't be interested in seeing how Joe and Katherine Jackson met, so I tuned up the tape to the scene where Michael is born. He balked at Michael's choice of a playmate ("I could *never* be friends with a mouse! *Yuck!*") and sang along and even imitated some of the fictional Michael's moves.

The only time he took his attention away from the TV was when the phone rang. He normally didn't answer my phone but knew I wouldn't mind tonight, given who he hoped would be on the other end.

123

LOVE
THE
ONE
YOU'RE
WITH

"Hell-oh? . . . *Hi, Daddy!* . . . I'm jood, how are you? . . . that's jood . . . uh-huh . . . I am . . . I'm looking at a movie about Michael Jackson, when he was a little boy . . . uh-huh, I finished it before I left Grammy's house . . . Mitch-hull said he's gonna help me with my vocabulary . . . uh-huh . . . no . . . okay . . . I will . . . he's right here . . . okay . . . Daddy? . . . Please come back home soon . . . I miss you . . . okay . . . okay, I'll be jood . . . I love you, too . . . okay, hold on, here's Mitch-hull."

He handed me the phone, grabbed the remote, and unpaused the film, settling back on the floor with his legs crossed and placing the popcorn bowl between his legs.

I walked toward the bedroom. "Hi, Pooquie."

"Hay, Baby. How you be?"

"Jood. How are things with you?"

"They a'ight."

I closed the door. "Where are you?"

"On tha set. Clemmy let me use her cell phone."

I stretched out on the bed, leaning up on my left elbow. "Ah. That was nice of her. So, how is it going on the set?"

"We been doin' tha same scene over and over tha past half hour."

"Which scene?"

"That club scene."

"The one where your character gets into a fight?"

"Yeah. They say my choreography is off. It's gotta be precise and it ain't. It's hard tryin' ta fake it and make it real at tha same time."

"I can understand how you could have a hard time fakin' it. You never have that problem with me." I giggled.

He sighed. "I hit tha other brotha a coupla times."

"You did?"

"Yeah."

"You didn't hurt him, did you?"

"Nah. I jabbed him in tha neck when I was s'pose ta be shadow-punchin' his jaw."

"He didn't hit you back, did he?"

"Nah. Ha, he better not had, cuz then we woulda been fightin' fuh real. They ready ta bring in a stunt double."

"Well, it's a standard thing in the industry. It's no big deal."

"It is ta me," he snapped. "I want this role ta be all me, Baby."

"It will be."

"Not if somebody else is fightin' my battles."

"Who will know the difference?"

"*I* will."

"Pooquie, it's not like you're Jennifer Beals in *Flashdance* having all your dance sequences performed by others. Or, better yet, in an action flick with Jean-Claude and havin' a hard time with the karate kicks. This thirty-second scene does not define who your character is."

"But it's still an important scene."

"Yes, it is. Every scene you're in is important. But it's not *the* most important scene."

"But, Baby, I feel like . . . like I ain't pullin' my own weight."

"Pooquie, don't torture yourself. So what if you don't get everything. There are others who don't get everything. Didn't you say that one of those actors is always fumbling his lines?"

"Yeah."

"Now, *that's* a major problem. But this is a minor thing, so don't turn it into something major. You'll get so focused on not being able to do this one thing and won't give your all for the rest of the shoot."

I felt him come down. "Uh . . . you right, Baby. Clemmy already told me all of this. But I guess I just needed ta hear it from you."

"I won't be any less proud of you if you can't do the scene. And the world won't know it's someone else; they do a jood job of covering that up. Besides, I would prefer they *did* bring in the stunt double."

"Why?"

" 'Cause, if the other actor hurt you, *I'd* have to hurt *him*."

He chuckled. "Baby, he taller and bigger than *me*. How *you* gonna hurt *him*?"

"Ha, the bigger they are, the harder they fall, Pooquie. That's what that scene is all about. And when you mess with *my* man, you better be prepared to be messed with back."

He giggled. "You cray-zee, Baby."

"About you? Most definitely."

"So, how you doin'?"

125

LOVE
THE
ONE
YOU'RE
WITH

"Jood. I'd be doin' better than jood if you were here. But Junior's doing a jood job of keeping me company."

"Befo' ya know it I'll be Black."

"I know." I looked at the calendar on the back of the bedroom door. "I'm countin' the days."

"Oh, Baby, I gotta go. They callin' fuh me."

"Okay. Don't sweat this. And if you need to talk again, just call."

"You know I will. Thanks, Little Bit. I love you."

"I love you, too, Pooquie."

I WAS DRIFTING OFF TO SLEEP WHEN THERE WAS AN erratic knock on the bedroom door.

"Yes?"

"Mitch-hull, may I come in?" Junior asked in a hurried voice.

I sat up. "Yes, you may."

He bolted in. *"Oh, I'm scared, I'm scared!"*

"Why?"

Just then, a flash of lightning illuminated the dark room.

He jumped. He covered his eyes with his hands and then aimed for and buried his face in my chest. *"That! That!"*

"The lightning?"

"Uh-huh," he sobbed with urgency. He was trembling.

I cuddled him. "You're afraid of lightning?"

"Uh-huh," he repeated.

I reached for and turned on the lamp. "You can look up now. The light is on."

He wouldn't budge.

"Junior, it's okay."

He inched his hands away from his eyes to peek. Seeing it was safe, he lifted his head.

Now, I could've given him the spiel about how he shouldn't be afraid, that we're inside and it won't hurt you, that it's only God blinking His eyes, and that it's one of those natural wonders that we have no control over but can be rather spectacular, even beautiful. I remember hearing all of those things when I was his age and also being frightened—and none of it made any sense, nor did it make me feel better. Instead of providing me with comfort, these explanations just made it more mysterious and made the anxiety grow. So, at this moment, the last thing Junior needed was a lecture (especially since I'm sure he's already heard it, more than once). It would be equivalent to convincing him the bogeyman isn't in his closet. I think it's important to help children overcome their fears, but there is indeed a time and place for everything, and trying to rationalize something so frightening when they are so young and want to be protected, not preached to, doesn't help.

I took his silence and that very panicked look on his face to mean one thing. I knew what he needed and wanted to hear right then.

I cupped his chin. "Do you want to sleep in here tonight?"

Those small eyes grew so wide I thought they were going to pop out of his head. "Can I, *pleeze*?"

"Of course. Come on."

He hopped in the bed, scooting under the covers and settling on his back.

I did the same. "I'll leave the light on, okay?"

"Okay. Thank you." He smiled.

"You're welcome."

He grabbed my hand and squeezed it tight. "I love you, Mitch-hull."

I squeezed back. "I love you, too." I kissed him on the forehead. "Jood night."

"Jood night."

A POLITE RUB TO MY SHOULDER WOKE ME UP. I opened my eyes to see Junior's smile.

"Jood morning, Mitch-hull." He was already dressed.

I sat up. "Jood morning. How did you sleep last night?"

"I slept okay." He grabbed my right hand, pulling me out of bed. "Come on. Wash your face and brush your teeth so you can eat your breakfast."

"Eat my breakfast?"

"Yes."

Junior knew better than to mess with the stove, or work any other electrical appliance. I had to see what "breakfast" for him would entail.

He had set a place for each of us at the dining-room table. There was a box of Wheaties, a glass of chocolate milk (for him), a glass of

127

LOVE
THE
ONE
YOU'RE
WITH

orange juice (for me), a banana for each of us, a stick of butter in a dish, and a jar of jam.

"I didn't want our toast to get cold," he explained. "All I have to do is pull down the button and it will be done."

I walked into the kitchen. There were four slices of bread in the toaster. I smiled at him. "Well, isn't this nice. I'll scrub up and be right back."

"Okay."

We ate and then we watched an episode of the Jackson 5's cartoon series (it's on my special Michael Jackson compilation tape, along with his famous moonwalk on *Motown 25,* clips from their variety specials, and appearances they made on *Soul Train, American Bandstand,* and *Midnight Special*). We were out of the house just before noon and trekked on down to downtown Brooklyn's Fulton Street Mall and Strip.

Like Gene, Junior likes to shop-till-u-drop. Pooquie was outdone when we all went Christmas shopping last year; after two hours, he decided to wait (more like sleep) in the car while Junior and I finished (we legged it for another two). As I soon discovered, Junior had been paying close attention to what I purchased for myself. He'd been able to read me so well that he figured out my taste. And he managed to not only choose the right item but the right store to go into; he's never fooled by those "Going Out of Business" and "Everything Must Go" signs, which are just ruses to entice you inside and get you to buy shit you don't want or need (half the time the store isn't folding; they're just trying to unload all the merchandise that hasn't sold).

So I let him take the lead. Because they were having a blowout on summer wear, he decided we should venture into Dr. Jay's, a spot for those looking for the latest designer urban gear at somewhat reasonable prices. We weren't in there thirty seconds when . . .

"Ooh, Mitch-hull! Look at this!"

It was a brown-and-gold tropical short-sleeved shirt. I took it off the rack.

"I think you would look jood in that!" he exclaimed.

"Do you?"

"Uh-huh."

"Let me see . . ."

I turned to a mirror mounted on a wall behind the clothing rack. I held it up to my chin and admired the way it complemented my own skin color. "I believe you're right, Junior." I raised my eyebrows. "Do you think your daddy will like this?" I already knew the answer would be a definitive . . .

"No." He pointed to another shirt. "Daddy would like *that* one." It was a *very* bright orange.

"Hmm, I think you're right." I checked the tag on the collar. "And it's the right size."

"A double extra-large?" he asked.

"Yes." He knows his daddy, all right . . .

After getting a sweater and a pair of overalls for himself (he grows so fast that it's best not to buy him summer clothes in the winter), we found a cashier. He was more like an assistant manager—at least that's what his name tag said. It was pinned to a turquoise turtleneck above his right nipple, which, like his left, was very visible and *very* hard. He had skin the color of butterscotch, a short natty 'fro (I assume he was locking his hair; I could smell beeswax and Indian hemp), soda-bottle-cap-sized eyes, a silver hoop through his left earlobe, and lines shaved through his eyebrows (the "jagged" style that would become very popular a few years later).

"Good mornin'," he said, flashing those pearly whites (and a gold crown) at the both of us.

"Good morning to you, too," I replied.

He took the items. "Looks like y'all got some good bargains here."

"Yes, we did."

"And y'all got here at the right time. The crowds usually don't show up till one or two."

"Oh, good." I glanced at Junior, who was giving the man . . . well, it could best be described as an evil eye. I never saw him wear a scornful face like it before.

"Is that gonna be cash or credit?" he asked.

"Credit." As I went into my pocket, he turned to Junior. "So, little man, what's yo' name?"

Junior was stone-faced and silent. Hmm . . . did he not like being called "little man," which is similar to Li'l Brotha Man, the title his daddy christened him with?

"What's ya name?" the man repeated.

129

LOVE
THE
ONE
YOU'RE
WITH

He still wouldn't answer. In fact, he wouldn't even look at him.

I palmed his shoulder. "The man asked you a question."

"Oh," he feigned. He shifted his body in the man's direction, but his head didn't move with it. "My mommy and daddy told me to never talk to strangers."

The cashier and I nodded at each other.

"It's okay. He might be a stranger but you're not alone."

Junior peered at me. "Junior," he coughed, still not looking at him.

"Ah. I'm a Junior, too. My first name is Tazmaine. Folks call me Taz. How 'bout you?"

No answer, again.

"Junior, the man asked you what was your first name."

"Oh," he feigned again. "I . . . I don't wanna say."

That was a switch: the kid who is so proud of his name, who delights in not just saying it but *spelling* it for anyone who'll listen, not wanting to disclose it?

I was a little embarrassed by his behavior. "I'm sorry. He must be a little tired."

" 'Sa'ight." He held out his hand. "I'll take that."

I looked down; I still hadn't given him the credit card. "Oh, sorry."

"No prob."

While we waited for the confirmation, he continued to make small talk. Junior huffed.

"Hope to see ya again . . . *real* soon." He winked, handing me the bag.

"You keep having sales like this and you will," I assured him.

"Ha, don'tcha worry—we will," he promised. "Oh . . ." He came from around the counter and handed me a card from his back pants pocket. "Whenever ya come back and need some help, just ask for Taz."

I took the card. "Well, thank you, Taz. You have a nice day."

Junior tugged on my arm.

"You, too." He watched us leave with his hands folded across his broad chest and a grin just as broad on his face.

When we were outside, I confronted Junior. "Is there something wrong?"

He frowned. "I don't like that man."

"You don't?"

"No."

"Why? He didn't do or say anything bad to you."

He shrugged. "I still don't like him."

Hmm . . . could Junior sense when someone was trying to get next to me in *that* way? Maybe he recognized the way his daddy looks at me in Taz's eyes. Or it could've been Taz's body language. Or how Taz said what he said. Whatever it was, that friendly, affable aura that is very much a part of his personality disappeared, and he became cold and curt. Pooquie has reacted in the same way a few times when he peeped someone checking me out. It appears that even when it comes to the green-eyed monster, Junior's a chip off the old brick wall. Wait till Pooquie hears this . . .

Junior's sour mood was erased when we browsed through Toyland and stopped in McDonald's for a Big Mac. Then came the highlight of the day: after dropping off our packages at the apartment, we hopped the bus to the Billie Holiday Theater to see *The Wiz*. After he'd watched a young-adult Michael Jackson in the film version, I thought Junior would love seeing it performed live, and he did. We were in the second row in the center section, so he had a perfect view. The whipped cream on his slice of sweet-potato pie, though, was meeting the actors and getting their autographs. Of course, Junior was most interested in Tyrrone Weatherly—the actor who, like Michael, portrayed the Scarecrow.

And when Junior was being tickled by Dorothy (who couldn't get over how cute he was), Tyrrone let me know that he was interested in *me*.

"Would *you* like my autograph?" Tyrrone asked.

"Uh, no, that's all right."

"That's too bad. I was hoping to sign my *real* name and include my phone number with it."

I blushed. Junior wasn't the only one being tickled. "Hmm . . . I wonder how many other people you've said that to."

"The truth?"

"Yes, the truth."

"Quite a few."

I laughed.

"Hey, but that's only because I've had the honor of being in the presence of so many fine spe-ci-*mens*."

131

LOVE
THE
ONE
YOU'RE
WITH

"While playing this role or during your career?"

"This role *is* my career, so far; this is my first professional gig."

"Really?"

"Yup. Just graduated from SUNY Binghamton last year. Been in this production since November."

"Well, you were quite good."

"You enjoyed my performance?"

"Very much."

"Does that mean you *do* want my autograph?"

I giggled.

"Believe me, I *never* dress like this, I *never* wear makeup, and I do have *real* hair, even nappier than this stuff," he explained, pulling on the straw attached to a large black Kangol cap. His face had brushes of yellow across it, and a few glittery silver stars dotted his cheeks. And the costume—a checkered tan corduroy vest, a mustard-colored sweatshirt, tattered light blue jeans, and a stained pair of Timbs (this was definitely the hip-hop version of the show; instead of the traditional pumps, Dorothy clicked her heels three times with some red jelly-heeled shoes)—made him look more like a hobo on the Bowery than a stick man in a corn patch. Four things that couldn't be disguised: the gorgeous chocolate complexion; those big, expressive light brown eyes; that sexy, poked-out bottom lip; and that round bootay (like me, he's a slender guy with a big seat). "You've just caught me at a bad time."

"I could take the autograph but not the number. My boyfriend wouldn't like it."

"Well, this ain't about what *he* likes; this is about what *you* want. And he's not the one I want to give it to."

"I know that. But as intriguing as you are, I couldn't."

He threw his hands up, as if to surrender. "Ah. A'ight. I don't need a house to fall on me, like the Wicked Bitch of the West."

I chuckled.

He lightly slapped his forehead. "The Scarecrow has a brain"—that hand found its way to his chest—"but his heart is once again broken."

He's a charmer, ain't he?

I smiled. "You're a very talented man. And funny. I bet you're gonna go far."

"With you? Ha, one of these days I surely hope to!"

We both laughed on that one.

Junior rushed back up to us. "Mr. Scarecrow, can I have a picture with me, you, and Mitch-hull, *pleeze*?"

Tyrrone peered at me. "Mr. Scarecrow would love that very much." I don't know how Junior missed *that* glare; I guess he was so excited it went right past him.

Dorothy was enlisted to snap the shot. Tyrrone and I sat down in the first row while Junior stood between us. Tyrrone allowed his arm to reach across my seat, pulling me closer.

After we cheezed it, he and I stood—and his hand somehow managed to make its way across my ass.

He bent down toward Junior. "Well, it was great meeting you, Junior. I'm glad you had a great time."

"Thank you. I did!"

"You be a good—oh, sorry—*jood* little boy, okay?" Ha, Junior made another convert.

Junior nodded. "I will."

Tyrrone zeroed in on me. "Mitchell . . ." He held out his hand. I shook it. "It was great meeting you, too. I hope you enjoyed . . . the company."

I nodded. "Yes, I did. Very much, thank you."

"You two have a *jood* night." He pinched Junior's left cheek. As he walked away, he gave me a once-over that gave me chills.

When we got back to the house, the phone was ringing. Junior raced to answer it.

"Hell-oh? *Hi, Daddy!* . . . I'm jood, how are you? . . . That's jood. Ooh, Daddy, guess where Mitch-hull took me? . . . To see *The Wiz!* . . . It was better than the movie. And the man who played the Scarecrow, he was better than Michael Jackson. He gave me his autograph, and he took a picture with me and Mitch-hull. I had such a jood time . . . uh-huh . . . uh-huh . . . okay, I will . . . I don't know . . . okay . . . okay . . . Daddy? . . . I miss you . . . okay . . . I will . . . I love you, too . . . okay, here's Mitch-hull . . . bye bye." He handed me the phone.

"Junior, get your bag and make sure you've packed everything. Then wash up for dinner."

"Okay." He skipped off.

I sat on the couch. "Hi, Pooquie," I puffed.

133

LOVE
THE
ONE
YOU'RE
WITH

"Hay, Baby. What's up?"

"You, that's what's up. How are you?"

"I'm jood. You?"

"I can't complain."

"Uh-huh. He wore you out, didn't he?"

"You know it. If it ain't one Rivers man wearin' me out, it's another."

He chuckled. "And ya know it."

"Where are you?"

"On tha set."

"Clemmy let you use her phone again?"

"Nah, Malice."

"Malice? The rapper?"

"Yeah. One of his boyz is in tha flick, so he dropped by."

"Ah. So, how was the last twenty-four hours?"

"Jood."

"What happened with that scene?"

"I got tha job done."

"You did?"

"Yeah. They had that stunt guy rehearse it wit' me. He showed me a better way ta stand and crunch when I swing. I got it right on tha next take."

"Oh, that's great. I'm so proud of you."

I could feel the glow. "Thanks."

"What else y'all been doin' today?"

"Court action."

"The real easy part."

"Ya know it, Baby. Now I know how brothas in tha NBA feel. Ha, ev'ry time I score a basket, I can just hear that *cha-ching*."

"Well, I know you're havin' fun, Pooquie, but remember not to let it all go to your head."

"Whatcha mean?"

"Don't start to get a big head."

"Ha, I already *got* one of those!"

"You are just *so* nasty."

"Yo, I was talkin' 'bout my dome," he snickered.

"Sure you were," I groaned.

"Uh . . . was I really soundin' like I'm gettin' a big head?"

"A little."

"Even a little is too much, Baby. Whenever you see it or hear it in me, you make sure you bring me back down, a'ight?"

"I will."

"So, you 'bout ta take him back Uptown?"

"Yup, right after we eat."

"What you cook?"

"I made some baked chicken, peas and rice, and broccoli."

"His new fav'rite vegetable, thanks ta you."

I beamed. "All I have to do is heat up his plate."

"Sounds jood. Wish I was there ta chow down on it—and then chow down on you."

"You will be soon."

"Yeah. Well, they only gave us five minutes. I gotta jet."

"Oh, okay. Thanks for calling, Pooquie. I love you." I gave him a smack.

He smacked me back. "I love you, too, Little Bit. I'll call ya tomorrow nite at yo' mom's."

"Okay. Bye."

"Bye, Baby."

I hung up the phone. I had taken our food out before we left for the show so we could nuke it when we got back. I put Junior's in the microwave first and, after heating it for two minutes, placed it on the dining-room table along with a glass of apple juice.

"Junior?" I called.

There was no answer.

"Junior, come and eat."

Still no answer.

Thinking he was in the bathroom, I made my way up the hall; the door was open and the light out.

I entered the bedroom and there he was, asleep on his back. It figures he passed out—he did get up earlier than I did, we did have a full day, and he didn't take an afternoon nap.

I took off his sneakers and covered him up with the comforter. I kissed his forehead. I'd just have to be a little late to Gene's bash.

135

LOVE
THE
ONE
YOU'RE
WITH

11

"So . . . Mama Bear was finally able to pry herself away from Baby Bear, huh?"

I arrived at Gene's two hours late. Of course he wasn't pleased, but there really was no need for me to show up at eight, the time he expected me to. The festivities didn't get under way until ten, and most folk wouldn't be arriving until around midnight (the Children *always* have to make an entrance). There was nothing to clean—Gene hires a "day maid" (a beefy brutha named Kelvin who wears next to nothing and I'm sure gets more than a monetary tip for his services) to come in twice a month to sweep, scour, scrub, and simonize the apartment (as he has often testified: "I only get on my hands and knees to do *one* thing—and it does not involve ammonia or Comet"). And there was nothing to prepare—the party was being catered (a soul-food spot in Harlem called Shortening Bread) and B.D. made both the strawberry cheesecake and the double-layer coconut birthday cake.

But judging from the face he wore when he let me in, you'd think I'd shown up two hours after the party *ended*.

"Don't look so gloomy," I consoled, taking off my coat. "Domestic duty called."

"Uh-huh." He embraced me. He was wearing a Versace ensemble—dark blue slacks and sky blue silk shirt. He was steppin' in some black patent leather Kenneth Coles.

"Don't be mad because nobody wants to play house with *your* bitter ass!" said B.D., waltzing up the hall.

Gene rolled his eyes. "If you weren't one of my

very best friends, I'd tell you where to go. But since you are, I'll just let you guess."

As Gene breezed off with my coat, B.D. stuck his tongue out at him.

He hugged me. "Honey, I am *so* glad you're here. I am not a grounds-keeper and I *refuse* to move any of those dead animals out of the parlor."

I chuckled. "So how are you?"

"I'm quite fabulous, as you can see." I could—he was giving much fever in a silky dark olive Moshood suit with black dress sandals. And the face was beat*en*: the eyebrows were plucked, the eyelashes combed, and the strawberry blush made his very light plump cheeks red, à la Saint Nick. "And I understand you've been a *fab*ulously bad boy."

"Huh?"

He pulled us toward the kitchen. "I heard about the *spin* you took on the dance floor last week."

"All I did was dance."

"Uh-huh. All you did was dance for not one, not two, not three, but—"

"Four hours straight," Gene enunciated with him as he emptied ice from their trays into both a large bucket and a white Styrofoam cooler.

"Uh-huh, with some strange man who, according to *my* sources, was quite a sight."

"You'd think they were conjoined twins the way their hips were glued to each other," added Gene.

I shrugged. "I was just having fun."

B.D. wasn't buying it. "Gyratin' with *one* man for two hundred and forty consecutive minutes without an intermission?"

Gene peered at him, floored.

"Yes, I *do* know how to tell time *and* add, thank you very much."

"Wonders never cease," snapped Gene.

B.D. rolled his eyes. "An-ty-way . . . dahling, you weren't just hav-ing *fun*—you were having a *fiesta*."

I defended myself. "It's not like I went after him; he started danc-ing with me."

"And from all press reports, you did *very* little to stop him."

"Well, Montee was—is a great dancer."

"Montee, huh? Why do I get the feeling that is his nickname . . . ?"

They both glared at me.

137

LOVE
THE
ONE
YOU'RE
WITH

I confirmed his suspicion. "Yes. His first name is Montgomery."

They nodded at each other in unison. "Mmm-hmm."

"It was just one night. I'll never see him again." I didn't tell Gene about our chance encounter on Wednesday—and given the third degree I was receiving, I didn't intend to.

"You may never see *him* again, but he will show up in another form. They always do, hon. Remember: *It* knows everybody's name."

So I am learning.

I had to change this subject. "Where's Babyface?"

"He's setting up the back rooms," Gene answered.

"I'll see if he needs help."

As I walked out, B.D. opened then closed one of the cabinet drawers in frustration. "Chile, I *wish* you would get some silverware up in this place." He had apparently forgotten where he was. A spatula is Gene's only kitchen utensil—and it, like the whipped cream, is in the bedroom ("It's used for mashing and flipping pancakes—but not the ones you cook on the stove").

"Bitch, you ain't the Galloping Gourmet. But you *do* bear a striking resemblance to Miss Julia Child," Gene bellowed as I headed up the hall.

Babyface was in Gene's entertainment room, inserting blue bulbs in the track lights. While folks did their rump shakin' to house music in another room, they could do their slow jammin' in this one (I made the tapes for this). He had on the same outfit as B.D. (it complemented his chestnut-colored skin); he opted for black casual shoes instead of sandals. His dark brown, just-above-the-waist locks were tied back near the base with a black scarf.

"Hi, mister."

"Hey, Mitch."

He came down off the ladder (which he didn't really need; he clocks in at six feet five inches). We embraced and kissed.

"How are you?" he queried.

"I'm jood. Can't complain. How about you?"

"Same. How's Raheim?" He climbed back up on the second step.

"Fine. It's been a tense week for him, this being his first film and all, but he'll get through it."

"Ah. And how are you dealing with it?"

"I'm . . . okay."

"Just okay?"

"Well . . . the separation . . . I miss him terribly."

"I'm sure."

"I don't know. It's only been a week and two days yet it feels like a year."

"You may have to get used to it. He'll probably be spending a lot more time on that coast."

I sighed. "Yeah."

"Have the sharks started surrounding you yet?"

"The sharks?"

"Yeah. They always know when your partner isn't around, when you're wadin' in the water without your paddle. I've been there. I know."

"You mean, you've . . ."

"No, I haven't. But"—he remembered those times with a mischievous grin—"boy, did they try!"

"So, how did you handle it?"

"I just enjoyed it."

"You did?"

"Of course. The attention was nice—and telling. It was so funny watching all those folks who wouldn't acknowledge I was alive when I was single suddenly decide I'm now worth their time and doing everything they could to get next to me. And their interest made me appreciate what I have more."

"How?"

"They were seeing the man I had become *with* B.D.—and I wouldn't be the man they wanted if I weren't with him. One *does* become more attractive, more desirable, when they're married." He smiled. "And you are no exception."

I blushed.

He hopped down. "Besides, if I were to commit adultery, it would be with another married man."

"Why?"

"The question you should be asking isn't *why* but with *who*." He winked.

My cheeks burned—*both* sets.

139

LOVE
THE
ONE
YOU'RE
WITH

"But B.D. wouldn't be upset that it happened; he'd be upset that it happened without *him*!"

We laughed.

I nodded. "And considering that Pooquie wouldn't mind taking a dive inside B.D., and you've had dreams about Pooquie . . ."

He replayed that dream. "Now, *that* would be something else: a Black gay version of *Bob & Carol & Ted & Alice*."

B.D. popped in. "Yoo-hoo, lovelies. The first guest has arrived."

That first guest was (and always is) Horace Cleveland. He's known as Sleeveless Cleve or the Sleeveless Wonder because he loves to show off his immaculate arms and chest, which are deltoid deep and pectoral perfect. It doesn't matter the season: it can be below freezing (as it was this particular evening) and he'll peel off a coat, a sweater, and a thermal undershirt to reveal one of his many silk sleeveless blouses (or, as he has on other nights, muscle Ts). He always comes at the designated start time and leaves at the quoted finish. He doesn't like to miss anything—or take a chance that his delts and pecs will be missed *by* anyone.

Like Horace, all of Gene's oldest friends are in their late thirties to midforties (I'm the baby at twenty-eight; B.D. and Babyface are both thirty-one) and are very youthful (they probably partake in the same kind of rigorous beauty rituals Gene does). And each one, like Horace, has a special title bestowed upon him by the other members of the Looney Toons (as they dub themselves). Gene is known as M.D.—Mack Diva (no explanation needed). The other unusual usual suspects in no particular order:

A bus driver by day and aspiring actor by night (and after seeing him perform, you know why he is *still* aspiring), Jesse MacDougal is Holy Mackerel, since he has holes in his ears, tongue, nipples, bottom lip, right eyebrow, and left nostril. And he fills those holes up with nothing but silver. He was inspired to get pierced when he and Gene planned on attending LaBelle's "Something Silver" concert at the Metropolitan Opera House on October 6, 1974. Everyone was asked to wear that color, but he didn't feel his galactic see-through jumpsuit and platform boots were enough. I still can't believe he did it: being poked with needles in ten different places on your body couldn't have been fun (this was years before that zip gun was invented) and this is a man who still faints when he nicks himself shaving. But no sacrifice was or is too great for Miss Patti, whom, like Gene, he worships. They each have several framed pics with her taken over the years (including one on that silver night) and they share a copy of a gold record for "Lady Marmalade" (the first six months of every year, it can always be found above Gene's dresser).

Jackson Graves, a VP in charge of business loans at a Queens branch of Citibank, is Jumpin' Jack Flash—and not because he loves to do jumping jacks. He loves for the boys to jump (i.e., sit) on his jack; unfortunately, the excitement makes him come in a flash. He's only had sex in that position his whole life and the others have argued that if he'd branch out maybe he'd be able to sustain an erection longer than thirty seconds.

The owner of a hair salon called Weaves-R-Us in Harlem, Edmond Zimmer is the Walking Conflagration. B.D. might be a flame but Edmond is a *blowtorch*. He scorches a path as he walks by—and his tongue is just as fiery. That blazing autumn sunshine 'do is also a tell-tale sign that if you play with him you will get burned.

Jerry Perry is Dr. Do Little because he is in fact a doctor (a veteri-narian) and has to do little to make the boyz bow down to him except unzip that fly and allow that thirteen-and-a-half-inch tube steak (which Gene swears he ties in a knot to fit into a pair of underwear, including boxers) to do the talkin'.

And then there's Alan Simpson, the Grand Canyon. He's a thick man who wears his weight well (very chunky, not chubby) and is, as he will tell you, "a hundred and one percent bottom." Well, to the crew, he's more like a bottom*less* pit. He can apparently take it without a squint (he and Jerry had a tryst some years ago and that was the one and only time Jerry claims he broke a sweat). Alan had defensive-end dreams, but instead of playing for the team he promotes it: he's an assistant marketing manager for the New Jersey Caravans. They may not be the most popular platoon in the league, but their logo and mer-chandise still pull in a jood amount of green each year—and Alan's paid nicely because of it.

There's a sexual tension between Gene and Alan that hangs over them like a storm cloud. Everybody sees it—except Gene. Or maybe he doesn't want to; as the designated hit-and-run member of the

141

LOVE
THE
ONE
YOU'RE
WITH

group, he probably senses that he wouldn't be able to just hit Alan and run. For over twenty years they've been fucking each other—with words, that is—and they never stray far from the script.

"Alan, I dis*tinctly* remember crossing you off my guest list, so *what* are you doing here?" Gene frowned in his very best Margo Channing twang, sizing Alan up as he stood at the front door.

"Come on, G.R. You know I couldn't miss the opportunity to help you celebrate your twenty-first birthday . . . for the forty-fourth time. You should be receiving your first social security check any day now, right?" Alan is the only person in Gene's circle who can shut him down.

And whenever he's been trumped by him, Gene resorts to stock comebacks. "*Fuck* you," he blurted, stomping off.

And, as he always does, Alan went after him, chortling: "Ha, I want ya to, but you won't!"

Alan is always the last to arrive—and the first to get drunk (it doesn't take much; one swig of vodka and cranberry juice and he's floating in the air like a puff of smoke). And he always comes solo.

But not tonight.

"So . . . we meet again," he said.

"Yes, we do."

"If I didn't know any better, I'd say you were stalking me."

"Stalking you?"

"Yeah. First you show up at my dance spot—"

"*Your* dance spot? I didn't know it was copyrighted under your name."

"—then you just *happen* to be in the *exact* same building at the *exact* same time I'm making my runs—"

"Believe me, that was a coincidence."

"—and now here you are."

"Yes, at *my* best friend's birthday party."

"Right, *not* yours. My grandma always said, 'There ain't no such thing as a coincidence.' Things don't just happen. But don't get me wrong: I don't mind being pursued. It feels kinda good."

I just shook my head. "May I have your jacket?"

He took it off. "Is there anything else you'd like to have?"

"Excuse me?"

"You heard."

Okay . . . I'll toy with him. "Why, yes, there is . . ."

"Well, all you gotta do is ask for it . . . and it's *yours*."

"All right . . ." I moved in closer; we were almost nose to nose. "Your hat, please."

"Say what?"

I tapped the flap of his brown leather cap with my forehead. "Your hat."

He took it off without taking his eyes off of me.

"Thank you."

"You're most welcome."

"The food and drink are in the kitchen. After I hang this up, I'll fix you something."

"Oh, you will?"

"Well, you are a first-timer. I know how to treat a guest."

He snickered. "Uh, does that mean I get first dibs, too?"

"You don't get first *or* last dibs."

"Okay, seconds will do. That way you're already broken in but still a little ripe."

I stepped back and out of his way. "I'll be there in a moment. It's the first arch to your right."

"I'll be waiting." He walked backward in that direction, keeping his eyes on me.

After I made him that drink ("*Sex* on the Beach"), he went to mingle—and as soon as he stepped into the living room, *the men all paused*. Montee wasn't the only new meat, uh, man at the party (everyone except Alan came with two friends/acquaintances/colleagues/new or hopeful boyfriends–fuck buddies–pieces, and there were a dozen other freshman in the group, a third of the entire party), but he was the only one eyed by just about everyone, including Babyface ("Now there's a boat *I'd* love to row!") and B.D. ("He may as well change his name to SAM—Sexy Ass Motherfucker"). And why wouldn't they be all in his mix: he was just as phyne as he wanted to be in a cream-colored knit long-sleeved shirt, tan pleated corduroy pants, and mahogany-brown unlaced leather British Knights. (I was wearing a similar ensemble, except my shirt, corduroy pants, and BK boots were all dark gray.) His 'fro had grown an inch since last week but wasn't sprouting up but around his head, a

143

LOVE
THE
ONE
YOU're
WITH

very compact and attractive style. And the gold choker with a crucifix that sat below his Adam's apple told you he was a God-fearing man but not a man you'd have to fear.

But, as a few remarked during the evening, Montee only had eyes for me. He never said anything; he just watched me from afar. Whenever I felt his eyes on me, I'd turn and there he—well, *they* were. But I figured I was home free when, after Dr. Do Little, the Sleeveless Wonder, and the Walking Conflagration struck out, one of the other newbies—a hunky, handsome fella from Haiti with mocha skin, green eyes, and shoulder-length locks named Garrick—made his move. After a half hour of intimate chat (as each minute passed, Garrick moved in closer and closer), they became *the* couple on the dance floor, claiming it as their own for over an hour (at one point everyone else stopped and surrounded them as Montee shook that ass like he did at Body & Soul).

Sometime later I was putting ice trays in the freezer when he appeared.

"Could I bother you a moment?"

"Yes?"

"Garrick wants a screwdriver and I don't know how to make it."

"Okay."

I retrieved two new plastic cups and filled them up with ice. He stood directly beside me, his left shoulder leaning into my right. I looked at him.

"I just want to see how you make it so next time I'll know," he reasoned.

Sure he did. "Would you like another Sex on the Beach?"

"I'd really like to have sex on the beach with *you*." A slight grin formed across his face.

I made them. I faced him. He reached for the drinks . . . in slow motion. He grasped my hands instead of the cups.

We stood in silence, our eyes locked.

"*A-hem.*"

We turned. It was B.D.

He released me and finally took them. "Thank you."

"You're welcome."

He eased past B.D.

B.D. walked toward me. His disapproving expression turned to a smile. "*Slut.*"

"Nothing happened between us."

"If I hadn't entered when I did, *something* would have."

"There's nothing between us, B.D."

"The fact that you feel it's necessary to explain tells me there *is*."

"I . . . I . . ."

The buzzer rang. Saved by the bell.

"I'll get it." I sighed with relief.

"No, *I'll* get it. It should be my surprise for the Ice Princess. I'll be right in. Everyone's waiting to sing 'Happy Birthday.' "

"Uh, okay."

When I entered the room, just about everyone was paired up (including Carl, who came with Ivan; I guess he passed Gene's inspection). And Garrick, who was a little taller than Montee, was leaning on his left shoulder.

B.D. carried in the cake. He placed it on a card table in front of Gene. He snapped his finger. "Oh, we need a candle."

"Only a *brain-dense* child like you would forget the candle," snorted Gene.

A voice bellowed over the crowd's giggles: "I got a candle fuh ya— and a few other thangz."

All heads and eyes turned to the door as a path was cleared for a very buffed, bald gentleman who was dressed as Zorro—black eye mask, skintight spandex shirt and pants, steel-toe boots, and cape.

He made his way toward Gene, his sword extended and aimed at the birthday boy's chest. "Gene Roberts?"

"That's me," Gene anticipated, his eyes taking in every inch of the fine form in front of him.

Zorro threw down the sword (which was a fake). "Well, you wanna blow out *my* candle"—he grabbed his dick—"and eat some of *these* cakes?" He spun around, bent down, and flung his cape over his head to reveal his big bare light brown booty (the pants had a Ziploc pouch in the back, like a pair of underalls).

The crowd went ballistic. Zorro jumped up and yelled, "Hit it!" Off of Patti's "Feels Like Another One," he flipped and dipped, twirled and swirled, and did several eye-opening splits, slipping out of each

145

LOVE
THE
ONE
YOU'RE
WITH

article of clothing and throwing them all in Gene's lap as if he were a clothes hamper.

And Gene . . . he just couldn't control himself. He was sweating like a swine, never took those wide eyes off of Zorro, and that tongue wagged during the entire performance, with saliva dripping from his mouth like a wolf about to devour a lamb. When Zorro jiggled his crotch in his face, Gene gnawed at it. When Zorro wiggled that ass in his face, Gene buried his face in it. And when Zoro rubbed up *on* him, Gene rubbed up *into* him, eliciting screams from the crowd.

When the song ended, Zorro wore nothing but his mask and a G-string and had Gene straddled in a chair, riding him as if he were a buckaroo and Gene a bronco. Everyone applauded, hooterin' and hollerin' for more.

"I'm sorry, fellas, but tha only one who gets a encore is birthday boy"—he clutched Gene's head and gazed into his eyes—"and *that* will be in *private*."

"Ooh," we all choralized.

"And it not only feels like another one," he added, grinding slowly, "it feels like a *big* one."

Gene blushed.

Zorro clutched his face. "Happy birthday, from B.D." He planted a real sloppy one on Gene, who attempted to swallow and have him right there.

"*Ow,*" "*Yeah!,*" and "*Woof Woof Woof!*" filled the room.

"All right, you two, that's enough," B.D. interrupted. "The birthday boy can cop some more feels after we've sung and he cuts his cake."

Gene slapped Zorro's ass as he bent over to pick up his clothes.

"I'm talkin' about *this* cake, you fool," said B.D., pointing to the one he made.

Gene stood. "Of course *you* would give me something tawdry like this. And I *adore* you for it." He fell into his arms.

"Aaaaaaw," the group moaned.

B.D. was also taken aback by this show of affection. "My, my, my, age must be wearing down that iron will. You're almost acting . . . *human*."

The group laughed. Gene pinched him on his left arm.

"Is there a bathroom I can use ta freshen up and change?" Zorro asked me.

"Sure. I'll show you."

He grabbed his bag and followed me. When we reached it, I turned.

Zorro was unmasked—and "Oh, my God!" was all I could muster.

"Zorro" was Angel, Pooquie's homeboy. "Ha, I been called *that* befo', but *never* outa bed!"

I hugged him. "I . . . I'm just so surprised to see you. And to see you *here*."

"I bet. It's been a while, hunh?"

"Too long a while. After we sing 'Happy Birthday,' we can talk."

"A'ight."

As the cake was being cut and eaten, Angel and I went into the kitchen. I fixed him a drink and a plate of food.

"So how long have you been doing this?" I inquired.

"Like five months."

"And how did you come to do it?"

"This guy stepped ta me on tha street, sayin' I could make a lota money strippin', bein' an escort. I thought he was tryin' ta hustle me. But he was right. I'm tryin' ta make enuff green fuh school."

"You're going to school?"

"Yeah. Baruch in September."

I hugged his neck, since he held his plate in his hands. "Wow, that's fantastic! Congrats!"

"Thanks."

"What are you going to major in?"

"I'm stuck between computer science and business administration."

"Ah. Hopefully Pooquie will be following your lead soon."

"I hope so: I'm gonna need somebody ta copy answers from. He is one smart mutha-fucka."

We laughed.

"Uh . . . what does being an escort entail?"

"You know, goin' out wit' folks, bein' their date, or doin' a private striptease. I know it's a fancy name fuh a male prostitute these days, but I don't be sleepin' wit' my clients. But . . . I might hafta make a exception tonite."

"Oh, really?"

147

LOVE
THE
ONE
YOU'RE
WITH

"Yeah. I was always attracted ta Gene. But he was wit' somebody when we met at yo' place last year."

That's right, they met at the surprise party Pooquie threw for me. Now, this would be too funny, not to mention bizarre: Gene hooking up with Pooquie's homie. *That* would make for some interesting double dates. "Looks like he's very attracted to you."

"Yeah. He ain't *say* nuthin' ta me then, but I could tell he was."

"How?"

"Tha way he was lookin' at me. Ev'ry time I turned around, there he was wit' his eyes on me. Nah—wit' his eyes on my *ass*. I tell ya, they like laser beams."

"Yes, they are."

"So . . . you enjoy my dance?"

"Yes, I did. Of course, I always knew you could shake that money-maker." I slapped him on that meaty thigh.

He grinned.

"I see you do private parties. Do you only do parties for men?"

"Nah, I do women's parties, too."

"Ah. And I don't think I ever asked you before: Are you bisexual?"

"Well . . . I've slept wit' men and *a* woman. So I guess some folk would say I'm much, *much* more gay than bi. But I don't see myself as neither. I just like what I like. And I don't discriminate. I'll do Black parties, parties fuh tha boricuas, white parties, straight parties, gay parties, bisexual parties . . ."

"Bisexual parties?"

"Yeah. I did one wit' this girl last week. That shit wasn't off da fuckin' hook, it was disconnected. It was nuthin' but a orgy. Ha, I made so much money in tips I could pay my rent fuh two months."

"Do you enjoy it?"

He thought on that one, chomping away. "I don't know if I enjoy it. I sure as hell enjoy tha funds I collect. It's just a job, ta take care of me 'n' my Anjelica. Ooh . . ." He put his plate down and opened up the gold heart-shaped locket hanging around his neck. Inside was a profile of a smiling Anjelica in pigtails.

I smiled. "My, she is such a beautiful girl. How old is she now?"

He beamed. "Three, goin' on thirteen."

We giggled.

"I bet."

He closed it. "That extra cash always comes in handy. She growin' so fast. So I'm gonna do it until school starts. That should tie me over fuh a spell. And if things get real tight, I can always go back ta it. I'm already rackin' up a large list of admirers. Ha, Rah ain't tha only one wit' fans."

"Mmm . . . does Pooquie know?"

"Nah, he don't. And I *don't* want ya ta tell him."

"Why?"

"I . . . it's . . . well, he would probably come down on me cuz he done already said that if I need some help, ta just ask. But . . . a brotha gotta do it fuh himself, ya know what I'm sayin'?"

"I do."

"And he got enuff ta deal wit'. I ain't about ta be one of them friends wit' his hand out. If he wanna give me sumthin', he can. Ha, I ain't gonna turn down a gift. But it's just like my moms always say: 'If ya don't wanna lose a friend, money you should never borrow or lend.' "

"Indeed. I understand. Your secret is safe with me."

"Thanks. And how is he doin', anyway?"

"He's doing jood. The shoot is going okay and he should be home next Sunday."

"We should throw him a jam ta celebrate."

"We should. He'll probably be too tired to party when he comes back Sunday night, so it'll have to be the following weekend."

"A'ight. He might be too tired ta party wit' us when he gets back Sunday nite, but he *ain't* gonna be too tired ta party wit' *you*."

I playfully punched him in his left arm.

"And just *what* is going on here?" Gene was perched in the entry-way of the kitchen with his hands on his hips.

"I was just making sure your . . . gift was taken care of."

"Uh, *that* is *my* job."

"Okay. I'll leave you two to get . . . acquainted." I winked at Angel. I left the kitchen as Gene took a seat on Angel's lap.

I helped B.D. with the cleanup in the back, taking folks' dishes. Missing? Montee and Garrick. When I headed back to the kitchen, I realized why I hadn't seen them: they were on the sofa in the living

149

LOVE
THE
ONE
YOU'RE
WITH

room, Garrick sitting between Montee's legs, feeding him cake with his fingers, which Montee would also nibble on after each serving.

No way was I going to ask them if they were finished.

A half hour later, while Babyface and B.D. and two other couples dragged to "Don't Ask My Neighbors" by the Emotions, Garrick was pinned up against a wall, twitching and sighing in ecstasy, as you-know-who performed a little oral surgery on his mouth, neck, and ears. The way Montee's lips pursed, puckered, and popped, and his tongue darted in and out, circled and stabbed, licked and lapped . . .

At three, the party was over. There was little to clean. I wrapped up what food folks didn't take (you know just about everyone left with *two* paper plates wrapped in aluminum foil in either a brown paper or shopping bag) and put away the beverages they didn't guzzle (it was BYOB and each person brought a minimum of two bottles, leaving Gene with a considerable amount of vodka, rum, and gin for his collection). I was tying up the extra-large Hefty when Montee and Garrick passed by the kitchen; Garrick was leading him by the hand. Was Montee leaving with him? And if so, wasn't he going to say good-bye? After I heard muffled voices and coats being put on (yes, I'm somewhat ashamed to admit, I tiptoed to the entryway to eavesdrop), the front door closed. The Sleeveless Wonder exited right after them with one of the other newbies, a Cuban cutie named Luis, whose arms and chest were just as gorgeous as his.

Five minutes later, the front door opened as I was having a slice of cheesecake. I sprang up and stepped out into the hallway. It was Montee.

"You scared me," I breathed.

"Sorry."

"I thought you left with Garrick."

"Leave without sayin' good-bye? That's what *you* do, not me, remember?"

I frowned.

He leaned against the refrigerator. "Besides, I just met the brother; why would I leave *with* him? I ain't that kinda guy."

I stood against the sink. "You're not what kind of guy?"

"The kind that meets you and eats you on the same night."

Okay . . . I asked for that one. "But you don't have a problem tonguin' 'em down on the first night . . . ?"

"Hey, gives me somethin' to look forward to. And I'll know after the kiss whether or not I *want* to see him again."

"Oh?"

"Yeah. Some brothers can seal it with the kiss, some can't."

"And did Garrick seal it?"

"Ha, you saw for yourself: What do *you* think?"

Whoops . . . I was scoped scopin' them out. Time to change the subject. "Uh, I was having some cheesecake. Would you like a slice?"

"Sure." He took off his coat and hung it over the back of the chair opposite mine. He sat, resting his hat on his lap. I cut him a slice.

He chomped. "Mmm. This is really good. Did you make it?"

"No, B.D. did."

"Ah. I'm surprised you didn't. After all, it's really sweet—like you."

Uh-huh. "You know all the wrong things to say, don't you?"

He shrugged. "Since when is telling a truth like that wrong?"

"And, you never know when to quit while you're behind."

"And *behind*, I do got, as you felt last week."

At that moment B.D. pranced into the kitchen with Babyface behind him. "We're outa here, hon."

"All right." I stood to hug and kiss them.

B.D. turned to Montee. "And, *Montee* . . ." He held out his right hand for him to kiss, which he did. "It was in*deed* a pleasure." His eyes fell on me. "But I hope it won't be *too* much of a pleasure for someone else later this morning."

Montee chuckled. "Good to meet you, too." He shook hands with Babyface. "Good meetin' you, brother."

"You, too. You came with Alan, right?"

"Yes."

"He's knocked out on the love seat in the Blue Light room."

"That's okay. I don't live far."

"I'm driving. Would you like a lift?"

Montee glanced at me; was he expecting me to answer for him? "That'd be nice. Thank you." He didn't sound too happy about accepting the offer.

151

LOVE
THE
ONE
YOU'RE
WITH

B.D. pointed to his cake. "Well, wrap that up, hon. And did you get a plate or two?"

"No, that's okay."

"There's plenty left."

"No, that's all right. Could I just use the rest room a quick minute?"

"Of course. Your cake will be ready to go when you get back."

He left.

"*We* are *saving* you from the *sins* of your *soul*," preached B.D.

I wrapped Montee's cake. "Huh?"

"Don't give me that coquette act, okay? You two won't be able to sit up in this kitchen for long before you return to the living room—which happens to be your *bedroom*—and hear voices off in the distance encouraging you to also satisfy those carnal instincts."

"Voices off in the distance?"

"Gene and Zorro," Babyface piped in.

I had completely forgotten about Angel—and they seem to have forgotten they met him before. I refreshed their memories.

"*Ah* . . ." B.D. began, putting the other pieces of the evening's puzzle together. "*That* explains why he stuck around and they were carrying on like dogs in heat. Around two o'clock, Mr. Angel transferred all the presents into Gene's bedroom—and never came out. Then Miss Thing ducked in there ten minutes ago. We're waiting for her to bid us good night when we hear slurpin', suckin', sighin', spankin', and moanin'—along with Roseanne's big-ass mouth. When Zorro said only the birthday boy could get an encore, he wasn't kiddin'!"

"I guess we'll be hearing about it later today."

"Ha, *you'll* be hearing about it this *morning*. Gene is *loud*. He's wanted some papi cock and Rican rump for the longest time. So, *you'll* probably have to turn on a TV, too."

Montee returned.

B.D. kissed me on the cheek. "We'll speak—*soon*."

"Okay."

"Good night, Mitch," said Babyface, picking up the large tinfoil pan of food they were taking home.

"Good night."

I handed Montee his doggy bag. He held out his hand.

"Good to see you again." He smiled.

"You, too."

As B.D.'s eyebrows rose, we let go. That shake lingered longer than it should have.

He threw on his coat and hat. He noticed the garbage bag. "Do you want me to take this out?"

"That would be nice. Thanks."

"No prob." He grabbed it with one hand.

I walked them to the door. Montee was the last out; he paused before stepping outside. Did he want to say something?

I locked up, took a shower, and laid out my clothes. I turned off all the lights, set the alarm on the travel clock Gene must've brought out of his room and placed on one of the end tables (he might've been serious about gettin' a nut but at least Gene didn't forget about me), and collapsed on the couch.

But I couldn't sleep—and it wasn't because of the sounds emanating from Gene's bedroom. As the bed knocked out a slow and steady then quicker yet still rhythmic beat against the wall, and a grumble or growl from either or both of them followed each stroke; and as Angel's cries of *"¡Sí, papi!," "¡Cómeme el culo!," "¡Pégame duro!," "¡Clávamela! ¡Más dentro, sí!,"* and *"¡Fóllame, papi, fóllame!"* were answered with Gene's declarations of *"¡Dame tu culo!," "Ponte boca arriba y levanta las piernas," "¡Te voy a follar duro!," "¡Así me gusta!,"* and *"Me encanta tu culo"* (he was loud, not to mention bilingual—and he would know all the freaky phrases), I wished I was gettin' some jood stuff like they were.

But the person I envisioned givin' it to me *wasn't* Pooquie.

153

LOVE
THE
ONE
YOU'RE
WITH

"Mitchell?"

My eyes popped open. "Are we here?"

The *we* being my brother, Adam, and my mother, who had tapped me and woken me up.

And the *here* being D.C.

I got up at dawn (I only slept three hours) to meet Adam at the family home in Jersey so we could drive down. We've been making the trip the past seven years to honor my father on his birthday. His remains are in Evergreen Cemetery in Brooklyn, but we travel to the nation's capital to pay our respects at what has to be the largest tombstone ever erected: the Vietnam War Veterans Memorial, known as the Wall. And visiting it has been and continues to be the most spiritually and emotionally wrenching experience I've ever had.

I've watched every Vietnam War—based, —themed, and —inspired film there is—from the so-called A-list flicks (*The Deer Hunter, Coming Home, Apocalypse Now,* and *Platoon*), to the not-so-revered cinematic clips (*Hamburger Hill* and *Hanoi Hilton*), and even the very entertaining (though exploitative) adventures of Colonel Braddock (Chuck Norris) and Rambo (Sly)—and have yet to see an image that actually reflects what Black soldiers may have faced. And why would I: anytime the story is told through a white man's eyes (and it always is), you know it is a distorted view of not only his own reality but everyone else's—especially us Negroes. And while Black soldiers were featured in *Tour of Duty,* a drama series set during the war, they were usually front and center for one reason and one reason only: to confront (what else?) racism. And despite the KKK-ish attitudes and behavior of their white comrades, they were always expected to be humble and forgiving, playing peacemaker in the end (no thanks to some white Hollywood liberal writer, who can't for a moment allow a Negro to be both justified in and unapologetic about his anger). These whitewashed presentations are an insult to the disproportionate number of Black men who served, were injured, and killed in 'Nam.

So you know I couldn't wait to check out *The Walking Dead*, which sought on some level to do what these other projects didn't, wouldn't, and couldn't. But the film was more of a morality play, analyzing the wars the Black soldiers were fighting (or running away from) inside of themselves, not so much the politics of the conflict. And I read Wallace Terry's *Bloods*, the first (and still one of the few) comprehensive accounts of African-Americans serving in the war, a half-dozen times—but as gripping a book it is, I still felt disconnected from the war and, most specifically, my father's role in it.

But the first and every other time I've come to the Wall? I will never know what my father went through, what he was up against, what he was thinking, what the final moments of his life must have been like, but when I see his name on that city-block-long, rectangular mass of black marble . . . I can *feel* him. The absurdity, the horror, the immense tragedy of the war embraces you, engulfs you, almost smothers you (at one point during that first visit I was gasping for air; it seemed I couldn't breathe). But so does the courage and dignity he and the fifty-thousand-plus others whose blood was spilled (or who are still missing in action) had to possess in order to fight for an unknown cause (fighting the spread of communism in such a remote part of the world?) in an unknown part of the world (like many of his comrades my father not only didn't know where Vietnam was, he didn't even know such a place existed) under a well-known yet hollow mantra (that "We're America, Land of the Free and Home of the Brave" crap). It's no wonder that to this day, so many are still divided over why we were there, whether we should've been there, and whether or not it was worth it. But forget the politicians, historians, cultural critics, and warmongering, flag-waving schmucks: for a true expert opinion, ask the millions of people who are still coping with the grief and bitterness over their husbands, wives, fathers, mothers, brothers, sisters, uncles,

155
LOVE
THE
ONE
YOU'RE
WITH

aunts, nephews, cousins, lovers, and friends being sacrificed (the term *lost* doesn't come close to describing it), and the tens of thousands who survived the war (only to return home to fight another for their right to be viewed and treated as American heroes and heroines).

The Wall finally allowed the nation to face the past and grieve. Its design is not spectacular by any means, but its brilliance and power is in its simplicity. In its very own peculiar way, it's brought me closer to my father than I was when he was alive (my last memory of him is at five, waving good-bye as he got on a bus to be transported upstate to be sent overseas), and I'm sure it does the same for so many others. And it's the closest I ever want to come to the hell he had to endure. More than any other war memorial erected, the Wall says what it is supposed to: War is fucked up—and this was truly one *fucked-up* war.

I stretched and yawned. I looked at my watch. "Wow, Mom, you musta been doing eighty. We got here in record time."

"Well, I got us through Jersey, but your brother took over in Wilmington and zoomed us here. Given all those Indy 500 dips, loops, twists, and turns he performed, I'm surprised you didn't wake up." She climbed out of the car. "You musta really had a great time last night."

I hopped up out of the backseat and closed the door. I smiled. "Yeah, I did."

She glared at me. "Hmm . . . and just how great was it?"

"What do you mean?"

"*You* know what I mean." She nudged me in the side with her elbow. "Don't even think about cheating on my son-in-law. *I'll* turn you in if you do."

I laughed—she didn't. She was serious. I changed *that* topic. "So, where's Adam?"

"He went to get some flowers." She spotted him. "Here he comes."

The older my brother gets, the more he resembles our father—especially since he's let the hair grow on both his head (he now has a two-inch afro) and face (a trimmed beard). In addition to his appearance, there's also the habit he's recently adopted—crunching on ice. It's a transformation that started with our visits (has our father's spirit invaded him?). My mother sees it, too; we were both smiling at him as he approached. He carried a bouquet of gardenias (my father's favorite flower).

He appeared uncomfortable by our gazing. "Why y'all lookin' at me like that?"

We just giggled.

With my mother in the center, we take the walk together, hand in hand. There were several dozen people on the grounds; it was just before noon and the masses hadn't shown up yet (it gets very crowded). Many of them were veterans, dressed in their respective uniforms (all four branches of the military were represented). Family units of all colors and generations were present (one little girl, probably no more than three, was sitting on the lap of a man in a wheelchair who had to be almost a century old). There were red, white, and yellow roses, violets, tulips, daffodils, sunflowers, and daisies inside the plot holes along the Wall's base, as well as American flags of various sizes. And, of course, there was a soundtrack of muffled sobs and prayers.

By the time we reached my father, we were also in tears (which wasn't unusual). We clung to each other for a few minutes, swapping hankies and hugs.

My mother arranged the gardenias. Then I took a blue colored pencil and a piece of light gray granite paper from my knapsack and did what has become a rite of passage here: I bent down, placed the paper over his name—he's in the fourth panel, sixth row from the bottom—and "shaded" it. I gave it to my mother, who will date and place it in her Bible later tonight. She collects them as a memento of each trip; she must have six by now.

We each spend time with him alone. Clutching his photo and the Bronze Medal he received posthumously, my mother usually sings him a few tunes like she used to back in the day. I remember her lullabying me to sleep; I inherited my voice from her (she stopped singing after he was killed and didn't start again until we began visiting him here). "At Last" by Etta James was his favorite song and that's always on her playlist. Adam just sits in silence, with his head in his lap. He doesn't remember him—and not having any memories has to be worse than trying not to forget the few you do.

I always write him a letter. When my mother and Adam took their walk, I bent down on both knees and read it out loud (but not so loud that I attracted or disturbed others):

Hi, Dad,

Happy birthday. Hope the past year has been a blessed one. I've been in very jood health and spirits.

Let's see, there's so much to tell you since our last meeting. Probably the most important news: I found a job. I'm teaching at a school just blocks from my apartment. No more racing out of the house to catch a train or bus. I'm teaching creative writing for the sixth through eighth grades. It's a challenge, to say the least. But I am realizing one of my dreams. I don't think I ever told you that. Being a teacher was one of my goals. Somehow I let it get away from me. But now it's got ahold of me and I am enjoying it so much. You've got two sons who are shaping the minds and bodies of tomorrow.

Speaking of that other son: you should see Adam, Dad. He is the spitting image of you. He's a lot thicker than you were; I tell him all the time he should seriously consider becoming a professional bodybuilder. I know he feels cheated that you were taken from us before he had the chance to know you. I didn't really know you, either, but at least I can replay some of those moments we had. He doesn't like to talk about his feelings, but the fact that he is literally changing into you before our eyes tells me that your spirit lives on in him. You'd be so proud of the man he has become.

Pooquie and I are still together. He's in Hollywood right now making his first film. He's going to be a star. It leaves me wondering where I'll fit in when that happens, though. He hasn't tried to hide me, but he hasn't told the world about us—not that I expect him to. But I know that the bigger he gets, the harder it will be for and on us. No matter how many strides gay people have made, people just aren't ready for a man like him declaring who he is and publicly acknowledging his beaufriend. And Pooquie isn't at that point himself. But I love him and I know he loves me. He makes me so happy, and so does his son, Junior. Junior came to visit me on Friday. We had so much fun together.

Pooquie's father reappeared last spring. Pooquie is suspicious of him and I guess he should be—the man walked out on him and his mother when Pooquie was five. I don't know why he came back, but I told Pooquie that he has a chance I don't. I have to remind him how

james
earl
hardy

lucky he is. How I wish I could really talk to you, really laugh with you,
really hug you—not as a little boy but as a man. He can have that if he
works through the anger. I'm kind of jealous but happy for him.

Say hi to Grandma Ada, Grand Pop, and Uncle Russ. I love and
miss them. And I love and miss you,

MC-20

That's what he called me. When he came home from work, I'd fly
into his arms and he'd carry me through the house. He was my sky as I
puttered and whizzed with delight, my body erect and arms extended.

"That DC-10 has nothin' on my MC-20!"

"No, it don't, Daddy!"

In that one playful moment, he made me feel like I could do anything.

After my mother, Adam, and I said a final good-bye and prayer, we
got something to eat at a diner. We all had salads. They both quizzed
me about Pooquie's adventure in L.A. so far, while my mother filled us
in on some of the family gossip (my father's very youthful-looking
seventy-eight-year-old aunt, Cecile, got married to a fifty-two-year-
old man last weekend; u go girl!).

"And, while we're on that subject: Did your brother tell you the
jood news?" my mother sang as the waitress took away our dishes.

I chuckled. "What jood news?" Our attention turned to him.

"Lynette. I asked her to marry me."

"And?"

"And she said yes."

"That's terrific!" I bellowed, slapping his hand. "When's the date?"

"We haven't set one yet. But we're leaning toward June next year."

"Great. I know Lynette can't wait . . ."

"And *I* can't wait to be a grandmother," my mother squealed. "It'll
be nice to hear the pitter-patter of little feet around the house again—
and know that, at the end of the day, those little feet will be going
home to Mommy and Daddy. "Hmm . . . I guess she's not counting
on *me* in that department. She's accepted who I am—her concern for
Pooquie and our relationship is proof—but I'm sure that deep down
inside, she wishes I were heterosexual (not that I would *have* to be to
give her a grandchild).

159

LOVE
THE
ONE
YOU'RE
WITH

She rose. "Ah, excuse me. I have to go to the ladies' room." She headed off, pinching Adam's cheek as she walked by him.

I studied him with a smirk.

"What?"

"I'm just picturing you as a married man. And a father."

"Are they hard to picture?"

"Not at all. You'll make a jood father and husband. And I'm sure Lynette will be a jood wife and mother. I really like her." And I did: she's an incredibly smart (physics professor at Columbia), sexy sister. At thirty-six, she's a decade older than him (you can't tell), but that's not an issue for either of them (the age-ain't-nothin'-but-a-number credo is a family thing—my mother and I are both roughly seven years older than the men in our lives).

"Seems like she's the only woman I dated you ever liked."

"No, I liked quite a few of your lady friends. Simone was really sweet. So was Theresa. And the model from St. Thomas, what was her name?"

"Roshamba."

"She was a living doll." And she was: Barbie dipped in chocolate with black hair straighter than a horse's tail (it probably *was* a horse's tail).

"I don't recall you kidnapping any of them the first time you met and keeping them on your arm the whole night, like Lynette."

"That's because they were all nice but—if I may be so bold—just a *little* too high maintenance."

"Huh?"

"Like . . . they were contestants at a beauty pageant, all gussied and glamoured up. Stunning to look at. But just a little too . . . tight. You try to cut up with them and they'd look at you in horror. Just a little too prim and proper."

"And Lynette?"

"Lynette's a homegirl *with* class, not to mention beauty and brains. The right mix. And when you two are together . . . I can clearly see that you are into her. I didn't see that with any of the others."

"You didn't?"

"Nope. *Especially* Jayne."

Jayne. A white high-school dropout from Sheepshead Bay working in her uncle's air-conditioner business as a cashier. No, I didn't like my brother dating a white woman—but not because she was white. It was because she's *wasn't* Black. Not two weeks after he testified that sisters were "too demanding and difficult" (and how many times have we heard brothers say *that*?), he shows up at my mother's July Fourth barbecue with Jayne. And Jayne was *plain*—skin as white as typing paper, her dark brown hair done in a sloppy short bob, and a nonexistent chest and backside. I took one look at her and thought: He's not dating her because she's *a* white girl but because she is *the* white girl. I've seen the syndrome before: *it don't matter what they look like, so long as they're white*. Present a brother with a sister with the same body and bio as Jayne and he'd most certainly balk. Black gay men aren't the only ones who can be snow queens; their hetero and bi brethren participate in that pathology on an even larger scale (you can count on just a few hands the number of pro-sports players and entertainers who have Black wives/girlfriends). So, while I was more than hospitable toward her (she was a pleasant woman, just not very bright), I was more than cool toward him. He knew I could see right through the masquerade. We never saw and he never mentioned Jayne again—and, lo and behold, one month later he met the woman who apparently restored his faith in sisters: Lynette.

"You never gonna let me live that one down, are you?"

"I just call them as I see 'em."

We sipped our hot chocolate.

"Mitch?"

"Yeah?"

"I want you to be my best man."

I beamed. "I'd be honored, little brother."

"Will you cut that little-brother noise."

"Well, you *are*—"

"My little brother," he finished with me, then continued, "Yeah, I know."

"Well . . . I guess it would be kind of silly to continue calling you *little* and you're practically a married man. And Little Adam Junior will be running around soon. No sense in confusing him." I winked.

He nodded. "You think Rah will be one of my groomsmen?"

"Of course. I'm sure he'd love that. I would, too." Funny how he and Pooquie immediately hit off when they first met, like Lynette and I. Hmm . . .

161

LOVE
THE
ONE
YOU'RE
WITH

My mother returned. "So, you two ready?"

"Yeah," we replied.

"Okay, then. Let's hit the road."

I was about to climb into the front seat when my mother cleared her throat. "Uh, aren't you forgetting something?"

"Huh?"

"Your luggage?"

It hit me. "Oh." I walked around to the trunk, took off my knapsack, and dropped it inside. Why? That would be revealed when we were back on the road, just outside of north Philadelphia.

"Do you two see what I see?" my mother asked, looking through the rearview mirror.

We both looked back. A New Jersey State Police vehicle was a couple of car lengths behind us.

"Damn. We haven't even officially gotten into Jersey yet," Adam grunted.

I turned around. I sighed. "Here we go again . . ."

It never fails. You're driving along a highway, freeway, expressway, city street, or country road, minding your own business, and suddenly you're tagged by a trooper or cop for no reason. Oh, sure, they try to come up with one—you made an illegal lane change, you made a lane change without signaling, you were driving over the speed limit, one of your taillights is cracked, your headlights weren't on, your license plate appeared obstructed, your gas tank is leaking—but you know and they know it's a bogus charge. And you don't fit the description of a suspect they received an APB on—you fit the description of the criminal they *know* you are.

After all . . . you're Black.

I'm sure the Driving While Black daymare my stepfather, Anderson, experienced with my mother is one of the reasons why he doesn't take the trip with us. Eight years ago, he and my mother visited his relatives in Richmond. They usually took Amtrak, but decided to drive that time—a decision they would both regret. Just outside of Trenton, they were flagged down by a trooper.

"Is there a problem, Officer?" Anderson innocently asked. My mother knew that that was the wrong question to ask—you don't challenge someone who, by the authority of the government, can take your life with impunity—and that if the officer had any mischief in mind when he stopped them, it would be carried out with much more glee now that, in his mind, Anderson had given him a reason to fuck with them.

And that's exactly what happened. Because he had the nerve to inquire as to why he was pulled over, Anderson was ordered out of the car (which he initially protested, but my mother urged him to), handcuffed, and forced to sit on the side of the highway. My mother was escorted to and placed in a police vehicle while drug-sniffing Dobermans canvassed every inch of the vehicle. It didn't matter that Anderson owned the car he was driving. It didn't matter that he was current on his insurance. It didn't matter that the car hadn't received a single citation, not even a traffic ticket. It didn't matter that he was a federal employee (he's a mailman). And it certainly didn't matter that he didn't have a criminal record, for we all know that any Black man without a criminal record is just a Black man who hasn't been caught yet, right?

The only "drugs" they found was a bottle of Tylenol (which happened to be empty) and my mother's vitamin supplements in the glove compartment. After being detained for ninety minutes (much of that time was spent waiting for the illegal search squad to arrive), they were allowed to leave. No sorry-for-the-inconvenience, no explanation, no apology, not even a good-bye (at least they didn't tear out the seats or junk the trunk, leaving it all sitting on the road for them to put back together; I understand that has happened to many). To add insult to this injury, Anderson was issued a ticket for "driving erratically." Neither one of them said a word during the rest of that drive back home. My mother just held his hand and wiped his tears as they poured down his face. It was the first time she had ever seen him cry.

And that was the last time he drove on I-95.

The "War on Drugs" (which is nothing but a war on and against Black and Brown people), as well as the already widely accepted misbelief that most crime is committed by us, has given law enforcement the perfect excuse to harass and humiliate citizens whose only "crime" is riding down the road in the wrong skin. The only racial profiling that should exist is the kind that weeds out white cops who believe niggers have no rights.

163

LOVE
THE
ONE
YOU'RE
WITH

After they blipped their siren and lights, my mother pulled over. She didn't have to tell us to be cool and let her do the talking; she had already schooled us on the do's and don'ts when interacting with cops (any Black parent who hasn't/doesn't is committing child abuse). Having come across more than a few Bull Connors in her time (including being shot at by one Nazi-like country bumpkin who didn't appreciate her and other "colored rabble-rousers" coming into the Deep South to help register voters in the late sixties), she doesn't trust them—even if they are Black (as she argues, "You can change the complexion, but you can't change the culture"). So she gave us both, at the age of eight, the ten-commandments-for-survival lecture on what to do if we're approached or stopped by police: don't run; stay calm; keep your hands in view at all times; do not exhibit body language that could be construed as "threatening"; don't resist or struggle with them; only speak when you're asked a question; be polite and respectful—even if they aren't; if you're arrested, call her; don't make any statements until she's arrived with an attorney (she's kept Henry Kleghorne's number right beside her phone and in her purse the past twenty-plus years); and if we are lost or need help and see a police officer, go in the other direction.

Two troopers—both white, in their early forties—approached the car on either side. One stopped just in front of Adam's door. He had that unattractive handlebar mustache and looked as if he were about to drop twins. He stood with his arms folded over his kangaroo pouch, a toothpick in his mouth. He reminded me of Sheriff Buford T. Justice in *Smokey & the Bandit I* and *II*.

"Could I see your license and registration?" the other one asked my mother, minus the *please*. He was thin, shorter, dorky (very Barney Fife–ish) and, like his partner, was wearing tinted glasses. He took them off and peered at my brother and me (we sat up right with our hands folded on our laps, as if we were in grammar school) as she retrieved the requested documents from her overhead pocket. She handed them to him.

He looked them over. "Uh, Mrs. Walker, where you comin' from, Florida?"

Translation: *Are you transporting drugs from the Sunshine State up north?*

"No. We're coming from D.C.," she answered.

"And what type of business did you have there?"

"We were visiting my first husband, their father, at the Vietnam Veterans Memorial."

His eyes bugged. "Uh, the Wall?"

"Yes. Today would've been his fiftieth birthday." I was truly loving this; she was going to make him feel like shit for pulling us over when he knew he had no right to. I held back a chuckle.

But he had to try to save himself, so he turned his attention to my brother and me. "So, these are your sons? Uh, do they have ID?"

Mind you, he asked *her* if *we* had ID. We were certainly one of the reasons—if not *the* primary one—why he stopped us (if there's more than one Black man in a car, they gotta be on their way to or from trouble), but not important enough to address directly.

She nodded. "Yes, they do."

Instead of going into our pants or jackets, we both reached into our shirt pockets and drew them out. Of course we waited until he was at our respective windows before we did (his partner didn't budge). You cannot rely on a cop (especially a white one) to warn a Black man *not* to reach for something. How many times have we heard in cases where a Black man has been shot, "He made a suspicious move and I thought he was going for a gun"?

He gave them to his partner, who returned to their car. You'd think he would have at least had the courtesy to say something like "This will only take a few minutes"—or, better yet, explain why we were stopped—but, of course, he didn't.

After a few minutes, the other trooper returned. "They check out okay," he grumbled, almost sounding disappointed that my mother wasn't driving a stolen car and that neither one of her sons had an outstanding warrant.

The thin one's face became flushed; he was embarrassed. But he tried to mask it with a very fake smile. He trudged back over to the driver's side and handed everything back to my mother. "Uh, I think that will be it. You can go."

She dropped it all in her lap. "Thank you. Have a good night." As he shuffled away, she rolled up her window. When we were back on the road, she frowned: "Officer Giardello."

I giggled as I passed my brother's ID to him. "Did you memorize his number, too?" I asked. I knew she had. I pulled down the over-

165

LOVE
THE
ONE
YOU'RE
WITH

head compartment above my seat and retrieved the emergency pen and paper.

She grinned. She recited it. I wrote it down.

Adam huffed. "It's a good thing you didn't have that knapsack. They would've wanted to search it." Indeed. And because of that "suspicious-looking bag" that I was no doubt "trying to conceal," they could argue they had "probable cause" to have all of us get out of the car and strip it. My mother has filed four complaints with the New Jersey State Police (including one over the incident with Anderson, although Anderson didn't want her to) and reported them all to the ACLU. If they ever decide to take on this cause (contrary to Caucasian consensus, these aren't just "isolated incidents"), she'll be the first to sign on to a class-action lawsuit and testify at congressional hearings.

The remainder of our journey was an uneventful one. When we got back to Longwood, we were treated to a delicious Sunday dinner prepared by Anderson: steak and garlic potatoes, glazed peas and carrots, and banana pudding for dessert. After the meal, my mother took a nap (she had to do the midnight shift; she's a nurse). Adam went to see Lynette, who lives in Newark. Instead of heading back to Brooklyn, I planned to stay the night in my old room. So I helped Anderson clean the kitchen.

We were loading the dishwasher when I broke our silence. "Can I ask you a question?"

"Sure."

"Does . . . does it bother you that we go to see my father each year?"

"No," he nonchalantly replied. "Why would it?"

"Well . . . I guess . . . most second husbands wouldn't be so . . . so accepting of something like that."

"I guess I'm not like most second husbands."

"But do you feel . . . left out because we visit him each year?"

"No. You all were already a family before I came along and you didn't stop being that family when I did. So I believe it's important for you all to have . . . a reunion each year. I'd never tell your mother she can't have it." He nodded toward the living room. "Do you know why your father's picture sits on the mantel above the fireplace?" It's next to their wedding photo (they'll be celebrating twelve years this August).

"Yeah—'cause you don't want a frying pan upside your head." I snickered.

He chuckled. "No. It's because I wanted it there."

"You . . . wanted it there?"

"Yes, I did."

"Why?"

"Why wouldn't I?"

I stated what I thought was the obvious. "Because it's her first husband."

"Well, that's exactly why it's there. I don't have to tell you how much your mother loved your father . . . how much she *still* loves him. Her love for him didn't die when he did. And she has living proof of that love: you and your brother. So I can't expect her to leave him in a photo album, store that album in a trunk in the attic, and just forget about him. If she could just put him away like that, she could do the same with me."

Hmm . . . jood point.

"I couldn't love or fall in love with a woman like that, and that's not the kind of woman I love and fell in love with. So how could I be that kind of man? What kind of man would *I* be if I expected her to deny her past?"

"You wouldn't be."

"I know."

We smiled.

"Let me ask *you* a question," he said.

"Okay."

He seemed to be searching for the right words. "Do you think your father would be happy with how I've taken care of your mother, you, and your brother?"

I was taken aback. "Why do you ask that?"

"I . . . I just wonder sometimes."

"Yes. I'm sure he is happy that she found someone like you . . ." I then realized why he asked that—and whose opinion about his role as a husband and guardian he *really* wanted. "And *I* am happy she found someone like you," I added.

"You are?"

"Of course. You've made her very happy. And if she's happy, I'm happy. You've also been a great stepfather."

He was startled by that admission. "I . . . I have?"

"Yes, you have."

167

LOVE
THE
ONE
YOU'RE
WITH

He wasn't convinced. "That I don't know about."

"Why?"

"I didn't know what being a father was supposed to be like. Ha, I still don't know. With you and your brother, half the time I didn't know what to say or do. The other half I just let your mother handle things."

"Well, they must've been the right things to do. If you did the wrong things, we wouldn't have any type of relationship."

He considered that, then sighed. "I guess I was always afraid that . . . you two would hate me for trying to fill your father's shoes."

"Being our stepfather didn't mean you had to fill our father's shoes. It meant you had to be Anderson and you were. And that was always good enough."

He smiled. "Uh . . . don't you mean *jood*?"

I laughed. "Yeah."

"Thanks, Mitch. I appreciate you telling me that. It's *jood* to hear." He held out his hand. I shook it. We simultaneously pulled each other closer and embraced.

I exhaled deeply in his arms. "You're more than welcome."

13

"So, Mitchell . . . you ready?"

I was at the Hit Factory, one of the premier
recording studios in the world, to lay down vocals on
a track for Kevron, a twenty-three-year-old out of the
Cabrini Green projects in Chicago who is being
trumpeted as the new R. Kelly. Well, at least that's
how *he* views himself. He doesn't have R. Kelly's
songwriting talent or pipes. But he and MCA, his
record label, are smart enough to recognize a winning formula when they see it. Thanks to Kelly (and
groups like Jodeci), a new brand of Black male vocal-
ist has emerged (some would say *sub*merged) on the
scene: harmonizin' homiez. New jack swing has
given way to new gangsta swing, with singers taking
on a more thuggish exterior. Some are throwing on
football and basketball jerseys, baggy jeans and overalls, Timbs, do-rags, and striking that cool pose in
order to compete with and complement their hip-
hop contemporaries. Just a few years ago, Ralph
Tresvant was extolling the virtue of "Sensitivity" in a
man; today, it's all about the Bump 'n Grind. Getting next to her is not the objective now; getting all
up *inside* of her is. As a result, old school has really
become *old:* veterans like Jeffrey Osborne, Teddy
Pendergrass, Peabo Bryson, and Freddie Jackson
can't get a record deal, have found themselves on
nondescript labels that have little to no clout in the
industry, or have gone the soundtrack route (be it
movie themes, television series, or commercial jin-
gles). Even Luther's catching flak: he's still cranking
out platinum albums (I contributed to his last one,
Songs), but his sound has been dismissed as wilted
and wimpy, just a little too middle-classish.

With less of an emphasis on romance and more on raunch, the door was busted wide open for those with limited skills to croak and crack their way onto the charts—like Kevron. Legend has it he first tried his hand at rapping, but was apparently booed off more than one stage in his 'hood. So he switched genres but kept the ghetto gear. He hooked up with an indie called Inner City Soundz and produced a couple of hits with the not-so-subtle titles "Swimmin' in Your Sea" and "Lick You All Over." Both videos were shot in black-and-white and cost less than $25,000 each—and it shows. The direction is sloppy, the lighting too dark, and the hoochies look like real dime-store hookers he pulled off their corners for a few hours. Yet despite this (or probably because of it), they became favorites on both BET and MTV. Add his faithful yet uninspired cover of the Isley Brothers' "Between the Sheets" (which continues to receive heavy play on Quiet Storm/Midnite Luv stations), and it's not hard to see why his debut, *Kev's Freak Show*, went triple platinum. In today's rap-saturated market, that's no small feat for a Black male singer, and the big white wigs took notice: after a bidding war, he signed a three-album deal for a reported $8 million, which included a $500,000-cash signing bonus.

I still find it hard to swallow that he's a better singer than a rapper: he sounds like someone is trying to choke the song out of him. He tries to disguise his gurgling by pulling a Barry White, speaking many of the lyrics in that bass-boomin' bedroom voice, but even there you know he's fakin' it because he has to. So why has he gotten over? His looks. In rap, being a pretty boy wouldn't score him points, but in R&B it does. So the ladies (and men) swoon even though he can't croon.

Neither his vocals (or lack thereof) nor his appearance are what he's *most* famous for. Not since the days of Run-DMC, Slick Rick, and Salt-N-Pepa has an artist adorned himself with so much jewelry. He's always draped in gold rings, gold ropes, gold watches, gold bracelets, gold caps, gold anklets (which he wants you to see by having his left pant leg rolled up a few inches below his knee), and one gold earring (two would certainly get folks to talkin' . . . not that they aren't already).

And tonight was no different. The producer, Bryant Bledsoe, introduced us. He was a big man—a *very* big man. We're talkin' Shaq-Attack Big. Stocky and stately, he was Snicker-bar brown and wore black horn-rim glasses. He could've been Kevron's bodyguard. Kevron's *real* bodyguard—a wide brutha just as tall as Bryant who wore a permanent scowl on his scarred face (had he been slashed?)—blocked my path as I attempted to enter the room.

"Can I help you?" he snarled.

Bryant interjected. "It's all right, Mack. He's the session singer."

"Mack" moved to the side but never took his eyes off me.

They both rose as I approached.

Bryant and I did the "brotha shakembrace" thing. "Good to meet you, Mitchell."

"Same here."

"Mitchell Crawford, this is Kevron. Kev, Mitchell."

"Good ta meetcha, brotha." Kevron smiled, exposing a top row of gold as he halfheartedly shook my hand, opting instead to encase me in his left arm.

"You, too."

Kevron was even more gorgeous in person: six feet tall, skin the color of a Planters peanut, an oval face, light brown eyes that sat far below his square forehead and an inch above his plump cheeks, a perfectly cut trail-line-thin beard and goatee, very thick lips that glistened like his bald head (which a gold-and-black bandanna was tied around), and a very pumped-up bod (the Jordan jersey accented his buff chest and arms, which were both decorated with tattoos: his name on the left and LUVA BOYEE on the right). The loveliest features, however, were that *huge* ass (we're talkin' two halves of a watermelon attached to his backside, okay?) and that very visible bulge (which grew as we hugged). Both could barely be contained in his red "snap-off" sweatpants (the snaps traveled from the bottom cuff up to the waist); those trousers were packin' so much in I was just waitin' (and anticipatin') for those top buttons to pop open and off. And he smelled *heavenly:* the sweet aroma penetrated my nostrils like a cough drop. But all that jewelry—*two* rings on each finger except his thumbs, a watch on each wrist, a dozen chains around his neck, the lone ranger in his left earlobe, and a few anklets—was unattractive and distracting. *This* is the reason he has such a hulking hunchback for a bodyguard.

Bryant shuffled together some papers on the table. "I'll be right

171

LOVE
THE
ONE
YOU'RE
WITH

back. I'll call upstairs to make sure things are all set." He scooted out of the room.

Kevron and I smiled at each other and turned away as if we were shy students meeting on the first day of school. There was a very awkward moment of silence.

"Yo, you want somethin' ta drink?" Kevron asked.

"Uh, some water would be fine."

He turned to his bodyguard. "Yo, Mack. Get tha brotha some beverage."

Mack trounced out of the room, causing pictures on the walls to shift.

"Yo, I wanna thank ya fuh doin' this on such short notice." He gestured with his hands.

"Sure."

"You listen ta my music?"

I wanted so bad to say, *You call what you make* music? but restrained myself. "Yes, I do."

He assumed the homie stance: upper body bent back and slightly to the right, right leg forward, left hand under his right arm, and his right hand under his chin. "Got a fav'rite cut?"

You *know* I didn't have one, but just to make him happy (and not get fired from this gig) . . . "You're Gonna Love What I Got." I would've said "Ass Bonanza," Pooquie's fave (he loves to be plowed as it's played), but knew *that* could lead to a place we didn't need to travel to . . .

"Ah . . . that's tha dopest cut on that CD. I wanted them ta release it, but you know how da Man is: it's his way or tha fuckin' highway."

He then started croaking and cracking it—which made me *cringe*. It's one thing to hear him on CD—it's quite another to hear him in person. He sounds worse in the flesh. (At least he has the sense to know he cannot sing in public—his only "live" musical performance has been on Showtime at the Apollo, and he talked through both songs. But given the buildup he's about to receive, he'll have to take some voice lessons *fast*.)

After the first verse, he warbled to the chorus: "I'm gonna swing it, tha way *you* want it, I'm gonna bring it, tha way *you* want it, don't worry, bay-bay, *you're* gonna love what I got." Hmm . . . in the song, he doesn't emphasize *you* or *you're* and actually says, *"Girl,* you're gonna love what I got." Was the man trying to serenade me?

If so, it wasn't working. But it was working for *him:* the bulge I didn't think could get any larger or longer did.

Thank God both Mack and Bryant returned. Kevron's great eye candy and the idea of being hit on by a celebrity like him was flattering, but I wouldn't have been able to stand one more bad note.

As Mack handed me a bottle of Evian, Bryant clapped his hands. "Well, gents, it's time to get buzy."

We made our way through a maze of a hallway, zigzagging so much I just knew we were lost, until we arrived at the control room.

As Mack stood guard outside and Kevron stared me down, Bryant briefed me on the song. It was called "All the Man You Need." Immediately I thought it would be a variation on Whitney's hit (which Luther had just recorded), but it wasn't. A smoky ballad, it contains an interpolation of Bobby Brown's "Rock with You," so I'm sure all those hip-hopsters will warm up to it. But considering some of the other songs Kevron's done, this one was tame when it came to sexually suggestive lyrics.

The chorus:

> Come on girl
> I'll take the lead
> Let me show you
> that I'm all the man you need
> Come on girl
> Your hunger I'll feed
> just let Kev be
> all the man you need

And the bridge:

> I promise
> it'll be an unbelievable night
> I promise
> you'll want it over and over again
> for the rest of your life

173

LOVE
THE
ONE
YOU'RE
WITH

Tantalizing yet tasteful, it was very similar to Boyz II Men's "I'll Make Love to You" in tone and flavor. But, once again, it has to be all about Kev: I'd bet my session check that the songwriter didn't pen it *for* him.

Because it wasn't as sexually explicit as his other tunes, Bryant believed "All the Man You Need" needed, as he put it, "a softer anchor." He had already recorded it with two of his regular female session singers but felt they were a bit too soft. So he called up Jimmy Newland, the brother who "discovered" me when I performed Stevie's "You & I" at Babyface and B.D.'s wedding last year. Jimmy raved about my range and said he could get me some session work; as far as Pooquie was concerned, Jimmy really wanted to *do* some session work on me, and not the singin' kind. But he's never made a move on me and has come through with those moonlighting jobs with folks like Will Downing, Pebbles, Regina Belle, Faith Evans, and Phyllis Hyman (it would be one of the last songs she recorded before committing suicide). Both Bryant and Jimmy graduated from Howard in '88 with degrees in music management, and Bryant knew that Jimmy would be able to locate a singer whose voice would be recognized as male but had "a little feminine flair to it"—and who would come quick and cheap (figuratively speaking, of course). And after years of screaming along with Aretha, Chaka, and Patti, I fit the bill.

After listening to the track twice (as usual, Kevron croaks and cracks up a storm), doing an a cappella run-through and an instrumental-track sing-along, Bryant taped me. I suggested that instead of repeating the entire chorus at the end, I could riff off of "All the man you need," particularly since Kev was *bad*-libbing "I'll take the lead" and "Your hunger I'll feed." They appreciated the change.

I got comfortable in the studio, sitting on a stool. I put on the headphones. I took a very deep breath. "I'm ready."

Bryant did a countdown. "Five, four, three, two, one . . ." He pointed to me.

When the red light went on and the "Recording" sign flashed, I closed my eyes. I always think of Pooquie while singing. And, more than any other song I had been asked to sing on, this one fit us like a G. I could see us getting very freaky-deaky off of this. And I guess that visual helped bring out what they wanted.

For, five minutes and eleven seconds later . . .

"That's a take," Bryant bellowed. "We're gonna play it back."

We listened to it.

Kevron was thrilled with the result. "Yo, Money, them vocals was *tight*."

Bryant agreed. "Yeah, Mitchell, this is *exactly* what we need. Jimmy was right—you were the best choice to help us out on this track."

"Thanks. Does this mean I'm finished?"

"Yeah. I still have some mixing to do, but you're done. Just make sure you sign the register so you get credited."

I took off the headphones and I stepped out of the studio. Kevron and Bryant were no longer in the control room.

Montee was. What the hell is he doing here?

He grinned, slowly spinning left to right in one of the black leather swivel chairs. "Thanks for making my song sound so good."

His presence truly worked me; all I could muster was a very weak . . . "Your song?"

"Yeah, my song. I wrote it."

"*You* wrote that song?"

"Yeah, *I* wrote that song."

Silence.

"Well . . . it's a great song," I congratulated.

"Thanks. You made it *sound* great."

"Thanks," I gushed.

"Welcome. You make *him* sound good—and *that* ain't an easy thing to do. That brother thinks pitch is only something Dwight Gooden does."

"Indeed."

"It's obvious you don't. Alan was right: You got a voice on you. I wasn't gonna come down tonight, but *some*thin' told me to. I'm glad I did."

Silence.

"So . . . who were you thinking about?" he asked.

"Huh?"

"While singin', who was on your mind?"

"What makes you think I was thinking of someone while singing?"

175

LOVE
THE
ONE
YOU'RE
WITH

"Singin' that song the way you was? Don't even try to front. I know. *I* been there."

I shrugged. "Maybe I was . . . maybe I wasn't."

He grinned. "Was it me?"

I frowned. "No, it wasn't."

He studied me. "You sure?"

"Yes, I'm sure."

" 'Cause if it was . . . I was just gonna say that . . . the feelin' is mutual." He rose and stood in front of me, our faces just an inch apart. "With me writin' 'em and you singin' 'em . . . we could really make some *beautiful* music together."

We gazed.

I stepped back. "I . . . I'd better go."

He followed me out of the control room. "Mitchell, wait . . ."

I stopped.

"I'll be singing at a club called Oasis this Friday night. I play there once a month. I'd love for you to be my special guest."

"I . . . I don't know."

"Just think about it, okay? After sharing your gift with us, with me . . . I just want to return the favor. And I'd really love to know what you think of me, of my act."

"I . . . I . . . I'll think about it."

That was jood enough for him. "Great." He took out a business card; he wrote on the back of it. "This is the address. If you need directions, you can call that number."

I took it. "Good night," I mustered, breezing up the hall. When I knew I was out of sight, I stopped to catch my breath. I felt flushed. They say it only takes a minute to fall in love, but it only takes a second to *fall*—and I almost did just that.

I needed some water. I had left my bottle in the studio, but wasn't about to go back in that direction. I dipped into a nearby bathroom, failing to notice the "Out of Order" sign. It turns out it wasn't out of order. It was placed there for a different reason.

As I was standing in the vestibule, the first thing I remember was the smell. Kevron's smell.

And then the slapping. Something was being slapped. Slapped repeatedly. Slapped *very* hard.

And a yelp followed each slap.

I carefully pushed open the door leading to the stalls.

Whack!

"Mph, Big Poppa, spank dat azz!"

Whack, whack!

"Oooh!"

Whack, whack, whack!

"Oooh oooh!"

I was frozen. What do I do? Part of me wanted to see, *really* see, whether or not the rumors (from Gene and Pooquie) I heard were true. And if he was *really* trying to serenade me.

I crept to the final stall, stopping a head's peek away.

"I'm gonna get one mo' lick befo' I stick ya . . ."

Slurpslurpslurp.

"Ssss, *yeah*, eat dat *azz*, eat it all up, *yeah!*"

I peeked. I *geeked*.

Holding on to the top of the stall, Kevron was kneeling on the handicapped handlebar attached to its wall, his big azz stuck out and being eaten out by Bryant. Both were naked, although Kevron had on his sneakers, do-rag, and (of course) the jewelry.

I thought Bryant was jerkin' off as he feasted, but he was actually rolling a condom down his dick. Now that's what you call *skill*.

After arming himself for battle, Bryant stuck one, then two, then three, then all four fingers up Kevron's hole, preppin' it for the real thing.

"*Ooh*, come *on*, Big Poppa, *yeah*, give it ta me, come *on*," Kevron begged as that booty shivered.

The position was perfect; Bryant didn't have to rise on his toes, stoop down, or maneuver Kevron's ass (Hmm . . . I got the feeling they'd been there before). He just aimed for and slid that very long and very thick dick all the way inside. No red or yellow lights, no yield or stop signs.

Kevron took it all—with a big ol' smile. "Oh *yeeeeaaaah*, Big Poppa . . ."

"Ha, ya like dat dick, huh?"

"*Mmm-hmm.*"

Kevron liked it so much that he started twirlin' and twistin'.

177

LOVE
THE
ONE
YOU'RE
WITH

"Uh-huh, yeah, work dat dick," Bryant demanded.

Relaxin' for the ride, Bryant crossed his arms behind his back and started bumpin' 'n humpin'.

"Uh-*huh*, Big Poppa, *mph*, take *all* dat pussy, *yeah!*"

"Ha, don't worry, this pussy gonna be *all* mine . . ."

Bryant slid in and out, teasing Kevron.

"Nah, nah, *nah*, Big Poppa, don't fuck wit' me like that, now, *she-it!*"

"Ha, I'll *fuck* witcha any way I want . . . now take *that!*"

He plowed inside.

"Ooh *yeah*, Big Poppa, you da man, *yeah!*"

"Yeah, I'm *all* the man *you* need, right,?"

"*Uh-huh!* BP, bang it like ya *knooooow!*"

He did.

Bryant began violently banging Kevron (or, rather, his head and shoulders) into the stall wall, never missing a funky fucking beat.

"*Ya better act like ya know! I . . . better . . . not . . . EVER . . . hear . . . you . . . singin' . . . a . . . song . . . fuh . . . some . . . OTHER . . . nigga . . . like . . . that . . . A-GAIN!*"

And all through that, the brother's glasses never moved, even though they were hangin' right on the tip of his nose.

Every word was accented with a *THRUST* that I know had to be so painful it couldn't be nothin' but pleasurable.

And Kevron showed just how pleasurable it was: he started *sangin'*.

That's right, *sangin'*.

I mean, this boyee was *wailin'*, okay? Starting off in the low basement bass register and going so soprano high, my ears popped. The harder Bryant bootay-slammed him, the louder and higher that voice soared.

With Bryant pumpin' up that jam (*"I'm gonna FUCK that song right OUTA yo' AZZ!"*) and Kevron sweepin' the scales (*"I'm singin it fuh you, bay, I'm singin' fuh YOU, bay, ya know I'm singin' it JUST fuh YOU, bay, so keep on DOIN' it 'n DOIN' it 'n DOIN' it RIIIIIIIIIIIIIIIGHT!"*), I almost busted out laughing. I had to get out of there before I did.

Kevron *does* know what pitch is. If Bryant could only get him to sing like *that* on CD . . .

14

"Hello?"

"Hay, Baby."

"Hi, Pooquie. Where are you?"

"Back at tha hotel."

"Why? The show isn't over yet."

"It is fuh us, Baby."

"Ah."

"I can't believe them mutha-fuckas."

"Well, I know you were rooting for Warren. And he really deserved to win both. But the Queen and Salt-N-Pepa were overdue."

"Yeah. But at least I got ta meet him."

"You did?"

"Yeah. He madd cool, Baby. And y'all could be twins."

"Really?"

"Uh-huh. You'll see. I took a picture wit' him. He invited us ta a party at his spot later on."

"Us?"

"Yeah. Me 'n' Malice. And his posse."

"Mmm. You meet anybody else?"

"Yeah. Snoop, Dre, Yo Yo, Ice Cube."

"Boy, the whole West Coast crew. I know you were in heaven."

"And I met one of them brothas from Boyz II Men, tha real skinny one."

"Shawn Stockman?"

"Yeah. He had his Grammy. And I ran inta that fella hostin' tha show."

"Paul Reiser?"

"Yeah. I was comin' outa tha bathroom and he was comin' in. He is one *un*funny mutha-fucka."

I chuckled. "I agree. He was a bad choice. I'm sure he won't ever be asked back."

"They shoulda got somebody like Martin Lawrence."

"Ha, he'd be too much for them. He's not tame like Paul."

"Don'tcha mean borin'?"

"Uh-huh."

"You still watchin' tha show?"

"Uh-huh. But with the sound down. Never know when a Negro may pop up. How did the scene go this morning?"

"It went a'ight."

"How do you feel about it?"

"Well . . . it ain't like all my bizness was out there fuh tha whole world ta see. My back was ta tha camera."

"Ah. So the world will get to see Raheim Rivers's rump, huh?"

He sighed. "Yeah."

"I don't think you should worry about it. It's not as if they had you all do it just because. Men do walk around nude in a locker room."

"We'll see what ratin' they give it now. It was guaranteed a R wit' all that cussin'. But wit' us walkin' 'round butt-bootay nekkid, they prob'ly gonna slap it wit' a NC-17."

"As many times Kevin Costner has shown his pale ass in a film? I don't see why they would."

"C'mon, Baby. We talkin' 'bout brothas, not some white boy. They gave them folks behind *Jason's Lyric* grief over a movie poster. I can imagine what they gonna say about this."

"Well, it's really a *man* thing, not a Black thing. They tripped over how Jada was positioned on the poster. If it were Allen Payne, they wouldn't have cared. And speaking of Allen: when *Rebound* is released on video, I'll have two of the most beautiful asses ever captured on film in my collection." I giggled.

"*I* better be number one."

"You know you are." I kissed into the phone. I could feel him blush. "You just have two more scenes to do, right?"

"Yeah."

"Do you need to go over your lines?"

"Nah, cuz I only got one line in both scenes."

"Mmm . . . when it comes down to it, they actually paid you to shoot hoops and walk around nude in a locker room."

"Uh-huh. Tha easiest green I ever made. So, how was yo' day?"

"It was okay. Nothin' special. Just went to work and came home."

"Ah. How my homie, Willoughby, doin'?"

"He's doing fine. You'll be happy to know he received the highest grade in the class this term."

"He did?"

"Yup."

"Wow, Baby. I know he gonna flip."

"I'm sure the ones who will flip are the parents of some of the other students when they see their children's grades. I'm gonna get an earful tomorrow."

"Oh, yeah. It's open school night."

"Uh-huh."

"You better not fuhget yo' Tylenol this time."

"Ha, I already have my pouch ready. I'm not gonna be caught off guard again."

"Jood. Any word from Jozie?"

I sighed. "Well . . . she didn't receive the agreement today. They said they need another week."

"Another week?"

"Mmm-hmm."

"Why?"

"As Jozie expected, it all comes down to language. They are trying to put things in a way that puts them in the best light. And, as they're no doubt discovering, that ain't gonna be easy. But Jozie told them they have to show her something by Monday so we can see what direction they are headed in— and if they are going the wrong way, point them in the *right* direction."

"A'ight. You feelin' better about it?"

"I . . . I guess I am."

"You should, Baby. They'll know better next time ta fuck wit' one of us. When I get home, we gonna celebrate."

"How you think we should?"

"Ha, you know how." He giggled.

"Uh-huh. Now, you know we never need a reason to do *that*."

"Nah, we don't, but that's as jood a reason as any."

"Yes, I suppose so. Oh, at least *your* papers came today."

"Did they?"

"Yup."

181

LOVE
THE
one
YOU're
WITH

"Didja look 'em over?"

"I started to."

"Whatcha think?"

"Your rental agreement looks okay. Are they really giving you the last month free?"

"Yeah, cuz I'm payin' a full year up front."

"I just knew that was a misprint. But if they're gonna do that, they can at least do something similar with your mom's co-op. Since you're paying for it in cash, they should knock five or ten percent off the purchase price and give you some kind of break on the closing costs."

"A'ight. Did they say when her apartment is gonna be ready?"

"The letter says you'll be able to show it to her in a couple of weeks, after they finish the bathroom."

"Jood. You think she gonna like it?"

"She's gonna love it."

Silence.

"Little Bit?"

"Yes?"

"I miss you."

"I miss you, too, Pooquie."

"Uh . . . how 'bout givin' me some mo'."

"Huh?"

"Gimme some mo' of that long distance love."

"Don't tell me you want a repeat of last week . . ."

"Yeah."

"You can't make it to Sunday?"

"*Hell* no!"

I laughed. "You got enough time? What time are they supposed to be picking you up?"

"In a half hour."

I considered it. "So . . . are you in your birthday suit?"

"Yeah."

"You are?"

"Been in it all this time."

"Hmm . . . you got on the Timbs and the cap?"

"Yup. And I done already assumed tha position."

"Well . . . when you all oiled up and ready to go, how can I refuse?"

15

Now I know how *my* teachers felt on open-school night.

The last thing a parent wants to hear is that their child has done something wrong. It's not that they can't believe it—after all, I'll bet many have whooped their kids for disobeying and misbehaving—it's that they don't *want* to believe it. I get two earfuls of that disbelief during parent-teacher conferences, the most common refrain expressed being: "Oh, *no, not my* child!" The sisters have it down to a science: that neck starts to twistin' and those hands get to flailin' and those eyes get to jumpin' and those teeth get to knashin' and those nostrils start to flarin' and those temples get to pulsin' and that forehead gets to perspirin'—and they just *implode*. Not only could their child *never*, under *any* circumstances, talk in class, be late for class, disrupt the class, be caught doodling during class, not complete their homework assignment, not turn in their homework on time, not turn in their homework at all, cut my class, or play hooky from school altogether, but you, the teacher, are more than mistaken for even suggesting their child is capable of such things—you're insane.

"Are you crazy?" several have said in a joking manner, but I knew they weren't joking. One would *have* to be crazy to accuse their baby, their baby boy, their baby girl, their baby cakes, their cupcake, their Pooh bear, their honey bear, their sweetums, their candy cane, their candy apple, their apple tart, their apple dumpling, their cream puff, their muffin, their angel cake, their angel face, their angel, of anything. I don't like to be the bearer of bad news, but I often have to shatter that glass bubble they're living in.

Some of these kids have their parents so hoodwinked, so wash-bucked, so bushwhacked, so bamboozled, so snowed that even when the evidence is presented to prove the charges, they still can't (or won't) accept it. I see just how manipulative children—and how gullible their parents—can be. But it's usually the parent that has duped themself—and they expect you to join them in the delusion.

I do temper the not-so-good news with the positive in a tone that isn't judgmental (I don't plan on being mowed down like that obnoxious teacher was by Kathleen Turner in *Serial Mom*). But that still isn't good enough for some. In addition to being personally offended, a few have the gall to demand that you admit their child is your favorite. All teachers *do* have favorites—and I am no exception. There are those students who literally light up the moment I walk into the room—their notebooks are opened, their homework assignment ready to recite to the class, and they're rocking in their seats with anticipation. It's a joy to see them so excited, and that gives *me* joy. And there are students who are a little rough around the edges, challenging me to work a little harder to reach them, and when I do, the payoff is great for the both of us. But while I may have my favorites, I don't *play* favorites; I make sure each student gets the attention and receives the adulation they need and deserve—and with three classes that each have no more than twenty students, this isn't hard for me to do. But playing favorites is exactly what I would be doing if I, like other teachers, disclosed to any parent that their child is the top—and because I don't, folks get indignant.

Too often, what should be a brainstorming session to determine how we can work together to ensure their child's performance improves or continues on its current path turns into a trial in which I, the accused, am expected to explain, justify, defend my right as a teacher to run my classroom the way I choose. Now, I can understand not understanding my technique, or the system I use to rate a student's work. But I gather some of these parents are used to teachers just rolling over and going along (that *is*, after all, how so many kids graduate from high school barely knowing how to read or write). As they throw a tantrum, one has to wonder who is the parent and who is the child—sometimes the kids act more grown-up than the grown-ups. And their parent(s) being a pain in the ass means I can always count on leaving school that night (or afternoon) with a pain above my neck.

But at least it's an ordeal that only lasts for two to three hours once every two months. In fact, it's a minor irritant considering how much I love to teach. And who would've thought that a man I despise would be responsible for providing me with what's turned out to be the opportunity of a lifetime?

IF THERE'S ONE THING FOOLIANI HAS DONE AS THE MAYOR OF New York City that I agree with (and there's *only* one thing), it's his giving the green light to Knowledge Hall. Located just a few blocks from my apartment in Fort Greene, Brooklyn, in a three-story building where New York's firefighters were trained in the 1970s, Knowledge Hall is a charter school conceived and run by Elvin Macintosh, a forty-four-year-old Black Republican and former Wall Street wiz. Many view Elvin's being crowned the "director" (principal doesn't sound important enough for him) of Knowledge Hall as a quid pro quo for the work he did on both of Fooliani's mayoral campaigns as a field organizer (not to mention the $25,000 in campaign funds he's alleged to have contributed). But it turns out that Elvin (who doesn't have children and isn't married) was so disgusted with the tales he constantly heard from friends about the education (or lack thereof) that their children were getting attending overcrowded, understaffed, underequipped public schools that he drafted and began shopping the plans for Knowledge Hall in the late eighties. But he couldn't convince either Ed Koch or David Dinkins, the former mayors, or the Board of Education to support the plan.

That all changed with Fooliani's being voted into office in 1993. Barely two months after he was sworn in, he announced that a dozen community-run schools would open around the city in the fall of 1994, and one of those would be Knowledge Hall. Many educators and liberal politicos vehemently opposed the proposed institutions, viewing the projects as a not-so-veiled attempt to privatize the school system with public tax dollars (minus a voucher program). They also warned that parents would be playing a dangerous game of Russian roulette with their children's futures, not knowing what kind of people could be teaching them since some of those recruited (such as

185
LOVE
THE
ONE
YOU'RE
WITH

myself) would not be accredited and have little to no teaching experience. But since each school had the backing of the community it was located in, and many parents were already very familiar with the incompetence and corruption that plagued the schools their kids already attended, they were more than willing to take a chance on something formed outside of the bureaucratic, bankrupt system.

Fooliani has never been a fan of the Board of Education or the United Federation of Teachers union, so you know he relished pushing forward with the charter school plan and giving both entities the middle finger. And I have no doubt that Elvin is serious about providing students with a viable alternative to what is being offered. But Knowledge Hall is a stepping-stone for him; he has his eyes on becoming a major player on the political scene, making a name for himself within the Republican Party, and winning himself a prime job in the administrations of our newly elected Republican governor, George Pataki, or, as he predicts, our next president, Bob Dole. And what better way to do that than to open a school in a Black neighborhood and outshine the others by producing students who can outperform their peers?

It's still too early to tell if Knowledge Hall is actually achieving that goal; after all, its doors have only been open for six months. But in those six months, Elvin has gotten a lot of press (from *Newsweek* to *Both Sides* with Jesse Jackson) and received a lot of hosannas for his courage and chutzpah. As a gesture of goodwill and to prove his dedication, he's waived his salary for the first two years (which isn't really such a big deal since he's a millionaire). And the school's motto—"Your altitude depends on your attitude"—has so caught on that like "Just say no," it's fast becoming another mantra adopted by the sound-bite-heavy conservative crowd.

Since I believed in his mission (if not his politics), I threw my résumé into the pot when he officially put the call out for staff. What did I have to lose? I was still very much unemployed after leaving *Your World*, and the search was becoming a very frustrating one: the publications that wanted to hire me didn't think my experience warranted the type of position and salary I knew I deserved (I *quit* a job because I was undervalued and underpaid . . . *hello?*), and the few positions that appealed to me were in different parts of the country, the closest being Atlanta. While they were great opportunities and there was a lot of room for growth, I hadn't lived anywhere else in my life (and I have been spoiled being able to just hop on a train or bus, or just walk, wherever I want to go). Most importantly, I wasn't about to pick up and move away from my family—Pooquie and Junior. Pooquie and I discussed it and he felt I should do what would be best for my career, but I knew he didn't want me to take any of the positions because he knew he'd probably lose me if I did. And the feeling was mutual. I had already tried the long distance thing—and once was enough.

Elvin called me a week later and we scheduled an interview for the next day. Well, you can't even call what I went in for an interview. After introductions were made and some small talk about the weather ("It's rather warm for spring, isn't it?"), our conversation went like this . . .

"You've done a lot of work as a journalist and editor," he observed, perusing what I assumed were the résumé and clips I sent. He was even more unattractive in person—a very long thin face, pug nose, a chin that protrudes out an inch, and large eyes that look awful lonely (for some reason, he has no eyebrows).

"Yes, I have."

"I'm very impressed. I've heard of that publication you were an editor for. It's really made current events hip and kids love it. Do you think you could make them feel the same way about writing?"

This was my chance to impress. "Yes, I do. Many view writing as an insurmountable task, a chore, a bore. I believe this view stems from the rather unimaginative ways in which some educators approach it; as much as I enjoy it, many of the assignments given to me in grade school through my college years didn't make what I was doing or learning fun. I believe the key is to present it as the joy it can be so students can get joy out of it. Seeing how powerful one's own words can be will be very affirming, encouraging students to look at both writing and reading in a whole new light."

He cleared his throat. "You don't have any teaching experience," he said rather dryly.

So much for wanting to hear my opinion. "No, but I do have a teaching proposal and a sample lesson plan prepared if you'd like to see them." I had worked on them all weekend.

"Sure." He didn't sound too enthused. I had the feeling he only agreed to look it over because I had them, not because he was gen-

187

LOVE
THE
ONE
YOU'RE
WITH

uinely interested, I just knew my phone would be ringing in a few hours with the news that I hadn't gotten the job. But I opened up my leather case and pulled them out anyway.

He took them. "We can go over them next week when you come back in to be processed."

"Processed?"

"Yes. You're hired."

I was stunned. "I am?"

"Yes. Unless you've been convicted of a felony or happen to be a registered sex offender"—he finally looked up—"and I happen to know you haven't and aren't."

But of course he would. Being the left-hand man of Fooliani, who practically runs the Gestapo—uh, police department—I'm sure a thorough background check was done on me.

He picked up a slim manila envelope and handed it to me. "This will explain the position, your working hours, salary, benefits. And there's an overview about Knowledge Hall, what we plan to accomplish and what we expect of our personnel. Miss Hanson will set up a meeting next week for you to sign the contract and for us to start work on the fall semester."

I was still stunned. "Oh. Great." We swapped packages. I rose. "Thank you. Thank you very much."

He rose to shake my hand. "Thank you. I believe this is going to be a great project for all involved."

After I set up another appointment, Miss Hanson buzzed him. "Your eleven-forty-five is here."

"Send her in."

Miss Hanson turned to a sister wearing a dark blue dress and black pumps. "You may go in." She did, closing the door behind her.

At first I was ready to dismiss Elvin as being unemotional, somewhat detached, but he was doing what I'm sure he had to do in the very high-stakes and high-stress world of the markets—make decisions based on your gut instinct that will allow you and your clients to flourish. Time is indeed money and you can't waste either. And he was wasting no time getting his new ship up and running: everyone—the 11:45 he was debriefing, the 11:50 who was waiting to be seen, the gentleman I passed on the way out who announced he was his 11:55, and all those who came before and after—was getting job offers. If what he saw on paper complemented his vision, you were chosen. His clients in this case are the students, and his main priority was that he choose a staff that showed a passion for what they'd done in life; whether he genuinely liked the person sitting across from him during the "interview" was of no consequence or importance (most of us thought he didn't like us during that initial meeting—that is, until the words *you're hired* came out of his mouth). And time and money were indeed factors here as well: folks were predicting the school would fail (the feeling was that it wouldn't open its doors on time) and half of the school's five-year, $25 million budget (stocking it with computers, wiring it for cable television, and ensuring every child has the textbooks and tools needed to prepare them for the twenty-first century) was fronted by outside entities. So while his no-nonsense approach threw me and took some getting used to—he's very much a "team player" kind of guy—I respected where he was coming from.

Besides the great salary (we're paid almost twice the $30,000 base most first-time teachers in the city earn) and perks (you can't beat having all legal holidays off, as well as one week for spring break and a two-month summer vacation), I can now walk to work (I'm sure it must be a bit unnerving, though, for some of my students that their teacher not only lives in the same neighborhood, but on the same *block*). I also love the fact that the racial makeup of the staff is the same as the student body—ninety percent Black. In addition, half of the teachers are also male (to say that this is rare would be a gross understatement—if you run into a Black adult male in a public school in New York, chances are he's a security officer, custodian, or cook). This commitment to diversity would certainly score Elvin major points in the community (for years the Board of Ed has been blasted for its dismal record of hiring and retaining male teachers of color) as well as quell the fear that he only planned to employ his conservative, Republican friends, most of whom are white.

My mother was thrilled that I was returning to the ranks of the employed. My brother was, too—but when he found out what my new career was, he didn't mince words.

"Do you have any advice for me?" I asked him. He teaches sixth-grade physical education.

189

LOVE
THE
ONE
YOU'RE
WITH

"Yeah: Don't do it!" He had so many "beat up the teach" horror stories (one kid, unhappy about being benched after he fouled another player in a basketball game, kicked him in the shin so hard he still has a small bruise some two years later) that he started smoking.

I wasn't worried about being verbally or physically assaulted: the hundred and fifty students at Knowledge Hall were hand-selected (i.e., their parents or some other adult knew Elvin personally and had their child's name on the list before it was even drawn up) and are considered the cream of the crop. Most were reading at or above grade level, only a few had received written reprimands because of their work habits or behavior, and none had ever been suspended or expelled. So the chances of us ending up with a rotten apple in this group was slim.

But even in a so-called good school, you're gonna have your problem kids—or, rather, your kids who cause them—and Knowledge Hall is no exception. Jesse Price loves to tease other students when they get a wrong answer. Annabelle Garland believes that because she is the tallest student in the school (just over five feet), that gives her the right to boss others around. And Treena Bloomington and her twin sister, Teena, try to fool us by pretending to be each other. No serial killers in the bunch, just mischievous and crafty.

And then there's Willoughby Grant.

Every class has its clown (most not as funny or as clever as they think they are) and Willoughby willingly took on that title in mine. In fact, he was the jokester in all of his classes. Our first day of school together was reminiscent of the initial meeting between Mrs. Sherwood (Anne Meara) and Leroy Johnson (Gene Anthony Ray) in *Fame*. I had barely slept the night before because I was so nervous; not even a pep talk from Pooquie and a "jood luck" card from Junior (he crossed out the *g*) could calm my fears (more than anything, I believed my nightmare would come true: I would freeze in front of the students and not be able to talk). But aside from one student smacking gum and another throwing a minor fit because someone else was in *her* seat (she apparently staked out the first desk in the third row in all her classes so she could sit right in front of the teacher), the day went rather smoothly.

But as soon as Willoughby strutted into what was the last class of the day, I knew all of that was about to change. Instead of a boom box, he had a Walkman. But he did have the same chip Leroy Johnson had had on his shoulder. He headed straight for the back, dropped his book bag on the floor, plopped himself in a chair, leaned back, and shut his eyes.

I was going to nip this before class started. I walked over to him. I tapped him on the shoulder.

He jumped. He just stared at me, still grooving.

I pointed to my ears.

He took the headphones off. "Yeah?"

"What is your name, young man?"

"Willoughby. But they call me Will."

"Well, Will, I'm Mr. Crawford, your teacher for this period. And I'm sure you know that listening to a Walkman during class is against the rules."

"But class ain't start yet."

"Class starts the minute you step into this room."

He shrugged. "A'ight." He rose and started to walk out.

"Where are you going?"

He turned. He looked at his watch. "It's two-oh-two and class don't *officially* start for another three minutes, so I'll just wait out here till then." And he did just that.

I could feel a headache coming on.

At 2:05 he returned, headphones off.

I tried to smooth over our previous encounter. "Glad you could rejoin us."

"Yeah, right." He snickered.

He wasn't going to make this easy . . .

I took attendance and then gave them the same spiel I had two other times that day.

"In every other class you take in this school, you will be expected to solve a problem, memorize facts and figures, and perform a task where there is only one right answer. But in this class, there isn't just one right answer. There are many. Twenty-five, to be exact. Each and every one of you will have a correct response to every assignment because only you have the answer to it. Here, your voice counts, and it isn't my job to restrain or restrict it, but help you find it."

191

LOVE
THE
ONE
YOU'RE
WITH

Willoughby's hand went up.

"Yes, Mr. Grant?"

"Uh, what if we wanna express ourselves with mu-zac?" He grinned, holding up his headphones.

The class giggled.

"I only accept work submitted on loose-leaf paper."

He shrugged off the response.

"In addition to your regular individual assignments, you'll be producing a newspaper and a literary magazine. You'll be doing a lot of writing *and* reading, so this isn't going to be a class you'll be able to, as I've heard many of your peers say, breeze. An A won't come easy. It's going to cost. And right here, today, is where you start paying."

"Yo, teach, you ain't Debbie Allen!" Willoughby shouted.

The class burst into laughter.

I had to chuckle at that one myself. "No, I'm not Debbie Allen. But after you had a taste of me, you'll wish I was. She came on television once a week; you'll be seeing me *three* days a week."

That disclosure wasn't lost on him.

"Now, your first assignment is to write an autobiography of yourself in fifty words or less."

The class reacted with grumbling and hissing.

Willoughby made his displeasure known the loudest. "Yo, we gotta do homework on the first day?!"

"In the future, do not address me as *Yo*. And, yes, you will have homework on the first day. Get used to having it *every* day."

"Yo—"

I glared at him.

"Uh . . . Mr. C?"

I nodded. "Mr. C is fine."

"Don't you know Lincoln freed the slaves in 1863?"

More laughter from the crowd, uh, class.

I smiled. "You are a witty one, Will. And smart, too. I look forward to seeing that humor and intelligence displayed in your homework—starting with tonight's assignment."

I did see it in that assignment, and many others: a haiku about Jesse Jackson ("MLK's homeboy helping us keep hope alive and our eyes on the prize"); an essay about his mother, who died when he was a baby; and a commentary on girls playing team sports with boys (his argument was a sexist one—"Girls just don't want to do what boys do, they want to *be* boys and they can't be"—but he presented it in such a convincing manner that it's easy to see how even the most non-sensical ideas can be made to *sound* sensical). But while he turned in near-perfect work, he was determined to test every teacher in the school. The comic outbursts and flippant air were getting him a C across the board in both behavior and concentration—and you know what happens to Black boys who are labeled "difficult," "aggressive," and "abrasive," as some teachers had Will. I surmised he learned at a younger age that the best way for him to get people's attention was to be a smart-ass—and given how invisible Black boys are meant to feel, I can see why some react in such a way. This is why I give the boys just a little bit more time than the girls—Black boys are more likely to be "tracked" into remedial classes, placed in special education (instead of educators, most of whom are white, taking the extra time to work with them), and harshly disciplined for the most minor offenses, such as talking back or making noise (instead of being diagnosed with "attention deficit/hyperactivity disorder" and receiving a prescription for Ritalin or some other kiddie drug like their white peers). Such events scar them and make school a very unpleasant and unappealing experience, leading many to lose interest and drop out by the time they reach high school. It's my job to both undo the damage that may have already been done and lead or keep them on a path to realizing their own potential.

So, at least once a week during that first month and a half, I kept Will after school.

"What am I going to do with you, Will?" I asked for the umpteenth time.

"Whatcha mean?"

I gave him a "don't even try it" look.

He twirled his tie. "I don't know."

"You do, too, know."

"Uh . . . maybe I'm just lazy."

"You're not lazy."

"Maybe I'm just stoopid."

"And you're not stupid, either."

193

LOVE
THE
ONE
YOU're
WITH

"Maybe I just don't care."

"Oh, you care. You care enough to act up, so I know you care."

Silence.

I sat down in front of him. "Run out of excuses, huh?"

"What?"

"I know and *you* know you are not lazy or stupid, and that you do care. This is about your wanting attention."

"I don't want no attention."

"You say that but your actions tell me something different. There's a right kind of attention and a wrong kind of attention, and the kind you are constantly seeking isn't the right kind."

He looked down.

"I've noticed that the higher your grades get, the more you act out. Are you afraid your friends won't see getting good grades in school as being cool?" Although I hadn't heard any student say it at Knowledge Hall, that "acting white" charge is very much alive in some quarters of Black America. I got the label "Oreo" when I was in grade school because I excelled and that was almost twenty years ago, so I can't imagine how much harder it would be for kids growing up in environments today where the so-called role models are either in jail or livin' the (high) life selling drugs.

But apparently this wasn't the case. "No," he mumbled.

"Are you sure?"

"Yeah. I'm sure."

"Are you afraid that others won't like you if you don't act that way?"

"No."

I sighed. "Well, help me out, here, Will. What is it?"

He fidgeted in his chair, tapping his fingers on the desk.

"I'm going to tell you a secret. You can't tell anyone, okay?"

He nodded.

"According to the report card you'll be getting in two days, you'll have the highest grade point average in your class."

He looked up. He seemed surprised. "I will?"

"Yes, you will. But you could have the highest GPA in the sixth grade—maybe even the highest in the entire school—if you'd only chill out." I leaned in toward him. "You may think everybody likes you because you make them laugh, and they probably do. You're a likable young man. But you've got to be careful: if you play the fool too well, people might start believing you are one."

"I ain't no fool," he insisted, pointing to himself.

"*I* know you're not. But that's how people are reacting to you, especially the faculty."

He sucked his teeth. "Teachers in this school can't take a joke."

"Maybe some of us can't. But we're not not laughing because we don't have a sense of humor. We're not laughing because it is not funny the way you are screwing around with your future. There's a difference between telling a joke and making *yourself* the joke."

He shot me a contemplative glance.

I was breaking through. "Think about it."

He thought about it, and what I said must've had an impact—he's mellowed considerably. The old Will still makes a guest appearance every once in a while, but now people are no longer laughing at him but with him.

That my laid-back approach (allowing Will and others to call me Mr. C) was winning over the students wasn't lost on my colleagues. Some found my style as well as my teaching methods to be a bit unorthodox. To one in particular, they were downright disgraceful.

"We are trying to prepare these students to be doctors and lawyers, *not* rappers or actors in ghetto films," cried Henrietta Drake, in that dragging, monotone voice. A public-school science teacher for twenty-five years who came out of retirement to join Knowledge Hall's staff, she's a stout sister with freckles dotting her cheeks and a mop of wispy black hair. We were in Elvin's office.

"With all due respect, Miss Drake, I don't know what a ghetto film is, but if any student's goal is to be an actor or rapper one day, why shouldn't we recognize and nurture that?"

"*Because*, Mr. Crawford, this is not the High School for the Performing Arts."

"All the more reason for us to do it. My class is the only one where they get to express themselves freely, to use their imaginations and be creative."

"*Here* is an example of your allowing them to use their imaginations and be *creative*." She held up one of Will's papers and adjusted her reading glasses, which had been planted on her very big bosom.

195

LOVE
THE
ONE
YOU'RE
WITH

"And, I quote: 'I wish Drake would give us a break, give us a breather for goodness' sake, / The way she talks about the planets and the stars, you think she was once livin' on Mars, / I betcha she's an alien, in this world she wasn't born, / All I wanna know is, how does she hide her fangs and horns?' "

Elvin giggled to himself.

She was not amused. "I don't find that the *least* bit humorous, Mr. Macintosh."

"Believe me, Miss Drake, I wasn't tickled by that rhyme," he managed to get out without cracking a smile.

"I would hope not." Her eyes rested back on me. "But I know I couldn't think the same of Mr. Crawford."

I nodded. "Well, that's the first thing you've said that I agree with."

"I don't believe you are taking this seriously."

"Taking what seriously? That you have a problem with a student composing a rap in which you are the butt of a joke?"

"That you would even pass this off as educational and imply that one shouldn't be insulted by both the assignment and its execution is a joke."

"What *I* find to be a joke is a nonexpert in the area of creative writing telling me what that can and cannot constitute."

She shook the paper in the air. "This *trash* has *no* place in a classroom!"

"This is not 1975, Miss Drake, it's 1995. It is our job as educators to adapt to the times. And since you aren't a student in any of my classes and don't know what my students do or do not receive, you are not in a position to make such claims."

"I've been a teacher a *lot* longer than you, young man, and—"

"And you would want to save that paternalistic tone. Your many years as a teacher and many, *many* more years on this earth do *not* give you the right to talk to me in that manner."

She heaved in disgust while Elvin grinned.

"The bottom line is that my students are learning the value of the written word, beautifully crafting it in ways that explore the worlds they live in—and they have the grades to prove it." I turned to Elvin. "If that'll be all, I have a class in five minutes I must prepare for."

Elvin nodded. He wasn't the least bit moved either way by our debate; he didn't care one way or the other. He'd only held the meeting to appease Miss Drake. But I knew that if push came to shove, he wouldn't suggest I tone down or change my approach—especially when the newspaper the sixth-grade students produced, *The Hall Monitor*, had just been featured on FOX-5's morning program, *Good Day New York*, and CNN's *Reliable Sources* (Will was the star in both reports).

"*Good* day, Miss Drake," I bellowed in my best Maggie Smith à la Jean Brodie voice, closing the door behind me with a thud.

I believe the real problem with Miss Drake is jealousy. Because of her much-ballyhooed appearance on *Oprah* a few years back and the two Teacher of the Year Awards she won from the National Education Association, she's used to being numero uno and has been campaigning to defrock those she feels have dethroned her—namely, myself and Miss Ramos, who teaches math. I don't think she'd find many supporters amongst the students (I can be stern and strict, but only when I have to be, and they know it), but if she were to have any success having me ousted, her allies would surely be outraged parents—and open-school night would be the best time to identify and rally them to her cause.

YOU'D THINK AFTER VISITING ME TWICE DURING THIS school year, these folks would know me by now—and would just *know*. But, no, there are those who always have to try me. Miss Reyes disagrees with how I evaluate her daughter, Alma, attempting to use my not speaking Spanish as the reason why her little girl doesn't get the grades she deserves (she thinks *bilingual* means Alma should be able to do all of her schoolwork in Spanish). Mr. and Mrs. Edmundson are convinced their son, Harold, will be a future publisher (à la Earl Graves Sr.) and, given that, deserves to be the publisher of his class paper (never mind the boy can't *spell* the word *publisher*). And Mr. Morrison just doesn't think his son, Prince, is special (with a name like Prince why wouldn't he think that?); he feels Prince deserves special *treatment* (he's a national-science-project champ who has an ACT-SO prize from the NAACP).

Mind you, they all know their child *deserves* something, but it's a sense of entitlement that has everything to do with what the parent wants, *not* what the child needs. I will say one thing for these and other parents who are fanatical—at least they've chosen a jood thing

197

LOVE
THE
ONE
YOU're
WITH

to be obsessed about. Instead of a bunch of brats who do little to no work and are constantly in the principal's office (and whose guardians are probably always missing in action), I've got a flock of overachievers whose parents consider it a personal affront if their child isn't deified as The One. Give me an overinvolved parent over an uninvolved (or, worse, unconcerned) one any day.

It was five minutes to nine when I decided to close shop. If anybody else was coming (my last parent left at 8:25) they would have already shown up. I erased my name from the blackboard, stuck the bottle of Tylenol in my pants pocket (I only popped one; I usually need two), and started loading the students' work into my briefcase when a set of footsteps came marching up the hall.

I turned as they—or, rather, *he*—stopped in front of my door.

He was so tall that he had to duck before entering the room, so wide that his shoulder blades bumped the door's entryway coming in, and so thick that one could clearly make out the mountainous mounds of muscle under his dark blue suit and pink shirt.

"Mr. Crawford?" the forceful yet friendly voice asked.

My mouth opened; nothing. I tried again. "Yes?" I yelped.

He extended his *big* light brown hand. "I'm Willoughby Grant Senior, Will's father."

"Why, Mr. Grant, it's a pleasure to meet you." I shook it and *it* shook *me*—smooth and hard as finished wood.

"The pleasure is all mine," he insisted, licking those reddish lips. Like the lips, that sleepy left eye, dime-sized mole on the right cheek, and gray eyes ran in the family. Unlike his son's crew fade (buzz on top, shaded on the sides), his head was dotted with dozens of twists, each one no more that a half inch in length.

I had to catch myself; I was *leering*. "Uh, you got here just in time. I was about to leave."

"I'm so sorry I'm this late. I just flew back in from the West Coast, and it took forever to get out of Newark Airport."

"Thanks for coming, but you certainly didn't have to. I'm used to seeing Will's grandmother, and she was the first one here tonight." Like she always is.

"Uh, could we just sit for a moment?"

"Sure." I was about to get a crick in my neck, gazing up at him. We both sat.

"Will's always been a precocious kid. He always got good grades, but they began to slip two years ago. I think he started to resent his mom dying when he was just a baby and me not being around to raise him. So he lashed out and became the comedian. Transferring him to this school was the best decision we made. He's really blossomed over the past six months and it's all because of you. Will really likes you, and he loves your class. I think it's given him a voice he never really had—or helped him find the voice that was always there. So, I just wanted to come up and personally thank you for all you've done."

Now, hearing *that* was worth getting a migraine.

And I was stumped. "I . . . I really don't know what to say."

"Well, I hope you'll say yes to a cup of coffee."

Hmm . . . "A cup of coffee?"

"Yes, or a drink, whatever you prefer."

I was still stumped. "I . . . was on my way home."

"Have you forgotten I live not far from here myself? My mother and Will have said they've seen you out in the neighborhood. We don't have to go far."

I was *still* stumped. "I . . . really have a splitting headache. As you can imagine, it's been a long night."

"Maybe we can do it tomorrow night."

No, he's not asking me what I think he's asking me . . . is he?

"Mr. Grant, I—"

"Please, call me Will. Well, I guess you'd have to call me *Big* Will."

Uh-huh . . . *Very* Big.

"I really appreciate the offer. But I couldn't."

He eyed me curiously. "You don't date widowers?"

"No, that's not it."

"You don't date men over six feet?"

I giggled. "No, that's not it."

"Ah . . . then it's the one I feared the most: You're involved."

Bingo. "Yes. I'm currently in a relationship." Damn . . . I've said that more in the past two weeks than I have in the past two years.

He didn't seem surprised by that bit of information. "Of course. A man like yourself would be."

"Even if I wasn't, I don't think it'd be a good idea to get involved with the parent of a student."

He chewed on that one, playing with his striped light blue tie.

199

LOVE
THE
ONE
YOU'RE
WITH

"Mmm . . . ethical. A caring, considerate man, thinking of what impact the actions you take will have on your students—or at least one of them. But you won't be Little Will's teacher forever. And, not that I'm hoping it happens, but maybe you'll be available one day, too."

"You're a very charming man. Thank you for making my night."

"You're more than welcome."

I had to know . . . "Uh . . . do you mind if I ask you something?"

"Go ahead."

"We . . . we just met. How . . . how . . ."

"Elvin has been singing your praises. And he also mentioned that you were . . . my type."

Oh, did he? I always had my suspicions about Elvin and I guess he's had them about me. Did that background check also include info on my love life? I wouldn't put anything past Fooliani.

"Sorry if I kind of put a rush on you," he gushed.

"That's all right. It was a good rush."

"If you don't mind and don't think it would be any trouble, I'd like to walk you home."

Hell . . . why not? "That would be nice."

It's a short walk, but it seemed longer this time. He offered the résumé—thirty, Florida A&M U grad, accountant for the stars (i.e., the new jacks and jills in the music biz), works out twice a day (no kidding!), loves sushi, R. Kelly (one of his clients), August Wilson plays, and John Sayles movies. Hard to believe we had been living blocks from each other for five years and didn't know it. Never found ourselves on the same line at a store, or doing our laundry. Never passed the other on the street or rounding a corner. And if we had, I would never forget it: You couldn't miss a constellation like him! That we would meet in this way, at this time . . .

As I watched him bop up the block, zeroing in on that big booty—which had more stories than the Empire State Building—I sucked my teeth in disgust, thinking:

Life can be *so* cruel sometimes, can't it?

16

Oasis occupies the first floor of a two-story building (a CPA rents the upper level) that is nestled between a twenty-four-hour Korean grocery and an Indian restaurant called Curry in a Hurry on Lexington Avenue in Gramercy Park. Only in New York could three different cultural stations like these be neighbors.

Given that this is a residential area—and a lily-white one, at that—it seemed the oddest locale for a rhythm-and-blues club (actually, the recorded message described it as a "rhythm blues cabaret"). And it's such a nondescript establishment that you can pass right by it—like I did. I was expecting town cars, Jeeps, limos, and taxicabs parked in front, and the proverbial velvet rope and a bouncer or two trying to keep a noisy, rambunctious crowd in line. But the streets and sidewalks were deserted (was the party over?), and there wasn't even a mini-marquee with the club's name emblazoned on it. After checking the address Montee wrote down for a third time—and seeing that the address I was in front of matched for the *third* time—I reluctantly opened the rickety and somewhat rusted steel door and stepped inside.

I was greeted by a white woman, midtwenties, wearing a strapless polka-dot dress (skinned right *off* the dalmatian, okay?) and no makeup, not even lip gloss (not that it would've helped). The straight blond hair was teased a bit too much.

"Good evening," she chirped, standing behind a black podium, the kind you'd see in a lecture hall at a university.

"Good evening. I'm here for Montee Simms's set."

"Your name, please?"

"Mitchell Crawford."

She went down the roster. "Ah, yes." She checked off my name and retrieved a menu. "Please come with me."

I followed her through a heavy bloodred curtain. A bank must have occupied this spot before Oasis: the teller station was now the bar and the four customer self-service posts were SRO tables, which formed a square around a dozen other tables. The gray walls were painted with palm trees and covered with framed posters of legends like John Lee Hooker, Robert Johnson, Lavern Baker, Etta James, Ruth Brown, Dinah Washington, and Ray Charles. Smoky (cigars and pipes were being puffed, and incense burned), packed (just about every seat and bar stool was filled), and buzzing with chatter and laughter (much of it coming from the bar, where a posse of brothers were huddled together), it was a very intimate, festive setting.

The hostess led me to a table—front row, center—just footsteps from the stage (which was a cement-block-high platform). A single yellow rose sat in a thin black vase. Propped up against a burning white candle was a brown envelope with my name on it.

"Do enjoy the show," she advised, removing the "Reserved" placard.

"Thank you."

No sooner had she left than a fifty-something waitress popped up popping gum. While the patrons and the few personnel were in semiformal attire, she wore a gold lamé blouse with green stretch pants and black knee-high leather boots, hoops as big as her pudgy face, several dozen silver bracelets on her left arm (none on her right), and a foot-high, beehive hairdo. Yeah, a real tart. She looked like she'd be more at home serving drinks at a 1950s drive-up malt shop, à la *Grease*. But with Jane Doe manning the door, I suppose they had to have *someone* a little more colorful up in here to brighten the spot.

And that she did. "Hay, sugah," she sang, chomping that gum like a cow. "I'm Janine. Can I get ya somethin'?"

"Uh . . . a Long Island iced tea, please."

"I'll be right back."

After she swished away (she was a tiny woman with a not-so-tiny rump), I opened the envelope.

Mitchell,

I hope you enjoy tonight's performance. I chose each song with you in mind.

Montee

Hmm . . . I was used to singin' for or to the men in my life. It would certainly be a different experience being on the receiving end.

Janine returned with my drink, cackling with two of the brothers from the bar who each climbed on the stage (one behind the drums, the other getting his bass in position). The glass was formed and ridged like a pineapple. "Here ya go."

"How much is that?"

"All your drinks are on the house, honey."

"They are?"

"Mmm-hmm. As the *very* special guest of Mr. Simms."

"Ah." That was nice of him.

"If I can getcha anything else, you just let me know."

"I will. Thank you."

"Enjoy the show."

"I'm sure I will."

The lights dimmed. A figure came from behind a black curtain and slid onto the piano stool. He began to play. The intro sounded familiar. Then came the first verse. Hmm . . . Montee is a bold one to do this particular Aretha tune.

"And I really gotta tell them . . . exactly how I feel . . . and make you understand . . . that love ain't playin' this time . . ."

He turned to the audience—or, rather, *me*—with the song's title: "This is for real . . ."

Yes, he was.

His voice favored Sam Cooke—the same timbre, the same throttle, the same flourishes, the same clarity, the same molasses-soaked soulfulness, the same spiritual intensity, the same gospel-deep power.

Heavy but hearty. Strong yet sweet. Tough yet tender.

The other two gentlemen joined in. And when he got to *the* part— ". . . and make you understand . . . that Miss Re ain't playin' this time . . ."—he replaced *Miss Re* with *Montee*. It was a perfect substitu-

203

LOVE
THE
ONE
YOU'RE
WITH

tion. He almost stole the song from Aretha (once she sings a song, it's damn near impossible to stake a claim on it).

One thing's for sure: Her version never made me *moist*.

"Good evening, ladies and gentleman," he said after the applause ceased. "I want to welcome you all to Oasis. I am Montee Simms—"

"*We know, baybay!*" screamed a sister seated two tables to my left, waving her hands as if she were a traffic cop.

Montee blushed. "Thank you for that. That's Stan 'The Man' Grady on drums . . ."

Short, stocky, and dressed in all white (including a bandanna tied around his forehead), Stan raised his hands, crossed his drumsticks, and tapped a beat on them.

"And that's Cool Cal Cooper on bass."

Tall and thin, Cal tipped his teal-colored wide brim hat (which matched the silk shirt and slacks he wore) and bowed.

"And we are the Simms Trio. We hope you'll enjoy the words and music we'll be throwin' at ya this evening. We invite you to groove with us, to groove with the one you're with—or the one you're next to."

Some took that invitation to heart: in addition to those same-gender couples holding hands and exchanging loving glances, one female couple did their own slow screw against the wall, another swayed in each other's arms by the bar, one male couple was parked up against one of the SRO tables (one brother melded his back and back*side* into the other's front), and another slow-dragged to just about every tune. Funny, but I hadn't really noticed that most of the pairings weren't heterosexual when I first walked in. It certainly was refreshing to see such intimacy displayed by Black Same Gender Loving people in a non-dance-club setting like this.

In addition to encouraging the smooching, the lineup of tunes—Randy Crawford's "I'm Under the Influence of You," Donna Summer's "Fascination," Phyllis Hyman's "The Answer Is You," Will Downing's "Closer to You," Dionne Warwick's "Where My Lips Have Been," Stacy Lattisaw's "I've Loved You Somewhere Before," and Lalah Hathaway's "Smile" (which really gave me a chill, since it was the song I sang for/to Pooquie moments after we first met)—signaled that he *did* choose tonight's repertoire with me in mind. In fact, at various points during the evening, he was singing directly *to* me—something that wasn't lost on the audience.

The highlight of the night was his "blues medley." Actually, it was a *crying* medley—the songs featured were about shedding tears.

"You know when someone really loves you? I mean, really *really* loves ya?" he asked.

A brother in the back shouted: "Yeah—when they'd mortgage their house for ya!"

Even Montee laughed. "No. It's when they don't only want to share the pleasure, but the pain." And with that he dove into "Cry Together" by the O'Jays.

"I'm sure many of you have lost a love so good you really knew what having a broken heart meant . . ." was the interlude before Alexander O'Neal's "Crying Overtime." And he prefaced the pop/jazz standard "Cry Me a River" (on which he scatted up a storm) with the very pointed words: "Take you back? *Take you back?* Ha, as Ashford & Simpson advised: 'Get out your handkerchief . . . you're gonna *cry*!' "

Then he did two songs *by* Ashford & Simpson—"Add It Up" (on which he tackled, not tickled, those ebonies and ivories) and "All for One"—and closed with a rocking version of Bill Withers's "Grandma's Hands" that had everyone on their feet. Several folks (including me) begged for an encore, but since he had another set at one A.M., he declined.

He went around to each table, thanking folks for coming out. Handshakes and shoulder rubs to most of the men, hugs and kisses to most of the women, including that very enthusiastic sister, who also squeezed him on the ass and slobbered him with a kiss (he didn't seem to mind). She was very attractive (she's the first woman I've ever seen with an hourglass figure), but the weave was a wove (very Art Garfunkel-ish) and the brown leather halter top was cut *so* low those two torpedoes attached to her chest were about to blast out. He tried to ease from her grip, but she wouldn't release him. He whispered something in her ear; she gave me a twice-over and nodded. She pecked him on the nose, groped the butt one last time, and let him go.

The sideburns were gone, but the mustache was thicker and so was the 'fro. He had on a dark gray pin-striped suit with a black shirt, and wing-tipped black shoes. He worked up a serious sweat: some ten minutes after the performance, he was still dabbing his forehead, and drops of perspiration continued to slowly make their way down his chest (his shirt was unbuttoned, midchest up). I would've loved to have done the dabbin' for him . . .

He sat down. He placed his stretched-out elbows on the table and clasped his hands under his chin. "So . . . what did you think?"

I leaned in. I smiled. "You were jood."

"Huh?" he inquired, rather puzzled.

"Jood. Better than good."

He nodded. "Ah. Okay. I gotta remember that one. Any song in particular you enjoy the most?"

"I can't say I enjoyed any one song more than the rest. But I enjoyed the way you interpreted each one. You have a brilliant voice."

"Thanks."

"And that moan of yours . . ." And what a *moan* it was . . . "That's gonna be the thing that hooks people, that folks listen for. They'll know it's you immediately. It'll rival Ronald Isley's 'La-da-da-da-da-da.' "

"I don't know about that," he gushed.

"It's already setting hearts afire. Take your groupie over there. She cried out every time you did it."

He acknowledged her. "Reena . . . she's a special friend."

Hmm . . . how "special" a friend is she? I wanted to ask, but it was really none of my business. So . . . "And I see you love Ashford & Simpson."

"How could you tell?" He smirked, dabbing the chest. "Yeah. They're one of the greatest—and *underrated*—songwriting teams."

"I agree. It's interesting that you chose songs they composed for others. Any reason why?"

"You can't sing any song they recorded together solo. And I don't think Stan or Cal would be willing to sing soprano."

I chuckled. "And you put a hurtin' on that Steinway."

"Thanks."

"How long have you been playing the piano?"

"Since I was eleven."

"You taught yourself, didn't you?"

"How you know?"

"I just got that feeling. You play it like it's . . . a natural thing. Like it *came* naturally. I always wanted to play."

"Maybe I can teach you." He reached out and took my right hand.

"You've got the fingers for it. Long . . ." He caressed each one. ". . . soft . . ." He peered into my eyes. ". . . and sexy."

Janine interruped this intimate moment. "Oh . . . I hope I'm not disturbing anything."

Montee released my hand. We both blushed.

She placed drinks in front of us. "Y'all enjoy."

"Thanks, J, we will," he replied.

I leaned in. "She seems a little out of place . . ."

"Janine? Ha, I guess she does. But she's real cool. Besides, when your nephew is the owner . . ." He pointed to a white man who resembled Ray Liotta, standing near the bar.

I sighed. "I really couldn't drink another one of these."

"Why—you feelin' a little buzz?"

"Yes, I am. And I don't need to feel a *lot* of buzz."

"Don't worry. I'll make sure you get home okay." He grinned.

I bet you will—to *your* home.

He held up his glass; I followed suit.

"To a sweet man. I appreciate you coming out. You made my night."

I nodded. We clinked. We drank.

"So, tell me, is this a gay nightclub?" I inquired.

"No."

I surveyed the room—the smooching was still going on. "Ha, you wouldn't know it."

"As they say, birds of a feather. Some of these folks are my regular peoples, others heard about me through the grapevine."

"Does the owner mind?"

"So long as folks are spending money on drinks and his famous hot wings, Joe don't care *what* way you swingin' it."

As if she knew that was her cue, Janine popped up again—with a batch of those famous hot wings.

"Thanks, J."

"You more than welcome." She palmed by back. "Enjoy, hon."

"I will, thanks."

He immediately scooped up five and dropped them on a plate while tearing into a sixth. "I am one hongry Black man. I haven't eaten since lunch."

"Why?"

207

LOVE
THE
ONE
YOU'RE
WITH

"Butterflies. I always get nervy before a concert. My stomach be doin' the cha-cha."

I noticed some sauce about to drip onto his jacket and caught it just in time with my napkin.

He was pleased with my deed. "Thank you, sir. You saved me from looking like a slob the rest of the night."

I nodded a *you're welcome*.

"Ain't you gonna join me?"

"Uh, no. I ate not too long ago."

"Hmm . . . it's all right. I don't mind if you enjoy watching me eat." He winked.

What is he, psychic?

"Back to your audience," I continued. "Is that why you switched up the identifications in some of the songs, but not in others?" On "Cry Together," *Me and my woman* became *Me and my baby*, but he didn't change *boy* in "Where My Lips Have Been" or "The Answer Is You."

"Yup. You not only have to play *for* your audience, you gotta play *to* them."

"After you make it big, I guess you won't be playing for gay audiences anymore . . ."

"*Hell* yeah."

"You will?"

"Yeah. Why wouldn't I?"

"I don't know of any Black male singers who do."

He shrugged. "Guess I'll be the first."

"Do you think your manager and record company will approve?"

"As long as I'm puttin' money in their pockets, why should they care *where* it's comin' from?"

Hmm . . . "So, are you going to be an openly gay singer?"

"No. I'll be an openly *bisexual* one."

That he's bisexual didn't surprise me; that he planned to be open about it in the industry did. "You think the world is ready for that?" I was being facetious.

"I don't know what the world is ready for, and I ain't much concerned. I do know what *I'm* ready for. If MeShell Ndegéocello can do it, so can I."

"Well, she *is* a woman. It's easier for some folks to digest her as bisexual."

"True. But I wouldn't be trying to reach them. I ain't trying to change folks' opinions. I just wanna make good music, and whoever wants to go along for the ride can."

"Will you record songs that are gender specific?"

"It will depend on the song. And it'll also depend on how I feel it. Like, some songs you just can't switch up. Take James Ingram's 'You Make Me Feel Like a Natural Man.' *That* was a mistake."

Indeed. And of *all* the Aretha tunes he could have covered . . .

"I can even do both versions and release them. Nothing says I can't. That way I've got both bases covered. I can play the big houses, packin' in the straight sisters, and do the gay circuit and Black Pride events."

"Mmm . . . sounds like you've got it all planned out."

"If you don't have a plan in this business, you ain't gettin' very far."

He chomped; I sipped.

"You're a brave man," I observed. "It will take a lot of courage and will to go up against that machine."

"Hey, I gotta do what's right in my soul. Besides, even if I don't get a major label to sign me, I can do my thang on an indie. Or the royalties from my songs can bank my own start-up. However it will happen, I don't know. But I do know that it will happen."

I not only believed him, I believed *in* him. And I was also proud of him: he could easily play the role or he could just pass and, after a few successful albums, test the waters and see how the public would accept him "coming out." But he refuses to participate in that charade. That's the mark of a man with integrity.

And, yeah, it was turning me the *fuck* on.

Just then, a man—a *burly, brawny* man—crept up behind him, swatting him on his neck. Montee spun around, irritated. But that changed once he got a jood look at who it was.

And *I* got a jood look at him. Is *that* who I *think* it is?

While Montee rose to greet him, the brother literally snatched him out of the chair and into his thick left arm.

"Yo, whazzup, Son?" the man asked.

"Same ol', same ol'. How 'bout you?"

"Just chillin'. Nigga, where yo' azz been? You been off tha fuckin' radar fuh weeks."

"Man, *you* the one been off the radar. And you always know where to find me."

209

LOVE
THE
ONE
YOU'RE
WITH

"Ha, that I do."

"What you doin' in town?"

"I'm visitin' my peoples up in money-earnin' Mount Vernon. It was a last-minute thang. You know I don't be rollin' up in da Big Apple wit'out givin' *you* a holla."

Montee was *so* engrossed that he forgot I was there. When the brother motioned my way with his head, Montee caught himself and did the introductions. "Oh, I'm sorry. Mitchell, this is Noble. Noble, Mitchell."

It *was* him.

Noble (aka Frederick Mannings) is a twenty-five-year-old rap artist from (of all places) Des Moines, Iowa (I didn't know Black people *lived* there). Instead of braggin' about bein' a player and a pimp, he waxes poetic about his favorite pastime: partying. His gold hits— "Get on the Floor (1-2-3-4)" and a remake of Chaka Khan's "It's My Party"—are ear-friendly, PG-rated dance jams that pop radio warmed up to. The debut they were culled from, *Where Da Party At?* (which was one of only nine rap CDs released last year *without* a "parental advisory" sticker), earned him a double platinum certification, a Grammy nomination, and a Soul Train Music Award. He's got rapid-fire verbal skills (the hip-hop community has tagged him one of its fastest ever) and the "right" rap résumé (son of a single mother, high-school dropout, former drug dealer, several run-ins with the law, and three kids out of wedlock by three women), but it's that rugged, ranch-hand stature—a V-shaped torso; muscle-pumped, vein-bulging arms and legs; and a robust, armorlike chest—that has gotten him the most attention. Last year he was picked by *Ebony* as one of its Most Eligible Bachelors, and last month became the first rap artist to grace the cover of *Playgirl* (there were *many* ass shots— and the brother do got some *serious* back—but he decided against frontal nudity because "When white folks look at me, they see a big black dick anyway").

I'd never heard any "stories" from the Children about him (à la "*Of course* he's gay . . . on such and such night/day, in such and such city, at such and such locale, we/my friend and him/my *friend's* friend and him did such and such . . ."), but the way he greeted Montee told the *whole* story. That wasn't a booty pat he gave Montee, the one brothers sometimes lay on each other when they embrace—it was a booty *pluck*. That huge left hand covered—and *clenched*—Montee's entire right bun.

He leaned in sideways and shook my hand, with the other hand *still* attached to Montee's butt cheek. "Whazzup?"

"Nice to meet you." I shook his hand; that copper skin was so soft and sheen.

"Mitchell sang background on the song that Kev just cut," Montee said, making it clear to Noble how we *didn't* know each other.

Noble finally ungripped Montee's ass and both hands found their way to (where else?) his crotch. "Ah. A'ight. What Seymour song didja sing on?"

My eyes darted over to Montee. "Seymour?"

"Uh, yeah, that's my middle name," a somewhat embarrassed Montee admitted. He frowned at Noble. "Yo, man, I done told you not to be tellin' folks that."

"Yo, sorry, brotha." Noble shrugged, not much concerned.

"It was 'All the Man You Need,' " I offered, trying to direct the convo back to the music.

"And Mitchell gave it just what it needed," Montee added. "He really is a good singer."

"Yo, *some*body gotta make that nigga sound good. Tha way he be hackin'? He could wake tha *dead* 'n' shit. Me 'n Malice was just talkin' 'bout his no-sangin' azz."

"That ain't stop either one of y'all from workin' on his new album."

"Man, *this* nigga ain't stoopid," he trumped, bumpin' up his chest. "If there's green ta clock, I'm ready ta rock."

"So, how long you in town?"

"Just tha weekend. I head back out Monday in tha A.M. I missed ya first set, but I'm gonna stick around fuh tha next one. And maybe we can, uh, nibble on a little sumthin', sumthin' afterward." He quickly darted that very *long* tongue out of his mouth.

He was *not* talking about them sharing a batch of Joe's famous.

A female admirer of Noble's appeared. Well, we heard her giggle before we saw her.

Noble turned. "Hay, sweetheart."

She continued to giggle.

211

LOVE
THE
ONE
YOU'RE
WITH

He pointed to a pen and a letter-sized envelope she was holding in her right hand. "I guess you want me ta sign that, huh?"

She continued to giggle.

He eased next to her. He bent sideways and held out his arm (she was a petite thing and, hunching over her in a lime Nike sweatsuit, he looked like the Jolly Green Giant). "Why don't we go someplace where there's a little mo' light so I can do that."

She stopped giggling. Her mouth dropped open. After receiving a nod from him telling her that she had in fact heard him right and that she was not dreaming, she cautiously looped her arm in his.

He turned to me. "Nice ta meetcha."

"You, too."

"Yo, I'll *see mo'* of ya later." He winked at Montee.

"Ah, a'ight."

He escorted the young lady, whose mouth was *still* open, toward the bar.

"How do you know Noble?" I asked.

"We met at Hit Factory last November," Montee explained, sitting down.

"Were you working on a project together?"

"No. He was remixin' a track with Malice. Alan was showin' me around, introducin' me to folks."

"Ah . . . isn't he dating Brown Sugah?" She's a rap artist out of Oakland, a true glamour ghetto gurl—you know, fixed up (she wears leopard-skin jumpsuits and pumps, her face is always painted, and the weave whipped) but still a little fringy (you can take the girl outa the ghetto, but you'll never get it *out* of her). Rumor has it that she is a lesbian, if not bisexual (when *hasn't* a female rapper been rumored to be anything other than heterosexual?). Noble produced her debut, *Sweet 'n' Sour*, which just went gold, and they have been romantically linked. But since the gossip started (she was apparently seen at a lesbian hangout around New Year's in Newark called Lady Day's, a nod to Miss Billie), they're no longer a duo—at least in public.

"As far as I know."

I wanted so bad to ask whether Noble was one of the people Montee was "involved with"—from what I just witnessed, *something* was goin' on between them—but decided not to. "Is he going to produce you?"

"He may do a track or two."

"Well, with him producing and Kevron recording one of your songs, it seems you've got all the right connections. And you've got the talent. So you're going to do all you want to and more."

"You think?"

"Yes, I do. And you've got a fan in me."

"Hmm . . . would you like to be the president of my New York fan club?"

"Mmm . . . I might."

"You might?"

"Yeah. How much does it pay?"

His eyes widened. " 'How much does it pay?' You're supposed to do it because you *a-dore* the artist. And, you'll get all the free CDs, concert tickets, and T-shirts you want—not to mention private performances from the artist himself."

"Is that what you're going to promise *all* your fan-club presidents?"

"No. Just a very special one."

He peered; I blushed.

He finished his last wing; I finished the rest of my second drink.

I pushed the glass back. "I should be going."

"Why?" He checked his watch. "It's only a few minutes before midnight. What you gonna do, turn into a pumpkin?"

"No," I chuckled.

"So, stay awhile longer."

"No, I . . . I better go."

"Uh . . . okay. Can I walk you to your car?"

"I don't have one."

"Then can I walk you to your carriage?"

I laughed. "My *carriage* is the 6 train."

"Then, may I . . . ?"

"Yes, you may."

He got his coat. We were silent walking those three blocks to the station. We stood near the turnstiles, a foot apart, facing each other.

"You don't have to wait with me."

"I want to."

"Your public awaits."

"Let 'em wait."

213

LOVE
THE
ONE
YOU'RE
WITH

"And Noble is probably waiting on you."

"*He* can wait."

Silence.

"Thanks again for coming."

"No problem. Thank you for making me your special guest—and making me feel so special."

"You're more than welcome. It was easy to do."

Silence. He stared at me; I focused on the token booth.

"Sure you can't stay . . . ?" He was almost begging; he wore that wounded puppy-dog face too well.

"I . . . I can't."

"Uh . . . okay."

Silence.

Wind from an incoming train swept through the station. I pulled my token out, ready to drop it in the slot when . . .

"Mitchell?"

"Yes?"

His hands in his pockets, he stepped to me. "I'm gonna do something *really* stupid right now, but I would feel even *more* stupid if I didn't do it. I think you are one fly brother and . . . I get the feeling that I may never see you again and . . . I . . . I . . . I would *love* to spend the day and night with you. No hanky-panky, no spanky spanky, just . . . just us two, catchin' a movie, just chillin' at my spot. I would cook you the *best* dinner you ever had. And I'd love to play a few of my other tunes for you, see what you think. I promise, I will be a complete gentleman. Just twenty-four hours out of the rest of your life, is all I'm askin'. Will you, please?"

Just *who* does this man think he is? I came to hear him, I supported him, and now he wants more? I tell ya, you give an inch and folks try to take a yard. He should be happy I came, for I didn't have to.

"I can't. Maybe if we had met, as you had sung tonight, in another place and time . . . you are a special man with a special talent and I wish you all the best in the future. Have a good show and a good night."

That's what I *should* have said. *This* came out instead . . .

"Where and what time do you want to meet?"

17

I had "the story" all figured out.

I would be working on an article for *Vibe* about the "gay flava" in hip-hop, doing a little shopping, then spending the rest of the day (and the night) with Adam (who, I would let it slip, was getting married and wanted him to be in the wedding party).

This is what I planned on telling Pooquie about my not being around today. But no matter how much I practiced it and tried to convince myself that what I was about to do wasn't a big deal, I couldn't escape the truth.

I was about to "cheat" on my beaufriend.

I've dated several men who told "the story" so well that when they were telling the truth you didn't believe them because the tales they told *sounded* better. Being involved with some of the most talented liars in the world, though, didn't make this task any easier. I had never deceived Pooquie before and doing it made me very uncomfortable—which is why it took me all morning to come up with "the story."

It was also taking all morning to tell it to him— or at least three hours. I had called a half-dozen times—four times at home and twice at a pay phone at the corner of West Fourth Street and Sixth Avenue, just footsteps from the court where Pooquie used to play basketball and the spot Montee wanted us to meet—and the line was always busy. We briefly spoke last night before I went to the concert; he had just got in from shooting all morning and was exhausted. He said he might go out later to celebrate completing his first film (of course, the *real* celebration would happen when he returned home tomorrow). Did he just decide to stay in and take the phone off the hook so he wouldn't be disturbed?

Not only could I not reach Pooquie, but Montee was twenty minutes late. Maybe these were signs that what I was about to do was a big mistake.

I cocked my heels to head back toward the subway when a yellow motorcycle blared up Sixth Avenue and swerved to a stop in front of me, causing me to jump back. With the motor still running, the driver took off his helmet.

It was Montee. He was wearing the standard biker drag—faded blue jeans, a worn brown leather jacket, black steel-toed boots, even fingerless black leather gloves and a double-link silver chain subbing as a belt, looped around his waist.

"I'm so sorry," he apologized. "I overslept."

I just stood, bewildered.

He waved me on. "Well, just don't stand there. We got a *lot* of ground to cover today."

I approached him. I did the baby-step thing he'd shown himself to have mastered at Body & Soul.

He chuckled. "You don't have to be afraid. I'm not a Hell's Angel."

I was finally standing in front of him, but I was still speechless.

"Say somethin'!" he cried.

I sighed. "When you said you'd be taking me on a trip . . ."

"I'm a man of my word."

"Indeed. You're also a man of many suits."

"That I am."

"And *I'm* a man who's never ridden a motorcycle before."

"You won't be doin' the actual riding—I will." He handed me the helmet.

I took it. "What will you wear?"

"Nothing. I'll be okay." He nodded toward the back. "Hop on."

I adjusted the helmet. It wasn't a perfect fit but snug enough. I leaned on his right shoulder and threw my left leg over the cycle, positioning my seat on the seat.

"You're gonna have to sit closer than that."

I inched up.

"Closer."

I inched up again.

"Closer."

I pushed up into that booty.

"Ah. Now *that's* better. *Feels* better, too." He winked. "Hold on to me."

I maneuvered my arms under the jacket (which was opened) and clasped my hands against his belly.

"You're gonna have to hold me tighter than that."

I tightened the grip.

"That's better."

He took some shades out of his breast jacket pocket. He put the pedal to the metal.

"Here we go."

And we were off. I admit that I was . . . *scared*. Most of the men I've seen ride have been much, *much* heftier (Humpty-Dumptys, to be exact), and while it may seem like an easier vehicle to steer, I'm sure the extra weight gives one more leverage to ride like the wind, not let the wind ride them (there were moments when I thought I would be knocked off because of the tornadolike breezes we faced). But Montee never once lost his grip, his focus, his balance, his stride. He directed the cycle with ease, flowing in and out of lanes, zipping through traffic, yet always obeying the rules of the road. And he never forgot about me, asking every few minutes: "You okay back there?"

"Yes," I'd reply, all the while thinking: With a man like you at the controls, how could I *not* be? After the anxiety subsided and we zipped through the Queens Midtown Tunnel, I started to soak up the sights and the smells, and the mix of the gas, the burning rubber, the leather, the cologne he wore—not to mention the friction being caused as his ass melded into my dick—was making that temp rise.

When we pulled into the parking lot of a movie theater, I realized I had never stopped to ask *where* we were going.

"So, didja enjoy your first ride?" he queried.

"Yes, I did."

"Good. I have the feeling you'll be experiencing a few more firsts today."

"Oh?" Hmm . . . what else did he have up his sleeve?

217

LOVE
THE
ONE
YOU'RE
WITH

He purchased tickets for *The Shawshank Redemption*. Given the other choices—*The Brady Bunch Movie* (I never cared for the series) and *Pulp Fiction* (a movie lauded for being innovative and revolutionary when in reality it's a gory blaxploitation flick in whiteface)—he made the right one. But why did we come all the way out to Queens to see it? I'm sure it was playing somewhere in Manhattan. I guess he wanted to *really* take me for a ride . . .

We had a half hour to kill before it started, so we ducked into a coffee shop directly across the street from the box office. We slid into a booth. We both ordered tea with honey and lemon and shared an apple Danish.

"How long have you been riding motorcycles?"

"I've only ridden one. I've had Blaze for three years."

"And why a Kawasaki and not a car?"

"The practical answer is that it's easier to maintain and manage, not to mention park. The personal answer . . . I always wanted one, ever since I saw Peter Fonda and Dennis Hopper in *Easy Rider*."

"Have you hit the road like they did in the movie?"

"One of these days I will."

"Are you a member of a cycle gang?"

"It's not a gang. Just a group of brothers who ride."

"The Panthers?" There was a panther on the back of his jacket.

"Yeah."

"Are they a local group?"

"There are mini-chapters in L.A., San Fran/Oakland, Miami, D.C., and Philly."

"Sounds like *whole* chapters, not minis."

"We're not an organized posse. It's not like we have a president, or a headquarters, or a set of bylaws."

"Ah. Do you meet with them on a regular basis?"

"Like once every couple of months. We just get together to hang, party. Or we'll ride someplace like the Poconos."

"Ah. Do you have a tattoo?" That's the one thing all cycle men and women seem to have.

"I do. But it's in a place only special people have seen. Maybe you'll be one of those people."

Yeah, maybe . . .

I HADN'T BEEN TO THE MOVIES SINCE . . . WELL, SINCE
Pooquie and I saw *What's Love Got to Do with It*. It was our first—and,
in a way, our *only*—date. I got a very strong sense of déjà vu about that
evening when Montee led us to the center of the very last row. They're
the perfect seats in the house to see the show, but they also give you
the perfect excuse to get close to your date—and Montee didn't let
this opportunity slip by. First the right arm went around my chair.
Then it made contact with my neck. Then it rested on my shoulders.
Then *around* my shoulders, occasionally pulling me closer.

Not to be shown up, I slowly eased my left hand onto his meaty
thigh, squeezing it every now and then (and it was *only* every now and
then, for every time I did, that bulge would bump up).

But we never took our eyes off the screen (not even to dig into the
extra-large popcorn, which was on my lap, and sip on the jumbo
orange drink, which sat between us in the beverage holder on the
armrest), and the reason why could be summed up in two words:
Morgan Freeman. Now I know why he received so much acclaim and
was nominated for Best Actor—and Tim Robbins *wasn't*. Much of his
"screen time" is off-camera—i.e., as the narrator of the story. But it's
a voice of undeniable power and quiet authority. Not only do you
believe everything he says, you know that no one else could tell the
tale. He's the anchor of the movie, its heart and soul—and the fact
that the story is *really* about Robbins's character being convicted of a
crime he didn't commit is a testament to Freeman's talent (the character he plays was originally an Irishman in *Different Seasons*, the
Stephen King novella the film was adapted from; another example of
brilliant "nontraditional casting"). He truly is one of the greatest
actors of all time.

The other revelation was James Whitmore as a senior inmate who
finds it hard adjusting to life on the outside; he should've gotten a
Supporting Actor nod. Add the well-written script and well-paced
direction, and you could almost forgive the filmmaker's somewhat
sanitized depiction of prison life (not that I *wanted* to see it, but I'm
sure Black inmates were not treated the same as whites in Maine from
the 1930s to the '60s), and that manipulative, annoying score, rising
at the most predictable moments.

219

LOVE
THE
ONE
YOU're
WITH

But the title!

"That is one *stupid* name for a movie, especially one that good," argued Montee as the credits rolled.

"It sure is. When I first heard about it, I thought it was a religious epic. And while watching it, I still thought Charlton Heston would pop up as Moses."

We laughed.

"And I don't see the redemption in the story."

"You don't?"

"No. Do you?"

He thumbed his chin. "I believe the redemption was about having faith. Even a man serving life in prison without parole has to have *something* to hold on to, something to believe in; otherwise, how could he make it through each day?"

"Even if that something is plotting his escape?"

"Ha, *especially* if that something is plotting his escape. What else could a condemned man hope for?"

I nodded.

"That James Whitmore . . . he's come a *long* way since *Them!*"

"He sure has."

"And Morgan is a magic man. He made all those rather simple sayings sound so . . . so . . ."

"Profound?"

"Yeah. Things we might've heard before but not in those words and not in that way."

"I agree." One in particular resonated: *Get busy livin' or get busy dyin'*. That was what I was doing at the moment (although one could argue that I was livin' a little dangerously).

"I hope he wins that Oscar. But knowin' how those folks are, they won't be able to resist givin' it to their new Every White Man, Mr. Hanks."

"Indeed."

"My only problem is that Disney-esque ending. I mean, they meet on this sandy beach to live happily ever after?"

"Uh . . . I got the feeling they were lovers."

"Really?"

"Yeah. There never was anything overtly sexual about their dealings or between *anyone* in the movie, and that's unbelievable. I mean, you're a lifer, there's little to no chance of your getting out, and you don't have a boy, a mate, a lover? I think their connection went beyond just friendship, but showing that might've turned it into a *very* different movie."

He chewed on that one. "Now that you say that . . . what a great observation." He smiled. "See, I knew I'd be seeing this film with the right person. I'm glad I saw it—and I'm glad you saw it with me."

"The feeling's mutual."

"Alan said I'd like it."

"Gene told me I would, too."

"The birthday boy, right?"

"Yes."

"I think Alan said he saw it with Gene."

Did he? Well . . . those two might be closer than I think.

"I never got the chance to thank him."

"For what?"

"For such a great time. I'd never been to a party with a stripper before—well, a *male* stripper, anyway. That was something different. He seemed to enjoy it—even *after* the party was over."

I guess when he went to the bathroom, Montee *heard* the after party in Gene's bedroom.

"You, Gene, Babyface, and B.D . . . you all seem very close."

"We are."

"Babyface and B.D. . . . they good people. And that Gene!"

People are usually at a loss to describe Gene, so I knew what he meant. "Yeah. He's a special man."

"Any man who uses Baby Wipes instead of toilet tissue has *got* to be."

We smiled.

"And with all those animals around that apartment, I was expectin' Jack Hanna to walk up in there any moment!"

I nudged him in his side. "Now, now, don't be talkin' about my best friend like that."

"I don't mean it in a bad way. I'm just glad he and Alan are good friends. I wouldn't have seen you for the third time." He squeezed my hand.

He had kept a count. I did, too.

221

LOVE
THE
ONE
YOU'RE
WITH

HE SAID HE DIDN'T LIVE FAR FROM GENE—AND HE doesn't. Seven blocks, to be exact.

"How long have you lived here?" I asked as we headed into the five-story, red-brick walk-up.

"Like five years. I moved in a few months after I first came to New York."

To think Gene and I had been passing by his building all these years and never saw him . . .

He lived on the first floor in the rear apartment. Both units on his floor are studios. They used to be a single apartment; when other abandoned buildings on the block were renovated and new businesses started moving in, the current landlord divided them knowing he could make more money. So while the front studio has the fireplace, Montee has the only one with access to the backyard (which was, at the moment, blanketed with snow and ice).

And it's a jood thing he has another space to walk into, for his pad is a tad too small ("sixty/sixty"—as in feet). A sofa futon with a black metal frame sits across from a thirteen-inch color TV (planted on a couple of milk crates) and a shelf-model Aiwa stereo system (which is on the floor). Near the door leading to the backyard is his MUSIC STATION (so the white license plate posted on the ridge just above one of two windows announced): a parched-wood piano stool, a synthesizer with a digital piano and amplifier, a studio mike with a recording track, and four CD trees, each holding fifty titles. And opposite this is his kitchen: a small countertop, two oak cabinets directly above the sink, and a single drawer, sandwiched between a refrigerator and stove. A compact steel pushcart on wheels sits to the right of the stove; on it was a microwave and some of his cookware. Upon seeing this, I could just hear B.D. shriek: "Chile, ain't enough room in here to let my titties *out*, let alone sling 'em!"

But, as I would later learn, he knew how to work what little space he had.

Montee placed the helmet on one of the hooks attached to a brass coat stand by the futon. "This is my very humble abode. It's a box, but it's a clean, *cheap* box."

It was. Crowded, but not cluttered (if it had been, he'd be walking into himself). Everything seemed to be in its rightful place. The only things decorating the off-white walls were seven framed flyers, programs, and posters from his concerts in Atlanta, D.C., Newark, New York, and Detroit. And a pleasant lemon scent seemed to be coming from the coffee-with-cream carpet.

One thing *did* shake me up, though: a postcard of Pooquie in his All-American boxers. Of *all* the things he could've had posted on that fridge . . .

He helped me off with my jacket. "I may *finally* be getting a one-bedroom. A tenant on the third floor is supposed to be moving in a couple of months, and I'm next in line."

"Thank you." I smiled as he hung it up and took off his own. "But you might be able to buy this building in a couple of months, if not the next six."

"You really think the song Kev recorded is gonna hit big, huh?"

"I do."

"Well, if you liked that, you'll *love* what I'll be playing for you later." He motioned toward the futon. "Please, make yourself comfy. Would you care for something to drink?"

I sat. "What do you have?"

He opened the fridge door and hunched over (now why he wanna stick *that* out?). "There's some orange juice, ginger ale, raspberry Snapple, and red Kool-Aid."

"Red Kool-Aid?"

"Yup. It's my fave."

Mine, too. I hadn't had it in so long. "I'll have some of that."

"Wise choice."

While he washed his hands I checked out the videos and books that sat in another milk crate by the futon. On one side were *Columbo, Banacek,* and *McMillian and Wife* teleflicks, and theatrical films like *Murder on the Orient Express, Death on the Nile, Chinatown,* and *Murder by Death;* on the other, novels by Agatha Christie, John Grisham, and Walter Mosley. "I see you're a crime-mystery buff."

"Sure am."

"I bet you can't wait to see *Devil in a Blue Dress* later this year."

"You know it. I think Denzel was the wrong choice to play Easy,

223

LOVE
THE
ONE
YOU'RE
WITH

but, hey, it probably wouldn't have been made if he didn't star in it."
He handed me a jelly jar. "Too bad I didn't meet you six months
from now. *Devil* would've been a more romantic movie to see
together."

He held up his own jar; I did, too. We clinked; we drank.

"*Mmm,*" I hummed. "This is *great!*"

"Thanks."

"I bet you used a pound of sugar."

"That's the only way to drink it." He pointed toward his music station. "Choose some sounds while I get started on dinner."

I obeyed. The problem was what to play. All the names I knew
would be in his collection were there, making it hard to select. It was
almost identical to my own—except for the inclusion of one title.

"How did you get this?" I held up Annie Lennox's *Medusa*. It
wasn't slated to be released for two more weeks.

"I got my connections." He snickered.

I slid the disc in and scanned the program.

"There's something odd about those songs, isn't there?" he asked.

There was. I considered each one again.

I joined him in the kitchen. "Annie is *fierce.*"

He was seasoning some lamb chops. "Oh? How so?"

"The nine covers were originally recorded and made famous by
men. *That* is the mark of a true diva."

"And *you* are a man who knows his music."

"What are you doing, testing me?"

"*Test* you? That I would never do. But *try* you? Oh, yeah."

Leaning against the fridge with my back to Pooquie, I devoured
two bowls of his slammin' shrimp salad (feeding him a heaping table-
spoon every now and then) while he gave me the bio as he buttered
and breaded, chopped and chucked, diced and spliced. Up until last
night, I didn't even know his last name.

The oldest of four, he was born in Little Rock, Arkansas, on a very
peculiar date: February 29, 1964.

I stated the obvious. "You're a leap-year baby."

"That I am."

"I've never met someone born on that day before."

"Ha, there's yet another first."

"That's kind of . . . weird, isn't it? I mean, the actual date you were born only comes around every four years. On what day do you celebrate it during the other three?"

"The last three days in February and the first three in March."

Hmm . . . is this why he wanted me to spend the day with him? "Well, happy birthday."

"Thank you."

"Have you always celebrated it that way?"

"No. I always thought my day was the twenty-eighth; that's what my parents told me. But then I saw my birth certificate when I was about to turn sixteen."

"How did you handle that?"

"I was a little angry and even confused, but I understood why they didn't tell me. Trying to explain to a kid that your birthday only comes once every four years . . . that could've been traumatic. It was for my father."

"He was born on the same day?"

"Yup. The same day, the same *time* of day, *and* in the same hospital."

"Mmm . . . is that him with you in the photo on the wall?" It was the only picture displayed.

"That's him."

"You two are almost identical." And they were. The only difference: The elder Simms was bald and a little stockier.

"Yeah. We are alike in many ways."

"Uh . . . how does he feel about his only son being bisexual?"

"He doesn't mind."

"He doesn't?"

"Nope. Why should he? Like I said, we are alike in *many* ways."

"*He's* bisexual, too?"

"Yup."

"You're kidding!"

"No, I'm not. I take it you never knew of a father and son who were both bisexual, huh?"

I laughed. "Uh, no."

"Like I said . . ."

"Yes, another first. How and when did you find out about him? Or he about you?"

Was this a painful story? Sorrow registered on his face. "There was a . . . family friend. I . . . we called him Uncle Blue."

225

LOVE
THE
ONE
YOU'RE
WITH

"Uncle Blue?"

"That's the only color he would wear. Even to his wedding and funerals. Including his own."

"Uh . . . I'm sorry to hear that."

He nodded. He sighed. "My father was a wreck when he passed. They knew each other since they were in their cribs; they were closer than brothers. But I didn't know they were *that* close. Well, I did."

"Whatcha mean?"

"One day I was sent home from school early because I was sick. I had a stomachache because I ate too many Ring Dings at lunchtime."

"I used to woof those down at lunchtime, too."

"I was upstairs in my room asleep when I heard voices. I went downstairs and saw them on the living-room sofa. Their backs were to me, but I could see them from their shoulder blades up. They were both shirtless. And they were . . . I didn't know *what* they were doing, but whatever it was, it was making them moan. So I snuck around into the kitchen, where I knew I could get a side view of the action."

"And what did you see?"

"They were both naked. And they were both *so* beautiful. Uncle Blue was paper-bag brown, so their tones complemented each other. And my dad was . . . well . . . massaging his feet."

"Massaging his feet?"

"Yeah. Uncle Blue's left leg was crossed over his right and my dad was massaging his left foot. And Uncle Blue was massaging my dad's dick. And I got there at just the right time, because my dad . . . he erupted. He . . . it just spurted up and up and *up*, like a gusher. And Uncle Blue kept saying, 'I love you, my brother. I love you.' And then . . . he embraced my dad and kissed him square on the lips."

"How old were you?"

"Eight. I never told anyone that story. Not even my dad."

"Why not?"

"Because . . . he's from another time. Folks didn't talk about it, even if they knew about it."

"To some extent, that's still true."

"It is. But it's not like it was twenty, thirty years ago. He wanted his other life with Uncle Blue to be his and his only. He didn't talk about him after he died. He still hasn't. He never wanted any of us to know about it."

"Including your mother?"

"Oh, *she* knew about it."

"She did?"

"Yeah. In fact, Uncle Blue's wife was *her* girlfriend."

Say what??? "You have *got* to be pulling my leg."

"I'd rather pull on a few other things," he groaned.

"I bet . . . so, your mother was bisexual, too?"

"She still is."

"Hmmph . . . I guess it truly is a family affair."

"It is. One of my sisters is bi, and another is a lesbian."

"And when did you all come out of the closet to each other?"

"The bag that finally let that cat out was opened when my dad and I ran into each other at a gay club in Phoenix."

"No!"

"Yup. He was dancing with this brother, who was my age."

"How old were you?"

"Twenty-two."

"*That* must've been a sight."

"It was—especially since I had *my* eye on him!"

We laughed.

"Not only are we alike in many ways, we like the same kind of men."

"Ah . . . would *I* be his cup of tea?"

"You wouldn't only be his cup of tea—you'd be the kinda biscuit he'd wanna dip in it."

I grinned.

"After that discovery, everything else came out. Well, every*one* else did, including the youngest, my fifteen-year-old sister."

"Wow. Y'all musta had a *big* coming-out party."

"We did. We invited all of our friends—and our *friends*. It was a blast."

"And is that when your mother's girlfriend was officially intro-duced to you *as* your mother's girlfriend?"

"Yeah. My aunt Bette Jean. Unfortunately, I couldn't do the same with her son."

"You were seeing her son?"

"Yeah. He couldn't face his father's death—or himself. I know . . . he loved me. He always loved me. We were as tight as our fathers were."

"How tight is tight?"

227

LOVE
THE
ONE
YOU'RE
WITH

"We planted many of our *own* seeds in the fields."

Okay . . .

"And the things we did inside, against, and *on top of* his pickup truck." He had a flashback that made his entire body tremble. "*Damn.* Ain't *nothin'* in this world like a pickup-truck fuck." He snapped out of it. "Uh, Little Rock is known the world over as the pickup-truck capital of the world."

"I see. But I bet the world *doesn't* know that many of those trucks are being used for activities other than drivin'."

He chuckled. "Mmm-hmm. Just about everybody I went to high school with lost their virginity in a pickup."

"Including you?"

"Including me."

"And you lost it to your uncle Blue and aunt Bette Jean's son?"

He sighed very heavily with a smile. "Yeah."

"What's his name?"

"Lancelot," he crooned. "And boy oh boy, did he like to do it a *lot!*"

"A lot being . . . ?"

"Every day, sometimes twice a day."

"That *is* a lot. And how long did you two . . ."

"We were both fifteen when we became . . . lovers. It lasted five years."

"You were high-school sweethearts."

"Yeah. And he had such a sweet heart—not to mention a sweet dick and a sweet ass."

"And you two would go buck wild in the truck?"

"*Uh-huh.* Usually after he had football practice. He was a linebacker for Central State, and then with the Razorbacks at UA. I was a cheerleader at both schools. I'd cheer him on on the sports field—then cheer him on in the cornfield."

"How was it, going to a school like Central?" Embedded in my memory bank: that photo in my high-school history textbook of a bespectacled sister walking through a very hostile crowd of white youths, with one white girl shouting something at her.

He knew what I was inquiring about; he considered it. "Let's just say that the more things change . . ."

I nodded. "Ah. And why did you two break up?"

He heaved. "He said he saw how hard his father loved mine, and that he didn't want to have that and lose it. But I think he really felt that if we continued, one of us would end up dying like his father."

"And what did his father die from?"

"AIDS."

"Oh."

"My father is negative, and so are my mother and aunt Bette Jean. So, Uncle Blue contracted it from someone else. That's probably another reason why my father was so devastated by his death. The betrayal . . ."

"Have you spoken to Lance lately?"

"I have. Just last week."

"Is he still in Little Rock?"

"Yeah. Married to his *other* high-school sweetheart, who doesn't know about him—so they say. He says he's never been with a man since me, but . . . knowing how much he loved it . . . I can't believe it. I just tell him . . . if he is, to be careful."

"And has your father found love again?"

"He has. A brother just a few years younger than him. They've been together now for three years. They're living in Phoenix."

"Did he divorce your mom?"

"No."

"Is she still with your aunt Bette Jean?"

"Yeah. They're living together now."

"Well, they don't have to be married anymore. I mean, the kids are all grown. And the secret *is* out."

"True. But they still love each other. Why get divorced?"

"They're not living as man and wife anymore."

"No, they aren't. But that doesn't mean they don't *feel* like man and wife. All the property they own, the ties they have . . . it'd be better just to stay married. They took the 'Till death do us part' vow seriously. That's the only way they plan to be divorced. And if Uncle Blue was still alive, Aunt Bette Jean wouldn't have divorced him."

"Mmm . . . to think they all found each other and made this kind of . . . pact."

"It goes on more than people think. Especially in small big-city towns like mine."

229

LOVE
THE
ONE
YOU'RE
WITH

"Did you ever find love again like you had with Lance?"

"He was my first; you can never have love quite like that again. But . . . I think I've come close." He peered at me. "And with others, *dreamed* that I could."

That made me tingle.

He checked the lamb chops. He turned them over. "Those should take about fifteen more minutes. What do you say we make some music of our own?"

He refilled our Kool-Aid jars. He shut off the stereo. We ventured over to his music station. He sat down at the keyboard.

I noticed the stack of music sheets on the windowsill. "Did you study music in high school and college?"

"Yeah." He began to play Beethoven's Ninth. "Did a few recitals. Even played for the mayor once."

"Really?"

"Yeah. At his inauguration. I played for both the school chorus and choir."

"When did you start writing songs of your own?"

"I was . . . twenty. Would you like to hear the very first Montee Simms composition?"

"Sure."

The lyrics were . . . well, depressing:

> Sometimes I cry
> because I feel so all alone
> And sometimes I weep
> for I feel that I can't go on
> And sometimes I wonder
> will you ever return
> And then I realize . . .
> There'll be no more roses
> delivered to my door
> And you won't ring my phone
> anymore
> And it's all so unfair
> Sometimes I wish
> you were still there

"So, whatcha think?" he asked when he was done.

"You must've had the blues when you wrote that!"

"*Had* the blues? I *was* the blues."

"Uh . . . Lance?"

He nodded. "But I got over him. And I vowed to *never* write another song like that again. Once was enough!"

And judging from the other selections he performed, he hadn't. A bubble-gum-pop, up-tempo track, "I'm Not That Kind of Guy" does what very few (if any) songs do: extol the virtue of abstinence for males. I could see a New Kids on the Block clone taking it to number one, sending preteen girls into fits of frenzy.

Then came "It's a Miracle," an inspirational tune. Its scope and the melismas sprinkled throughout make it a prime Whitney/Mariah or even Tramaine/Yolanda belter (he didn't do a bad job himself).

"This is the one I *really* want you to hear," he admitted before going into song number three. It had a new jack vibe, very Jodeci-ish. But K-Ci couldn't tear it up the way Montee did. Near the end, he even scatted.

"Is it called 'Where Have You Been All My Life'?" I asked.

He grinned. "That's what it's called."

"Who were you in love with when you wrote it?"

"What makes you think I was in love when I wrote it?"

"It has that feel."

"I wasn't in love. I . . . I wrote it a few days ago."

He's even written a song *about* me. I was blushing big time—and so was he.

He ended the gushing. "Did you ever watch *Name That Tune*?"

"I never missed it. That was my favorite game show."

"Me, too. Would you like to play?"

"Sure. Do you have the game, or episodes of it on tape?"

"Nah. All we need are these keys." He tapped out a melody. "I'll play, you guess."

"Oh, okay."

The catch, though, was that I wouldn't receive any verbal clues. I did get to decide how many notes I'd receive. I always chose four—fewer would surely stump me but any more than that wouldn't allow

231

LOVE
THE
ONE
YOU'RE
WITH

me the chance to really show him how deep my ocean of musical knowledge was.

The first two were simple: "Higher Ground" and "Ain't No Way."

The next four were a bit more challenging—"Guess Who I Saw Today?," "Smoke Gets in Your Eyes," "I Try," and "Stuff Like That" (of course, he *would* sneak an Ashford & Simpson tune in there)—but I guessed them.

Seven wasn't a lucky number. I got my usual four notes. Nothing.

Then he doubled that number of notes; nothing.

Then he *tripled* them; *still* nothing.

I recognized the music but couldn't place the lyrics. So he played an entire verse.

When I realized what it was, I harmonized the chorus with him: "*I* hope and pray that I will, but *to*-day I am still just a *bill*!"

And we laughed so hard we were in tears.

"That was the first song I ever learned how to play," he revealed.

"Really? For most people it's 'Chopsticks' or 'Happy Birthday.' "

"After I saw that *Schoolhouse Rock* episode . . . it just stuck in my head. And I'd sit at the piano, trying to figure out the keys. After a week, I got it. I would sing it *every* day. It drove my family crazy."

"It'd drive *me* crazy, too."

"My mother started beggin' me to start playin' hymns again. I knew she'd had enough then. Hymns always rubbed her the wrong way."

"Oh? Why?"

"She . . . isn't a religious person. She and my dad rejected the traditions of their families. Hers Baptist, his Catholic."

"So they didn't bring you up to believe in God?"

"Of course. They just told me to create that relationship outside of structured conventions. Don't look for God in a church or a book some *say* He wrote; locate Him inside your heart. So we didn't go to church and we never listened to gospel or spiritual music around the house—until I started buying records by the Winans and Walter Hawkins."

"She must've thought you were being converted."

"*Brainwashed* was the word she used. More than anybody, I loved to imitate Sam, and some of his best work was with the Soul Stirrers. I didn't even know he fronted a gospel group. But I didn't sing them when she was around. They brought back . . . bad memories for her."

"I'm sure she would've really flipped if you walked up in the house quoting Scripture."

"More like lapsed into a coma. The only Bible allowed in our house was *Jet*. You know if Black folks don't read about it—whatever *it* is—in there, it ain't true."

We cracked up.

"But she and my dad . . . they were told God *hated* them. And things haven't changed much since then. Folks still say that, but others try to temper their disdain for who you are with 'God loves you, even though He is *mad* about what you do.' *Yeah, right*. If God is mad at you for being gay, does that mean He's *half*-mad at me for being bisexual? That don't make no sense, and persecuting folks because of who they are and how they love don't either."

"Is there a particular hymn you enjoyed singing?"

He went right into "He Looked Beyond My Fault." I joined him when he repeated the main verse a second time and we "battled" on the chorus, each trading licks and runs.

He surrendered when I hit a Minnie Riperton octave. "Now, see, we could *really* have some church up in here. But it's time to eat."

After washing up, I returned to find a card table draped with a blue velvet cloth, situated in the center of the room. He was placing an ocean-blue vase filled with lilies and daisies between two thin lighted white candles. Two places were set, one beside the other. A bottle of red wine was opened. The room light was off; the ceiling fan above the futon lit (it had a variety of colored bulbs in its five sockets, creating a rainbowlike glow).

He stood by one of the pulled-out chairs. "Please sit." I did.

He made our plates (the way smoke escaped from them, you'd think it was coming from a chimney). He sat them down.

He filled our glasses. He settled in his chair.

He clutched my left hand. He bowed his head; I followed suit.

"To the Most Honorable, Glorious, and Gracious of All. We bow our heads at this moment, giving thanks for this meal, this time"—he squeezed my hand—"this fellowship, this life. Ah-men."

"Amen."

233

LOVE
THE
ONE
YOU're
WITH

He tapped the remote on the table and the stereo began to play all five of Anita Baker's CDs. The first song: "Caught Up in the Rapture."

Dinner was . . . well, one of the best . . . no, the *fourth*-best meal I've ever had (the other three having been prepared by my grandmother, mother, and aunt Ruth, in that order). The meat just crumbled (it didn't fall) off the bone, the broccoli cream soup was stupendous, the succotash was even better than mine (I bet Pooquie and Junior would even give it a higher mark), and the corn bread actually tasted like bread dipped in corn batter. I couldn't conversate while eating this meal—any questions or statements he made were all answered with mumbles of *uh-huh, I agree, yes,* and *no.*

He soaked the dishes (I offered to help but he refused; after a feast like that, I'd do his dishes for a *month*) and we retired to the futon with slices of his Death by Chocolate cake. I've had it before in restaurants, but this actually tasted . . . *deadly*. Mouthwatering wouldn't even begin to describe it . . .

I was ready to pass out, but he had other ideas. He didn't bother to place the dessert dishes in the sink; he put them on top of the video/book crate.

"Mitch?"

"Yes?"

"Can I massage your feet?"

"Huh?"

"Can I massage your feet?"

"Why do you want to do that?"

"It's somethin' I love to do, remember? Like *father* . . . we've always had this thing for pretty feet."

"You've never *seen* my feet; how would you know if they're pretty?"

"Because, I can tell."

"How?"

"You ask a lot of questions, don'tcha?"

"Well . . . no one has ever asked if they could do that before."

"No one knew *how*." He reached down. "May I?"

I nodded yes.

He had me sit up diagonally so my feet were hanging off the futon. He took off my right boot. He hesitated with the sock—I guess he was preparing himself. He pulled it off *slowly*, prolonging the unveiling.

And when he saw the foot . . . the eyes bugged, the tongue rolled out, and he let out a joyous sigh.

He cupped it with his left hand and analyzed it for a hot sixty seconds. He glanced up. "I'm *never* wrong." His fingers walked across each piggy, from the smallest to the largest. "*And*, I'm a *sucker* for manicured toes."

As he rubbed and ribbed, kneaded and knuckled, I gave up my life story (between the many *mmms* and *aahs*). While the love affair with my gymnastics coach in high school was discussed in juicy detail, *the* love of my life wasn't (he didn't ask; I didn't offer).

I *did* disclose the reason we ran into each other in Manhattan last week.

"I know who *I'm* gonna be hittin' up for demo money," he ribbed.

"I haven't gotten paid yet."

"You will soon." He eyed me with concern. "That experience . . . that musta been hard to deal with."

"It was."

"You've probably heard it before, but you *did* do the right thing. The real question now is when are you going to return."

"When am I going to return? To what?"

"To what you were placed on this earth to do."

"What makes you think I'm not doing that now?"

"Because, you don't talk about teaching—or singing, which, by the way, you also do very well—with the same passion you do writing."

I became a little defensive. "Teaching *is* something I always wanted to do."

"Wanting to do something and being *called* to do something are two very different things."

Yes, they are . . . "But I haven't stopped writing."

"No, you haven't, but it isn't the same just freelancing. You don't receive the same kind of reward like you do working on a publication whose mission you believe in. Hell, you'll soon have a little seed money—you could start your own magazine."

Damn. Now how did he . . . "You know . . . that's always been my ultimate goal."

"Well, nothing says you can't do it."

No, it doesn't.

235

LOVE
THE
ONE
YOU'RE
WITH

When he finished fondling my feet, he pulled off his blue, cranberry-dye-lined sweater (leaving on a crisp white undershirt that fit his frame nicely) and his shoes but not his gray thermal socks ("Trust me, *I* don't have pretty feet"). I sat up on the sofa with my legs crossed as he lay across them, his back leaning on a pillow up against the armrest of the futon. I rested my hands on his chest, occasionally tapping or patting it. It was as if we had gotten into this position a million times before (well, *I* had—with Pooquie).

"How long have you known you're bisexual?"

His eyebrows rose. "How long have you known you *weren't*?"

"Uh . . . since I was six."

"Ditto. Having those feelings for both sexes . . . I thought everybody felt like that. I still do."

"You think we're all born bisexual?"

"I don't know if we're born *anything*. But I do feel that given how sexual human beings are, it's silly to think one has to be either gay or straight."

Hmm . . . "Are you talking about identity, behavior, or both?"

"Is there a difference?"

"I think so. You may be oriented toward one sex, but because of societal pressure feel you have to be with the other. Just because a gay man sleeps with a woman and a lesbian sleeps with a man doesn't mean who they are on the inside changes."

"Ah. But the fact that they can sleep with a person of the opposite sex . . . that tells me that even if they aren't bisexual on the *in*side, they are on the *out*side. If one is oriented toward one thing, that doesn't mean they can only express themselves sexually in one way. Sexual identity may be fixed, but sexual expression isn't."

"And you like to express yourself sexually with both sexes . . ."

"Sexually, emotionally, spiritually. Hay, I like chicks and dicks—and sometimes chicks *with* dicks."

"Chicks *with* dicks?"

"Yeah. Some brothers are more chicky than the females." He chuckled.

"Do you normally refer to women as *chicks*?" He'd said it a few other times earlier in the day.

"Yeah. Why?"

"It just seems a bit . . . old-fashioned."

"I'm an old-fashioned kinda guy."

"Old-fashioned as in sexist."

"What's so sexist about calling women chicks?"

"The term isn't exactly endearing."

"It isn't?"

"No, it isn't."

"I don't use it to slight women. If I wanna insult a woman, I'd use—"

I put my left thumb to his lips. "*Don't* say it."

He puckered up; it made my fingers warm. "Why not say it? I heard your friends use it a hundred times last week. If there's any word that shouldn't be used as a term of endearment, it's that one."

I've never used it in that manner, but . . . "Point well taken."

"I think that's one of the reasons why I don't have many gay friends."

"Oh?"

"Yeah. All that *bitch* this and *girl* that and *Miss Thing* . . ."

"*All* gay men don't talk like that or address each other that way."

"All of y'all don't, but a lot of y'all do."

"What is a lot? Many? Most? The majority?"

"The majority of the ones I've been around."

"Uh, I know you like to think of yourself as a *worldly* man, Mr. Simms, but you certainly haven't met or known enough of us to make that judgment. In fact, you never could."

He nodded. "Okay. Point taken."

"You said that's *one* of the reasons why you don't have many gay friends. What are the others?"

"No others. Just one. I've found too many gay men to be biphobic."

"*Bi*phobic?"

"Yeah."

I snickered. "Like there is such a thing . . . ?"

"Yeah, there is. I don't know if I'd say gay men *hate* bisexual men, but quite a few sure don't like us."

"And why do you think that is?"

237

LOVE
THE
ONE
YOU'RE
WITH

"Because, according to many of the ones I've come in contact with, I am a confused brother who can't make up his mind. *Or,* a confused brother who is just denying his true feelings."

"Those feelings being . . . ?"

"That I'm actually gay and in denial about it."

"Ah . . ."

"I'm sure there are folks out here who are gay calling themselves bi because they know that identifying as that will make them . . ."

"Seem less threatening?"

"Yeah. All of us aren't like that. But you let some of these gay folks tell it, we're all just perpetratin'. Gay folks complain all the time how straight folks won't respect who they are, yet turn around and treat *us* the same way straight folks treat *them.* I mean, we're always an afterthought—if we're thought of at all."

I laughed.

"What's so funny?"

"Oh, I was just thinking about a line from a movie."

"What movie?"

"*California Suite.* Maggie Smith plays this Oscar loser whose husband, Michael Caine, is bisexual. But in her eyes, he's more homosexual than bisexual, since he's not sleeping with her but is fooling around with men."

"That's funny?"

"What's funny is what she says to him when they're discussing his sexuality: 'If there's anything I hate it's a bisexual homosexual—' "

" 'Or is it the other way around?' " he asked, finishing the joke.

"You've seen the film?"

"No. But it's been said to me by gay men before. *Now* I know where it comes from. I guess the reverse was true for some of the gay brothers I've tried talkin' to: they wanted me to pledge that I wouldn't be attracted to women when I'm with them. I mean, how am I supposed to turn off that button?"

"Not that I'm taking their side . . ."

"Of course not . . ." He winked.

"But maybe they wanted some assurance that you wouldn't cheat on them."

"If that was the case, why didn't they ask me to turn off the button that also attracts me to *men*?"

Jood point.

"If my steppin' out was the *real* issue," he continued, "that woulda been the issue across the board. But they only felt threatened by my attraction to women."

"Well, maybe that was because when they found themselves involved with a bisexual man, he always cheated on them *with* a woman."

"But what if he cheated on them with a *man*? Wouldn't that be just as bad?"

"For some it wouldn't be. I guess the reasoning goes: 'Why would he step out on me with another man when he's already got one?' He's more likely to pluck the fruit he doesn't have at home."

"Not necessarily. Some men are just straight-up *dawgs*. Whoever they can get it from and however they can get it, they do."

"Speaking of: Do you know what Gene says about your kind?"

"Hmmph, what, in his infinite wisdom, does he say?"

"Bisexuals are afraid to be *by* themselves, that's why they play in both arenas."

"See, there's the other myth: We want to have our cakes and eat them, too."

"Well, don't y'all?"

"Certain kinds of cakes, yeah." He eyed my rump. "I can't speak for all, but I don't see why I can't be involved with both sexes at the same time."

"Like now?"

"Yeah."

I recalled our exchange in the elevator. "What do you mean by 'involved with'?"

"I am currently dating two people, a man and a woman. They, too, are bisexual."

"And what does *dating* constitute?"

"I am seeing them socially—and sexually."

I decided to go there. "Is one of them Noble?"

"No."

"Have you two dated?"

"Why you wanna know, so you can write some exposé on the sex-capades of the stars?"

"No. Watching you two, it just seemed like . . ."

239

LOVE
THE
ONE
YOU'RE
WITH

He hesitated. "We've been . . . he's . . . you could say I'm his East Coast Hookup."

That wasn't hard to figure out. "When he's on the East Coast, you two hook up."

"Yup."

"Did you two hook up last night?"

"He wanted us to."

"And you didn't want to?"

"I'd be lying if I said I didn't."

"So why didn't you?"

" 'Cause . . . Noble is a Player with a capital *P*. He ain't the kind of brother you get all wrapped up in emotionally 'cause he don't feature that. But the more we . . ."

"Hook up?"

"Yeah. The more hooked I get on him. And the more hooked *up* I want us to be."

"And he don't wanna be?"

"No. He wants to see me, but he don't wanna see me like that."

"He just wants to *see* you between the sheets."

"It don't matter where. We done it everywhere *except* between the sheets."

Hmm . . . I wonder if they, like Kevron and Bryant, have also utilized that out-of-the-way, "out of order" bathroom at the Hit Factory . . . "Are you *hooked* on the other two people?"

"Mmm . . . not really. I like them both a lot and we have lots of fun. But . . . the sister doesn't want a relationship, which is fine with me. She goin' through lots of drama with her ex, the father of her son, and I ain't lookin' to be nobody's stepdaddy—at least not right now. And the brother . . . well, he's a little married."

"A *little* married?"

"Separated from his wife, seeking a divorce."

"Does that mean he is *actively* seeking the divorce?"

"He is. But not because of me. We met a year after they agreed to the separation and he moved out."

"Do these two people know about each other?"

"Yup."

"And they're okay with that?"

"Yeah. Why wouldn't they be? We're all adults. And we're not exclusively seeing each other." He held up his left hand. "Ain't no ring on this finger."

"Do you want to marry one day?"

"Yup."

"When you do, how will you handle not being able to have intimate relationships with other men?"

"Who says I want to marry a *woman*?"

OK . . . "So you would settle down with a man?"

"Of course."

"How would you handle not being able to have intimate relationships with a woman?"

"The same way any heterosexual or homosexual person would who is committed to their mate. I've been able to handle it before, whether I was with a man or a woman. It's not that hard. But sometimes I didn't have to put those feelings on hold."

"What do you mean?"

"Well, there *is* such a thing as an open relationship."

An open relationship. This is one concept I've never understood. But since he brought it up . . . "What's the sense of being committed to one person if you both plan on stepping out of the relationship?"

I guess he'd been down this road before; his tone was a little snippy. "In the kind of open relationship *I'm* talkin' about, we wouldn't be stepping *out* of the relationship. It would be a *part* of the relationship."

"You mean . . . you two would *share* this person?"

"*Share* isn't the right word." He thought about it. "*Experience together*. That's the best way to describe it."

"A ménage à trois . . . ?"

"Yeah." He frowned. "Don't look so disgusted."

"I look disgusted?"

"Yes, you do. I take it you've never been in one before?"

"No."

"Well, don't knock it till you rock it. Just like an open relationship."

"Uh . . . how long did this open relationship last?"

"Three years. It was the longest relationship I ever had—and the *best* one I ever had."

241

LOVE
THE
ONE
YOU'RE
WITH

"You were with Lance longer . . ."

"That's right, I was *with* Lance; we weren't *in* a relationship."

Mmm . . . "And, this open relationship . . . was it with a man?"

"Yes."

"A bisexual man?"

"Uh-huh."

"Why did you two break up?"

"He decided he wanted to pursue something with a woman, in the hopes of getting married."

"And the only men you two slept with were each other?"

"As far as I know."

"And when you both wanted a woman, you found one who would . . . be with the both of you?"

"Yeah."

"Was it hard to find a woman who would agree to something like that?"

"Not at all. Women can be just as if not more freaky than men; they're just socialized not to express it. Hell, a couple of the sisters we hooked up with got off watchin' us fuck each other!"

I'm far from being a prude and I didn't want to be judgmental, but . . . "I . . . I don't know. It . . . it still seems like cheating."

"How can it be cheating when you both accept it as a part of the relationship and engage in it as a couple? Winston and I just acknowledged up front that it's impossible for one person to give you everything you want or need. I mean, isn't that why you're here?"

I drew back. "I'm sorry?"

"You see things in me, want things from me, that you don't see or get from your man."

I became flustered. "You're being mighty presumptuous, not to mention arrogant."

"Maybe. But I don't think I'm wrong."

He wasn't.

"Many people would come down on you—and I'm sure your man would be one of those people—but I don't think folks should be judged so harshly for indiscretions. I think most people want to do the right thing, but . . . life is not a fairy tale. We don't live happily ever after. I learned that from my father."

"Then do you think it's a waste of time for any of us to commit ourselves to one person?"

"No, I don't. But it *is* a waste of time romanticizing that commitment. Shit just doesn't happen, people *make* shit happen—and it's always gonna make a stink. But we always seem to be so surprised when it happens, as if we're too special for it to happen *to*. I think it's better to recognize the limitations of love and our limitations *to* love. Not that I'm *endorsing* infidelity, but . . . sometimes people meet and . . . something happens. Ignoring it isn't always the easiest thing to do." He glanced at me. "Is it?"

No . . . it isn't. But I sure as hell wasn't going to admit it. Besides, he already knew the answer.

So I moved away from *that* subject. "Would you still be with, uh, Winston if he didn't want to walk down the aisle?"

"I would." He smirked, knowing he could've nailed me. "We were such a good match."

"Would you consider having such a relationship with a man who isn't bisexual?"

"Uh . . . I would. But it could get real complicated."

"Complicated?"

"Yeah. I mean, just because I want to kick it with some chick . . ."

I glared at him.

". . . uh, female . . ."

I nodded my approval.

". . . doesn't mean they can automatically go out and kick it with another man. It could turn into a game, and it ain't and can't be about keeping score, evening up the score, or getting even. So he'd have to be *very* secure."

"And would you want that kind of relationship with every person you decide to settle down with?"

He nudged me. "Are you asking this just to know, or for future reference?"

"Just to know."

"No. But I generally navigate toward folks who would be open to it or, at the very least, aren't repulsed by the idea—and I've found straight sisters and gay brothers to be the *least* likely candidates to fall into those categories."

243

LOVE
THE
ONE
YOU're
WITH

"Can you blame them?"

"Yeah, I can. They say they want you to be straight up about who you are, but when you are, they *still* trip. Bisexuals do have good reasons for . . . well, to borrow a phrase, staying in the closet. But I refuse to be one of those brothers living a double life or an invisible life just to appease or please others. I don't be carryin' other people's luggage."

"Are the people you're involved with now open to it?"

"We haven't had that discussion. We aren't serious enough yet."

"And . . . where does Garrick fit into all of this, if he fits in at all?"

He shrugged. "I'm still gettin' to know the brother. It's only been a week."

"Have you two been out since the party?"

"You know that's not what you wanna ask."

"It's not."

"No, it ain't. You wanna know if we got buzy."

"No, I don't. I'm just trying to understand . . . how you operate, relationship-wise."

He wasn't convinced. "We had dinner Wednesday night, drinks afterward. We were supposed to get together tonight."

Oh, really? "Why didn't you?"

"Because I decided I'd rather spend the evening with someone I long for than someone I lust for."

Okay . . .

Silence.

"By the way: How many gay friends *do* you have?"

"Three."

"One of them being Alan."

"Yeah."

"Well, I could be number four. Or better yet, your first Same Gender Loving friend." I had schooled him on the term earlier in the evening (his reaction: "Hmm . . . I guess that would make me an *Any* Gender Loving man, huh?").

He chuckled. "Yeah, you could be. But . . . I don't know."

"Why not?"

"I don't know if I could *just* be your friend. I could try it, but . . . it would be torture."

Silence.

He smiled. "I think it's time for my after-dinner mint."

He hopped off the futon and opened one of the floor-level drawers attached to its base. He rummaged through it and came up with a folded Ziploc bag.

Is that what I think it is?

He fiddled with the bag. "I bet you don't smoke weed, do you?"

"No, I don't."

"How adventurous are you?"

I didn't know what to say. I just shrugged.

"You don't have to if you don't want to. And if you try it and hate it, I can finish it all myself. *That* won't be a problem." He took a cigarette lighter and the only joint out of the bag; it was the shape and length of a cigar.

"I . . . I . . . I guess I didn't think a brother like you would . . . do that."

"A brother like me?"

"Yeah. I mean . . . it's not cocaine or heroin, but it's still an illegal substance. And it can still have an adverse effect on you. It could even affect your voice." I replayed what I'd just said—I sounded like his father.

And given that amused expression, he must've heard this lecture before, probably from his father. "Thanks for the concern, but I ain't a chain-smoker; I only do it once or twice a month. And I don't do it to get high."

"You don't?"

"No. I do it to lubricate, *not* medicate, my mood. At times like these . . . it's the cherry on top." He was about to light up; I guess I didn't look too pleased. "If you don't want me to do it, I won't."

"Hey, this is your house. You can do whatever you want."

"Uh-huh." He sat, yoga-style, on the futon. "So . . . I'm a bisexual who loves threesomes and smokes pot. Three things you hate."

"I wouldn't say I *hate* those things."

"You certainly don't hold them in high favor."

"I . . . I've always looked upon each with . . . dread."

"Ah. So I'm *dread*ful."

"You aren't dreadful. If you were . . . I wouldn't be here right now."

245

LOVE
THE
ONE
YOU're
WITH

"That's good to hear." He fired it up. He puffed. *"Mmm..."* He handed it to me. "You wanna join me?"

Rewind: my ninth-grade health-education class. There's Miss Flannigan, wearing a tacky flowered dress and orthopedic shoes, her straight white hair tied in a very tight bun and her hand planted firmly on her left hip, tapping the blackboard with a ruler and exclaiming in a deadpan tone: "Drugs can ke-ill you, so just say no."

Back to the present moment: Yes, they can kill you. I've never *seen* them kill people, but I've read the stories. And I've said no to them all my life. I've never even smoked a cigarette. But just because I do this one drug this one time does not mean I'm destined to try others, right? If I blow one blunt with Montee, does that mean I'll get hooked, lose my job, my friends and family, and flush my life down the toilet?

I bet that's what most people ask themselves before they take the plunge—and I bet most, like me, also convince themselves those things won't happen to them.

Since this was a day of many, *many* firsts, why stop now? Besides, I'll probably hate it—if I can't stand the smell (and I never could) I certainly won't be able to stomach the taste.

So, unlike President Clinton, I inhaled.

It felt as if I were ingesting—don't laugh—toothpaste mixed with collards (not that I've ever mixed the two before). A little tangy and a little pasty and a little ... grassy? It was a *strange* taste and it was giving me a *strange* feeling. I've felt a buzz, a little light-headed, even been slightly drunk. But this was a different kind of ... buzz. A different kind of ... light-headed. A different kind of ... drunk.

And one whiff was all it took—I was high.

We couldn't talk during this—no, *I* couldn't. All I could do was laugh. No matter what he said, a giggle or guffaw escaped before I had the chance to even think about a response, and I'd bowl over on the futon.

Finally, he gave up trying to engage me in conversation. "You could never smoke for real. You'd be one fucked-up mess."

Maybe so, but I was smart enough to know that when that joint got down to being a roach, it was every man for himself—and having seen others puff till it poofed out, I knew how to suck it dry.

And Montee wasn't happy about that. "*Yo*, Mitch! What's up with that?"

Yeah, I just laughed, tossing the microscopic roach into the ashtray.

"You think that's funny?"

Yeah, I just laughed, rolling myself up off the futon. I staggered a bit to catch my balance. Realizing I was indeed high, I clasped my hands to my face in embarrassment—and laughed even louder.

"Ha, I'll give yo' ass somethin' to laugh about . . ."

He grabbed me with his left arm and began tickling me, his right arm behind my back.

I might've been floating, but my sense of tickle sure wasn't dead. "*No! Stop!*" I screamed.

"Ha, you know you like it. I knew you were the ticklin' kind."

"*Stop!*"

"And how did I know *that* was the spot!"

"*Stop! Stop!*" I fought, trying not to laugh.

"You know you wanna laugh. Come on, come on, laugh . . ."

I did. And he did, too. Then he stopped tickling me. But I didn't stop laughing, and he didn't either.

And he didn't let me go.

Silence.

He sighed. "Ya know . . . I got a confession to make."

"You do?"

"Yeah. I . . . I was tryin' to make you jealous at Gene's party."

I had a suspicion . . . "You were?"

"Yeah. When I was dancin' with Garrick, I was hopin' you would cut in."

"Really?"

"Really. But I'm savin' the *special* dancin' for you."

"You are?"

"Oh, yes. I already know how you rock it. Now I wanna know how you *knock* it." He squeezed me tighter.

"What do you mean?"

"I want to slow-drag with you."

"Why?"

"Even when you high you Mr. Twenty Questions. Because I want to. And because I know *you* want to."

247

LOVE
THE
ONE
YOU'RE
WITH

"I—"

"And *don't* say you *don't* want to."

"No. I was going to say I *can't*."

"Not *wanting* to do something and not being *able* to do something *ain't* the same thang."

He was right. I breathed a chuckle. "You . . . you are incorrigible."

"That I am. I'm also just your average horny little devil." His scowl was similar to Jack Nicholson's in *The Witches of Eastwick*.

Horny? Yes. A devil? Indeedy.

But little? Judging by that snake creepin' across his pants that is heating up my ass . . .

NOT.

He released me. He went over to the stereo. He slipped a cassette into the tape deck. He pressed play. The elegant piano-string-laden intro of Ashford & Simpson's "So So Satisfied" filled the room. He roped his left arm around my waist and palmed my back with his right. I wrapped my arms around his neck.

Forehead to forehead. Eye to Eye. Pelvis to pelvis.

We swayed . . . *in, out, down, around. In, out, down, around. In, out, down, around. In* . . .

"So full . . . so warm," he brooded like Nick.

Given that this was a duet and he already stated he couldn't sing songs Ashford & Simpson recorded together solo . . .

"Like being dried out after the storm," I finished along with Valerie.

"New birth . . . runnin' . . . runnin' through my veins," he and Nick declared.

Valerie and I followed again. "Looks like that clear day finally came . . ."

"Feelin' *high*," we all soared together. "So, so satis-fied."

We were.

The A&S Quiet Storm parade continued with "I'm Determined," "Ain't That Good Enough," "Time" (which, ironically, I had included on Pooquie's "Missing U" tape and sung to *him* on the phone Monday night), "I'm Not That Tough," "Love It Away," "We Can Make It Work Again," "Experience (Love Had No Face)," "Send It," "It Seems to Hang On," "Is It Still Good to Ya," "Stay Free," "Crazy," "My

Kinda Pick Me Up," "I'll Take the Whole World On," "Believe in Me," and "Happy Endings." There were a *lot* of grunts, groans, and grumbles, yet we never missed a cue or a note, singing our hearts out to each other.

By the time "Somebody Told a Lie" rolled around, Nick & Val were on their own—we were too busy huffin' and hissin' to the grindin' and gropin', bumpin' up and pushin' into the other.

"Wanna take you there . . . gonna take you there . . . in my arms, babe . . ."

When Nick & Val sang the chorus for the final time and soared on *sky*, we both howled in ecstasy, climaxing simultaneously.

And when Nick & Val *"Oh"*- and *"Ooh"*-ed it up, we came down with some *Ohs* and *Oohs* of our own.

As their voices faded out . . .

"I see you do duets," he whispered

"Not until tonight," I breathed back.

"Mmm . . . yet another first."

"Uh-huh."

Silence.

He sighed real heavy. "Thank you."

"For what?"

"For *cum*ming into my life."

We giggled.

"And speaking of which: Maybe we need to get *un*sticky."

I nodded. "That's a good idea."

"Why don't you freshen up first."

"Okay."

We "kissed"—by rubbing noses.

I grabbed my little sack and went into the bathroom. I took a quick shower—three minutes—brushed my teeth, gargled, and dabbed Midnite, a sensual scent, all over. I slipped on an oversized T-shirt from B.D.'s dance company and some bikini shorts, both green.

I reentered the room. The futon was pulled out. He was lying on his back, his right leg hanging over the side and foot touching the floor (he still hadn't removed those socks).

"The bathroom's all yours."

No answer.

I crept up to him. He was out. *Knocked* out. His right hand was on

249

LOVE
THE
ONE
YOU'RE
WITH

his heart, as if he were about to pledge allegiance to the flag; his left at his side. Besides the socks, he wore ribbed light gray Hanes boxers. He was so . . . quiet. So . . . still. He didn't appear to be breathing at all. The sign he was? His lips parted.

I was kind of pissed he fell asleep—after all, it isn't a very hosty thing to do. But he *did* have a late night and an early morning, took us on a trip through three boroughs in the city, and cooked dinner. He should've fallen asleep on me sooner. And given the position he was in, he'd probably only planned to rest his eyes for a minute or so.

Truth be told, I was glad he zoned out, for it meant we'd avoid the inevitable. Sleep would've been the last thing on his mind after he showered up.

And I wouldn't have said no.

So I kissed him on the forehead—no moisture, no pucker, no tongue. I wanted to kiss him—many, many, *many* times—but knew it would really be over if I did (he's right; that *is* the way one can seal it). This was the only way I could without getting way in over my head (and end up *giving* him head).

I climbed in on the opposite side of the futon. It was rather toasty, so I didn't need the blanket that sat between us. I left it there.

"WHAT ARE YOU DOING?"

"What does it *smell* like I'm doing?"

The honey ham was in a dish in the microwave. I had just put the Cream of Wheat on a low boil. As Junior had done for me a week before, the four slices of bread were waiting to be toasted. And I was cracking four eggs into a bowl.

He approached me from behind; I think he wanted to hug me, but didn't. He just moved in very close, that dick brushing up on my ass. He breathed into my left ear. "Good morning."

I slanted my head slightly to the right. "Good morning. I don't have to ask how you slept last night."

"Uh, no. You don't." He stood in my spot by the fridge, his right shoulder leaning against it. "I have to apologize for falling asleep on you. I should've known . . ."

"You don't have to explain. I understand. It was a long day." I smiled at him. "A long, *lovely* day."

He smiled. He crossed his arms against his chest. He studied me. "You know you don't have to do that."

"I know. How do you like your eggs?"

"Uh, scrambled with cheese, soft."

Now, how did I know that?

I already had two slices of cheese out of their wraps, ready to be sliced up some more. "Why don't you wash up. It'll be ready when you get back."

He nodded, grinning. "Okay. I will." He jogged off, that azz jiggling along with him. *Mph . . .*

He put on *The Best of Bill Withers*, and what do you know, "Lovely Day" was the first song.

When he emerged from the bathroom, he was draped in a white towel and white socks. His body still glistened.

I pulled down the lever on the toaster. "You really don't want me to see your feet, do you?"

He paused Bill, who had just finished the first verse of "Lean on Me." "*I* don't want to see my feet."

"They can't be that bad."

"Believe me, they are. I'll tell you what I *will* let you see . . ." He started to unfasten the towel.

"What?"

"My tattoo."

"Ah. This isn't in a place that will make me lose my appetite, will it?"

He was thrown. "Say what?"

"I mean, we are about to eat. Like your feet, there's a reason why some things should not be seen." I laughed.

He didn't get the joke. He sucked his teeth, putting the knot back in the towel. "Kiss my ass."

I thought you'd never ask!

I was most definitely up to *that* challenge. "Bend over, spread 'em, and I will."

He was putting on deodorant. He stopped. I was serious—and he knew it. And he also knew he couldn't back down—after all, *he* opened *that* back door.

But he didn't have to consider it for long; in fact, he didn't consider it at all. He turned his back on me and backed that azz up just

251

LOVE
THE
ONE
YOU'RE
WITH

like he did on the dance floor at Body & Soul—except this time he wasn't takin' baby steps. I ripped off the towel.

Damn, damn, *damn* . . . what a *glorious* maximus it was.

As I marveled at his huge, hammy, hairless hamlet, he spread those legs so far apart I thought he was gonna do a split and bent *all the way forward*, planting his hands firmly on the ground and sticking his head through his legs, peering up at me with those eager eyes. He waved it at me.

And I waved right back with my tongue, flickin' at it, gettin' closer, and closer, and *closer* . . .

The tunnel to his love pulsed *in/out, in/out, in/out* as I came closer, and closer, and *closer* to landing, the pathway clear and the target marked.

When I finally landed he jumped up like a jack-in-the-box. I circled the runway, creating my own bull's-eye around *that* spot. He shook with anticipation, yelping like a dog, a very soft and sweet *aaay* following each tongue tap.

Then I grabbed those phat azz cheeks (causing him to cry *"Yee!"*), pulled them *farther* apart, and kissed that azz the way I wanted to kiss *him* for two weeks.

And *his* lips kept kissin' *me* back.

I can describe how he smelled (the Irish Spring mixed in with his own musky scent). And I can describe how he tasted (chocolate syrup).

But I *can't* describe what he sounded like. I mean, the brother was speakin' a foreign tongue, *not* a foreign language, and it wasn't Holy Ghost hosannas or pig latin (which other boyz have testified with as I tossed 'em). The utterances reminded me of a record being played backward: unintelligible and horrific (had a demon entered his body?). But in this case, they were also so damn mother-fuckin' *sexy*.

And ya know it was all turnin' me the fuck on *and* out. "I'm gonna stick my tongue so far up your ass, it's gonna tickle your tonsils," I promised.

And I kept that promise. The harder I stabbed and jabbed, the harder he pushed and mushed back, allowing my tongue to swim deeper inside. And the deeper I went, the more furiously he yanked on that third leg that swung *mighty* low between the other two.

He whirled and twirled and swirled and curled that azz like

crazy—and then I *hurled him* onto the table, pushing his thighs out around one of the corners.

I really feasted then, literally eating him out—gnawing, chewing, and chowing down—and burying my face so far up in it I almost suffocated (uh-huh, suicide booty).

And those *sounds* . . . they got even scarier and louder as he bucked the table the same way he must've bucked when fuckin' in a pickup truck back in the day.

It appeared the table was about to give when he started yodelin'—*on key*—and unleashed the gooeyest juice I'd ever seen on the table.

As he jerked, I scooted up to his head, which was awash in sweat. "Mmm . . . *just* what was missing from the breakfast buffet: buttermilk biscuits." I smacked them.

He giggled.

"Now that I've eaten you *on* the breakfast table, how 'bout us actually eating *breakfast* on the table?"

He giggled again.

I actually ate breakfast *on* his biscuits—the table was unstable after the pounding he gave it, so he lay across the futon as I balanced my plate on his azz.

And, unfortunately, we had to make do without the Cream of Wheat, because it burned (yet another case of déjà vu).

He had some of *my* biscuits after breakfast. I was on my back pulling my knees into my chest and squirming, squealing, and *screaming* with unpure delight (my words *were* intelligible and *very* naughty) as he slurped and slobbered all over and all up inside of me.

And as he snacked on my toes (a task he performed with schoolboy joy), I shot my load.

As I came down, he looped his arms around my waist. I locked my legs around his thighs, tapping a beat on his azz. I might've gotten high last night, but I was much higher right now.

"Isn't this hanky-panky?" I inquired.

"No."

"Then what is it?"

"More like licky-micky."

We chuckled.

253

LOVE
THE
ONE
YOU'RE
WITH

I became solemn. I sighed.

He eyed me. "You're feelin' guilty, huh?"

"Uh . . . yeah. But . . . not as guilty as I should."

"Mmm . . . maybe we need to go *all* the way, and then you will!" He bumped and humped me.

"That would do it." I managed a half smile.

He cupped my chin. "You don't *have* to feel guilty."

"How could I not?"

"Hay, I don't know the brother, probably never met or *seen* him before . . ."

So you think!

". . . but even if I did . . . the one thing I know how to be is discreet. How else could I carry on with a rap artist the past six months? I know how to keep it on the down low."

I nodded. "Hmmph, nobody has to know . . ."

"Right."

"But—"

"I know: *You* know, and no matter how much fun we had, you still feel bad about it. Well, that's okay. Feel bad about it—just don't make yourself feel *so* bad you feel bad about *you*. Feel guilty, but remember that that is what it was supposed to be—a *guilty* pleasure."

I ran my fingers through his hair. "You know, many men—be they bi, straight, gay, or otherwise—wouldn't have opened up and shared like you have, especially to a person they'd view as a one-hour stand."

His eyebrows rose. "Damn. *That's* how long they're lastin' these days?"

We cracked up.

He caressed my lips with his thumb. "It was easy to do. You're a very passionate man—not to mention devoted. He . . . he's a very lucky brother, whoever he is. I might've caught your eye . . . but he's got your heart."

We kissed with our noses again, for a jood minute.

"Oh." He leaned up on his hands. "And to think all of *this* happened because I wanted to show you . . ."

He knelt by my head. On his right cheek was the tattoo, in Old English style.

"Why 'Papa's Boy'?"

" 'Cause that's what I am," he trumpeted.

"Mmm . . . if he can eat ass like you, I may have to experience my first threesome."

He visibly recoiled. "Huh? I'm a freak, but I'm not *that* kind of freak."

"Okay then . . . I guess you'll just have to watch us from the kitchen."

He stroked his chin. "Hmm . . . now *that* kinda freak-*y* I *might* be able to work with."

AFTER A VERY LONG SHOWER (LOCKED IN AN EMBRACE as A&S played and the water cascaded between and on us) and a very long ride back to West Fourth & Sixth Avenue (it wasn't that long but it seemed that way) came the very long good-bye. We stood in the exact place and the exact spaces we had twenty-four hours before—but this time we were both vocally challenged.

A minute or so passed as we watched others walk by before . . .

I sighed. "Maybe . . . we'll see each other again."

"Maybe we'll *sing* to each other again. May as well give the world something to *really* talk about. They'd trip over a bi male singer; they'd trip *out* over a male singing duo."

"They would. Uh . . . jood luck in your career. I'm sure I'll be hearing you on the radio soon."

"Ha, we'll also be hearing *you* on the radio soon, too, if your prediction is correct. Thanks. I hope to be seeing *your* name at the top of a masthead."

"You just might."

Silence.

"Thanks for helping me officially enter my thirties. I had a very *jood* time," he enunciated correctly.

I smiled. "Thank *you* for both the ride and the high of my life—*literally*."

We laughed.

"Not to mention the jood movie and the *very* jood food," I added.

"Ha, which dishes—the entrée, the dessert, or the salads we had this morning?" He winked.

"All of the above, *especially* those salads."

255

LOVE
THE
ONE
YOU're
WITH

"You are most welcome. Hay, I aim to please, *and* I'm a man of my word: I said I'd take you on a trip, I said you'd be experiencing a lot of firsts, and most of all, I said I don't meet you and eat you on the same night."

I giggled.

"I guess I'll see you next lifetime," he predicted.

"You believe in people having more than one life?"

"No. I'm talking about another time in *this* life. The time was wrong—but we weren't."

Silence.

He tapped his helmet. "I get the feeling that neither one of us . . ."

"Then let's not say it."

"I can go for that. But neither one of us wants to be the first to walk away either."

I tapped his front wheel with my right foot. "*You* wouldn't exactly be walking away."

"You know what I mean."

I nodded. "I do. Well . . . why don't we both walk away at the same time. On the count of three, you go your way"—I pointed north—"and I'll go mine." I pointed south with my left elbow.

"Okay." He revved up the engine. "Who's gonna do the count?"

"I will."

"All right. I'll read your lips." He held out his hand; he searched my eyes. "Next lifetime?"

I folded his hand into mine. "Next lifetime."

We smiled. He placed his helmet on.

I took a very deep breath. "One . . . two . . . three . . ."

I repeated the heel turn I did yesterday as he zoomed up the block. I quickly spun around to watch him as he rode out of sight.

I cheated—again.

18

"So . . . ," B.D. began, after I had told him the *entire* story, "do you have any regrets?"

"Well . . . I do regret doing it."

"Mmm-hmm. But you *don't* regret *enjoying* it."

A grin formed across my face.

"*That*, no one *ever* regrets," he declared. "What would be the point of doing it? But you *do* regret doing it . . . at least that says you have a conscience."

We sipped our tea in silence. We were at Tiffany's, a restaurant in the Vill.

"I guess I'm trying to figure out why I did it," I confessed.

"Like I said before, the man is a Sexy Ass Mother-fucker—that ain't reason enough?"

"But I've been surrounded by SAMs the past two weeks; why him? I keep thinking that . . . there must be something wrong with what Pooquie and I have."

That he was *not* featuring; he wore the same frown Gene had given me during that infamous game of Truth or Shade. "You fooled around; don't be no fool about it."

"What do you mean?"

"*You* know what I mean. That is the trap most folk like to conveniently fall into: they stepped out-side of their union because something is wrong *with* their union. I mean, they gotta blame what they did on *something*, right? But they know that ain't the case—and so do you. You didn't do it because you fell out of love with Pooquie. Or because you fell out of *like* with him. Or because the spark you two share is no longer there. Or because you were feeling neg-lected. Or ignored. Or *bored*. You did it because you *wanted* to. The question you need to be asking is not what this says about your relationship with Pooquie, but what it says about *you*."

"What do you think it says about me?" I mumbled.

"It says that you are just like the 999,999 other folks who also decided to cheat on their significant others the same time you did: human."

I nodded.

"You stepped out on Pooquie, but at least you didn't step out of *yourself*. You creeped, but you creeped with a man who could clearly see you belonged to someone else and, in his own way, respected that boundary. Y'all only talked about certain things—and only *did* certain things. Believe you me, if your lips had so much as grazed his, you and Pooquie would *not* be celebrating eighteen months together in a couple of weeks."

"I wouldn't throw away what I have with Pooquie—"

"Uh-huh, this from the *same* man who emphatically stated that no other man could turn his head. Not only did Montee turn your head, he turned your *tail*."

Indeed.

"Montee knew he could only go so far with you; if he stepped over the line, he would've been in over his head—and his heart. The man didn't want to break up your happy home, he just wanted to borrow the welcome mat for a while—and he knew *exactly* where to lay it down."

He sho' 'nuff did.

Sips. Silence.

He tapped his teacup. "You two meeting . . . it must have been fate."

"You think so?" I was wondering about that myself . . .

"Sometimes the universe presents us with opportunities, *just* to see what we will do. And, if my calculations are right *again*, you and Montee kept running into each other every three days—and things usually happen in threes."

Wow . . . that we were running into each other often, I noticed; that it was happening in a particular numerical sequence, I hadn't. B.D.'s not as ditzy or dense as he pretends to be.

"*And*, given the way you two . . . *connected*, he *could* be your soul mate," he predicted.

My eyes bugged. "My soul mate?"

"Yes, your soul mate."

"I don't feel for him the way I feel for Pooquie," I objected.

"Who says that the way you feel for *Pooquie* is the way you're *supposed* to feel for a soul mate? A soul mate doesn't necessarily have to be someone you fall in love and settle down with. Babyface isn't my soul mate."

"He isn't?"

"Nope. And I'm not his."

"Then, what are you two if you're not soul mates?"

"Partners in love—and in life."

Hmm . . . "Then who can a soul mate be if he isn't someone you fall in love with?"

He put on his thinking cap for this one. "It can be someone you immediately recognize—but have never met or seen before. Someone whose eyes tell a story you've only seen played out in your dreams. Someone you feel such a seismic bond with, it's scary. Someone who may only appear for a brief moment—but makes a lasting impression, maybe for a lifetime." He shot me a quizzical glance. "I take it by the expression on your face that Montee falls into one if not all of those categories . . . ?"

"Uh . . . yeah."

He nodded. "Mmm-hmm. Fate. He came into your life—*now*—for a reason."

"Why?"

"Maybe this was a test of will—or better yet, will*power*. To prove to you that love don't love *no*body. Not only can you get hurt, *you* can cause some of that hurt." He paused. "Are you gonna tell Pooquie?"

"I . . . I don't know."

"You more than likely will. You're just not the keeping-secrets type."

He knows me well . . .

"But if you're gonna tell him, tell him at the right time," he advised.

"And what would be the right time?"

"After he tells you about *his* affair."

"You think he had an affair?"

He shrugged. "As you yourself learned over the past two weeks,

259

LOVE
THE
ONE
YOU'RE
WITH

anything is possible. But some stones are better left unturned, so don't rock the boat unless you are ready to be knocked out of it with*out* a life jacket."

Silence.

"Your secret's safe with me," he promised. He raised his cup. "Just another page in your life . . ."

I lifted mine. "Yeah."

Clink.

"Pooquie?"

"Yeah?"

"Are you okay?"

"Yeah. Why?"

"The last time you gave it up like that . . . ha, was the very first time you gave it up."

I slapped him on the right booty cheek. He giggled.

"You were workin' that back out somethin' fierce. I thought you were gonna break it!"

He laughed. "You should talk, standin' on yo' shoulders givin' it up. *Day-um.* I ain't know you could do that."

"There's a lot of things I can do you don't know about."

"Oh, yeah?"

"Uh-huh. Very special occasions call for very special positions."

"They sho 'nuff do."

Smack, smack, smack.

"Not to mention a very special drive home from the airport," I purred.

"Yeah. I knew I was gonna see you in tha backseat of that limo, but I ain't think you was gonna be *butt bootay nekkid*!"

"I wasn't *totally* naked—I was wearing a big red ribbon around my waist."

"Baby, pleeze. Like that ribbon was coverin' up anythang?"

I giggled. "I asked Gene if he would be our chauffeur, but the last thing he wanted to hear was us smoochin'. He heard enough of *that* when we were on the phone at his house."

"I bet. B.D. ain't seem ta mind. He was prob'ly enjoyin' da show."

"Oh, he was!"

"And that 'Welcome Home, Pooquie' sign B.D. was holdin' . . . that wasn't no sign, it was like a billboard!"

We cracked up.

Silence.

"So how does it feel?" I queried.

"What?"

"Doing your first movie."

"Uh . . . I don't know. It was a lota work, but it was madd fun. And now that it's over . . . it all happened so fast, but it went so slow."

"Whatcha mean?"

"You know. It's like . . . when you in tha thick of it, time just goes so slow. It was a long-ass two weeks."

"I know."

"But it was only two weeks; it wasn't like it was two months. Even tho' it felt like it."

"I know. *Believe me*, I do." I sighed. "We'll have to get used to your being away . . ."

"Yeah. But it ain't gonna matter how long we apart, or how far apart we are. Long as I know you waitin' right here . . ."

"That I will be."

Smack, smack, smack.

I glanced at the nightstand. "It's almost nine o'clock. You know Junior is just waiting by that phone for you to call."

"Ah . . . yeah. I'll call him in like five minutes. I just wanna lay like this wit' you a little while longer."

"Okay."

Silence.

"Little Bit?"

"Yes, Pooquie?"

"I missed you much."

"I missed you much much."

"Much much?"

"Yup. Twice as much."

"Then I guess you gonna hafta show me twice as much." He squeezed my ass.

"You know I will."

Smack.